Praise for

THE LAST STORYTELLER

"A vivid portrait of Ireland."

—*The Star-Ledger*

"Delaney has spun a magical tale. . . . A trilogy to be read and re-read. What a saga!"

—Bookreporter

"A charming mix of cotton-candy romance and history."

—*Kirkus Reviews*

Praise for

THE MATCHMAKER OF KENMARE

"Delaney re-earns his reputation for total reader engagement with his latest deeply thought-out novel, which weaves together various strands of the general theme of searching."

—*Booklist*

"An adventure into the underside of World War II, complete with spies, intrigue, and danger . . . [Delaney] skillfully portrays the physical and emotional effects of the changing world."

—*Historical Novels Review*

"World War II–era Ireland is the lush setting for Delaney's tale of intrigue and romance."

—*People*

"A spectacular mystery, an engaging history, and a tragedy written with sometimes great humor and sometimes great humility. Once picked up, the only reason to put this book down is to keep it from ending."

—Bookreporter

Praise for

SHANNON

"A gripping story . . . Delaney again shows himself to be a master user of language, a master at historical fiction and a master storyteller in the Irish tradition." —*Winston-Salem Journal*

"Delaney makes his lovely, battered country a character of its own."

—*USA Today*

"Delaney handles Shannon's therapeutic journey with sympathy and skill, introducing a diverse cast of Irish characters and layering the narrative [with] arcane native lore—historical, cultural and geographic."

—*The Washington Post*

"The Tipperary-born Delaney sends Shannon on an Irish American Odyssey across a mysterious landscape filled with eccentric characters, treachery and, ultimately, redemption." —*The Star-Ledger*

"Frank Delaney's *Shannon* will delight your senses with description and capture your attention with storytelling." —*The Free Lance-Star*

"*Shannon* is a delightful and engrossing read, overflowing with Delaney's passion for his country's beauty, history and traditions."

—*The Star Tribune*

"A well-crafted, satisfying work of historical fiction, as are all of Delaney's novels; respectful of the facts while not cowed by them, and full of life."

—*Kirkus Reviews*

Praise for

IRELAND

"Delaney gracefully collects essential myths—and invents a few, too—in his heartfelt ode to the oral tradition."   *—Entertainment Weekly*

"An epic novel of history and storytelling."

—U.S. News & World Report

"Dramatic, adventurous, heroic, romantic, slyly comic."

—The Philadelphia Inquirer

"Wonderfully engaging . . . History, legend, memory and myth come seamlessly together."   *—The Washington Post*

"A remarkable achievement . . . Frank Delaney has written a beautiful book."   —EDWARD RUTHERFURD,
New York Times bestselling author of
The Princes of Ireland

"An absolute masterpiece. With this extraordinary novel Frank Delaney joins the ranks of the greatest of Irish writers."

—JACK HIGGINS,
New York Times bestselling author of
Edge of Danger

THE LAST STORYTELLER

The Last Storyteller

A Novel of Ireland

FRANK DELANEY

RANDOM HOUSE TRADE PAPERBACKS

NEW YORK

2013 Random House Trade Paperback Edition

Copyright © 2012 by Frank Delaney, L.L.C.

Published in the United States by Random House Trade Paperbacks, an imprint of The Random House Publishing Group, a division of Random House, Inc., New York.

RANDOM HOUSE TRADE PAPERBACKS and colophon are registered trademarks of Random House, Inc.

Originally published in hardcover in the United States by Random House, an imprint of The Random House Publishing Group, a division of Random House, Inc., in 2012.

LIBRARY OF CONGRESS CATALOGING-IN-PUBLICATION DATA
Delaney, Frank
The last storyteller: a novel / Frank Delaney.
p. cm.
ISBN 978-0-8129-7975-6
eISBN 978-0-679-64422-4
1. Ireland—Fiction. 2. Ireland—Politics and government—1922–1949—Fiction. I. Title.
PR6054.E396L37 2012   823'.914—dc23   2011037154

Printed in the United States of America

www.atrandom.com

2 4 6 8 9 7 5 3 1

Book design by Dana Leigh Blanchette
Title-page illustration: iStockphoto.com

Author's Note

The classical mythologies had conspicuous purpose—to teach us how to live. Not only that, it was to their design that we built the drama that entertains us on film, on the page, on the stage. Action, betrayal, murder, romance, politics—the gods had it all. Every archetypal figure known to us—for good or bad—had a legendary beginning: the sage, the hero, the villain, the virgin. Every plot that stirs our blood, whatever its technological sophistication or contemporary reference, can first be found in the antics of Zeus and all who sprang from his forehead (or elsewhere), or the deities of China, India, Indonesia, Peru, Scandinavia—gods put their feet everywhere. Every fictional ingredient that we relish today was first savored at the feet of those mythic figures—heroism and cowardice, deed and retribution, revenge, obsession, passion, unrequited love, gain, loss, remorse, grief, redemption. Mythology was a bible ever before there was a Bible.

The Irish own an especially rich seam of mythic literature. If its themes consist in common humanity, it has a personality like no other. Warriors, naturally, play leading roles, as do impressive women, jilted lovers and wise men. Beautiful apparel features, and exquisite jewelry, and gorgeous horses, and food, and bards, and evil magicians—but to find where Irish legends differ from other mythologies, look for ambiguity, and a capacity to feel conflicting passions with equal force.

And the Irish keep regenerating their mythology. In the middle of the twentieth century, as though to keep the warrior forces of their legends rolling onward, revolution broke out again, twenty years after most of

the island believed that ancient matters with England had been somewhat resolved. The Partition, if not a wholly satisfactory result to many,
had at least proved workable. Some gods, it seems, thought otherwise.
And when matters turned bloody, the Irish saw, once again, the greatest
and subtlest of all mythology's ingredients—irony.

PART ONE

✻ ✻ ✻

The Living Legend

1

He comes back to my mind when I smell wood smoke. We had a clear and crisp October that year, and a simple white plume of smoke rose through the trees from his fairy-tale chimney. The long, quiet lane ended at his gate. My nose wrinkled as I climbed out of the car. *Applewood? Not sweet enough. Beech? Possibly, from the old mansion demesne across the road. Could it be elm?* Twenty years later it would be, as the elms died everywhere.

A white fence protected his small yard and its long rectangles of grass. He had a yellow garden bench and rosebushes, pruned to austerity. Around the side of the house I counted one, two, three fruit trees. If, on a calendar, a tourist brochure, or a postcard, you saw such a scene, with the golden roof of thatched and smocked straw, a pleased smile would cross your mind.

Not a sound to be heard, not a dog nor a bird. My breathing went short and shallow, and I swallowed, trying to manage my anticipation. Somebody had polished the door knocker so brilliantly that my fingers smudged the gleaming brass.

They said that he was eighty. Maybe he was, but when he opened the door our eyes came exactly level, and I was six feet three and a half inches. He shook hands as though closing a deal, and I was so thrilled to meet him at long last that my mouth turned dry as paper.

"Do you know anything about houses like this?" he asked as he led me into the wide old kitchen.

I knew everything about the house, I knew everything about him—but I wanted to hear it in his words, his voice.

"It feels nicely old," I ventured.

He laughed. "Hah! 'Nicely old'—I'll borrow that." Then, with some care, he turned to survey me, inclined his head a little, and smiled at me as though I were his beloved son. "I'm very pleased to meet you at last."

I said, "I'm more than pleased to meet you, sir."

He waved a hand, taking in the wide fireplace, the rafters, the room.

"This was what they called a 'strong farmer's' house. Now with 'all the modern conveniences,' as they say. I suppose you know what a strong farmer was?"

"Wasn't it somebody who supported his family from what he produced on his farm?"

"The very man," he said.

He showed me the walls—two feet thick: "They keep in the heat for the winter, and they keep out the heat of the summer—those boys knew how to build. And look, I can put wide things on the windowsills." He lifted a great bowl of jade, glinting with dragons. "Feel the weight of that. I carried it all the way back from Ceylon in 1936."

Looking up, he stretched an arm and patted a beam.

"Did you know that people used to hide weapons in their thatch?" He had a habit of nodding when he made a statement, as though agreeing with himself.

Such endearing pride: he drew my attention to everything—the floor of huge flagstones, shaped by a local stonemason; the handmade chairs from a neighboring carpenter, who had also built the long table dominating the middle of the room. He rubbed it with his hand. "In the original they'd have used a timber called white deal. I had to settle for pine."

"When did you buy the place?" I asked.

"Twenty-eight years, two months, and four days ago. When I finally came in off the road." He surveyed the walls. "There was only the shell here, it was burned out by the redcoats in 1848—there was that bit of a rebellion that year, and evictions everywhere. When I bought it you could still see the black streaks at the top of the walls where they'd burned out the straw on the roof."

He gave me the tour—but let me cut this short and give you the essential fact. This man, regarded (and jealously guarded) by the Folklore Commission as the most powerful remaining storyteller in the country, and possibly in the world, had restored fully an old farmhouse of considerable proportions. The conservationists, while allowing for the modern plumbing and electricity, had applauded him. "An elegant and authentic reconstruction," they'd said, "solid, proud, and wholeheartedly traditional." And that's what I mean by "the essential fact": the house was the man, and the man was the house.

He stood with his back to the fire. "So I'm to be yours now, am I?" he said. "How's James doing?"

"I believe he's holding on."

Mixed feelings were always going to leak into this visit. For years, my superior, my mentor, otherwise so good to me, had kept this man for himself, and I had not been allowed to visit him, write to him, have anything to do with him. But now my mentor had bequeathed him to me because he himself, the inimitable James Clare, lay silent and still in Dublin, his lungs closing down day by day to emphysema. That morning I had made a note in my journal: *I think that James will die soon.*

"He won't hold on long," said Mr. O'Neill—full name, John Jacob Farrell O'Neill. "What color do you think Death's face will be when it comes for James?"

"Gray," I said, without thinking, "It'll be gray." I knew that color. From the war.

"That's what I think, too." He nodded, and turned his head around to look into the fire. When he turned back he said, "Then you'll be ready."

My mind asked, *Ready for what?*

Even though I didn't speak the question, he answered it.

"Ready for everything."

He couldn't have known what "everything" would come to mean—or could he?

2

I wasn't ready for anything—and in particular, not for the events of the next day, when I halted for a pub sandwich in the little town of Urlingford.

It was the siesta time, and raining. Nothing should have been happening, and nothing was. Using no energy, I eavesdropped on the silence around me, punctuated by snatches of idle conversation.

"They say she will." This came out of the blue from an old coot at the bar, his nose hooked as Punch's.

"I bet she won't," said his drinking companion.

"She told Midge Corcoran," said the barman, "that all he wants to do is look at her."

"God, then he's paying dear for that," said Punch, whose pal had wide-open nostrils like little gun barrels.

The pal said, "There's fifty-two years between them."

To which Ted, the fat and fatuous barman, said, "One for every week of the year."

I knew these people well—not as individuals, but as a culture. Filthy old cords, worse boots, scant hygiene, no (you can bet on it) underwear. Every day of the week I saw men like them. Sitting at some bar everywhere, gossiping like knitters, stitching and bitching. Doing no work because there was no work, rarely a job that one could call a decent hire. Just sitting there talking. Talking, talking, talking. Or being silent. *Silent in the hatred of their lives* was what I'd always figured, until I realized that their emotions stood at zero. Their needles flickered only for sport or gossip.

In their faces I could see the blue veins of perdition, lines on a map of the country. That's why I listened but kept my distance: I didn't want to be infected with their ruin or catch their low-rent banality. Shallow as a saucer, they had no value to me in terms of what I collected.

Yet they caused some affect. For no reason that I could identify, I felt my chest tighten, and I heard the question in my mind: *What's making you anxious?*

Ted the barman had a smarm to him, aiming to please everyone. In the past, before I'd mellowed down, I'd have needled him, picked a fight. The frosted glass panel beside me hadn't been cleaned in a generation.

Most Irish pubs had a snug, a little room shuttered from the world, open only to the barman, where, typically, ladies were supposed to do their drinking because it was too indelicate for them to be seen in the public bar. Thus, I often found the snug a useful place to sit and listen.

My anxiety climbed. I fought a pricking of my thumbs and turned my ears inward. A frigid Saturday in late 1956, in my struggling, depressed native land.

Silence fell. We had a cough or two, a clink from a glass, a match being struck to light a cigarette. The rain no longer lashed the window. Weak sunlight spread a mild and yellow fire on the roofs of the houses across the street. With a clang of a latch rudely lifted, the pub's front door burst open. Jimmy Bermingham flew in, landed, and came straight toward me. Thus began the most dreadful part of my life.

3

Once upon a time, and it was a long time ago, when boys were boys, and girls were girls, and bears combed the fur on their coats, and the soldiers of the north carried spears of ice, and giant frogs who spoke in rhymes ruled our hemisphere, there lived a man who had a love as noble as the mountains, and as deep as the deep blue sea.

The story John Jacob Farrell O'Neill told me on that night of my first heady visit to him took so long that we didn't part until three o'clock in the morning. With the comfort of the chair by the fireplace, and the logs he kept heaping on the broad orange flames, I felt so safe.

"What's that you're burning?" I asked.

"Believe it or not," he said, "cherry. For the aroma. I had an old cherry tree out the back—I tried for years to save it, but it wanted to go. And

do you know what? When they took it to the sawmill they found a musket ball in the heart of the wood."

From the mantelpiece he took down a small white dish, in which, like
a little iron eye, rested the old musket ball. We marveled together.

He cooked for me. From a pot hanging over the fire he produced an
excellent meal of lamb stew, with onions and carrots and potatoes. He
moved around his large kitchen with the agility of a girl. The silver watch
chain on his vest caught the light from the fire.

His various tics interested me. I've mentioned the nodding, though
he didn't nod after everything he said, and soon it calmed down—perhaps
it was a shyness response. Now and then he fiddled with his breast-pocket
handkerchief, rebunching it. When listening to me (not that I spoke
much), he pursed his lips into a small bow.

I looked at him, thinking, but not saying, *I wonder if he has always
cooked, if he never married?* And he said, "I've always cooked. You can't
have a wife if you spend your life on the road—'twould be unfair to a
woman. So I never married."

Here's a note I made that night: *Such a practiced voice, educated by the
universe, every word clear and warm. But—he's an uncanny man. Don't yet
know how or why.*

James Clare had said to me: *It all comes together in this fellow. He's the
culmination.*

This is what James meant: in his years and mine, traveling as collectors for the Irish Folklore Commission, James and I had heard all kinds
of things: herbal cures, rambling ballads, family curses, jigs and reels
played on fiddles and pipes, nonsense verse, riddles and recitations—and,
above all, stories. Call them legends, call them fragments of mythology,
call them, simply, "lore"; they had become my staple diet.

Some descended from family traditions—a handed-down account,
say, of a row over an inheritance. (Such tales, a few generations old, customarily began with the droll comment "Where there's a Will, there's a
lawsuit.") Others, probably most of the stories I collected, came from the
deep and ancient past, from prehistory.

Frequently they had fused, and I'd heard many contemporary versions of tales first scribed by holy men of the fifth, sixth, and seventh
centuries. These clerics had been taught to write so that they could copy
psalms and church doctrine, but they hadn't been able to resist preserv-

ing the ancient stories they'd heard around their childhood firesides. (And perhaps they'd even invented a few.) Those epics became the basis of our literature in Ireland.

Most of the storytellers I'd visited hadn't known or fussed over the provenance of their tales; they cared only for the telling. My man, though, had spent a lifetime drinking from all the fountains. He had, naturally, pored over the monkish volumes, but he had also heard many of his stories in the old ancestral way, in his own home.

Furthermore, he truly did have tales from everywhere: material picked up during his travels in Burma, or Peru, from old men in Australia, or anecdotes of local history told to him here and there across the world.

Most exciting of all to me, I had always heard that he was from a mold cast in Ireland before the Romans had an empire. Meaning that John Jacob Farrell O'Neill was a fireside storyteller in the "old style"—he narrated in the ancient way: his voice orotund, his words full of ornament and color. He was a true, performing descendant of the bards who had entertained kings and chieftains long before Christ was born.

For that, and all the other reasons I've listed, he was, indeed, "the culmination."

4

Children, you have asked for this final account of my life, and eagerly I give it to you. As you already know the terms of my Will—"I leave everything I possess to my beloved twins, Ben and Louise"—therefore we can, I suppose, call this a Last Testament. There's no fear in me that I shan't live long enough to finish it; I have more than enough energy.

In advance I ask your forgiveness for a somewhat jagged beginning to this, the final phase of my *confessio*. Yes, my tongue is in my cheek as I use that pompous old medieval term, but I think you'll come to see why I chose it, and I think, I hope, you'll also come to understand this early jaggedness you might feel; it is deliberate—because this is a sharp-edged and dark side of my life that I have to tell.

Already you know the essence of your father's story, and that of Venetia, your dear mother, but there's so much that you don't know. For instance, John Jacob O'Neill: I placed him at the very beginning of this account. The reasons, as we go along, will become plain to you.

If you ask why I've never mentioned him in our conversations, I'll confess the selfish truth. I feared that were I to share him—with anybody—I'd have dissipated his power over me. Even after my involvement with him had long ceased, I was afraid that I might lose the spirit of him in me, like those legends where the magic figure must disappear before dawn. And I was the mortal in that legend; in my middle years he put the final shape to my life.

There are other things I haven't told you: the shadows that lay ahead of me, and the vile dealings and revelations; the fear, the awfulness of what I did, the loving strangers, the glorious light that also shone on me. In greater detail, I haven't given you, for instance, a full account of Jimmy Bermingham, and his role in your sad and appalling bereavement.

Nor have I ever told you in true depth my own loneliness and desolation when, having first lost your mother, I walked the wet roads of Ireland, mistaken for a young tramp, laboring for any farmer who would hire me, or often without work and therefore with no bed for the night.

In those days, and many times since, I kept myself alive by self-interrogation. For example: *How should I be kind? How does one grow kind? How might I learn to be loving and watchful?* I asked such questions when I had nobody for whom to care, but always, I admit, with Venetia, your mother, in mind. Yet I also said to myself, *You failed. She's gone. You didn't protect her.* And I'd fight back from that melancholy fact with *But one day, I believe it in my bones and my blood, one day we'll be together again.*

It didn't matter how futile my hope. It didn't matter whether she was dead or alive. It didn't matter, even after I'd met her again, that she had married another and was raising the two of you with him. The life-giving hope endured; the dream lived on.

Every day, imagining a great moment when she and I would once again belong to each other, I planned all sorts of caring things. I invented promises and anticipated the time when I could put them into practice. Those thoughts—they warmed me, I wrote them down, and I could always hear them, even above the never-ending drums of accusation.

I can hear them still. *For our winter fireplaces I will have a woodpile. And a workbench for fixing things. I will be impeccable in my hygiene and my manners. You will never see me looking as decrepit as I do now. I promise to shave every day. I will never leave the house with unpolished shoes. And never, never will I go out without telling you where I'm going. I will be so kind to you, tender beyond your most romantic dreams.*

How I will spoil you. Buy you things. Make you laugh, and never make you cry, unless through the telling of a touching story. I will come home to you with news of the outside world, and the strange things I hear in my daily work, and I will watch your eyes widen in wonder and delight and awe as I tell you. I will love you for being my finest audience, and for the talk we shall have, and the thoughts we shall share.

There the fantasy ended and the bitter reality took over, because I had long known what I wanted and had never had the courage to do anything about it. Here's the colder fact: I stood back from it. A coward. In depth. Constantly ashamed. And rightly so. For many reasons.

5

First impressions of Jimmy Bermingham: thin like a dancer; quicksilver flicks and twitches; seedy hint of the gambler. A long time after these blood-spattered upheavals, a friend of his said to me, "Do you remember the clothes he wore?"

I do indeed—and the guns he carried.

He had a camel coat on him that day, draped across his shoulders like a cloak, brown velvet tabs on his collar, and a pink shirt and a pink striped tie. *Pink? In the Irish countryside?*

Jimmy Bermingham looked me up and down. Can you believe—can I myself believe it?—that this man would lead me around my own country by the nose? He was twenty-eight then, fourteen years younger than me, in his shiny black shoes, socks with clocks on them like a bandleader, and the sultry dark eyes of Marlon Brando.

He sat down on my bench and drew the skirts of the camel coat loosely about him, like a young emperor arranging his cloak. "Now, Captain? I'm Jimmy Bermingham." He offered a hand, slim, quick, and cold as a fish. "And I know who you are. Ben MacCarthy. By God, I do, and I have a ton of respect for you."

Surprising? Not entirely. I had traveled around this island; many people knew me, and many more had heard of me.

"Captain, you collect stories." (He was often going to call me "Captain," regardless of my never having fired a shot. At least not a shot that I'd ever tell him about.) "D'you want to hear a real good one? Actually, I suppose it's more of a joke, really."

"Jokes can be stories," I said, in a soothing, hushing tone, "and I'm always in the market for a good joke."

He leaned back. His hands had been manicured, something I had never seen in an Irishman at that time (except doctors). I had met a German officer during the war who had also had impeccable fingernails, but back then in rural Ireland, daily soap and water still challenged some folk.

Jimmy Bermingham squared his shoulders and prepared for his little performance.

"There was a man up in Galway one night, and he was just getting ready for bed when a knock comes to the door. He goes back downstairs muttering, Who the blazes is this at this hour of the night?, and when he opens the door there's a snail on the doorstep. A big snail, nice shiny shell, and the little gray, greasy horns sticking up. And the snail says to the man, 'Good evening to you, sir. I'm sorry to disturb you, but could I interest you in buying a set of encyclopedias?'

"Well, Jesus God, the man is only livid and he still has his boots on, and he kicks the snail off the doorstep. Big strong kick. Snail goes sailing through the air, hits the far ditch. And the man closes the door, and he goes back up the stairs, and goes to sleep.

"Two years later, two years nearly to the day, the man is getting ready for bed again, and again the knock comes to the door. So he goes downstairs, and he opens the door, and who's there only the snail, on the doorstep again, big shiny shell on him, little sticky-up, greasy-gray horns, and the snail looks up at the man and says, 'What the hell was that for?' "

I laughed and laughed, so much that I had a coughing fit, and then I laughed some more. Jimmy Bermingham looked as pleased as a child. In his three-piece chalk-striped suit and his pinks, he seemed somewhere between an executive, a young con man, and a doubtful bookie.

"That's my test of people," he said. "Most of 'em don't laugh because they don't get the bit about how it took the snail two years to get back up on the doorstep. But they're buck stupid. What are you drinking, Captain?"

I said, "I've had enough for today."

He said, "In that case, I'll only have lemonade." He stood and called to the barman, "Ted! Lemonade for the cripple in here."

When he sat down beside me again, he said, "Now, tell me about your name. I've a great interest in what we have to call people."

He savored each detail, interrupting me as I told him.

"Ben? That's a nice name. Is it 'Benedict' or 'Benjamin'? No, not Benjamin, I'd say, there's not that many Jews down around here, is there? So it has to be Benedict." Then he said, "But MacCarthy, though? Ah, God. Great old name, great old Irish tribal name. Decent people, the MacCarthys. What does 'MacCarthy' mean if you translate it from Irish?"

I told him, "It means 'beloved' " (I've always enjoyed saying that), and he clapped his hands in delight.

"Great! And are you beloved yourself, Captain Ben?"

I said, "That's a long story."

6

In every family there's the shrub under the oak, the one who gets overshadowed. Here's what I mean. How do you carve out a champion's place in your own life if your brother is the most daring hunter, the most fearless warrior, and the most eloquent lover since the day the plates of the earth parted and Ireland rose to the surface of the sea, already green and beautiful, with sheep dotted like white mice on the faraway hillsides and birds singing long, melodious songs in the trees? Did you know that there are certain birds that fly just for their own delight? They whirl about the air above us in their slow and flitting dances of mystery.

John Jacob O'Neill's pipe glowed, his hands lay folded across his tweed vest with its watch chain. The flames leaped to a steady height. My cheeks grew warm. For reasons of length, I can't reproduce here the entire tale he told me that night; it lasted six hours. I hope, though, to give you the main thrust of that legend, and at the same time convey some idea of John Jacob O'Neill's power and narrative glamour.

Well, in my story of the man whose love was as fathomless as the deep blue sea, with all her silver shoals and floating tendrils, the overshadowed fellow has the name Malachi, or Mal MacCool. He was the younger and only sibling of the mighty Finn MacCool, the greatest man who ever lived, Finn MacCool, a fellow so egregious and remarkable that from the time he was eight years old the gods had been eyeing him as a recruit. Do you know what the word "egregious" comes from? It comes from "grex, gregis," the Latin word for "flock," and "e" or "ex," meaning "outside of."

So, in the MacCool family, Malachi became the one who stayed at home and worked the farm. He was the boy who gave his parents their dutiful due and made their sun rise every morning. Unlike his famous brother, Malachi was a shy fellow, grateful for the long, shiny eyelashes that birth had given him, because they helped him to keep his gaze downcast. They had named him perfectly—"Malachi" is an old word meaning "the messenger of the gods."

He had his own gifts, though. Many a time his bare white hand swooped down and scooped a pink-and-silver salmon from a fast-flowing torrent. His slingshot became an object of muttering and fear among the bad and the mad. His smile, they said, could melt the ice from the mountain streams when spring was overdue.

And Mal had his own talents as a warrior. When rapscallion neighbors tried to steal fields from him, he turned into a reluctant though nonetheless rousing fighter. He didn't want to go to war, but when he did, bravery became his signature, fearlessness his stamp, and valor his seal, and he grew famous throughout the land. For seven long years he waged the fight for his green fields, and when the war ended he went back to his farm and his parents.

When they passed away, Mal stood alone. Some men weaken under the pressures of solitude, some prosper; it's a matter of character. Mal strode the land, burgeoning in his spirit, a gentleman respected and admired. He built a great house, and he modeled it on the mansions you see in the morning when you look up at the cities and towns in the clouds above your head. The clouds, after all, were the first castles in the air.

Mal's house had colonnades and architraves and clerestories and cloisters. So marbled did he make it, and so brightly did it gleam, that people came from far away to see it. And they also hoped to catch a glimpse of this fine and famous man, so handsome, so tall—in his robes, with his neat, trimmed beard and his big jeweled bracelet and his great rings—in this mansion fit for the gods. They went away swooning with wonder.

Among those who came to view were the women of the world. "But look," they said, "he's all alone in that big house, and he has no wife, he hasn't chick nor child."

Such a vacuum gives offense to every woman. Mal might have been a mighty landowner, with rolling acres and woodlands barbered like a bishop's jowls, and he might have been as handsome and as rich as the man who owns the sun, but he was all alone.

He would dearly have liked to marry—but a chap who has been on the battlefield gets to know himself very well, and Mal knew that he had not yet seen the woman who would take possession of his heart and hold it in her soul.

And then one day, a day of sun and roses, a mercenary blacksmith came by with his beautiful daughter, Emer.

7

How should I describe the inside of my mind the next day? It rang with the music of John Jacob's voice, it lit up with the brilliance of his word-pictures, it thrilled to the antiquity of his tale, first noted down, perhaps, in some long-ruined, limestone abbey, Mellifont, Durrow, Clonmacnoise.

Yet there I was, sitting in a pub, a lower world, and thus robbing myself of the previous night's elevation. On a damp and slovenly day I had subscribed to a cliché: I had allowed myself to be drawn into a classic Irish conversation, random talk, half an inch deep, about everything and nothing, where strangers exchange snatches of knowledge and gossip and faux intimacy.

So I told Jimmy Bermingham about Venetia. Because he asked. He said, "Listen, you can't say to a man, 'That's a long story' and then not tell it."

How many times had I told it? In love when I was eighteen with a beautiful actress named Venetia Kelly. Whom I married on a ship in Galway Bay, when she wore flowers in her hair on a day of bliss. Stolen from me by her ruthless, murderous family. I searched high up and low down for her. Long thought her dead. Murdered. I dug woods and mountainsides looking for her grave.

And then I found her again. Met her many years after, on a beach in Florida. She'd had twins by me, Ben and Louise, one named after me, one after my mother. I walked away. Away from Venetia. Couldn't handle it. Away, therefore, from my children, too. And thus I'd never met them, never even seen them. That's the story I told him. A true story.

"Never even seen them?" he echoed. "Jesus, that's bad. How old are they?"

"Their mother is back in Ireland now."

He twisted toward me on the bench. "Where is she?"

"They're in their twenties. Not small children anymore. Born 1933."

"Ah, shag it, Captain, go look for her," said Jimmy Bermingham. "Go on. I'll come with you. Moral support."

Since that day I've shunned "moral support" with all my strength.

I said to him, "There's a show going around—*Gentleman Jack and His Friend.*"

"Oh, yeh, I saw posters on a lamppost somewhere. Catchy name."

"Jack Stirling is his real name," I said. "She's with him now."

"So is she the 'friend'?"

I hope you never know pain such as the anguish I encountered because of Gentleman Jack. And I don't mean mere jealousy.

"Yes," I sighed. "She's the friend, all right."

Jimmy Bermingham said, "I'll kill him for you if you like. And nobody'd know."

Next, in this newfound ersatz profundity, Jimmy Bermingham told me about his own deep and abiding love.

"My pet name for her is 'Dirty' Marian," he said.

"Well, that's some term of endearment," I remarked. He ignored it.

"Wait till you meet her, Captain—you'll see what I mean. But, God, she keeps me at a distance. She's as haughty as a cat."

"Is that because you call her 'Dirty' Marian?"

He said, "What chance has a fellow but to fight back?"

Now the asteroids began to crash.

First, a girl walked in. We'd kept our snug door wide open, so Jimmy and I retained a full view of the pub's general space. The girl, pretty as a rosebush, glanced all around.

Hmm. She's hunted-looking. Searching for somebody? But hoping not to find them?

We all stared at her tight red sweater.

Whatever she sought, she didn't find it, and she bit her lip. She stood back against the closed door, her hands behind her back. As adrift as a loose boat, she began to cry. She dragged a toe back and forth, drawing marks on the sawdust floor.

This is wrong. There's something bad here. Is this why I've been feeling anxious, this damned prescience again? And last night's names are bells in my head: Malachi MacCool, Finn MacCool, the beautiful girl's name, Emer . . .

Beside me, I felt my new friend freeze. Through the door of the snug she saw Jimmy, too—insofar as she saw anybody. As quickly as she'd arrived she wanted to go, and she reached for the front door's latch.

Jimmy called out. "Come over here and talk to us."

She shook her head. "I can't. Honest."

"Of course you can." This, as I would learn, was Jimmy's response to every difficulty. He stood up. "This is my great friend Ben," he said, as though we'd trekked the Himalayas together. "What's your name?"

The girl hesitated. I thought, *She's between heaven and hell*—and I figured it more accurately than I yet knew.

Looking all around the bar, she took a half step forward.

"He'll kill me this time—he'll kill me stone dead."

Jimmy said, "Well, I'd better do something," then whispered to me, "Isn't she a trigger, Captain?"

I stood and thrust an arm across him. "I'll do it."

In two strides I was with her.

"They're following me," she whispered from a chalk-white face.

I opened the pub door and pointed.

"See that car over there? That's mine. Go and sit in it."

"No. They're here in the town. They'll see me."

I insisted: "Keep your head low. I'll be out in a few minutes. You'll be fine."

"Come with me."

"No, they'll notice two people. Run."

I watched until she had opened the car door, clambered in, and ducked down.

Said the barman, ponderous as an ox, "Her name is Elma. Elma Sloane. She's twenty." He slavered a little and repeated her name. "Yep. Elma Sloane."

Jimmy said, "She looked terrified."

We sat down again. The barman closed the snug door, and we didn't stop him. But the door ended four feet from the floor, and minutes later, looking under it, we saw the boots.

Three pairs. They tramped in, heavy with menace, and stood. Big boots, brown-gray dirt on them. Boots that could kick a man to death. Two of them were outfitted with gaiters, the cut-off tops of Wellingtons sheathing the leg from knee to ankle. The third pair of boots shone with polish and rain.

Hook-nosed Punch, and his old-coot pal, and Ted the barman—they all fell silent. Then Ted said, "Hallo there, lads. Damp class of a day, huh? Whatchyou havin'?"

The boots stood side by side, a tiny, powerful regiment. Not a shift. Not a move. And no answer. We raised our eyebrows: *What do you think of this, eh?* How the boots hadn't seen Elma Sloane cross the street to my car, I just don't know. Jimmy Bermingham hunched his shoulders and half-sniggered.

How long did they stand there? A minute? Longer? I can't say. The door of the snug crashed open, a Neanderthal face looked in, as fierce and tangled as a briar bush, retreated from its glimpse of us, and closed the door again. They left. And closed the door behind them.

8

Malachi MacCool took one look at the girl and reeled back like a man kicked in the chest by a stallion. He had seen his heart's desire. Twice he had to look at her, because the first time a flash of forked lightning came down from the sky, got under his long, shiny eyelashes, and blinded him for a moment.

But when he opened his eyes, the girl hadn't gone away. Emer was her name, and she stood there like a pillar of the gentle light you see on a summer dawn. She was as sweet as cane sugar, thoughtful and serene, and yet playful, and of a fond nature.

Mal couldn't speak, except in his head, where he kept saying, "Oh." At last he took the girl's hand and welcomed her. She wore a green gown down to her ankles, the neck of it bound in gold embroidered braid. She had fingers as long and white as the lilies of the field. She was so lovely that Mal's heart tumbled like an acrobat inside his broad chest, and he smiled that innocent smile of eternal love that men smile only once in their lives. If they're fortunate.

Now and then John Jacob paused, carried on some business with his pipe, or gazed into the fire, his demeanor as peaceful as a child's. He had the countryman's face, his cheeks red as a pippin apple. Earlier he had put a match to the wick of an old oil lamp at the far end of the kitchen, and when he turned off the electric lights, we had only the lamp's yellow glow and the red power of the fire.

The blacksmith, looking on, believed that it would take very little work to secure this lucrative bridegroom. Knowing that the appetite increases when it is denied, he whisked his daughter away, taking their leave with courtesy. And no sooner were they up on their cart than the blacksmith, as gleeful as a songbird, said to his daughter, "There's your husband for you. We'll be important people yet."

But the girl, who had great spirit, retorted, "I'm not marrying any man as old as that."

Like so many Irish legends, the tale grew into a love story. The brother of Finn MacCool, in his advanced middle years, at last fell in love—with the daughter of a scheming farrier, "a ree-raw of a fellow," as Mr. O'Neill called him, meaning a rambunctious and hostile man, who set up his beautiful daughter as an asset to be cashed in.

Well, the blacksmith flew into a rage as high as a cat's back. When they got home, he hauled the girl down off the cart, dragged her into the house, lashed her with a swishing ash stick, and locked her in a dark closet until, as he said, she'd come to her senses. The poor mother never said a word—she was tired out anyway, having so many children to cook and wash and sew for.

As the tale developed, John Jacob sat up straighter and firmer, leaning and thrusting, in rhythm with the drama, hurling lines of the story like bolts across the gap between us.

The world took its turns that night, as the world always does, its clouds swirling around the moon, its blue oceans churning from pole to pole. Though Emer sobbed and wailed, the blacksmith's house quieted down, more in fear than from any other feeling. Later that same week, a messenger came to the door, a fellow spry as spring, with green eyes, and he said that Malachi Mac-Cool, the great warrior, the great farmer, the great landowner, brother to Finn MacCool, the greatest man who ever lived, wished to visit.

Now the house turned upside down. The angels of heaven never polished the golden staircase so brightly, and the twelve children had their teeth brushed and their noses pointed. Yet Emer stood as distant from all this as a tree above a river.

9

We walked across the wide main street of Urlingford to my car. Jimmy Bermingham had bandy legs like a jockey. With his coat draped across his shoulders and his thumbs deep in the pockets of his vest, he whistled a tune. Inside, I twisted. *My anxiety is so high. What's happening to me?*

When I opened the car door, Elma rose from her hiding place on the back seat and reached for my hand like a child. Jimmy Bermingham pushed up the passenger seat and climbed into the rear seat beside her.

"Why aren't you getting into the front?" she asked, shivering. Jimmy Bermingham took off his coat and wrapped it around her; she huddled into it like a mouse into cotton wool.

I looked back at her and smiled. "You'll be all right."

Little sting to the heart: Venetia had a smile as innocent as that.

And so three people, complete strangers to one another, set out on a coldish rainy afternoon in County Kilkenny in the year 1956, not knowing what on earth lay ahead.

I said, "Listen, I don't exactly know what's happening here."

"They want me to marry a man out the road here; he has a big farm of land. My father's after whipping me twice."

"Whipping you?" I said.

"Look." She twisted in the seat, leaned forward, and took down a shoulder of the red sweater. A broad weal, mauve with evil, ran under her straps.

"He's over fifty years older than me," she said. "But he has pucks of money."

"Did he whip you, too?" asked Jimmy.

"He says that when he looks at me he gets tears in his eyes. He says 'tis pure joy. But I think he has stomach trouble."

"Probably always had a bad bag," said Jimmy, sounding full of wisdom. "The stomach gets at you early in life."

"I take it you don't love him," I said.

"If I knew what love felt like, I'd tell you," Elma said.

"Hah, we're the boys to teach you that," said Jimmy Bermingham. "Aren't we, Ben?"

10

Emer turned Malachi MacCool down in favor of a younger man. Thus the drama sharpened. I thought that I heard an owl in the trees outside. Or was it the wind in the chimney?

"He's the son of a chieftain," Emer said to Malachi. "I hope you under-

stand. He's nearly the same age as me, and he will be the chieftain himself one day."

Mal, though stricken to the heart, nodded his head in agreement. Not so the farrier, who raged and ranted. He grabbed his daughter by the arm and began to shake her like a child shakes a doll. Mal, ever the gentleman, intervened. Holding the blacksmith at arm's length, he said to Emer, "Go to him, go to your young man." She kissed Mal on the cheek and stepped away from him.

Malachi MacCool locked himself in. He never again came out to walk his fields or inspect his beloved cattle. He kept his rooms dark, because he never again wanted to distinguish night from day. His cook left meals for him outside the door. Mal didn't eat the meals. He saw nobody, spoke to nobody, not even his trusted steward. Inside his chamber, he pined away, and if you do not believe that a man can die of a broken heart, then you do not understand the story of Mal MacCool and his love.

John Jacob drew near the end. His telling, though it had rambled across seven counties, never for a second lost the original thread. As he described Mal's decline, he powered up and grew more urgent. His voice cracked just enough, his eyes gleamed with tears, his shoulders reflected all the mourning of a great man brought low by love. This was grand opera, in solo recital.

One morning, after days of silence, the steward and his men broke down the door of the bedchamber, and they found Mal dead on his great gold chair. They buried him in his highest field standing up in a stone cairn. From there he could look out over the valley—a valley he had owned from horizon to horizon.

There was no inheritance, because there had been nobody to whom he wished to bequeath anything. His property was raided the day after the funeral and the house ransacked. Adjacent farmers staked claims to his fields and fought over them, killing men in their land hunger. Eventually they settled it all, and when their greed had subsided, every trace of Malachi MacCool and his estates vanished from the land as water seeps into the earth.

Now, in the final stages of the telling, John Jacob sat taller in his chair, and as his hands and upper body grew ever more animated, his voice took on a freight of regret.

Emer married the chieftain's boy, and they had three sons and three

*daughters. But, as some women do, she realized over the years that she had
married a bad egg, a worthless man who would rather talk than work.*

*She lived for her children, though now and then she allowed herself to
think of Mal and his proposals of marriage, and his frantic words of love to
her. And sure enough, bit by bit, she began to spend the rest of her life pining
for him. By the time her own journey to the next world had begun, she was
more in love with Mal MacCool than he had ever been with her. Whether
they reunited in the mighty and bright hereafter, I cannot tell. We are not
permitted to draw aside that curtain that reaches from the sky to the earth,
and from pole to pole, because we are not gods.*

*And so that has to be the end of my story of Malachi, or Mal MacCool,
the brother of Finn MacCool, the greatest man who ever lived. And as long
as I keep a clean heart and an open mind, another story will come along presently to fill that story's place.*

11

The rain slapped down, wide and flat, forcing me to reduce my speed.
Elma leaned far into her corner and closed her eyes. My good and familiar feeling of insulation returned. In my car I felt safe and sealed from the
world, and that activated an orderly side of myself that I liked. On this
"traveling desk" I had retrieval of all my pens, notebooks, and address
files, the tools of my trade.

Nothing ever cluttered the seats, in case I took aboard unusual travelers, such as the pair now dozing in my rear seats. Or gave a lift, as I often
did, to some walker on a country road, such as the man who suddenly
flagged me down in the driving rain.

Naturally, I stopped for him. That's what we did in Ireland in those
days—we gave lifts to hitchhikers in all their variety: students, housewives shopping in the local town, home-going drunks. I kept the passenger seat beside me covered with a special waterproof cover from a
mail-order firm in England.

And I needed it that day. The man, tall and angular as a long shadow, had been walking into the driven rain. It had soaked his coat, his hat, every cubic inch of him. In the wide, flat land around us now, no trees cushioned the skyline; he had no shelter or protection from that drenching gale.

I leaned across and opened the door. He scrambled in, knocking his hat half off. *He's exhausted. He's too old to be walking the roads in this rain. He's too well-to-do. What the hell's he doing?*

Lowering his sodden hat to his sodden knee, he pinched the water from his eyes.

"Thanks, oh thanks, thanks for stopping. There wasn't a soul on the road—you're the first car I saw. Thanks, thanks."

I said, "You're all right."

"Oh, thanks, you're my good luck today."

"Did you come far?"

"D'you know Urlingford?" he said, and as the words left his lips and hung there between us, I knew what was coming next. I glanced in the mirror and saw a frozen, wide-awake face, horror alive in her aghast young eyes.

The rain-soaked gentleman either caught my expression or felt the mood. He half-turned, looked back over his shoulder, and I thought that he would forever hold his head in that position. High drama may last for no more than a moment, but in our memories it lives on as an hour, an aeon. On impulse I slowed the car.

"God," said the stranger.

"Oh, God above," said Elma.

"What are you doing to me, Elma?" he asked in half a whimper. "What are you doing to me?"

"Dan, you're after me, aren't you?" she wailed. "Aren't you?"

"What-what?" said Jimmy Bermingham, also waking up—at which moment the stranger clasped his hand to his own upper body and said, "Elma, I think 'tis the case that you're after poisoning me."

At those words he turned back to face the windshield and began to convulse. He grabbed his left biceps and fought for breath as his face turned first red and then ash-gray. Twisting in the seat, he scrabbled a hand toward his door, as though to escape. Then he slumped. His head, heavy as a rock, fell onto my shoulder.

12

At a later time, I asked Mr. O'Neill where he had learned his trade. He gave me a curt answer: "It's not a trade, it's an art."

I could tell that he had read Homer. Where Homer repeats phrases such as "Dawn came with rosy fingers," he, in that first story, repeated three or four times, "Finn MacCool, the greatest man who ever lived," and "The world took its turns, as the world always does." I once noted down some tales from a man up in Mayo, out in the wilds of Bangor Erris, who repeated the phrase, no matter what the story, "Now a woman would never say that, especially a woman who had chickens to feed."

They did it, those ancient storytellers, to give our minds—and their voices—a tiny respite. Mr. O'Neill (his name, he said, means "descended from champions") followed his recurring phrases with a little pause: to fill a pipe, throw a log on the fire, or rub down fresh tobacco with the heel of his hand. And when he'd finished, we neither of us spoke until a log shifted in the fire and broke the spell. I thanked him—and my few words sounded meager.

He stood with me outside his door. The moon had reached the west and was quitting the sky.

"I'm glad you got here," he said.

All my life I have looked for leadership. I am drawn to those who lead, especially if they show a benign nature. By now I knew that I would have done anything for this man, any task he might have set me. I didn't yet know why.

"Mr. O'Neill, may I come to see you again?"

The pause he took made me panicky: *Have I done something wrong?*

Then he spoke: "I think you'll find that you have to."

I had no idea that night what he meant; I do now.

13

Elma Sloane ran her hands through her hair, then slapped them to her face like placards. She moaned without stopping for breath.

"Oh-God-oh-God-oh-God."

Like a taskmaster I said, "Elma!"

"It's-all-my-fault-it's-all-my-fault-it's-all-my-fault."

I snapped at her again: "Enough."

"Ben, turn the car around," said Jimmy Bermingham, "Cashel hospital."

No dramatics. No histrionics. Just find a gate and make a calm, three-point turn.

I've always looked beyond the idea of illness to the place of that ailment in the sufferer's story. For instance, my father kept falling and breaking limbs, and he had made so many missteps in his life. My beloved mother, always timid before the universe, suffered rashes on her face and hands.

I wish I had collected stories to illustrate my theory. Was there some legend—of some king, say, an unaware man with no insight who went blind? My friend Trigger McGowan, he had a sister who criticized him every time she saw him; he married a wife of similarly abusive gifts. And slowly, over the years, Trigger went deaf—for no diagnosable reason. But he could still play the concertina like a genius.

Here, in front of my eyes, my theories rose again. Sitting beside me, with Jimmy Bermingham trying to reach forward and stabilize him, was an old man convulsing within reach of the young girl to whom he had lost his heart.

I drove quickly enough to hurry, slowly enough to handle the rainstorm. Elma's weeping wasn't as silent as she thought. *Keep the old gentleman stable. He's still breathing. Jimmy Bermingham seems remarkably confident.*

"His name is Dan?" he asked Elma Sloane.

"Yes. Dan. Oh God."

Jimmy said, "Dan, if you can hear me, cough and keep coughing. Cough. Deep breath. Cough. Right?"

"Do you know what you're doing?" I said.

"Medical student. Nine and a half years."

Jimmy let go for a moment to stabilize his own crouching position, and the old man's head swung toward my jaw; spittle flew from his mouth and landed on the back of my hand. He breathed in rasps and gasps.

How many miles to Cashel? Thirty? Twenty? I've walked it often enough, I ought to know.

"Okay, Dan, okay?" Jimmy reclaimed the head, held it straight. "Dan, cough again, right? Keep coughing. Deep breath. Cough. Right?"

Good fortune defused our panic. In the short driveway of a farm I saw an ambulance with its doors open. The paramedics were unloading someone into the farmhouse, hurrying the wheelchair through the rain. I reeled the car off the road.

Minutes later, we were transferring our old gentleman from the car as though he were a frail child.

"Shouldn't maybe somebody go with him?" Elma asked.

The ambulance driver said, "I know who he is—his niece is a nurse with us in the hospital. He'll be fine."

As he closed the door I heard the old gentleman moan, and I knew whose name he called, but I said nothing.

Back in the car, Elma said, "Now look at me. Now look at what I'm after doing." Weeping openly, she was lost again.

"You did nothing wrong," said Jimmy Bermingham. He put his arm around her, took out his flashy handkerchief, and wiped her tears. She gave him her face like a child.

I said, "You can't be responsible for how he feels."

"But I never led him on," she said. "This is all my father."

Don't tell me that your father is a blacksmith. And that your name isn't Elma but Emer. And that the old gentleman's name isn't Dan but Malachi.

Jimmy Bermingham said, "We'll definitely have to hide you now, Elma, won't we, Ben?"

Silence again. And still came the rain, so heavy that I could have sucked it off the windshield.

Presently I saw from my rearview mirror that Elma had turned her head in against Jimmy's shoulder and closed her eyes. He tightened his arm around her.

To me she said, "Ben? Is that your name? I don't know you at all." She gave that involuntary snuffle that signifies the end of tears.

"Ben collects music and stories for the Folklore Commission up in Dublin, don't you, Ben? He had a lovely wife one time, and she ran away and left him. And now he's looking for love."

He shouldn't be telling her this. He's using information from my life to give himself power. I loathe that.

"Why is everyone too old?" murmured Elma.

Soon the rain began to ease. A lemon-colored light from the watery sun ran like a child across the bogland. Somewhere in that calm after the storm, Jimmy Bermingham leaned across and kissed Elma Sloane, and she made no move away. *Is Jimmy Bermingham a chieftain's son?*

14

Children, you know the name Randall Duff, don't you? You've seen the photographs: head like a hawk, eyes of fire. And you know that he's a very fine painter, and you immediately recognize him. You've seen two of his canvases on the wall of my workroom. Louise, I think you may have copied one of his pieces in your National Gallery classes.

I asked him once why he mainly painted fish, and he said, "See this lake? I've lived my whole life beside it. The Derga River comes into one end, and flows back out the other end—what more could any artist want?"

"Why did they call it the Derga? It doesn't seem red," I commented.

"Wait till the sun's going down," said Randall.

And when I said to him (this is all recorded in my notebooks), "Why do you use such a style? You paint the fish as if it's sitting on a platter, or lying on a table, or some clean surface, and then you rub and rub and rub, and what we see is a faint, gray image of a fish. Why do you do it like that?"

He didn't answer until late that night, the time when he calls forth the ghosts of his favorite philosophers; Aquinas, Hume, Bishop Berkeley, Voltaire all stand around the fireplace waiting for Randall's thoughts. And then he said, "I'm trying to get as close as I can to my own existence. There's a million colors kaleidoscoping inside me, and I'm trying to subdue them to match my actual life. Which is quiet, and rather still. And sometimes bleak. Don't misunderstand me—that's how I want to live. So I'm always trying to balance the two things, the excitement of the inner colors against the calm of the lake and the house and all these tall old rooms."

Randall loved company. He'd had an excellent education, Jesuits and Oxford, and he'd never had to struggle for money, though now the estate was difficult to keep up. All the older men of his father's time, trusted and respected, had begun to retire or die. The new help, he said, was "shiftless." And they always wanted more money.

No family—his beloved wife, Callista, had died during their first childbirth. One Sunday, full of whiskey and confidences, he told me, "I went to the hospital with her as a prospective father, and I came home childless and widowed."

One thing about Randall puzzled me; still does. He always had a dog, and, like me, he preferred big dogs—Bernese mountain, Newfoundland, Irish wolfhound, Great Dane. But their life span rarely exceeds seven, eight, nine years. They often die younger. Yet he gave each successive dog the same name, Callista. So that each time a dog expired—as many did while I knew him—his Callista died all over again. Randall kept no secrets. I could ask him anything. Yet I never managed to inquire why he had established and maintained this mournful cycle.

15

In the car not far from Duff House, some handiwork commenced between Jimmy and Elma. Elma saw me looking at them in the rearview
mirror. She pushed Jimmy's hand away (but not too far) and said to me,
"Ben, you must think I'm awful callous."

I shook my head and said in my pious way, "We should never judge
others."

Jimmy said, "Ben doesn't jump to confusions," and cackled at his
own joke.

"But you'll listen to me, won't you, Ben, you'll hear my side of the
story, won't you?" The pleading in her voice almost hurt.

"Let's get you safe first." And safe we did get—well, up to a point.

Randall greeted us as though royalty had arrived. Like all people of
good breeding, he seemed not one jot put out at three people descending
on him unannounced, in teeming rain and howling gale, and asking for
beds for the night. Or the week. Or forever.

I loved that wide hall with its large black and white tiles. And that
great broad fireplace in which I often stood and looked up the chimney
at the stars. Huge logs burned there this stormy day.

Randall blurted, "My, my, what a pretty face!" He kissed Elma's hand,
and she giggled. He then put an arm around Jimmy Bermingham's
shoulders.

"Ben, dear boy, how do you know this rascal?"

Jimmy said, "He's my friend for life."

When Randall stroked his beard I knew to expect a pronouncement.
He pointed one of those skeletal, paint-stained fingers at me and pronounced, "James, you'll be lucky to have Ben for a friend. Come on,
we're in the small drawing room."

Elma and I walked behind them. Randall kept his arm around Jimmy's shoulders, and they laughed at remarks we couldn't hear. He owned

a Canaletto, and a small Veronese. As we walked past I showed them—and others—to Elma.

She asked, "Has he a son by any chance?"—and then gasped as we followed Randall and Jimmy though a wide, mahogany doorway.

"If this is the small drawing room," she said, "what's the big one like?"

Annette, with red, billowing hair, and plumping out now in her forties, had been with Randall for as long as I'd known him. She appeared with a tray of amber decanters and sparkling glasses. Wind hooted in the chimney, causing the fire to leap and flare. The rain, heavier now, lashed the windows, making the room feel safe.

No, it wasn't safe. As Annette lowered the tray to a wide, low hassock, one of those crystal tumblers shattered.

16

I remember thinking, *The knot has come back to my chest? A bigger knot. Is this what I've been waiting for? But why? And from where? What have I been waiting for, anyway? Is it my imagination or did John Jacob O'Neill tell me the real-life story of Elma Sloane, a mere day before I witnessed it?*

I looked around that beautiful room, puzzling hard.

Elma had just told Randall her age: "I'm twenty next month."

He was saying, "But you're so poised" and looking at us, hands spread. And in that dramatic silence of Randall's speechless wonder, I saw something. Too fast to tell. A brick. A flying brick. Shattered the tall windowpane. Struck the silver drinks tray. Skittled a cut-glass tumbler. The shards fell on the rug like angry diamonds.

Nobody spoke. That's how we first heard the shouts. Vicious. Even in the distance. Even in the lashing rain. On Elma Sloane's face the chalk-white fear reappeared.

She whimpered, "Oh, Jesus, they followed us."

Randall rose to his feet.

Jimmy said, "I'll stay here with Elma." He crossed to the sofa and put his arm around her.

Then came the hammering. On the door. Randall strode from the room. I caught up with him just as he opened the great front door. Outside, two tall lumps of men backed away. Both shouted. One of them kicked the rear fender of my car. The other had a shotgun.

"What are they saying?" Randall asked me.

"It's just yelling."

"The habitual eloquence of the lout," said Randall. "What do you want?" he called.

"Where is she?" one of the men shouted.

Randall called, "Who?"

"You know who."

Randall stepped out of the house and moved toward where they stood. Rain slanted across him. He walked tall and slowly, like an old high priest. To the men he made a "calm down" gesture, pressing the flat palms of his hands downward.

The rough pair stepped back a little farther. I watched. *How did they get here? No car. Or did they park it down the avenue?*

Each man was bigger than me. Each one shabby. Thuggish. The one with the gun cocked and aimed it. He had old-fashioned whiskers, jet-black hair slanting in thick wedges along his cheeks. Randall continued his stately walk, looking at the gun.

The other fellow, the more vocal, had gathered some fist-sized stones at his feet. He picked up one. Threw it the five or six yards between him and Randall. Such aim. The rock hit Randall's glasses on the left lens. Randall recoiled. Jerked sideways. Then fell.

The men ran away. At the entrance to the avenue that would take them out to the road, one stopped, turned, shook his fist. Shouted what sounded like "We'll be back." The gunman fired a shot in the air, and the crack reverberated in echoes across the lake.

I began to give chase. For what? I have no idea. To take them on? Two against one? And a shotgun? Randall called me.

"Ben, I need you here," he said. He was trying to stand. I came back and helped him upright. He put his head back. Hands covering his eyes, blood in his white beard, he looked like a smitten Moses. His broken spectacles lay on the ground. I picked up the remains.

"Did the stone hit the actual eye?"

"Christ, dear boy."

"Can you see?"

"Bastards. If I were a pianist, would they have broken my fingers?"

I took Randall's arm. "Keep your hands on your eyes. I'll lead you back to the door."

Annette danced on hot coals.

"Warm water," I said. "Not hot. And a towel."

She rushed; I eased Randall to a chair; he kept his head tilted back.

"I am like Job blinded by the swallow's dung."

"That would make me a Job's comforter," I said, trying to keep it light.

"My mother was a Job's comforter," said Randall. "If I fell and cut my knee she'd say, 'Oh, poor you, I hope you won't be damaged for life.' "

Annette brought the water and towel.

"Call Jimmy," I said.

I eased Randall's hands away from his face. His left eyebrow had a violent bruise glowing through the white hair. Almost as I watched, it spread up his forehead. A minuscule sliver of glass glinted on the pad of flesh under the eyebrow. Above the eyelashes. I eased it away.

"I think your glasses deflected the worst of it," I said. "Open your right eye first."

Fear and shock had darkened and widened his pupil. I dipped the towel in the warm water and patted his face.

Randall said, "Thank you, dear boy."

"Now the second eye," I said.

Nothing happened. A faint tremor, perhaps of the eyelashes—but he wouldn't or couldn't open the lid. From the right eye slid a tear.

"I'm afraid," he said.

"All right, Randall. Take your time. There's no hurry. It's all right."

I stood there, my hand on his shoulder, waiting as long as it took. On the far wall hung a Randall Duff masterpiece: large, unframed canvas; chalk-gray ground; a great, glistening salmon, its pink as faint as a dream. What dominated the painting? The fish's eye.

I looked back to Randall. The unhurt eye had fixed on me. He nodded.

"Good," I said. "Take a deep breath."

He inhaled like a giant. As though handling a baby, I pressed the towel down on the general area of the closed eye. I held it there, soft as snow, for ten, maybe twenty seconds, maybe hours. When I took it away, he fluttered the eyelash. The eye opened. No shattered lens, no dreaded whiteout, not even redness. Tears, though—a good sign.

"How does it feel?" I asked, and Randall winked the eye.

He sat there for a few minutes more. A tableau began to form. Jimmy Bermingham arrived at last and walked to Randall's chair. Elma Sloane remained in the doorway, pinched and cold, arms folded tight to her young bosom, like a woman just come in from the harsh world. Annette appeared with a book-sized slab of marble in her hand.

"Dead cold," she said. "Press it to your forehead. It'll stop the bruising."

Elma Sloane said, "That was my uncle threw the stone. Everybody knows about him—he did jail for manslaughter. He killed a fellow with a brick he threw."

The tableau froze.

17

On that same afternoon of broken glass, the following incident took place more than a hundred miles to the north. Since two of the perpetrators are still alive, I'll change the location's name and call it "Brookbridge."

In weak sunlight after rain, a twenty-year-old man was repairing his tractor on a roadside. Three other men in a black van drove by. They stopped; they were wearing police uniforms; they marched back to the young farmer. He looked up from his engine, then stood erect; he had a screwdriver in his hand. Without a greeting they grabbed his hair, pushed him back against the tractor, and took the screwdriver. (Years later, one of the trio, having found God, told his conscience-stricken story to a journalist—who refused to testify.)

The first policeman tugged out clumps of the young farmer's hair and drew blood. The second man reached down, grabbed the young farmer by the crotch, and iron-gripped, then twisted the testicles. Nobody spoke; the young farmer screamed, but he was half a mile from the nearest house, his own home.

They marched him—his name was Joseph McConnell—to the van and threw him in the back, where one sat on his face. The others climbed into the front, and they drove the van in the direction of the Brookbridge police station. On the way, however, Joseph McConnell began to scream as nobody had ever heard a man scream before. They stopped the van, the men in front climbed out, and one opened the rear door.

"What's after happening?" they asked their comrade. He held up his hands—covered in blood.

"Bastard bit me."

Not the whole truth, as the volume of blood suggested. The policeman (whom we shall call Sammy) had knelt on Joseph McConnell's throat and gouged out Joseph McConnell's left eye with Joseph McConnell's own screwdriver. Apparently Sammy said with a grin, "Like the stone out of a plum."

The other two scowled.

"This is a right mess, like," said their sergeant.

To which the third man said, "I know how to fix it."

"You'll never put back an eye."

The third man shook his head. "Haul him out here."

They stood Joseph McConnell against a tree, blood a dark torrent on his fresh young face, his eye easing loose. From a few feet away, aiming at his profile, the third man fired a shotgun with heavy-caliber cartridges and blasted away his forehead and upper face.

"Nobody'll know about the eye now," said the man with the shotgun.

"Anyway, didn't he attack Sammy, like?" said the sergeant.

"He did so attack me," said Sammy. "He bit me, didn't he?"

They slung the young corpse into the van and drove away, back to Brookbridge.

The local doctor, a Protestant, name of Henderson, a decent man, concerned for all people of all persuasions on his rounds, examined the body that evening. Later, in the safety of his own home, he looked at his wife and sighed, "How can anybody think that such things don't have consequences?"

That was in November 1956.

18

Louise and Ben, I wish I'd told you more about the land in which you were conceived. I know this country as intimately as I know my own body. And, yes, I've talked to you about all kinds of interesting places—mine shafts and riverbanks and old abbeys; high villages, remote and forgotten; empty castles where they left the plates on the racks, the books on the shelves.

But I'm talking now about the spirit of the land, and in particular about a dimension of violence that was close to spiritual in its intensity. It took decades to build, and much of it had already lodged deep within me and, I submit, most Irishmen by the time these incidents occurred. The police and the screwdriver; the painter's eye—they didn't feel strange or untypical (and there will be more).

You'll think that I may have made the violence seem too commonplace. Well, it was. When I was on the road I saw it everywhere—ordinary, local, everyday brutality. All over the country. Ask the old-timers, they'll tell you. Scarcely a day ended without some row, brawl, or riot somewhere. And casual fisticuffs in many a bar and pub.

The week before I met Jimmy Bermingham, I watched a fracas in the little County Carlow town of Tullow, involving forty or fifty people. A farmer accused a tinker of trying to peddle a lame horse at the fair (the tinker limped while walking the dud animal toward the farmer), and everybody piled in. The fighting Irish; that was us.

I know you still struggle with this reality, because you grew up in Florida, where Venetia gave you an Emerald Isle view of Ireland, all castles and cottages and glossy brochures. As you know, I've tried to see it through your eyes and explain it to you, but I don't think I've done so particularly well—so let me try again.

The word I reach for is "adolescence." We were, in the south of Ireland at any rate, a new state. With notable violence we'd broken from England in 1922, and we severed the last ties when we declared our republic in 1948. Then, and on into the 1950s, we still resolved our difficulties as children and adolescents do: by violence. If guns had been freely available, we'd have been killing each other wholesale.

Our political immaturity contributed. We had two major factions who stood poles apart. One side, the republicans, believed that we should never have signed the treaty with England. *Fight on,* they said, *until we get back our last six counties. Become a nation once again.* The other side, traditional conservatives and peacemakers, shook its collective head and said we still needed England. *They're our allies. Our neighbors. Our chief trading partners. Don't anger them.*

That polarization trickled down and by the middle of the century was damaging us every day—because with it came poverty. The governing republicans banned exports to England—our biggest customer. Result: no jobs anywhere; we were fighting what our rulers called an "economic war" with vastly richer England. Laughable.

Do you have any idea how poor we were? I remained the only one of my graduating class who hadn't emigrated to England or the United States. If you stayed behind, you barely ate. We had a national culture of need.

As to the general quality of life, think of the simplicities you children took for granted in Florida. Most rural dwellers in Ireland had neither electricity nor running water, nor did the large villages, nor even some small towns.

Few people drove cars. We rode bicycles. Country buses helped; so did the train service installed by the Victorian English. Even though that was worse than ever. We used to have a joke: *What are the two things you know about the Dublin-to-Cork train? Answer: That it'll break down on the way to Cork. And that it'll break down on the way back to Dublin.*

We were a makeshift people. In a makeshift nation. We were a curious hybrid; we came from a glorious ancient past, and yet we looked and acted like a recently discovered tribe, settling our disputes with our fists and eking out, for the most part, an existence with few comforts. No wonder the Catholic Church throve—as do all major religions where affluence has not yet arrived.

Our food, too, reflected our state of undeclared poverty. The national diet continued: centuries of meat and starch, either bread or potatoes, with little variation. Some housewives cooked excellently, but from their mothers' and grandmothers' recipes, not from any new, cosmopolitan information.

And this island nation still hadn't discovered fish—which would have saved its people during the famine of the 1840s. On Fridays, when meat was forbidden by the church, eggs took over. Baking flourished: soda bread, pastry for pies, "shop bread" for sandwiches. Little else. The term "health food" had yet to reach Ireland—or perhaps even to be coined.

In the clothes of the adults you'd have found not a ribbon of chic. A handful of women, from old money, shopped in London. The rapacious *nouveaux riches,* the green greed crowd, hadn't yet been spawned, and if Dublin stores carried outfits for the wife of the surgeon, the barrister, the company man, they were rarely *haute* and never *couture.* In any case, fine dressing earned disapproval, because display of the body might lead to what the priests called, with a sinister grunt, "other things."

Those clergy—they had an absolute grip. They took command of the crucial arena between thought and feeling. Controlled both. Thomas Aquinas was the moral gold standard, with brides told, "No sex unless you're trying to conceive. Otherwise you're committing sin." The subtext was "Have as many little Catholics as you can, and to hell with the family economics." I visited a family once out in Barna, beyond Galway, the Quinlans—twenty-five children in a two-bedroom cottage.

The bishops called it "faith," but they told us what to believe in: heaven and modesty; the infallibility of the pope; transubstantiation. And of course all non-Catholics went to hell. "The big H," you'd probably have called it. Yes, that truly was what it was like, a revolution waiting to happen.

The politicians went along with it. They allowed a kind of social power vacuum, which the church filled. And as the church controlled most of the education, so the priests patrolled that fence, too.

Some of the support for them came because people felt they owed the church a debt. After Irish Catholicism was decriminalized, in 1829, the priests seized the moment. They rallied the people. They led the campaign to take back the land. On ramshackle village streets they gave fiery, dog-collared speeches. When they had condemned the English landlords, the priests then carried the fight to the parliamentarians. And won—and in 1956 the Catholic Church still held that intangible but real power.

Signs, though, had begun to appear, stirrings from the caves of the sages. The poet Yeats, the exile Joyce—even though dead by now, they had been pathfinders; they'd shown an entire people that the world of ideas belonged in the light of the sun and not in the dark of the pews.

To retaliate, the bishops increased the pressure for censorship. The government censor banned Irish novelists as a monthly routine. Newspapers published the lists, and we laughed out loud, because the works of serious writers appeared alongside *Playboy,* or *Madam Lash,* or *Lurid Girls in Wet Rubber: Issue 14.* Yes, we were makeshift all right.

You could see it everywhere. Consider that bunch of us in Randall's house. He came from the old world of Ireland, and everything in his presence and his possessions and his properties showed it. Fiercely anti-clerical, a committed and militant atheist, he represented the bridge from the ancient, mythological glories of kingship and chieftaincy to a brave new dawn that so many of us hoped might lie ahead.

I had come from the ancient MacCarthys, with my branch a well-to-do farming family that had held on to its land for centuries. That farm was mine anytime I wanted to return to it. My parents still lived and worked there, and they had no great passion for prayer.

Elma Sloane came from the beleaguered and impoverished peasantry. The children in her house couldn't all go to school on the same day because they didn't have enough clothes to go around. At mealtimes they had to take turns with the few spoons.

In Duff House that evening, we represented such class differences as Ireland could define: the old money of Randall; the safe farming of my clan; the savagely reared Elma Sloane; and the thugs throwing rocks to force her into marriage so that they could grab another man's fortune. Yes, we had it all that day.

As for Jimmy Bermingham—you may well ask. He dressed like a poor man from a rich country or a rich man from a poor country—which was it? He professed undying love for one girl, yet proved ready to jump on another. In short, Jimmy ran ahead of us all. He also ran guns.

19

When Randall felt strong enough to walk, we returned to the small drawing room. He rested on a sofa, again holding Elma's hand—a gesture she didn't contest. Jimmy Bermingham examined Randall's eye once more and said that the stone hadn't connected with the eyeball. Annette found a spare pair of spectacles and another warm, damp towel, which Jimmy held to Randall's eyes. We made small talk, seeking ease.

In time we went in to dinner, to a long dining room with its own echo. Randall kept testing the left eye, opening, it, closing it, fluttering the lashes.

Such a curious evening: the conversation drifted in bits and pieces; here, from my journal, are some snatches:

Randall: "Will I be blind, I wonder? They say if you lose the sight in one eye, you often lose the sight in both. But, of course, I haven't lost the sight in one eye."

Elma Sloane: "How did they follow us? Or did someone see us driving in here?"

Jimmy Bermingham: "Did you think he'd fire the gun at you?"

Randall: "Girls aren't often so beautiful so young."

And then we heard the drama of Elma Sloane. In its way, it counts as something I collected; does that widen the definition of "folklore"? In a hundred, a thousand years, might it not be legend, if preserved?

She lived, the oldest of twelve siblings, in what was called "a council cottage"—every county in Ireland tried to build affordable housing. A typical cottage had two bedrooms, a kitchen, and some kind of living room; the roof over their heads at a nominal rent gave people some self-respect.

Her father worked for the county council as a roads laborer; her mother jobbed for farmwives. Elma quit school at fourteen, though her teacher called her "highly intelligent and well-behaved." She chose not to emigrate—if she stayed she could help her mother, and even bring in some money.

"I always liked shoes," she said about having gotten hired in the local shoe store. "And there's something nice about helping people ease their feet. Most people who come in, their shoes don't fit them, and their feet are sore."

"Good girl," said Randall.

Her father came to the shop one day and crooked his finger, saying, "C'mere you." She winced as she mimicked him.

Out on the street, "a tall old man" waited. Her father said, "This is your husband. His name is Dan—he's a great man, a great hero. Shake hands with him."

The man put out his hand, and Elma took it. "Because," she said, "I was afraid my father would hit me."

That evening her mother smiled a thin smile and asked, "And are we to have a bride in the house?"

The father came home, sat down at the table, and said, "We did a good day's work today. This house will never again want for things."

That night Elma began to weep. Her mother said not a word—but Elma did: "I'm not marrying that old fellow." Elma told us, "My mother collapsed onto a chair, and she said, 'Oh, Jesus. Your brother, your brother.'"

Elma, again frightened, finished her tale:

"I had a young brother who died a few years back. He had an argument with my father, and he ran out of the house and my father ran after him. My father came back, but my brother never did, and we found him that night under a tree. His head was all crashed in, and my father said he must have climbed the tree to hide and then fell out of it."

20

As the fire began to die, Randall said to me, "You and I have unfinished business, Ben." Mystified, I walked with him down a long passageway. "Somebody," he remarked, "should scare the life out of that beast of a father. Why don't you do it?"

I said, "Randall, I'm only around here once a year or so."

"Avoidance again?" he said. "Old habits die hard."

My heart lurched from annoyance to shame. *Why don't you ask him what he means by "avoidance"—and "again"?*

He had converted the large old stables, replaced stone walls with glass. Dozens of finished canvases leaned in stacks against every wall of the studio. I counted six easels, all with work in progress. On the largest and most central stood a nearly finished nude study.

He means, doesn't he, that I have no guts, that when it comes to the crunch, any crunch, I sidestep? Or run? That is what he means, isn't it, by "avoidance"?

"Randall, why is this portrait familiar to me?" I asked, looking at the nude.

"You've just praised her cooking."

Annette! I hadn't known. Are the locals aware that she poses for him? They'd drum her out of the village.

"Good models are so difficult to find," he said. "I trained her. She now understands how to concentrate with her body." Then, as Randall always could, he surprised me further. "And I suspect that's a good model you brought with you."

"Which of them?"

He laughed. "Well, not Jimmy. Not that little narcissist."

"How do you know Elma could?"

Randall said, "Natural to her, dear boy."

And then he unfolded a plan, taking, as he always did, great leaps of life in a few sentences.

"Tell everybody she's gone to England. Let her stay here in seclusion with me. We'll teach her to model. She can always go to Paris then and make some kind of living."

Randall said all this while standing before a small canvas on a wide easel. I watched as he took a brush and scratched at the paint with the handle. On tiptoe I half-circled him. He peered at his work and blinked, blinked again, wiped his eyes with great care, closed the unbruised eye, peered with the other, then blinked again. In a moment his face began to rest; he had dismissed his anxiety.

I tiptoed away. He left the easel, looked around for me, and called.

"Our unfinished business, Ben." He beckoned, and I followed. At the large canvas of the nearly completed nude, he paused, and with a gentle fingernail adjusted one of Annette's eyes.

On a table nearby, next to an antique leather chesterfield, lay months of magazines, art gallery catalogs, newspapers. Randall picked up a thick folder leaking with press clippings and crooked a finger to draw me in close. He opened the folder and searched, then opened it wider and showed it to me: an old newspaper report of Venetia's disappearance in 1932.

"That's what I meant by avoidance."

And still I said nothing. *Don't answer. If you don't answer, you can't make a mistake.*

"She's back, Ben. Did you know that? She's touring the country. But I'm sure you know it. And you're avoiding it."

I nodded, shaken. "Why did you clip that?"

"Painters never forget beauty. I saw her traveling show back then." No words came to me. "D'you want to read it again?"

"No," I said.

Randall detached the old clipping and handed it to me.

"Put it in your wallet," he said. "Go after her. I saw her on the stage again three nights ago, and she's more beautiful than ever. But she's not happy."

"Where was she?"

"They're in Templemore." He turned to face me. "Go on, Ben. She's with a bad fellow."

Several hours later, restive under the gray fingers of dawn, I thought with some bitterness, *Thank you, Randall.*

21

Do you know the word "pusillanimous?" I enjoy it now, even if it still makes me uncomfortable. It literally means "being of small mind." Therefore of tiny spirit. How well I've known that word.

In my defense, I'll say that I'd had the stuffing kicked out of me long ago by losing Venetia. At least that's my excuse. Being pusillanimous is one of those conditions that you promise you'll fix in yourself one day, put right. But you never do.

Randall rises at six; so does everybody else in that house. Jimmy and I left after breakfast. My head bulged, my heart quailed, as the word "avoidance" tormented me.

On the doorstep I spoke to Elma.

"Randall says I'm to stay here. Anyway, my father knows I was threatening to go to England."

"You'll be all right here."

She shrugged. "Will I be all right anywhere?"

"Is there anything you need, clothes and things?"

"Annette is going to bring me shopping."

I gave her some money, and she flung her arms around my neck.

Jimmy announced in the car, "I told Randall we're going to talk to her father. Elma told me where he'll be."

Four miles from Urlingford we turned down a side road, until recently a muddy lane. Two men labored at a roadside wall. They had just begun their day's work.

"What are we going to say to him?" asked Jimmy Bermingham.

"The stone in Randall's eye?"

"Water off a duck's back," said Jimmy. "You heard what he did to his own son."

We drove past the two workers. In those days, cars drew attention, especially on small country roads. The two men stopped working and stood erect to stare after us. I turned the car, came back slowly, and parked fifty yards short of them.

"He's the tall fella," said Jimmy.

"I saw him yesterday," I said. "Him and his gun."

As we walked to him, Elma Sloane's father leaned across the wall and picked up a short crowbar. The forked hook on it could rip out a man's throat.

"Keep walking," said Jimmy, to my surprise.

Small country road. Pillows of snowy cloud drifting across the powder-blue sky. Fields bare in the wintry morning.

Sloane's coworker stepped away, then grabbed his bicycle and rode off in the opposite direction. He halted at a distance, his back to us: this was a man who didn't want to be a witness to anything. We walked closer to Sloane.

You could see the skull beneath the skin. He had a spider's web of veins on his cheekbones. The hand that held the crowbar—so relaxed. He'd done this before.

His eyebrows met, like a pair of black, dangerous insects. Calm as a candle he watched us. No flaring of nostrils. No chewing. None of fear's flinching. Boots square on the ground, perfectly apart for fighting. His hair was as short as barbed wire. Prominent forehead of a Neanderthal. Note that I haven't mentioned the eyes—because I couldn't look at them.

A sour taste rose in the back of my throat. I kept my hands in the pockets of my coat. He had fists as big as bowling balls. After the frozen moment in which we stopped and stood some yards from him, he spoke first.

"Will you look at the two fools," he said.

"How d'you make that out?" I already knew Jimmy Bermingham well enough to hear the tremor in his voice.

"Sticking your nose into other people's business."

"Mr. Sloane, I thought we might—"

I got no further. He didn't at that moment feel like talking.

"*Mister* Sloane." As he sneered the words he slammed the crowbar's fork down into the new tarmacadam of the little road and hoicked up a chunk. He spiked it on his crowbar and lunged it at us, as a caveman might offer meat on a stick.

"In a minute that's what your brain will be like," he said to me. He swore, blue and raw.

Jimmy Bermingham once asked me why I never used four-letter words. Answer: they unleash something nasty in me.

The crowbar gunslinger sneered again. "*Mister* Sloane. When everybody knows I'm Jody."

"Jody," began Jimmy Bermingham—and got no further.

With a downward whip of the crowbar, Jody Sloane flung the black knuckle of tarred road to one side, lurched across the gap between us, and hooked the forked iron tongue of the bar into the lapel of Jimmy's camel coat. He twisted, and the fabric began to tear.

My work across the Irish countryside took me through open fields, along farm avenues, unmade roads, small town lanes—therefore, I wore boots. Heavy, black, and laced high, they had rows and rows of glistening hobnails on the soles, as did Jody Sloane's, and I knew that he could stamp his daughter to death with those boots, jump up and down on that sweet and eager face, trample those breasts.

It will become clear to you as we go along that my cowardice, my pusillanimity, had a natural override. There was an automatic response that sometimes arose in me, and over which I had no control. If it happened once in a day, it tended to happen more than once, as though uncaged—and then didn't appear again for months.

It lit my mind in black and red, the black of savagery, the red of blood. And usually produced terrible results: brawling, shouting, mad violence, danger.

With the forked crowbar, Sloane dragged Jimmy up to his face and held him like a butterfly on a pin. To do so, he had to pull Jimmy to one side. That gave me a clear road to Sloane's knees.

My eyes went red from the inside, and I kicked him. Twice. Hard. Each knee. God, I kicked. With all my rampaging force. If you're hunting badgers or otters, you must put sticks down your boots, because if they grab your leg they won't let go until they hear the crack. I heard the crack. I heard two cracks. And a scream.

Jody Sloane fell to the road and lay on his back. He had no choice. You can't actually stand upright if your kneecaps are broken.

22

And he screamed at us all the way to the hospital. Jimmy turned to him at one moment and said, "Two against one, Jody. Your word against ours."

We told the nun who greeted us that Mr. Sloane had suffered a bad fall, hurt his knees.

The nun had a dry way. "From praying, I suppose," she said. After a moment's thought she added, "We know all about this gent—we get his wife and children in here from time to time."

And still he screamed; we could hear him as we walked out.

More shaken than we wished to admit, we got into the car and leaned back. Jimmy lit a cigarette.

When he'd smoked the last drag he said, "D'you want a drink?"

I shook my head. "You go. I'll pick you up in a while."

"I'll be at Mick Davern's," he said.

My car had a clock, a rare accessory. "It's nine in the morning, Jimmy. They won't be open."

"They know me." I drove him over to Mick's. Outside the pub, his coat tattered, he then said, "Come in with me, Ben. Big work needs big drink."

"Jimmy, I have to see a man about a dog." That was our national euphemism for private matters.

When they let him in, I drove away—to the hospital, back to the dry-witted nun.

"I forgot to ask, Sister. Yesterday the ambulance brought in an old gentleman. He might have had a heart attack."

"He's here, but he's a bit vacant," she said. "We'll hold on to him a while yet."

In country towns, we hadn't much by way of hospitals in those days. We could barely afford hygiene. And if we had any, it wasn't exactly stainless steel. Yet the sensitivity to illness and disease could not have been higher, because for many years the country had lived under the tyranny of tuberculosis. Thousands died, in ghastly sanatoria, to which people went as to the gallows. That deadly little cough, almost a politeness. That dabbing of the handkerchief to the mouth, almost demure. Those flecks of blood, almost a death sentence.

Let me say now, though, and it isn't relevant but I'll tell you anyway: we beat it. We trounced TB. Cleared it from the land. I tell you only because it shows that we could always do the right thing when we wished.

23

Imagine the kind of hospital you've seen in old war films: white-painted iron beds against beige walls; sheets crisp and white, but fraying; wooden floors waxed an inch high. Get that antiseptic smell in your nostrils anywhere ever after, and you're back among those wards. Where now I walked, unsure of myself. Again.

I saw him before he saw me. He sat propped up in bed, halfway down the shabby ward. How ancient he looked. Inert and lost, he stared ahead into some unknown land, his face as wrinkled as old stones, his gaping mouth a small cave.

At my mild cough he looked up, seemed to recognize me, and his face began to open. The striped hospital nightshirt barely framed his gaunt shoulders; his neck sagged, a blue-veined craw. Straightaway he drew me into his story.

"Is my girl with you, did you bring her?"

How much older than Cleopatra was Antony? Arthur than Guinevere? Here was their descendant, who saw no impediment in the age difference between a man and his love object. He felt all the ardor of a young buck, all the pain of a teenage Romeo.

I paused, trying to think fast. *Why am I here? What have I come for? My heart hurts for him. He's prepared to lose any dignity he has. And has already surrendered so much. There must be some good that I can do. But what is it?*

"Is she out in the car, is she? Is she coming in to see me?" He rasped his words, his eagerness overcoming his weakness.

"How are you feeling? My name is Ben MacCarthy, by the way."

He didn't care if I'd been christened Moby Dick.

"Is she with you?"

"I have a message from her."

"It's bad news, so," he said.

I said, "No—"

"If it was good news, she'd be here."

"She's gone over to England. Just for a while."

"Ah," he said. "She has an aunt over there."

"When she comes back, I'll bring her to see you."

Malachi strode the land, burgeoning in his spirit, a gentleman respected and admired.

"I'm aware," he said, with some effort, "that I'm seen by some people as doing damage. But I can offer her a very good life."

He built a great house, and he modeled it on the mansions you see in the morning when you look up at the cities and towns in the clouds above your head.

"But I might as well tell the whole truth. I'm not in my seventies; I'm in my eighties." He closed his eyes. "Her father's aware of this."

A different nun came by. "All right there, Mr. Barry? And is this your son?"

I smiled, we shook our heads, and as she walked on a bell rang in my head, and I said, "Mr. Barry? Are you the same Dan Barry—?"

And Mal had his own talents as a warrior. . . . Bravery became his signature, fearlessness his stamp, and valor his seal, and he grew famous throughout the land.

I stood and shook his hand. "I'm delighted to meet you."

"Will she write to me, do you think?"

For seven long years Malachi MacCool waged the fight for his green fields . . .

"I read the book of your fighting days."

"So did a lot of people," he said.

His mythic dimension grew in my mind. A generation earlier, this aged lover had been a famed and fierce guerrilla, known as far as China for his firefights in the Irish fields.

*His slingshot became an object of muttering and fear among the bad and
the mad.*

Mr. Barry began to weep a little. There was no sound, just a trickle of
tears down from each eye. I didn't know what to do.

"Listen," I said, about to tell him that I'd visit again. He held up a
hand and stopped me.

"The thing about the one true person in your life, the thing is this,"
he said. "Nothing is important except the trueness. It could be the other
way round. She could be eighty-five and me twenty. Doesn't matter a
straw. The one true person is the only person who fits exactly into the
shape of what's inside you. And that's her for me. I mean, if you put a
bullet into a gun, doesn't it have to fit the gun in order to fire it?"

With this he stopped. And so did the world.

I stared at him, and my mind's eyes began to swim. Alarm surged in
me. *Uh-oh. I know this feeling. Christ! Twice in one morning. Red rage.
Triggered now with no chance of escape.*

24

With my slow emotional metabolism, the flood builds and then the dam
bursts. At such moments a chair becomes a straitjacket, a room a prison.
When that mood took me—and it always had to do with Venetia—I
became unreliable. Unsteady. I had to act, but then I did things I
shouldn't have done. Mostly self-damaging. Now, and I knew it, I was
about to return to that bad pathway.

I could feel myself wishing to close my eyes and shake my head. If I
did, it would be a slow shake, from side to side. That has always been the
first symptom of serious disturbance. At any moment, awful fears would
rise in me, black and red and twisting.

Stop! Stop everything! Halt every thought! Too late.

Old feelings, long locked away, began to break out. I could physically
feel—I could see—the beginnings of a tornado inside me. On and on it
came, ripping the roof off my composure. Debris flew into the inner air.

The walls of denial that I had built for twenty-four years burst open. They'd done so only once or twice before, and they'd caused havoc.

In essence, there was a part of me over which, for many years, I had little or no control. I'm not proud of it. Truth, or at least truth I hated to face, triggered it. This old man—he was telling me my own story, telling me how I, too, had known such an exact fit and had lost it. If my rage at that fact of my life turned inward on me, I would not be able to keep myself safe.

Sad and defeated, Mr. Barry said no more. His hands, translucent and calm, rested on the white sheet.

"Listen here—" He opened his eyes and looked at me. "If a man ever feels like this in his life," he said, "it'll always be in him. No matter what he does or no matter what happens to it."

When I heard that remark—what chance had I left?

My beloved Louise, my beloved Ben, here's something else I haven't told you. I've never revealed my decision to kill the man your mother married. Brace yourselves. I'm about to describe the first steps I took to humiliate, and then slaughter, him whom you called "Dad," who raised you, out there along the long, empty, Atlantic beaches of Florida, where I once followed your mother down the path of the sun.

"I met someone who wanted to look after me," she said that morning. "His name is Jack Stirling." And she told me about you, both of you, for the first time. "There were—are—twins."

I said to her, "Didn't we joke about that possibility?"

"Do you want to know their names?" And she told me: Louise and Ben. My mother's name and mine.

I hated that Jack Stirling raised you. You were my children. Not his. I still hate it. Perhaps not "hate"—perhaps bitter regret. But those two feelings are close to each other.

I knew what he looked like, had already seen him—I'd waited outside your house in Jacksonville that morning and watched him go in. Couldn't bear the sight of him, that thin black line of mustache, that oily skin. He looked like some minor functionary, a deliveryman, a salesman for a low-rent outfit. Not good enough for your mother. Or my children.

25

On fire, blinking my eyes in confusion, I said goodbye.

"I'll be back to visit you soon."

"Don't come if you can't bring her with you," Mr. Barry said.

As soon as I quit the hospital, he left my mind. Greater forces moved in. My confused brain ran film of a sniper, a bullet, a gun, drawing a bead, with the music of death on the soundtrack.

In the old days, when the insides of my lips turned dry, that meant sadistic violence, vile and worthless. I had long banished it, and for a moment I had composure enough to track its pathway: from Randall's sarcasm about my avoidance, through his urging that I find Venetia, and on to the kicking of mad Jody Sloane.

Mr. Barry had capped it. He'd shown me my own truth, and my own failure to regain it. "Trueness." What else is there?

Randall had said Templemore—a long narrow town, easy to survey. Easy, too, to figure where the show would play every night; and easy to confirm from the posters.

Theatrical companies liked Ireland: good audiences, and not much by way of rival entertainment. Most towns had one or two bed-and-breakfast landladies who would take traveling entertainers. Not everyone did, because some troupes flitted by moonlight and never paid the bill.

The women who took the risk liked the shows and the performers. Often they had a little theater in their own heads—like Lily Egan in Templemore. I had known her for years: tall, rouged, and whispering, a ship in full sail when out in the street.

Sometimes I stayed at her place—Morning Glory: Select Bed & Breakfast—for the fun rather than the food; she had the best gossip in the county. She'd also hinted that she'd been a high-kicking chorus girl in London. That fact reached me late one night on half a bottle of Madeira.

"And you needn't ask me," she whispered, rolling those big velvet eyes, "if I had to take off my clothes. Because I won't tell you." At which she hoisted her bosom again.

I drove into Templemore that morning in a blaze of desperate confusion. Lily Egan greeted me with caution.

"Yes, they're staying here."

"When did they arrive?"

"Are you here to make trouble, Mr. MacCarthy?"

"What makes you say that, Miss Egan?"

"Well, everybody knows who she is."

"How is she?"

Lily Egan didn't invite me in at first. She looked up and down the street, in case anyone could hear.

"That isn't a happy lady." She saw—she must have seen—the anguish cross my face. "But are you going to make her any happier, I ask myself."

"What do you mean?" I said.

"They're not in, anyway."

"I can wait."

She pursed those fat crimson lips.

"On the grounds that a few hours won't make a difference?" When I began to speak she stopped me and said, "Don't you remember telling me the whole story one night?"

I didn't. But it was likely.

I said, "I miss her."

"The children are lovely," said Lily Egan. "They're like children you'd write away for. Great natural teeth," she added, tapping her own tall dentures. She narrowed her velvet eyes and measured me. "Yes, you are here to make trouble, aren't you?" She had a witch's chin. "Mr. MacCarthy, don't. Not in front of the children."

Some air left me. "May I come in for a moment?"

She opened the door, and I walked past her and leaned against a wall in the hallway.

"They went out very early," she said. "They're climbing the Devil's Bit Mountain; the children were intrigued by it."

"What's he like?" I said, meaning—as I now know—*Would he be easy to kill?*

Lily Egan looked me up and down as though about to make a purchase. "Well, he's not you."

And then I again asked the panicky question: "How is she?" The marks in my palms from my fingernails lasted two days.

"She's silent," said Lily Egan. "She hasn't said a word since she got here." Then she looked away.

"You're hiding something."

"This is none of my business," she said.

"But it is mine." I caught her hands. "What are you hiding?"

Lily Egan had always liked me. I knew that, and my touch to her hands succeeded.

"We had a woman staying here once who was very like her in temperament. Here for six weeks, and she never said a word. The man she was with used to hit her." I tightened my grip on her hands. "Stop," she pleaded because she saw me ignite. "Don't. You'll do nobody any good."

I said, "Are you sure?"

She eased from my grip but still held my hand. "The children are watchful. But the fellow—he has a terrible temper."

"Have you heard him speak to her?"

Lily Egan now rolled her velvet eyes and whispered at the top of her dramatic scale, "Like you wouldn't speak to a pig. Calls her stupid, thick, slow, an imbecile." She mimicked him: " 'Children, look at what your stupid mother has done now.' He called her a 'sow' the other day in front of me."

He had to die. I knew it. Children, forgive me. I know that he raised you. Forgive me.

We both fell silent. Lily Egan never took her eyes off me. I leaned back against her wall.

"What am I to do?"

"Nothing until you calm down."

"When are they coming back?"

"In time for the show," she said. "Why don't you go away and think about all this?"

"Maybe I will." I could feel my heat slipping away, and in the distance I saw my sanity rising like a peak above clouds.

Lily Egan read more books than anybody I knew, cheap romances. She kept stacks of them all over the house, as carefully shelved and classified as in any library. Doctor-and-nurse romances occupied the parlor; boss-and-secretary in the dining room; test-pilot-and-pretty-servicewomen took the stairs; cowboy-and-cowgirl, the main bathroom. She had once told me that she kept what she called "the real stuff" in her bedroom. "And nobody gets in there," she'd added.

Now, and not to my surprise, she asked me, "Do you still love her?"

I gave her the answer I had been giving myself over the years: "There's nothing still about it."

If you're wondering how she knew so much, children, remember that I had been traveling the countryside searching for your mother, and therefore everybody knew me as the young man whose wife had disappeared. See Ireland as a village and you will completely understand.

"Well," said Lily Egan, in her summarizing fashion, "if you love her, you'll find a better way back into her heart than causing trouble."

I said, "I doubt it," but I did leave.

Fifteen minutes later, I saw him. Alone. I knew him at once: thin as a plank, white raincoat, and that swagger. For some reason, you had all parted company and he'd come down the main street to a newspaper shop for cigarettes.

When he came out, fiddling with the packet, I stood in front of him, blocking his path. He thought it clumsy or accidental, but I blocked him again. After a question had crossed his face with a frown, he knew why I had come.

"Are you who I think you are?"

I nodded. Rocks cracked together inside my head. His English accent helped me. From the unsteady depths of our Irish history, I could demonize him. Not that I would need many reasons.

My more rational voice asked, *Why not maim him instead of killing him? For the rest of his life? Reduce him? Immobilize him? Scar him so that he'll be banished evermore from public view?*

The answer came back, obstreperous and clear: *Not enough. He has to quit the planet.*

Yet another voice, my sanest, said, *Don't do this, Ben. This is not for you. Stop.*

They say that when hired killers see their intended victims, they sometimes get qualms. Not me. He spoke again, his voice full of light and fright.

"This is personal, isn't it?"

Again I nodded, refusing to dignify him with my words. I had warned myself, *Don't speak. Not until his last moments, just before the consciousness quits his eyes. Then tell him. Tell him why. Tell him that he has no place left. Tell him that he deserves to die.*

He said, "Venetia, is it?"

I nodded again. The same slow nod. Never taking my eyes from his mouth. He said, "What good will it do you? She won't go back to you. The children don't know that you exist."

I hate the power of the banal. It controls our lives more than we acknowledge. The shop owner came out and spoke to Gentleman Jack.

"Sir, you forgot your change."

"Actually," said Jack, "I need something else," and he ducked back through the door.

PART TWO

❅ ❅ ❅

Gentleman Jack and His Friend

26

Jimmy Bermingham could sulk for Ireland—and had mastered that old Irish art form, reproach.

"An hour and a half I'm here. In the pours of rain."

I could have said to him, "Why didn't you wait inside?" But when "normal" I didn't possess a confronting spirit, not even with people I didn't fear.

Children, you will soon ask yourself, *How in God's name did my father get in tow with Jimmy Bermingham?* I have two explanations, one simple, one professional.

Remember that I met him just after my first visit to Mr. O'Neill. I think the afterglow blurred my judgment of character—I wanted to think everyone as fine as John Jacob. And I was flattered that he had known of me.

Secondly, as a collector of legends, traditions, and lore, I (obviously) kept a detailed official record. I also maintained a private journal, and I wrote it up almost every night. In it you'll find all kinds of people who never made it into any official report. At times it reads like a freak show, and the more eccentric the person, the more vivid my entry. That, if you like, was my private collection.

And that's how I first allowed myself to keep the company of wild men. Such as Jimmy Bermingham. He called himself a poet, but he never wrote a line of verse. He said he was a patriot, but he was paid as a mercenary killer. He thought himself a demon lover, but—well, we'll come to that.

I soon perceived a man desperate not to see himself for what he was:

a rake above rakes, a drinking, seducing fellow, weak and willful, a low-grade actor who could start a riot in an empty yard. Or turn a law-abiding man such as me into a criminal.

Under normal circumstances I wouldn't have given such a man the time off my watch, but I was lonely. My forty-second birthday had just sped by, and loss still filled me up like moonlight in a grove—all light, shade, and sometimes beauty. I believed that I had come to terms with it—up to a point. Slowly, but sometimes in a rush, I had learned how to take rewards from everyday life. Jimmy, exuberant and smart, looked like such a reward.

It also helped that I loved my job and felt secure in it. The Folklore Commission had only a few official collectors. I was a permanent and pensionable civil servant.

Thus, some of that ancient anguish had dulled. Its weight had changed. Once I had been as bowed as Atlas with the world on his shoulders; then it grew lighter, a heavy knapsack of grief that I could leave aside now and then.

Until I saw the Gentleman Jack posters. Until Randall needled me. And until, most savage of all, I saw what true yearning looked like in a man twice my age for whom love was a form of truth. Who could possibly wish to grow old as pained and tearful as that?

I asked Jimmy, "Where do you want to go?" The lapel of his shattered coat still hung loose.

"There's a tailor in Limerick," he said.

I swear to you that I picked up no ambiguity; what man in such a moment wouldn't have needed a tailor?

In the car he said to me, "I'm glad I found you, Ben." *Found* me?

27

Paddy Collopy was a tailor from a bad fairy tale. Cranky as a bitten mule, sitting cross-legged on a table, his waistcoat bristling with pins—if he'd ever stood straight he'd have made five foot three. Wires of steel-wool hair bristled from his nose. He had metallic skin on a face that hadn't smiled since before the war.

Collopy glanced from Jimmy to me, and back again—and then to me once more. He scrutinized my face as though trying to read something. Whatever he found gave him some challenge.

"You better know what you're doing with this article," he said to Jimmy Bermingham.

"He's no article, Pat," said Jimmy.

"Too many teeth for his own good," said Collopy.

He rose from his table. Bent sideways like an old nail, he limped across the room to a tall cupboard, then turned to glare at me again. He looked like a man who wanted to spit.

Collopy reached for the cupboard door. He turned again and said to Jimmy, "You're sure?"

Jimmy nodded. "Yeh. He's perfect for us."

The tailor took a small key from his vest pocket and unclipped the padlock. As a dignitary does at an unveiling, he stepped to one side and swung the door open. Inside stood a long crate whose wooden lid had been removed. Fake straw and other packing materials bunched on the bottom of the crate. Above them, in a chilling rank, six rifles caught the light on their polished stocks, their blue-gray barrels.

Collopy said, "The rest is in the yard shed."

Jimmy Bermingham turned to me and said, as though we had discussed it, "How many cases do you think, Ben?"

"Cases of what?"

"Four? Six? We could put two on the back seat and fling a coat over them."

I've always been able to feel consternation physically: the skin on my face tightens and shrinks. You know by now from recent Irish history that in 1956 a group of activists calling themselves by the traditional name of the Irish Republican Army opened up with bullets and bombs on the Irish border and ran their campaign until 1962. That day I saw their newly arrived weaponry, shipped as "machine parts" from Chicago to the port of Limerick.

"Are you joking?" Doubt and fury mix badly.

Another man in the room, wide as a black van, moved behind me and blocked the door.

I said to Jimmy Bermingham, "For Jesus's sake!"

"Calm down, Ben, would you?"

"Calm down? I'll tell you what's not calming me down. The full legal term is 'accessory before the fact.' That's what's not calming me down."

"Stop shouting willya," said Collopy, "or the whole parish'll hear you."

"Ben, come on." Jimmy had a new edge to him.

"Come on what? I met you twenty-four hours ago."

"The boys need this stuff."

"What boys? What the hell are you talking about?"

"Willya stop shouting," said the tailor again. He had more authority than I'd expected. "Listen to me." He dropped his voice. "You're in it now whether you like it or not."

"I'm in nothing. As a matter of fact, I'm out. Out of here."

I began to turn.

Collopy said, "Whatcha gonta do? Tell the cops? You can't step away from it. Jimmy and me know that you know. So if anybody official finds out, we'll know who to blame." He spoke those five sentences in a steady and clear-voiced pace; I reckon he had rehearsed them.

Jimmy held out his palms. "Ben, you're the ideal cover. We've to get these friends of ours"—he pointed to the guns; he would always call them "friends"—"a long way up the country. There's lads waiting for them."

In my eyes he saw refusal.

"Jimmy, what is going on?"

"Shhh. Lower your voice. This is new stuff," he said. "Big stuff. Just starting."

"Are you out of your mind?" I demanded.

Collopy said, "They have six counties of our land. It isn't over."

"Oh, for God's sake, grow up," I said.

Jimmy said, "Ben, there isn't much you can do."

"Watch me," I cautioned, and the wide, nameless man at the door jumped aside at the force of my departure.

28

What man in his right mind would let himself be dragged into some tin-pot, cack-handed, half-cocked revolution that was, even in its conception, anachronistic? We might have been a makeshift nation in those days, but were we yet, in the famous saying, a banana republic without the bananas?

Think of it. Jimmy Bermingham wanted me to run guns up to the Irish border, where a bunch of rebels were about to attack a dominion of Britain. The odd thing is, emotionally my politics were completely with Jimmy and his friends. Our island is a single geographic entity, and it should always have been allowed to determine its own independence, rather than have a bite taken out of it by a neighbor.

If I'd had to vote on the Anglo-Irish Treaty of 1921, which divided the island into the twenty-six counties of what is now the republic and the six counties of what is now Northern Ireland, I'd probably have voted to fight on.

After World War II, though, and its horrors in France, and bombed corpses, and body parts bagged by men with shovels, I would never again in my life have voted for anything that fired a bullet or threw a bomb, even in the cause of independence or nationalism.

Now I had been trapped. *Go along with it until you can think your way through.*

Jimmy Bermingham followed me onto the streets of Limerick.

"Just this one load, Ben, okay? Then you're out, right?"

"One load to where?" I needed to keep calm. *You're in, and you can't help it, but then get out.*

I never saw Collopy again. The wide, silent man brought out the crates. And so we set out, Jimmy and I, running guns.

It rained for the entire journey. I said scarcely a word. Jimmy found this a challenge and said so; it brought one of our few exchanges.

"Ben, you're not in a good humor."

"With a car full of your 'friends'?"

"We'll unload them tonight," he said, "and then you'll be okay."

At every road junction I looked all around me like a fugitive, expecting at any moment to be stopped.

29

The rain cleared, and a late sun wiped the sky clean. Many minutes from any major roads, we drove down a long lane through wild scrubland. Ours is a small island with a huge ego; we believe that the world revolves around us. This holds especially true of those who live off the beaten track. In their silent places, the liquors of their opinions ferment—patriotism, religion, politics. We had come to the lonely, low stony hills of impoverished County Leitrim.

I shall give no true names here; their children still live, so I shall call the couple to whose house we came "Bob" and "Maisie." And I'll call the welcome they gave me "mixed": in the kitchen, Bob thrust a glass of whiskey into my hand, and Maisie thrust a gun into my ribs.

"How do we know he's any good?" she said. She had iron-gray hair in a straggly bun and a university voice.

"If Jimmy says he's the goods, he's the goods," said Bob, who seemed to want little more in life than a new drinking companion. Maisie needed more; she thirsted for anarchy.

I asked, "Could you please pull back your gun?"

"Just reminding you," she said. Eyes like bugs, black in a white face, and she kept sawing her upper lip with her lower teeth.

"Tell him, Maisie," said Jimmy Bermingham. "Tell him about the B Specials."

"B Specials"—the Northern Ireland police reserve. They harassed and killed Catholics along the border. So we were told. For sport, we were told.

"A repressive power is always expressed through those whom it most wants you to trust," she said.

I looked puzzled at this proclamation.

"What are police for?" she ranted. "To protect the people and their property, right? To let the world go about its business safely, right? They're the officials we're most invited to trust, right?"

Bob, helpful and drinking, agreed: "That's the general picture, Maisie."

"So when they, in the course of their duty, are encouraged to destroy that trust—well, then you know what kind of regime you have."

Bob took another swig. "That's it. That's the picture."

I made the mistake of saying, "But it's in the north—it has nothing to do with us."

She hissed like an angry goose. "Where were you born? Is all of your native island not your concern?" Turning to Jimmy, she asked, "Where did you pick him up?"

Jimmy said, "He's actually okay, Maisie. And he knows the country like the back of his hand."

"How?" She festered with suspicion.

"I work for the Folklore Commission," I said.

This restrained her, and she laughed.

"Well, I bloody hope you brought your notebook."

That was the moment at which I should have risen from my chair and left that house. But I didn't, and it's in the not doing as well as the doing that we undo our lives.

"Are you sure he's one of us?" asked Maisie.

I said, "No, I'm not. Not at all."

Maisie, striding like a hiker, exited the room. She returned within minutes and walked straight over to me. In her hands she held an old-fashioned rifle, its heavy stock gleaming with wood polish, a Lee-Enfield.

"Here's your choice," she told me. "This?" She put the muzzle to my right temple. "Or this?" She thrust the gun at me so hard that I had no choice but to take it from her. "Which is it?"

Guns discommode me. Their facility alarms me. Point and kill. Ruin someone's life. Remove at a finger pull deeply loved people, as important in their spheres as the sun in the sky. The very weight of a gun disturbs me—an insolent object, insisting on its own importance.

Maisie walked away from me, clapping her hands.

"You're in now," she said.

I looked around, cleared a space on the kitchen table, and laid the rifle down as gently as a glass.

"Not me," I said. But I didn't storm and rant and rave as I should have done.

"Your fingerprints are on that gun," she said, looking out the window. "I won't be wiping them off."

From my pocket I took a handkerchief and began with foolish movements to wipe the gleaming wooden stock. She strode over and pushed me away.

"Listen to me." She was at that moment every spitting female revolutionary the world has ever seen. "The border is a few miles away. And we lost one of our best men yesterday. They gouged out his eyes. In the back of their van. We know the bastard who did it. A B Special called Sammy Gilpin." (Not his real name.) "That's what's going on here."

And I? The implications couldn't have been clearer or more dismaying: damned if I do and damned if I don't.

When *in extremis,* talk or stay silent. Shrewdness is knowing when to do which. I didn't know, so I turned my back on that gun, and on the three people in that house, and I walked out.

At the car, I halted and looked back. Nobody followed me. I opened the door, sat, closed the door. When I went to start the engine—no key. Jimmy Bermingham had taken it. I sat back, afraid once more.

These people had made their calculations. What could I do? Go to the police and tell what I knew? That I'd seen caches of guns in private houses? And that one of them had my fingerprints on it? Maisie and friends need only say, "He asked to join up."

And even if the police did believe my story, how long would I, an informer, a squealer, live? At my waist, on my hipbones, and slipping down from under my arms, I felt the feary coldness of sweat.

Not knowing where I was made it worse. Driving in, I'd been so intent on finding the place that I hadn't looked around. This area felt new to me. I got out of the car and went for a walk, and now that I could see the location, a sense of wonder eased my mood. Maisie's cottage, surrounded by trees and shrubs, had been the steward's house or the gate lodge of a great manor. I followed a high stone wall to a pair of huge, rusty gates leaning off their hinges. Lions, their proud heads wigged green with moss, squatted on the pillars.

The manor had long fallen. In the distance, piles of cut stone marked its collapse. To my left, the old garden opened up. How bizarre.

Twin trees marked where a wide door had stood. Beyond them, tall evergreen cones marched for hundreds of yards. From the feet of these trees radiated gravel pathways, like rays of gray light. I followed one; they stretched off into smaller enclaves, with smaller evergreens. Here and there, among these cones, deep circles had been cut into the ground—ornamental flower beds, perhaps. From God's view it must have looked like a formal geometric drawing with circles and their tangents.

At the end of the garden I climbed two steep flights of grassy stone steps to a high terrace, and from there I looked down. The ornamental circles seemed like the pockmarks on the moon. Dusk had begun to fall. Shadows were sneaking into the greenery. Some of the evergreen cones began to hide themselves.

Behind me I felt something, a presence, not ghostly but defined. I turned to look. A deer stood five feet away, unafraid. No flinching; it didn't even turn its head, not even when I walked toward it—because it was made of stone. Another illusion in my unreal life.

30

Back at the car, Jimmy waited, his elbows leaning on the roof, his face a white place in the closing darkness.

"Will we go, Captain?" he said. His tone sought to appease me.

"Where's the key of the car?"

"Sorry, Ben." He climbed in and, when I followed, handed me the key.

"You planned all this, didn't you?" I said. "You set me up." Moments later, I had this thought: *Why didn't I try to stop him from getting into the car?*

"I did," he said. "I did it deliberately."

"Why me?"

"You'll be invaluable to the cause."

"And I could go to jail for life. Or even be hanged," I said.

"That'll never happen, Ben."

"You don't know that."

"In every revolutionary movement, there's a man who survives everything because of his own stature, because of the kind of man he is. You're that kind of man, Ben."

"There isn't a movement!" I yelled.

"There is now," he said. "You saw it back there."

I shouted, "That madwoman, that manipulative bitch—that's no revolution!"

"Why wouldn't it be?" asked Jimmy Bermingham. In those days I could rarely distinguish calm from cold.

"Why me?"

"Who else collects our traditions? Who else understands our depth as a people?"

"What clowns you are. Clowns." By now I was steaming.

The facts are these. Relics of the guerrilla squads who had fought in the War of Independence from, effectively, the 1916 rebellion to the treaty of 1921, and then against their sons and brothers and comrades in the civil war for two years, had continued to rage against the Irish border. Many of them, articulate, capable, and educated, felt horribly denied. In due course, they spawned new blood. Time, they said, to start again. Strike at the hated partition and the forces who patrol it. Get back our six counties—only the full thirty-two counties can restore the ancient nation.

They had money, they had guns, they had volunteers. Maisie, for all her mad wildness, had been a professor of political science. They'd removed her for her views; she'd retreated, then disappeared—to this remote place near enough to the border to kick-start attacks. Nothing or nobody could have been farther from any choice of mine—for anything.

Jimmy Bermingham spoke directions and I drove: east and north. No light anywhere, not a house, not a candle. When we'd reached civilization by way of a straggling village with a lamp on a lone pole, Jimmy said, "We have to make a little bit of a detour, Ben."

"No detours. We're going to Dublin, I'm dropping you off in the middle of the city, and then I'm going down home to see my parents."

"Yeh, sure, Ben, after a detour."

Something in his voice snagged me on a spike of worry. I looked across. He had put his hand inside his ragged coat.

"What are you doing?"

"We have a little errand to run, Ben."

"No, we haven't."

He said, "Ben, we're heading for a place you might be familiar with. Glenboy. D'you know it?"

He pulled out a handgun and laid it on his lap. Catching my breath, I detoured.

It's difficult to call Glenboy a "place"—but it existed, north of Killarga, a nowhere cluster of houses at the edge of high scree. A retired school-master who lived on Saddle Hill had interesting legends here about ladies with long hair who rose from the nearby waters of Lough Melvin and Lough Allen. On my last visit, the snow had come in, and I couldn't get out of his house for two days; since he had talked nonstop, he'd nearly crazed me.

"What's in Glenboy?"

"There's a man I have to see, Captain."

"Don't call me that. Does he know you're coming?"

The anger of the morning hadn't yet dissipated. But it hadn't re-mained at a high enough level for me to fight back. I caved again.

Jimmy Bermingham said, "He'll know I'm there. Leave it at that."

I can't write down what I said to him—it's too obscene. And using profanity enrages me further.

He countered, "Think of it as your job, Ben. Write us up."

"Jesus Christ," I said. "There's a place in hell for your kind."

Jimmy Bermingham flinched and caressed the ugly gun on his lap. We reached a main road, and I headed north. I should have headed south, found the police in Dromahair or Drumshanbo, but I didn't. Wrong choice.

31

Clutching at straws and telling nobody, I decided to take Jimmy Bermingham at his word and keep a record. Here was my first idea: *I know this is crazy and lethal, but treating it as history might one day somewhat justify my stupidity in not running from them.* Next thought: *Am I going to dignify this scruffy insurgence by keeping a record?* And here is the actual extract from my first attempt; you'll see why I didn't file it for decades.

Verbatim account of James J. Bermingham (Jimmy) of his first involvement in the Border campaign of the IRA, December 12, 1956. Note: The IRA actions continued to February 26, 1962.

 We left Kildysart when darkness fell. [This is J.B. speaking.] *I felt proud and important—the designated assassin. Like one of Michael Collins's men in the old days.* [The War of Independence was run by the famous hero Michael Collins, later assassinated by his old comrades in the civil war of 1922–23.] *We knew about this B Special, Gilpin, we knew where he lived. Sammy Gilpin was his name. Maisie said as I was going out, "Two shots. Legs first, to immobilize him, then the head shot." And she said, "Good luck. For God and for Ireland."*

 The Webley was inside my coat; she was firing .455 slugs. We got her from a girl who smuggled it out of a British army barracks in Germany. Friends everywhere. You need that in a guerrilla war. Collins could have stayed in any farmhouse or cottage in Ireland and been safe. Maisie couldn't talk about Collins and not break into tears.

 Did I think about what it would be like to kill somebody? No. No point. And no worries on that score. The cause orders everything. The cause is my master. Get them off our island. Stop them persecuting native Irish people. Maisie says that the problem south of the border is that the people have gotten fat and soft, and as long as they're comfortable they don't care about anyone else.

Once we hit Belturbet I knew this was it. In deep. I'd been to a lot of the briefings, and I knew there was a big operation starting up that night. The boys were going after a transmitter in Derry. A courthouse somewhere else. And a radar station over on the Antrim coast.

The gun was warm from my handling it. I didn't load it yet. And I had to be ready to throw it out the window if we saw a roadblock up ahead. We weren't going to cross the border by an approved road, and there was a police barracks in Lisnaskea.

Maisie told us how to find the unapproved roads and we hit one or two that were blocked by barrels full of cement so we had to turn back, we couldn't get across the Border that way. In the end our driver [that was me, Ben MacCarthy: I took my own name out of this report] *got us over by going through the forest above Lisnaskea. When we came down onto the level road you could see in the light of the headlamps the water glinting on each side. A land of lakes.*

I'd memorized the details Maisie gave me. Anyway we had a map and a torch. The driver swung into a wood, and we followed a small road along by a stream. This would lead us close to the bigger road that the B Special boyo would take from the pub to his mother's house. He went that way every night. Our small road was parallel to his, with the stream between us. None of us knew was how wide was the stream.

They told us that he came home about half past ten. We sat there in that car. I loaded in the slugs and turned on the safety catch. Nothing went along his road nor ours. A dead-quiet night. Black as a cat in a coal hole. We knew that Maguiresbridge was over to our right. The Gilpin house was off to our left. We couldn't see either.

At twenty past ten, I got out of the car and shone the flashlamp on the stream. I'd have to walk through the water to get at him, and I had only shoes on, not even rubber soles. But I went anyway. That's what I mean by the cause. That water was freezing—a mountain river, I'd say, coming down into the lakes. The trouble was, if I went up on the road and the boyo had a light on him, he'd see me, and there was no bank to crouch on.

Maybe half an hour, maybe more, I stood in that water in my good shoes. God, it was freezing. Then I heard the footsteps, a strong heavy step, coming toward me along the road. Up I step out of the water when he's right near, and I says, "Is that you, Sammy?"

"Who's that?" says he, and I says, "A friend, Sammy, a friend who thinks

you shouldn't gouge out people's eyes." I shine the torch in his face, he shines a torch in mine, and I bring up the Webley and I squeeze off a shot. He dropped. I couldn't see in the dark where I'd hit him but he was down at my feet and twisting.

I stood over him to fire the second shot into his head and didn't the gun jam? Now, I'd never fired it before. And that was a mistake, not to practice with it, learn it, because it had a heavy, slow trigger. The handguns weren't all like that.

So I was slow, and he was down and I heard shouts. So I was gone, running like hell back across the stream to the car. My shoes were ruined, never the same again, I had to get a new pair.

Sammy Gilpin didn't die. He took Jimmy Bermingham's bullet in the side of the head, and it paralyzed him for life. Not elegant, was it? Nor heroic; not the stuff of history books.

32

The following day, a hundred and twenty miles to the south, I drove slowly along the short avenue into my parents' farm. Regrouping? Certainly. Seeking advice? No. I wouldn't have frightened my mother with such a tale, and my romantic father offered no reliable common sense.

My father was one of those men whose reaction you could never predict. He blew with the breeze. I'd hear him one day praise an acquaintance to the skies, swearing undying respect; next day, he'd damn the same man as a knave.

Did he hold his opinions to please others, or did he always tell us what he thought we wanted to hear? One thing I do know about him: he lived from jolt to jolt; he should have had his own private Jupiter sending him lightning bolts. If I wanted to thrill my father, I'd find a story of great drama or tragedy—a man isolated halfway down a cliff; a child in a well—and tell him slowly and carefully. His eyes would grow amber, he'd run his hands through that mass of hair, the red now whitening but the waves still heaving, and say, "God-God-God above, boys."

It took me many years to understand that this need for voltage had been the cause of his great truancy. Remember, children, that in 1932, when he ran away from home to pursue your mother, travel with her road show, I followed. And that deep infatuation notwithstanding, he still showed endless love for his own wife, my mother.

Venetia also told me that when he was with her he talked principally about me, his only child. I was then eighteen. So, in his mad mistake, my father had discovered that he was a family man, not some gallant from a Byronic age. In fact, you may recall that Venetia found herself first attracted to me *in absentia* because of the bonfire of talk Harry had built in my honor.

Alongside this need for lightnings, the other main feature of my father's life drove me craziest of all. Whenever I visited them, I never knew what life-changing scheme to expect. For example, he had put the farm up for sale at least five times, and then withdrawn it at the first offer. Or I'd discover that he'd been buying racehorses, one of life's more efficient devices for losing money.

Another time he was asking for a government grant to raise a statue to a blind poet who had stayed in our house two centuries earlier. The government, naturally, told him to pay for it himself. That brought on two years of Harry's vituperation, red-hot letters and white-hot telegrams proclaiming "You disgrace us, sir"—and he once delivered his practiced tirade in full stammering volume to a politician passing by.

He sounds dreadful at my hands—but he wasn't. Maddening, yes, and unsteady, and impulsive, yet superbly intelligent, and endearing, and funny, and sometimes so aware of his own shortcomings that he could, as he said himself, "Make-make-make God laugh" with tales of his mistakes.

Louise Hopkins MacCarthy, his wife, your grandmother, my dear and beloved mother—as a younger woman she was long and lean, and as neat and tight as a braid, and she took Harry in her stride. It needed many years and many tears to get her past the hurt he'd caused her by running away. And she never again allowed him to be alone with another woman.

His foibles, though, his schemes and opinions, his imagination and his brilliance as a self-sustaining farmer—that was her Harry MacCarthy, and, as far as she was concerned, when that Harry was on parade, there could be no better place than at his side.

By now, long after they've gone from the planet, it's clear to me how their relationship worked. Each thought the other the best person they'd ever met. Their intimacy, a serene and bottomless lake, sent out signals. Touches and glances at breakfast, or at dinner after their Sunday afternoon nap—those two people had a skin-to-skin closeness. Who loved whom the most? I used to think that my mother was the lover and my father the loved; now I'm not so sure.

Children, you knew your grandmother, you got to spend more time with her than with your grandfather. You may not have seen—you may not have been allowed to see—the iron in her. Yes, she felt shattered when her husband ran off. She had no warning—and no precedent, national, local, cultural, or personal. In hard terms, what in God's name was a middle-aged, settled, respected farmer doing pursuing an itinerant actress from a road show?

Her steel, however, still chills me. And her ferocious instruction: "Go out and bring him back. For me."

That same morning she fell into a despondence that changed her very appearance, but even as I looked at her face, gray, taut, and strained during those bad days, I also sensed that a river of fire flowed deep inside her. That's what kept her ferocity intact.

For a time in that fracas they lost everything—their farm, their marriage, their place in the world. And yet she was the one who led their march back to normal life. She never discussed it with me, not in depth; nor did she denigrate him to me.

Nor did I see her make any savage assaults upon his heart; she never, so far as I could see, plucked the strings of his considerable guilt. I suppose she didn't need to; in a constant mode of making reparations to her, he danced to tunes she never had to play.

My memories of her change every day: her tears of helplessness when laughing, bent double and breathless, often at something my father had said; her urgency to bring baskets of food and fresh linen handkerchiefs to an ill friend; her tact at a frail bedside; her unreachable concentration as she scrubbed her pigs with a long-handled, heavy-bristled broom.

She had little vanity that I saw, yet when she died I found in her possessions more than a dozen kinds of hand cream and as many eyebrow pencils, though my memory holds no recollection of ever having seen a trace of makeup anywhere on that face, with its high cheekbones and ivory skin. Now, as the house appeared around the bend in the avenue, it was her face that rose like the moon in my mind.

33

My father had a way of scurrying that said, "Embarrassed." As I climbed out of the car, I saw him do it. In the opposite direction. He crossed the stableyard and went into the house by the scullery door. Not a good sign; he usually hallooed me and came forward, talking already, in full spate, with some story: "Well, do-do-do you know what just happened?" or "Well, we were just-just-just talking about you."

Now he ran away from me, and I knew he hoped that I hadn't seen him. I also knew what would happen next: he and my mother would materialize on the front porch and walk out to my car together. When something difficult had to be said, she rode shotgun for him.

As she did now—and my heart plummeted. She embraced me—unusual in itself; this was not a demonstrative woman—while he hung back a little and said nothing.

"What's wrong?"

"I'd say that 'wrong' isn't the right-right-right word." He beat her to it. "In fact, 'right' may very well be the right-right-right word. Heh-heh."

Her face and eyes offered calm. "Come on in, Ben. When did you eat?" But she stopped in the hallway, put her hand on my arm, and said, "We've sold up." He walked on.

"You what?"

He turned back. "We-we-we got a great price," he said.

"Here?" I asked. "Not Ballycarron?" We had a second farm run by a manager.

"Both," she said. "We sold both."

They knew that I had no interest in carrying on the farm. The place would have given me too much pain. My memories of Goldenfields remained too imbued with recollections of Venetia, and our meeting in the woods, and my young husbandhood. Yet when they told me, the breath left my body, and tears surprised my eyes.

My father walked away, embarrassment daubing his face red. Mother stood in front of me, anxious and waiting.

"He can't do it anymore, Ben. He's not up to it."

My first words, as I look back, still appall me. "But where will I stay?" I wailed. "Where will I go? I have nowhere else."

Unbeknownst to myself, I had defined the word "home."

Mother gave me a timeline. I agreed to come back for the auction of the effects and contents. The house still contained many of my childhood treasures. And their new abode had a small guest room. "Anytime, Ben. For as often and as long as you ever need."

But that old and sometimes gilded life of mine was over, and I knew it.

My father never raised the subject with me. I stayed for two nights, the three of us ate our meals together, and the sale details never fell from his lips. I, perhaps sadistically, didn't mention it either. Or perhaps the weight around my heart felt too heavy.

I left in the middle of a bright morning, promising to come back in good time for the auction. As Mother walked me to the car, she said in the tone of a confidante, "Do you know that she's back?"

"Who told you?"

"Everybody around here went to see the show. Except your father." She half-chuckled. I said nothing. We walked on.

By the car door, Mother took my arm, her typical move with grave issues.

"Ben, he hits her. That fellow she's with."

I looked at her with eyes of stone.

"Mother, what are you talking about?"

"Ally Carroll's sister has a bed-and-breakfast in Mitchelstown. They stayed there. The police were called. She had a broken rib. He's a drinker."

For the next two hours I paced by the river. *A small guest room? No! I'm not seeing the water. I'm not looking for the flights of the birds. The children and grandchildren and great-grandchildren of the birds I first learned to love here. Now I'll be a bird, too, a bird of passage. He hits her. He broke her rib. How often do I have to be told? Failed again.*

As depression swept in like a tide of sludge, I took one last look at the house. Seen from the river, the chimneys stand up through the trees. That's the view I knew best, the view that had given me security and the lessons in how to be free of it, the view that still means the most to me in the world.

34

In my earlier days, after such a painful time, and wearing a huge sense of loss, I'd have avoided people; I'd have sought quiet places such as woodlands or mountainsides and wallowed in bleak groves. This form of retreat had a curious side effect, in that I became able to identify the legends I collected with the undulations of the land.

This time, however, I didn't seek the quiet places; I resumed work, went straight back into collecting, fulfilling the month of appointments I had made.

Indeed, that very day, I found a short tale in the next county. It's a little piece of mythology that supports what I've observed about the connection between legend and landscape. Here it is, as I took it down from a retired farmworker in County Kilkenny (not far from Randall's house).

Near Mooncoin, where the River Nore has a wide bend, there used to be a thick stand of trees on a height above the water. Long ago, the land was owned by an old Irish family, name of Riordan or O'Riordan. The farm was taken from them by a family of Scottish planters brought in by the English government. Jer Riordan, the oldest son, had to stand there and watch his parents carried out in a cart, the farm they'd worked on all their lives robbed from under them.

Now Jer Riordan was a quiet fellow, born weak, and not able to fight. So he went up to the man who was taking over the farm, a man by the name of Langden, and says to him, "I'm going to curse your family for five generations

*until we get our land back. Whenever you see a deer on that hill over there by
the trees, a big buck with fine antlers, then you'll know that a Langden is
going to die."*

*The following morning, Mr. Langden got up and went out his front door,
and there, across the river, he saw a big stag, with a rack of antlers you could
hang vestments on. And then he heard a shout above his head. He looked up
and saw his small son waving out the window to him. But the boy leaned too
far out and fell down at his father's feet and broke his little neck and died.
That kind of thing happened four more times in a hundred years—and
there's Riordans back on that farm again now.*

35

As long as I kept moving, I knew I'd begin to feel better. And Jimmy
Bermingham wouldn't find me. Five weeks had gone by since the shoot-
ing of Sammy Gilpin—five weeks since I'd shoved Jimmy out of the car
in Dundalk, south of the Irish border, the town they'd later call "El Paso."
And then, calmer, resigned, and even making plans in my head, I went
to watch the afternoon sunlight dancing through Randall's long windows.

It was one of those days when a hush hangs everywhere, heavy as
cloth. Nobody to be seen on the property, no workmen in the fields, no
housemaid cleaning the brasses on the front door. The lake spread long
and lovely, blue satin, to the tall red reeds on the far bank. I parked the
car on the terrace.

Silence everywhere. No answer to the long, echoing clang of the
doorbell. I opened the door and, reacting to the house's stillness, closed
it behind me with no noise. No dog barked. No Annette bustled. No
voice called.

I stood for a moment; how wonderful were those limestone flags in
their big, regular squares. A great portrait, which I somehow hadn't taken
in previously, hung on the darkest wall: a benign man of considerable
age, old enough for his blue eyes to have grown watery; his wooden chair

seemed a plain throne. No legend on the frame, just a date: 1786. An ancestor?

Somewhere, distant and reassuring, a human coughed. Through the farthest doorway in the hall's corner I followed the sound, walking without weight. I recalled the corridor—to Randall's studio. Another cough, closer now, led me to the studio door, ajar though less than half open.

Randall stood at his easel; Elma Sloane sat on the podium, which was as high and wide as a small stage. He had shown me this platform before; he'd had it built for tableaux when experimenting with painting historical pageants from Irish history. Sometimes, poets came and read from there.

I looked at Elma first—I stared. She sat upright, completely naked, as free as a child. Her arms rested on the chair's arms, her feet squarely and wide apart on the floor, her head high but not falsely so. That Randall had posed her so explicitly seemed likely; that she had embraced the pose without question also seemed true—because an animation came off her, a lively sense of involvement, and even joy.

I craned my head to see his work. He had stretched a large canvas, maybe ten feet by six. Two splattered palettes sat on the worktable next to him, and innumerable knives and brushes, and rags as colorful as a clown. But although he glanced up at his model every few seconds, he wasn't painting a great nude portrait. On his canvas, as large and silver as the river from which it might have come, gleamed a massive fish.

For several moments I stood at the door, looking in. It may not say much for my presence that neither Elma nor Randall noticed me. In fact, neither could see the door without a serious turn of the head. Naturally, my eyes kept going to her, and I found myself on edge. Her age never crossed my mind.

I knocked.

Randall called out, "Don't come in!"

Elma, however, said, "It's Ben." I recall listening for some excitement in her voice.

"Randall, sorry if I'm interrupting."

"Dear boy! Come in, come in. Not everybody is an interruption." He nodded to Elma. She sat back in the chair and didn't reach for a robe, though she did fold her arms and close her legs.

"Hiya, Ben, howya doing?" She had a smile as wide and bright as a window.

"I hope you'll stay," said Randall.

"May I look?" I asked. "Or are you superstitious?"

"I won't seat thirteen people at my table," said Randall. "But you may look."

A score of questions raced into my mind. *Why is the salmon's head on the left of the canvas and not the right? Does that suggest, say, that you are left-handed? How does a painter make such a decision? For what reasons? Did you work from colors on an actual fish to capture that iridescent pink that fades down? How did you remember how brilliant a fish's body can be? Did you have to learn to put a dot of white in the eye to generate light? Or was that something you knew by instinct? The size of the fish in relation to the rectangle of the canvas: what powered that decision?*

Over all these inquiries arched one question: *How did you paint a fish lustrous enough to make us gasp, while using as your model the naked body of a lovely girl not yet twenty?*

I bit the bullet and asked. Randall had been standing beside me as I looked at the painting. It still had some way to go. He called to Elma, "Would you, like a good girl, resume the pose?"

She sat forward again, placed her feet very deliberately on the stage—I saw that he had set down chalk marks—and sat up with her elbows along the arms of the chair, her head once more high.

Randall said, "Look at her. Consider her as if you were going to paint her portrait."

I looked. Beauty, desirability, excitement—I registered all of that, and after a moment felt any embarrassment slip away. She had a summer-colored face, all mallow and light and alabaster. Looking at her would have inspired any kind of portrayal, direct or unconscious.

36

Over dinner, Randall asked, "How long is it since you were here, Ben?"

No trace of bruising remained around the assaulted eye. He looked so like an eagle.

Elma answered my unasked question: "It's great, Ben."

I loved her natural happiness. Her bad family circumstances hadn't raped her uncomplicated spirit.

"Elma, tell Ben the rules we established when we agreed that you'd stay here?"

"That I'd pose for his pictures." She grinned at me. "Without any fuss or nonsense about being in the nude, that's what he said to me. He told me he'd teach me all he knew."

"And what else? Ben is to be trusted."

"That I'd never tell the outside world what goes on here."

I asked Elma, "What have you learned from Randall?"

She sought his approval; I saw the glance. *Is he exercising more control than he seems to be?*

Randall said, "What do you want to know?"

Clever, putting the onus back on me. I said, "The most interesting thing you've learned."

"That I'm up in the air," she said.

Randall translated: "That she's capable of anything at which she wants to excel."

"And fix it all," she said. "Always fix it."

He translated again: "That there's no such thing as a problem without a solution."

"I'll contradict that," I said, and not quite knowing what possessed me, I told my story of the guns.

When I had finished my account of Maisie and how she had compromised me, and Jimmy Bermingham and the failed assassination, they remained silent. Excitement danced in Elma's eyes, and she said, "Randall would tell you that you already know what to do."

Though I saw him nodding, I shook my head. "I don't know what to do. What can I do? I've already breached the law. Christ, I can go to jail. You've seen the newspapers."

Bombs had gone off. Men had been arrested.

Randall shook his head. "No. Let's think."

"That bloody gun. My fingerprints. Is there anything I can do?"

He said. "Dive back into the problem."

"What do you mean?"

"Ramp it up."

"Aren't things bad enough?" I said.

"That woman got your fingerprints on the gun so that she could threaten you with the police."

"Right."

"So—pull her teeth. Go to the police. Neutralize her. Shoot her fox."

"But won't she and her gang—won't they come after me?"

"How will they know?"

"Randall, they don't need to. If they're raided, they'll say it was me. And the gun will be there. With my damned fingerprints."

"Make a deal. Be a double agent. I'll make the introductions for you."

"This is unreal."

"Life is unreal, Ben. Especially in Ireland. Now I have a question for you." I watched him like a dog about to be kicked. "The newspaper cutting. Last time you were here."

"Yes."

Randall said, "Have you done anything about it?"

I didn't want him raising this topic, and I shook my head.

"You should," said Randall. "There was a goodness in her. It shone from the stage—and remember, I never saw her in anything but a rickety old village hall. But she could be acting from the back of a truck and you'd see it."

"Did she die?" said Elma.

"For a long time I thought she did," I said.

37

The next day, I said to Elma, "Come with me."

She didn't resist.

It was an enormous morning, of sun, wind, and heavy clouds.

"Can you guess where we're going?" I asked her.

She said, "He's still in the hospital."

"How do you know that?"

"Things cycle by us out here," she said.

As we parked the car, I remarked to her, "This is a great chance for you." Her eyebrow asked the question. She wore a black knit top with three buttons falling like teardrops from the neck. "A chance to be kind," I said. "A chance to make someone feel special."

She took a deep breath, preparing for an effort. We walked quietly along the hospital ward; he sat alone between two empty beds; she hesitated.

I whispered, "It's all right. I'll move us out after a few minutes."

Like some great, scrawny, mythical creature, he turned his head. His eyes lit up our path to his bedside.

"I knew it," he said, struggling to sit higher. "I knew it, look out at the sky."

By now the sun had gone high, and the clouds were racing past it like children past a teacher.

"Howya, Dan?" said Elma. She leaned in; I saw her fists tighten; she kissed him—on the forehead, on the cheek, and on the lips. Light and fast those kisses fell, and she stepped back to join me.

"Good girl!" I whispered.

She sat on the edge of the bed.

"Sit here beside me and let me look at you," he said.

Twenty years began to fall away from this man's face; a moment ago it had sagged like an old tent.

"Dan, you're still in here."

"Well, Elma, I had the damn ol' heart attack," he said, "and they're lettin' me home soon. Did you come all the way to see me?"

"I did, Dan, I did; a stray calf is what I am. Don't tell my father." She reached out and took his hand. "Look at you," she said, and she spoke like a bossy woman. "Why aren't you at home?"

He loved it. "Will you come with me?"

"Dan, I'd have to hoist different sails. I have a job now, a good job, working under a shiny kind of a man."

"What's England like?" he asked.

"Up the middle and down the sides," she said. "Level enough. I'm living in a very nice place."

And he said, "I didn't know they had any nice places in England."

"Ah, Dan, 'tis a long time since the English were here."

"Stand up for me till I see you," he said.

She rose. "Do you like my clothes?" she asked, and did a slow twirl.

"Ah, you're the loveliest girl. I'd fight them all over again for you."

I intervened. "They told us not to tire you out."

He said, "And tell me again—did you come from England specially to see me?"

"I didn't come to see nobody else," she said. "I'm going straight back." She took his hand and kissed it. "You're to look after yourself, d'you hear me?" She held the hand as though it felt important to her. "How will you be any good to anyone if the devil takes your pay? You're serious for us."

"Will you come back to me?"

She said, "We'll talk about that when you're better." I nudged her. "All right so, Dan." And she kissed him again, forehead, cheek, lips. From the look on his face I knew that he had never been kissed in his life.

Then came the surprise. We walked down the stairs together. I glanced across at her. Elma Sloane had begun to weep.

"Ben," she said, "will you marry me? Or will you get somebody to do the deed? Anybody?"

"What's wrong?"

"There's mistakes and mistakes," she said. "If I don't go to that old man's house with him, I might be making the biggest mistake I'll ever make. And I want to go and I don't want to go. Did I go too close to him? Oh, God!"

I said, in my most sanctimonious voice, "There's no such thing as too much kindness."

"Oh, will you listen to Saint Ben," she said.

38

The people in this next part of the story—you'll come to understand if I give them no names other than "Man One" and "Man Two." One of those names will change. To "Little Boy."

"Randall Duff's introduction," I said when I telephoned the police station in Newbridge. I hinted at, outlined, a story of guns and shootings. For political reasons.

Both walked me away, to a quiet room. Both spoke like boors. Both jostled me.

Man Two said, "Saving your skin, is that it?"

Man One: "Any friend of that old bugger has no friends here."

And yet, confident as cash, Randall had said to me, "They'll greet you with open arms."

Man One ran the county CID, Criminal Investigative Department; Man Two had come down from Dublin at the beckoning of Man One—who said, "You know they can hang you for this."

"By the neck," said Man Two. "Until. You. Are. Dead."

"Your bowels empty out," said Man One. "On the end of the rope."

"And your prick stands straight up for all to see," said Man Two.

How often in my life have I not known the right thing to do? Answer: over and over and over. It's a terrible feeling—and I had spent years roaming Ireland not knowing what to do, slopping out cowsheds, weeding beets and turnips, long lines of them in appalling weather on my knees, in drills that ran, it seemed, for hundreds of yards, an old jute sack folded at the corner to look like a cowl over my head as the wind whipped up the wet earth into my face inches below where I was kneeling.

In other words, I'd had superb training in adverse matters, and it made me superior to those two brutes. They could induce no bleakness of spirit, no fright, no fear I hadn't already known.

"Spill it, pal," said Man One.

I said, "I came here to 'spill it'—but I'm changing my mind."

Man One began to erupt, but Man Two, more experienced, held him back. They retreated a pace from their positions in front of me; they had stood me back against a gray and empty wall.

"Oh? Changing our mind, are we?" said Man One, and balled his fist into a club. "We can stop that happening."

Man Two again put out a restraining hand. "What do you want?"

"Not this," I said.

Man Two jerked his head at Man One, and they quit the room. I didn't move. They came back within a minute.

"Okay. Tell us what you want."

"Protection."

"You want our protection," said Man Two.

Man One: "People who ask us for protection always double-cross us."

I said, "Is this Chicago or something?" My stomach ached with tension.

"Jerry, get us a few chairs," said Man Two. When Man One had gone, he added in a more collegial tone, "The local fellows, they don't know how to handle this kind of thing."

"But you were the same as him when I came in here," I protested.

"Ah, that was only tactics," he said.

"Can we drop that now?" I asked.

He said, "Why would we?"

I said, "I came here of my own free will, and I can take back anything I said." And all the while I was thinking, *If they search my car they'll find my notebook, and it has incriminating details of my trip to the border.*

We got nowhere. Round and around we went, implying this, speculating upon that, suggesting the other; "what if?" and "suppose" carried the day. They hated me for it.

39

Shivering like a wet child, I left them, made it to the car, and drove away. James Clare had once said to me, "Ben, you have good instincts." For a long time I hadn't known what he meant, but here's an example. Expecting to feel stressed after the Dan Barry visit with Elma, and knowing that I'd feel straitened if I went to the police, I'd arranged by telegram a second visit to Mr. O'Neill after those events. Nothing would calm me as much.

My humility, banished by recent anger, came back when he opened the door. *He has no age spots. Does he always dress as though for an important appointment?* Less excitable—though still as thrilled—now, I could see him more clearly.

He fed me again. This time I observed his hands, large and wide. *I wonder does he use a pocketknife, like my father, to pare those nails. They're so straight-cut.* We lunched on potato soup and the national dish of bacon and cabbage with white parsley sauce. Cooked perfectly. With glasses of milk. I complimented him.

"I'm not as good as I was," he said. "We're all getting older."

No. Don't age. You don't wear glasses, you're as light on your feet as a dancing master, your voice sounds like a new bell. You're not getting older. Stay this age for another eighty years.

We drank tea after lunch. I asked, "When you were on the road, did you tell people stories about the places they lived in?"

By way of an answer he said, "Are you a good driver?" We left the house, directed by him. "I think you're going to enjoy this," he said.

As we drove through the countryside, he built a running commentary. "See that field? The week before the Battle of Clontarf in the year 1014, Brian Boru's army defeated a force of Vikings in there. They call this the hill of Crogue, and the historians have neglected that battle. Which is wrong of them, because if Brian had lost that day, Ireland might well be Scandinavian today."

A few miles later, he pointed to a tall ruin out in the middle of the fields.

"Now, there's something very interesting. We always think that these fortified houses, they were built by the MacNamaras and such families, that they're unique to Ireland. But I've seen very similar buildings in Spain—tall and powerful and capable of being defended easily. So were we imitating the Spanish or did they imitate us? Or was this something we both did at the same time because we're in part descended from the Milesians who came from the north of Spain when God was in his twenties?"

On and on he went. I wanted to drive him on every road in the country, and I told him so.

"Well," he laughed, "God knows I've walked every road in the country. And every one of them many, many times." He fell silent.

Soon I said, "Mr. O'Neill, the last time I saw you—something odd happened to me soon after."

He snapped his head to attention, and I told him the story.

"I used to know Dan Barry," he said. "He's a sensitive man."

He waited for me to make my point.

I said, "But the day before, you told me the story of Malachi Mac-Cool and his longing."

"Why do you call it 'odd'?" he said.

Of course I had no answer. I said, "Has it happened before?" I could feel my hands beginning to shake.

"Everything has happened before. You know that, Ben. And as you get older you'll find your own life repeating itself."

I asked, "For better or worse?"

Quick as a dart he said, "That will be up to you."

He reached into his pocket for his pipe. Caressing it, he brought it to his nose; he had filled it before we left his house.

"Look: stories are our oldest and best teachers. If you can get hold of that and use it, you'll have a happy life."

He sniffed into his pipe. "Mmmm," he hummed. "You can smell Kentucky," he said and held it to my nose.

I don't know what Kentucky smells like. Coffee. Brandy. Rich odors. Thick, sweet Madeira. Venetia. Or does it smell of time itself? And adventure? And peace? And sunlit fields?

I said, "That's some aroma."

He caressed the pipe again. "I've always loved," he said, "the strange experience of beauty. And I see that you know what I'm talking about. Now"—he changed tone—"to business. We're on the trail of a tale from history. From nearby times. About a mile from here, near Pallasgreen, take a left turn. Do you know where we're going?"

They'd said in Dublin, *You don't ask him. He chooses which story to tell you.* But my heart jumped because I guessed what he had in mind, and it couldn't have been more different from the first tale he'd told me.

Well, they'd said, *Expect anything.*

40

This is the most famous story in Ireland. At least it is to the people who live near here. I mean, you'd have to ride a donkey through Ballyneety to detect the place, because donkeys are very slow. But not everybody rode slow donkeys through here, and those who did had overwhelming cause to regret it. We'll get out of the car up there, at that bend in the road.

Horses pranced on the tie he wore. When he sat back in the passenger seat, pausing for a moment, he rested two fingers upright across his lips.

Again, I bring you an edited version; and again, as with the tale of Malachi MacCool, you can see the full report in the Folklore Commission archives. Before we got out of the car he pointed to a farmhouse in the distance, two stories high, black roof, green front door.

"There used to be decent people in that house," he said. "Always good for a bed for the night. Then a daughter-in-law moved in, and that was that. A thin woman. In every way."

"Did you stay there often?"

"I never abused a family with a welcome," he said. "The trick out on the road was to try and make sure you came to a house so rarely that they'd be delighted to see you."

"The people in that house—before the thin woman got there, did they know the story of Ballyneety?"

"Even if they did, they liked to hear it again," he said, and he began.

Until the cows come home and milk themselves, Ballyneety will be known as Sarsfield's place, because this is the story of Patrick Sarsfield and his famous ride to triumph.

Long, long ago, but not so long ago that the children of your grandchildren's children can't remember it, King Billy and King James were fighting like ferrets in a sack. Ireland was the rabbit the two of them were chasing, and they dragged that bag hither and yon, through field and stream, in mighty combat.

We climbed out together and buttoned our coats against the cold wind.

"There's rain on that wind," he said. "Stand here a minute and look to the northeast."

Farmhouses and hedges, bare now, their tough, webbed branches leaning east with the prevailing wind—that's all I saw, and large scuds of lowering clouds.

"We'll stay looking." He put his fingers to his lips again in recollection before resuming.

Came the day, a day when people moaned with fear, the day that King James's army was forced down the country, down and down, from high above Dublin. They came this way, from the direction we're looking, and they were bound for the walled city of Limerick behind us, a town where to this day the dogs of the streets can walk on their hind legs.

"Turn around now," he said, "and if we're lucky we can see the spire of St. John's Cathedral."

He seemed disappointed that we saw no spire, and he led me to the shelter of a tree beside a gigantic rock, a glacial erratic thrown there at random by an ice age that poured across County Limerick twelve thousand years ago.

When King Billy reached the city walls of Limerick, he surrounded them two hundred and seventy degrees, and he just sat there, a big round Dutchman, hands folded across his roly-poly belly, smoking his pipe. For weeks and weeks he didn't move, as patient as a fat fisherman who's looking to land a big, spiky pike.

Now, the people inside the city, they couldn't make out why King Billy wasn't attacking. He had fifty thousand soldiers pacing up and down between Limerick and his camp in Caherconlish, seven miles away from the city, and about twelve miles from where we're sitting now. That was twice as many soldiers as King James had. So why was Billy holding them to a siege?

Well, they soon found out—because an Irish soldier in Billy's army, a local man from Garryowen, deserted and got into Limerick. Billy, he said, was sitting tight because he was expecting what he called a siege train, with hundreds of guns and tons of gunpowder and cannonballs. And the deserter told them too that the siege train was expected in Cashel over there in County Tipperary, by Thursday—that was the tenth of August. Better weather than we have today.

Mr. O'Neill stood out from our sheltering tree to point northeast. He tested the wind with a wet finger, then stepped back in and began the elaborate arrangements of lighting his pipe. When he had it fully going, and the blue smoke was whipped away on the icy breeze, he squared his shoulders, leaned against the tree, looked into the distance like a seer, and continued.

When they heard this news inside Limerick, they told themselves that they were surely doomed. There was a little Frenchman with them; he had the rank of an officer, and he was the son of the Duke of Lauzun, in France. He looked at the walls of Limerick, on which they were all depending for protection, and he said that King Billy's army didn't need cannonballs; they could knock down the walls with roasted apples.

Now, there were a few Irish officers in that army, and one of them was a gentleman as well. An officer isn't always a gentleman, but this man was. His name was Patrick Sarsfield, and if you go around Limerick you'll see his name everywhere. To this day they name pubs and streets and children and bridges after him.

Sarsfield wasn't content to sit there waiting for King Billy to come in and wreck the place. He, smart man that he was, reckoned that if they could destroy Billy's guns before he got to use them, then Billy would have a sore jaw from a punch like that. But how could Sarsfield do that? He, too, sat trapped inside the besieged city, where nobody could get in or out.

But Sarsfield knew a fellow, a wild man, name of Hogan, from the long, quiet village of Doon. He was known as "Galloping" Hogan, and he was a rapparee—a bandit, a highwayman. He and his gang, like the outlaws in the Wild West, held up stagecoaches and trains; they robbed the rich to help themselves.

So Sarsfield sent for Hogan, who crept into the city, where Sarsfield, eloquent as an orator, mannerly as a diplomat, told Hogan what he wanted to do. Of course Hogan, who loved a bit of mischief, was delighted with this plan, and he knew every hill and hollow of these counties.

In the notes of my first visit to John Jacob, I reflected that he "seems to have more than one octave in his speaking voice." Now when he said, "He was a rapparee—a bandit, a highwayman," his inflection rose almost to a musical sharp; and the phrase "eloquent as an orator, mannerly as a diplomat" came out brown and warm.

Again he used his hands with the flourish of a conjuror. By his fireside that first night, the light had made shadowgraphs of his gestures on the whitewashed wall of his kitchen. And his fingers seemed like the ghosts of dancers, mumming and miming the tale he was telling. Here, I could see Galloping Hogan leaning down from his horse, listening to the earnest words of the tall, aristocratic, and bewigged Patrick Sarsfield.

John Jacob O'Neill puffed a mighty puff on his pipe, buttoned his coat tighter, and said, "Come over here with me."

Striding like a young fellow, he left the tree, walked fast by the great rock, and stood out in the open air. From a high piece of ground he pointed due north.

"Up there," he said, "that's where you have to look, and out of all the events in our history—God Almighty, I'd love to have been there."

He paused again; seen from a distance, he could have been a monument.

The year was 1690, and we had a nice and fine summer that year. So on the ninth of August, a Wednesday night, thirty secret men rode out through the north gate of Limerick. Their horses had bandages of thick cloth on their hooves so that they wouldn't be heard by King Billy's soldiers.

They rode up the western bank of the Shannon. Along the way they met other Irish soldiers who had been primed by Galloping Hogan's men. By the time they got to Killaloe, they were five hundred strong and fierce. According to their last report, the siege train had reached the town of Cashel in County Tipperary, thirty-six miles east of Limerick.

He pointed north, then described an arc eastward with the stem of his pipe.

The Shannon in summertime is low to this day at Ballyvally; that's up above Killaloe. There used to be a ford there, and in that dry weather Sarsfield and his men crossed to the Tipperary bank. They hid in the Silvermine Mountains, until Galloping Hogan's scouts came back with news of the siege train. They reckoned that the wagons and the big field guns were making about six to eight miles a day, and Hogan had reports of people watching it trundle across the country, and the soldiers with it sweating like pigs.

By now Galloping Hogan was able to guess the direction the siege train would take, and they only had to decide where to intercept it. So, Wednesday night they crossed the Shannon, and between hiding and riding they got to the slopes of Keeper Hill on Friday. Now they were in Galloping Hogan's home country, where he knew both sides of every leaf on every tree, and plenty of places to hide and get food.

Saturday night they rode again, and we're gazing directly now at where they were coming down from—up there north of us, and heading for this spot we're standing on. Those reckless horsemen—they were a rag, tag, and bobtail gang of outlaws and rapparees and highwaymen, galloping hell for leather, and all of them ready and willing and able and eager to give the fat king of England a poke in the eye.

And at the same time, heading across over here east of us, you'd have seen the fat king's army, a great column of soldiers and horses and donkeys and mules, dragging wagons of food and ammunition and explosives, and big, shiny, heavy field guns that'd knock down the golden walls of heaven itself.

Again I found myself torn: listen or hope to take an accurate note? The weather lost its meaning for John Jacob—by which I mean a typhoon could have struck and he'd have kept going.

Did I imagine it or did he seem to rise higher on the ground, proud as the little hill of Ballyneety itself? I'm certain to this day that a person passing by, down on the main road, might have looked up at us and thought that a statue had been erected on this historic site, or at the very least that a great actor had come here to perform.

I ceased to exist in my body, because as he rose to the high and wild climax of his story, my spirit ascended with him.

Now you're asking yourself, "How in the name of God could a force of five hundred horse soldiers go through the countryside and not get seen?" Well, they did get noticed. Protestants in Killaloe saw them and reported them, but the word didn't get to King Billy until the Sunday, and he sent out a sizable military party to find these wild riders, but he didn't find them. In any case, he was too late.

By then Sarsfield and his men were up there on those wooded hills. Look! You can see the same trees or their grandchildren, and hidden there beneath the branches, the leaves making dapples on their faces, Sarsfield and his riders could watch the siege train off in the distance, dust rising from it. Miles long it was, a hundred and fifty wagons, and they saw the head of the snake get to the village of Cullen, while the tail of the serpent was still back in the village of Monard.

The siege train camped that night here at Ballyneety. In the lee of this big rock they lit a great campfire. Those old stones over there—they're the remains of a ruined castle the men could shelter in. And they had only a dozen miles to go the next day to join King Billy's main army.

When the soldiers of the king put the horses grazing, they posted a few indolent sentries, they ate their supper, and they settled down for the night. Not for an atom of time did they suspect that five hundred tough Irishmen on horses were about to breathe down their necks—well, they say a good soldier never looks behind. Their sentries, most of them, fell asleep.

The ball hops to the winning team, and that afternoon Sarsfield got a great bounce. One of Galloping Hogan's men had a horse that threw a shoe, and the man had no choice but to get off and walk. He wasn't, of course, wearing a military uniform—why would he? He was a rapparee. So he could walk his horse along the road and nobody would suspect that he was part of a big raiding party.

He saw a woman ahead of him, and being a man who liked the ladies, he got into a chat with her. Dimpling her cheeks, she told him that she was the wife of one of King Billy's soldiers, and that she was going to see her husband in the camp at Ballyneety that night.

He said to her, "But will they let you in?" and she said, "I have the password." And he said to her, "What's the password?" and she said to him, "I'm not supposed to tell you." But he gave her the glad eye, and maybe a bit of a squeeze, and she told him. And d'you know what the password was? The password was the name "Sarsfield."

Galloping Hogan, Patrick Sarsfield, and the five hundred men formed up a few fields away from the siege train. They could see the glow of the campfire, they could almost hear the chomping of the horses grazing, they could smell the food. Slowly they rode up to the nearest sentry.

"Halt!" says this fella. "Who goes there—friend or foe?"

"Friend," says Sarsfield, cool as cress.

"Give the word, friend," says the sentry, meaning the password.

"Sarsfield is the word," says Sarsfield, "and Sarsfield is the man." Leaning down, he bisected the sentry with a mighty slash from his sword, and he and Hogan and their fiery hundreds rode into the camp.

Sarsfield's men rounded up the siege train horses, which were all saddled and bridled and armed, and prepared to rustle them home. They terrified the siege train soldiers into gathering all the cannons, the guns, and the gunpowder. When Sarsfield saw what he had captured, he danced on his saddle: a dozen pieces of large artillery, wagon after wagon of gunpowder, shot, and cannonballs—and matches to light them all.

Galloping Hogan ordered one of the gunners to demonstrate how best to explode everything. The gunner stuck the muzzles of half a dozen field guns into the ground, like geese in a field with their beaks in the clay, then stuffed the guns with gunpowder. They piled everything else on and around the field guns.

With the blade of Sarsfield's sword at his neck, the gunner ran a fat trail of gunpowder, thick as the spoor of a giant snail, along the ground to a safe distance. Sarsfield's men took all the horses from the siege train and all the mules, and they rode them away, far out of reach of King Billy's soldiers, because no decent Irishman would ever want to harm a horse.

Sarsfield turned to Galloping Hogan and said, "Mr. Hogan, to you falls the honor of lighting this fuse."

Hogan put a match to the trail of gunpowder, and they rode out of the camp like the wind and let the flame eat the fuse.

The explosion woke people out of their sleep for miles and miles around. They heard it in Tipperary, twenty miles away, where it broke windows. They heard it in Clare, thirty miles away, where it cracked a chimney. They heard it in Kilkenny, forty miles away, where it roused the birds from their nests. And they heard it in the city of Limerick, where they danced in the streets: Sarsfield was indeed the man. King Billy knew that the game was up, and it wasn't long until he finished the siege and went away home.

I tell you this, the most famous story in Ireland, just to prove to you that we have to be careful when we use the word "mythology"—because it might also be history. And what's the most important thing about history? The most important thing is: history is what's happening to us all the time, and it happens again and again. To each and every one of us.

41

All they'd said about John Jacob O'Neill had come true. All the times and all the days on the road, and all the legends had, for me, come down to this man.

Although he told me a news story from three hundred years ago, a story known in every Irish schoolroom—he yet told it as the bards had done in the courtyards of the kings. As the storytellers did under the banyan trees of Asia. As the weatherbeaten travelers with their brown, creased faces still do in the high villages of Peru.

We sat in the car. He looked exhausted. How much heart did it cost him to build that stage on which figures laughed, and rode horses, and tempted Providence? How much emotional energy did he commit to laying the trail of gunpowder, "thick as the spoor of a giant snail," across the grass and out of the camp, ending in a small pile to which that wild man, Galloping Hogan, then applied the flame from a tinderbox?

And where did he learn that he must show us the life behind and beyond the story? How the riders looked to a wife whose farm they rode past; how they lolled with their horses under the trees on Keeper Hill; how the brave sentry at the Williamite camp stepped forward with his challenge and then looked up aghast at Sarsfield's descending sword as it flashed in the light from the campfire.

My hand ached as I closed my notebook.

I asked, "You're tired now, Mr. O'Neill?"

"Not much of a story if I wasn't," he said.

I was about to ask, "Is there any correlation between the story and the tiredness after the telling?" when he said, "Big story—weary storyteller."

There it is again. He truly is uncanny. Is he reading my thoughts? Remember when he said, "I've always cooked . . . I never married?" Should I be nervous of this? Or is it benign? Think nothing of it, said my mind's sanest voice. *Perfectly logical. Shared thoughts at shared moments. Would he—would this gift of his—be of use to me? Help me to sort out my life?*

I shifted my feet, to check my stability.

"The next time you're here," he said, anticipating me again, "I want to talk to you about yourself."

I said, "You're the interesting one."

He said, "Go and see James."

42

Within days of the Sarsfield elation a new tide swept in, a sad, slow wave. When it swept back out to sea it took with it the dear person who for twenty-five years had been my safest, sanest reference point.

I wish you'd known the peerless James Clare. He met your mother—just once—and found her enchanting. I know that he would have loved you, too. Louise, he'd have held on to your handshake, looked all over your face, smiled at that head of frizzy red hair, and said, "Well, your father's apple didn't fall far from his orchard." And to you, Ben, he'd have said, "You have your mother's soft eyes—are they gray or are they blue?"

Nine o'clock at night: I parked on the street near Miss Fay's, because two cars sat in the small forecourt. *Visitors?* The front door stood ajar. Inside, every light blazed as though in a stadium. *This is odd. She's a demon with light switches.* Although I had my own key to Miss Fay's house, I always rang the bell during social hours. No answer.

In that house you can see from the hallway into all the rooms on the ground floor. Nobody anywhere. I called out a quiet "Miss Fay?"

Her head appeared around a door at the top of the stairs. Then she stepped into view, a tall and exotic bird more than ever before. She had dressed as for a gala dinner. A huge butterfly brooch sparkled on a light purple silk dress that hung royally on her bony, coat-hanger shoulders. She blinked through her great spectacles, and clasped her hands together.

At the top of the stairs, she held her arms out. I took both her hands and said, "Well, well—look at you. Lovely!"

She whispered, "James is dying. I'm wearing my best finery to see him off," and she began to cry, a phenomenon that I had never seen.

We looked into each other's eyes with that slow desperation of a complete and awful truth. The skin on my face began to tighten.

"Is he very bad?"

"He took a coughing fit at the weekend," she said, and patted her angular rib cage.

"Internal damage?"

"If he had the lung power, he'd survive."

"Is he lucid?"

She said, "I was about to try and find you." Her typical stoicism finally collapsed. She cried harder and her tears stained dark the light purple of her dress at the neck.

"May I see him?"

"D'you want to know my dilemma?" said Miss Fay. "My dilemma is—when he sees you, he'll feel it's all right to go." She won back some control. "But that's my selfishness."

These days, if I'm asked, I describe James Clare as a national monument. He certainly looked like one, with his long black coat, and his shiny boots—all of which I have myself emulated. And the bicycle—let us not forget the bicycle; was ever a bicycle so polished and gleaming? And did ever a briefcase seem so tidy, so beautifully kept, so magisterially important, as James's old black leather Gladstone bag?

To this day he remains the standard for folklore collecting. In his lifetime the Scandinavians honored him with medals and awards, as did Scotland. And Australia—how he regretted that he didn't have the strength to make that journey; he so wanted to meet "the dream people." Now I wanted to talk to him about John Jacob O'Neill.

And I wanted once again the wisdom of the real James, the man who saved my life, and to inhale the gigantic kindness he ever showed to me. James has been dead now for more than forty years, and I am unable to think of him without tears in my eyes. Among the many lessons he taught me, one remains the most important, the lesson he himself fetched from the life he perceived. Here's how he spoke it to me:

"Ben, every legend and all mythologies exist to teach us how to run our days. In kind fashion. A loving way. But there's no story, no matter how ancient, as important as one's own. So if we're to live good lives, we have to tell ourselves our own story. In a good way. A way that's decent to ourselves."

Whatever softness of nature you may perceive in me, I might not have developed any such quality without James. He was ever the figure in my mind, sitting in a chair across a room or standing in the distance, under a tree, of whom I would ask a crucial question.

"James, how can I give up drinking?"

"James, what should I do about Venetia?"

"James, should I interfere in the lives of my parents?"

And James, the real James in his black suit and white shirt, or the imagined James under the tree, would always come back with an answer that seemed to work.

I said to him one day, "James, are you aware that when I take your advice it always seems to work?"

"Ben, I don't give anybody advice. All I do is release the good thinking that's already inside of you. You're the one who acts on your own advice, and I have the pleasure of helping you reach those thoughts about yourself. So it's not me helping you—it's you helping you."

"But, James, how come it always works? Always?"

"Run a little test for me, Ben." He loved little tests. "Try to observe decisions that are taken out of kindness. Then try to observe decisions that are taken with a little negative kick to them. It is my profound belief"—he had a lot of profound beliefs—"that in the former you will find success, though perhaps not immediately. And in the latter you may find short-term success. But in the former, we make everybody feel good. In the latter, we make enmity. And as we all know, there's nothing eats up your energy as much as hostility. Do you know how acid is made? The manufacturers distill resentment."

And so we would talk, every time we met. Mostly, in recent years, we met in Miss Fay's kitchen, with her slinging in toothy observations from across the floor by the stove.

That night I would go to bed, regretting once again that James had retired, and that the Irish countryside no longer got the visitations of his great wisdom, from which so many people—they told me themselves—had benefited so much and so often.

Now I pushed the door of the bedroom with care and in silence. The doctor, blond as a young Viking, sat on the edge of the bed; the nurse, firm and starched, prowled.

James had been raised on the pillows, and even from the doorway I could hear that rasp that I so hated from his battered chest. His eyes were closed and his hands were joined, as if he were already making the undertaker's job less difficult.

Miss Fay whispered to the doctor, "He's here. Is James awake?"

The nurse looked at me, then reached in and stroked James's hands.

"Your son is here," she said. "What's his name, James?"

James, scarcely able to breathe, said, "His name is Ben."

The nurse and the doctor both beckoned to me at the same time, and I walked around the nurse, reached in, and laid my hands on James's folded hands.

"What are you doing?" I said. "I come all the way up from Limerick to see you, and this is what I find."

"I've decided to travel on, Ben," said James, and he opened his eyes.

"Not your best decision, James."

"What are you complaining about? I waited for you. How's the road?"

I said, "Up and down."

He tried to laugh; that was our old joke.

"Wouldn't we have the finest job if it wasn't for the hills," James used to say. "And the hills would be fine if it wasn't for the hollows."

The effort to laugh nailed him. He laid his head to one side and stopped. But his fingers tightened on mine, and I knew that I would be there, in that position, for several more minutes. So did Miss Fay, and she brought a chair from the far side of the room. I sat down and James said no more. Ever again.

The skin on his face had become rice paper. Thin lines I had never seen before ran down his cheekbones, small, ice-blue veins. His hair, dense as scrub, stood up, as uncombed as ever. Against the pallor of the skin, the insides of his nostrils seemed almost to glow red. And I saw, not for the first time, his deerlike eyelashes.

It's fair to say that I had long envisaged a scene such as this: James at last beaten back by the poor respiration he'd had since infancy; and we know nowadays that his sixty cigarettes a day didn't help.

I had long planned all kinds of words for this occasion.

"James, tell me what I should be collecting."

"James, are there great untold stories in the countryside that I should now be looking for?"

"James, tell me how to run the rest of my life without you."

Within those imagined sentences lurked slices of our history together. James was the one who had sent me on the road, who had first directed me into a world where people had strange and interesting chores, habits handed down through generations of their families, family cures efficacious for all kinds of ailments. James was the one who from time to time told me a great legend or a major slice of mythology that he had uncovered in some corner of some parish in some remote county somewhere in Ireland. Notably, he usually revealed it to me after he himself had collected it; however kind, James did not allow sentimentality to interfere with his competitiveness.

As for running the rest of my life without him, if I'd stopped to think about it I wouldn't have been able to do it. Knowing James was like walking down a staircase; hesitate—that is to say, imagine what life would be like without him—and you fall.

Time stood still in that room. Forgive the cliché, but that seems to me a truth that has stayed with me ever since. Four people, two of whom he loved and who loved him, Miss Fay and I, and two who were clearly impressed by him, the nurse and the doctor, stayed with James Clare until he quit the planet. We should all go like that.

He scarcely had enough breath to address the effort of dying. No movement came from him; now and then his throat rasped, or his head lolled into an uncomfortable position and was righted by the nurse. Miss Fay came around to the other side of the bed and laid her hands on top of mine, on top of his.

It seems to be the case that we have no rational thoughts at such moments. I was aware that something fabulously important was happening to me, but I feared too much the selfishness of the thought. And yet, I should have given the idea free rein, because I was losing one of the major components of my life, inside and out. From the moment he heard what had happened to Venetia, and how brutal had seemed the kidnapping, and how savagely our young, innocent lives had been wrecked, James had watched over me. No parent, no teacher, no priest could have been more vigilant.

I've known all my life the fabled difficulty of defining the precise, the exact moment of death. How we debated it in religion classes in school! When does the soul leave the body? How long may a soul linger here on earth? By and large, we were taught that the soul continues to dwell in the fading cadaver for up to twenty-four hours. Who determined that span of time has always been a puzzle to me, and it produced enjoyable debate. Now, though, I found myself unable to say the precise moment at which James left us, taking his great, informed soul with him.

Miss Fay, however, knew exactly. She withdrew her hands from mine and cupped James's face. Then she leaned in and kissed the dry line of his mouth, and pressed her forehead to his.

"Dear man. Dear man." She said it over and over. "My dear man. My dear, dear man."

For the next several hours—no, years—Miss Fay and I sat in that room, on side-by-side chairs. We said little; we ate nothing; we drank water. Eventually, Miss Fay remarked that we should get some sleep.

I rose; she reached for my hand.

"Ben, what do we do now? The two of us?"

Frozen to her chair, she removed her spectacles; I had never seen her without them, and the nakedness shocked me. So alone did she travel into her grief that, when she waved me away, I did exactly as she wished and went to what they'd both called "Ben's room."

And by the way, it is true that somebody's death can change your life forever. It was Christmas Day.

43

James Clare is buried on a hillside overlooking the sea at a place named Howth (rhymes with "oath"), north of Dublin. He chose the place himself, Dora Fay told me: "He said, 'History and mythology meet there.' "

The cemetery slants up along the hill, and on a clear day, especially in the diamond brightness of a frosty morning, I can see its whitened stones like a mouthful of small teeth across Dublin Bay from my front door. I'm pleased to be within sight of James's last resting place.

Thousands of people turned out. Dublin had no traffic problems in those days—not enough cars—but for James's farewell they bought, they hired, they begged and borrowed. Most came from distant counties, by bus, by train, by car, some on bicycles. Every taxi in the city, it was said, disappeared that day, following the hearse along the road by the sea north of the city.

At the neck of land they call Sutton Cross, the funeral stopped. Everybody climbed out of every conveyance, and for the last few miles we walked behind a lone piper. Hundreds of men took turns carrying the coffin. They made changeovers so smooth that not a pace did we misstep.

When my pall-bearing stint was done, I slowed down to let Miss Fay catch up with me. She was the only female member of the cortege; in Dublin, the women tended not to go to the graveyard, but try telling that to Dora Fay. She wore a deep black veil that fell from her hat.

"If he could only see it," she said. After a pause she added, "And thank you for not saying something stupid and platitudinous like 'I'm sure he's watching.' "

The name "Howth" derived from the Scandinavian, from the Viking settlers who lived here in the ninth, tenth, and eleventh centuries, and meant simply a headland or clifflike promontory.

We climbed up the slope, stumbling among bleached headstones. Ahead stood a crippled tree, also white as bones. We stork-stepped over the old mounds until we reached the brown grave where men still dug, their heads level with our feet.

I looked back at the road to Dublin. And nudged Miss Fay. For miles behind us stretched a long line of people, a tapering black snake.

"But they'll not all get in here," she fretted, anxious in her courtesy.

"The piper will stay until everybody has visited," I said. I'd been to funerals like this in the north and west.

"Then so will we," she said. "I have something to say to you, Ben, and this is the place to say it."

With my head bowed toward her, I waited. Nobody as yet had come to stand near us.

"James always wanted you to go back to Venetia."

I said, "I know."

"She's in Dublin. I've seen the posters."

"In the Olympia Theatre."

"Why don't you go, Ben?"

Never did I encounter a circumstance where it felt possible not to answer Dora Fay. I always spoke candidly to her—partly out of fear of her disapproval, but wholly to honor the deep role she played in my life.

Now I answered, "I'm afraid."

"Of?" The one-word question—always her best shot.

"I'm not sure."

"Then look for sureness. Find the true reason."

"Why do you say that?"

"Because you won't find it. There is no reason. James said you were a natural couple."

Why now, at such a moment? Why whisper this monumental thought over the deep rectangular hole in the ground that would shortly receive the body of her best beloved, the man of whom she'd once said to me, "I have only one god"?

"But I so wrecked my chances in Florida."

How that meeting haunted me. And, children, your mother had never looked more wondrous, and I, who had tracked her to Jacksonville, and had stalked her along the wide, wide sands, and watched her swim in the ocean, and then had come face-to-face with her, my heart pounding in my ears, couldn't stay and listen to what she so frantically wanted me to hear.

"There's no such thing as a wrecked chance with someone who loves you," Dora Fay said.

"But I stormed off. Full of my own injury."

"Yes, and the fact that you know you did—that enables you not to do it again. What did James say to you one night long ago in my kitchen?"

"He said so many things."

"I mean about fear."

I remembered and smiled. "When you're afraid, stand on your tippy toes—in your mind as well as your boots." She murmured the final sentence with me: "Make yourself taller and the fear will be afraid of you."

The priest and the acolytes arrived, in their black soutanes and white surplices.

"Oh, and there's this," Miss Fay told me. "James said you'd read it well." She pulled a sheet of paper from her pocket, her pointed nose now wind-tipped to blue. "It was his favorite piece that he'd ever collected."

The piper ceased. Voices rose and fell in the muttered and stuttered litanies of obsequy. Some of the prayers ran away with the breeze. Dipping a round-knobbed silver pestle into a small silver bucket, the priest scattered holy water on the coffin. Now the loss began to bite.

Miss Fay tightened her hand on my arm. We had one last chanted incantation, one last attempt to persuade "the Almighty to welcome the soul of thy humble servant, James Clare"—who'd been nobody's servant and never humble. The priest stepped back, Miss Fay nudged me, and I opened my mouth to speak.

To my surprise, my throat and my lips worked. I heard myself say, "James had one famous and favorite piece of folklore that he collected, and I'll read it now; it's very short."

Eyes blue as flowers, eyebrows blue-black and shining bright as the shell of a beetle, teeth as twin rows of pearls in her mouth, gold abundant hair woven into two tresses, each tress woven into strands, the point of each strand rounded by a little golden ball. Eyes dancing like stars. Each cheek glowing rosy as the berries of the rowan tree, lips gleaming red, each slender arm white as the may blossom, shoulders soft and high and white, wrists tender, polished, and white, nails pink and delicate. Neck arching long as a swan's and smooth as silk and white as the foam of a wave, thighs smooth and creamy, legs as true as a carpenter's measure, feet slim and dainty and white. Such was the beauty of the beautiful Princess Etain. And so we celebrate the beauty of the world, and beauty has no time limits.

I finished, and, all around me, people nodded their heads and I could almost hear them say, "Yes, that was James, all right."

Miss Fay said, "Well done." She tightened her grip on my arm. "He gave me that after one year together. He said it made him think of me."

I folded the paper.

Miss Fay murmured, "Keep your eyes closed and your head down. Do you know why?"

"Respect?" I said.

"There's more to it. At the funeral of a good man, the sky fills with angels. But we don't look up in case we don't see them," said Miss Dora Fay.

44

I escorted Miss Fay to the university hallway at Earlsfort Terrace. Music, stories, more music. Not too much to drink, just enough for hospitality's sake, because James, for all his conviviality, for all his ability to get the best stories out of people, felt uncomfortable near too much alcohol.

I didn't enjoy it much. James's friends hassled me. It didn't matter that I'd been doing his job—and my own—for the two previous years, since James had been off the road.

"You'll never be the man James was."

"You're not in James's league."

"You're wet behind the ears."

"James knew the world."

How James would have fumed. Miss Fay, when by my side, countered them for me. She didn't catch the worst of them.

I left the hall to take a break. And heard the voice behind me. "Well now, Captain."

Uninvited.

"What are you doing here?"

"I'm sorry for your trouble," he said, using the traditional condolence phrase in Ireland.

"How did you know?"

"Heard it on the news," he said. "He wasn't that old, was he?"

"I never knew his age," I heard myself say—and realized for the first time that it was the truth.

"What did he die of?"

Old joke: he died of a Tuesday. "Emphysema. Heart gave out finally. How are you?"

"Have you your notebook with you?"

We found a quiet corner at the end of a long corridor. Jimmy Bermingham was one of the few men I've ever known whose eyes actually glinted.

"What am I supposed to be taking down?"

"I'm only doing what you asked me to do, Captain, telling you what I was doing." And he did:

Do you know the town of Larne? A cold town, up there in East Antrim. Well, a bunch of the boys was caught out there last week. I was with them and we were interrupted in our very first job, which was to give a good hard kick to the British occupation of our country. This wasn't in the papers at all, so we have censorship now, and you're going to be the only person who has the full story, Captain.

Soldiers, police, tracker dogs, trucks, jeeps, tanks nearly, the occupying power, as we call them, mustered everything they had to catch us. We got trapped in a cave, a strange kind of a place up near the Giant's Causeway.

And the dogs outside were going mental, because they got the scent all right, but the soldiers and the cops were too frightened to come into the cave or even to the mouth of the cave. Because they didn't know how many of us were inside. And they didn't know how heavily armed we were.

Now, we were over that side of the county because we were aiming to wreck a big consignment of ammunition and guns that the soldiers were to unload from the dock at Larne. That cargo was being brought in from England to strengthen the garrisons all across the north.

If we could only have got down onto the port, our impact would have been mighty. Because there was meant to be very few soldiers there, and we'd plug them and then blow up the whole mixture. But with the explosions the night before, the English brought in hundreds of troops to protect the unloading. The rest of their soldiers went out chasing our boys.

And here we were now, in terrible weather, holed up in a deep hollow in the icy rocks of the northeast. On those same hills, that's where Saint Patrick served out his slavery. Herding pigs, he was, and he said he nearly froze to death.

We sat in the cave for three days. My legs were shafts of ice. But we were well equipped. I mean we had plenty to eat and water to drink; there was a spring and a pool in the cave near us, and we were armed to the teeth. The soldiers outside kept being relieved in relays, and we were stuck.

On the morning of the fourth day, nobody was making a move either way. It looked as if we might be trapped in there for four more days, and maybe even beyond that. Our commandant said to us, "Lads, we can't stay here much longer. We don't know what kind of stuff they might throw in here to gas us out."

We could tell at nighttime that the soldiers or the police had brought up big, huge lights and were running them off the engines of trucks. Anybody who came to the mouth of the cave would be seen immediately, and we all knew there would be no coming out with our hands up, no surrender—we'd be shot at sight.

Now one of our fellows was from around there in East Antrim, and he said that he'd always heard that these hills were honeycombed with strange caves and potholes. In his opinion, there was probably another way out of the cave, and he asked his commandant if he could go and look for one. He was given permission, and the lad was gone for twelve hours.

When the lad came back, he said that he'd been out in the open air. It was a simple enough route; you just had to be careful in one place with the underground water, but if you followed a stream it would lead you right out. In fact, he said, when they came out on the other side they'd find themselves looking down a hill straight into the yard of the very school he went to as a child.

Slowly and carefully, and it took several hours, the young lad led us out into the open air. We emerged blinking at ten o'clock in the morning. Straight in front of us down the hill was the school with the gate wide open. There were six of us, and we walked into the schoolyard and stole six bicycles.

We rode these bikes a few hundred yards across the open countryside, and then we made arrangements to split up and come back together again on the hill above the town of Larne. Six men on a bunch of bicycles with rifles on their shoulders? We had to hide.

If you're coming into Larne, you come down a hill, and you see the port down below. Well, we hid in various places along the same roadside, and when it was time to come together again, we followed the road, each one of us whistling or singing the same tune until we all met up. There we were, hidden in trees along by the road, looking down the hill at the port.

And what was happening at the port? Soldiers, hundreds of them, were guarding the dockers, who were unloading crates and huge equipment and machinery off a ship onto a series of trucks. We knew that we'd hit the jackpot.

We waited together—God, it took patience! We figured that the army trucks had to drive past us. This was the biggest road out of Larne. We all took up position, scattered down along the roadside, hidden in the brush, to ambush the trucks when they started coming up the hill.

The commandant dispatched two men to find a farmer's cart. They found one. The farmer wasn't there, but his wife was, and she was chatty. She said, sure, they could borrow the old cart, and she told them that she had a son who was a soldier and he was down there loading guns and all kinds of machinery onto the trucks for distribution across the province, and she was expecting him home for his dinner, because they were leaving the port at exactly twelve o'clock and he had two days' leave after his job was done. They thanked her for the cart, she gave them some homemade bread and some milk, and told them hurry up and go before her husband got home and changed his mind.

Our two boys wheeled the cart nearly a mile cross-country, to the place on the side of the road where they were all hiding. Now they had their timing: noon that day. So they ate the bread and drank the milk. And none for us. We reefed them for that later on.

When we saw the convoy of trucks leaving the port way down below, we settled down into our positions, a spread of about a hundred and fifty yards, and all on one side of the road so that we wouldn't hit each other with our own bullets. As the convoy started to climb the hill, two of the lads pushed the old cart out into the middle of the road, and they guessed right, that the trucks would be the first traffic to come that way. There weren't that many cars in East Antrim.

The first truck stopped, and we opened fire. We ran down the hill and we *fired at every wheel we could see, and we punctured every tire we shot. We hit fifteen trucks altogether, and none of the soldiers got a clear shot at us. Mission accomplished. Gone. It took two weeks before the British army could get over their problems. By that time we were back down across the border.*

45

After Jimmy left, Miss Fay and I made the most of the night. We saw all the people she needed to see. Many stiffened toward her. She had, after all, a doubtful status in Catholic Ireland, because she and James had never married, and he'd been staying in her house for thirty years. The least they said about her was "Ah, what could you expect from a Protestant?"

The hypocrites. Many of them, with their pious frowns, had borrowed money from James, and most had never paid him back. I discovered their debts in his effects long after his death.

A decent core, though, all men, acknowledged her as fully as they would any widow. His real friends. And she showed her gratitude. She also introduced all of them to me and made them pledge that if they could ever be of use to me, they would gladly do so. We listened to stories about James. We heard two of the tunes that he had inspired—a reel named "James Clare's Fancy" and a jig, "James Clare's Pony," which is what he called his famous bicycle.

When the last guests had gone, we went home to her kitchen table, a place where lives—mostly mine—were saved.

"What will you do now?"

"I will build a garden," she said. "Here. At the back of the house. There's plenty of room. And everything I put in that garden will have to do with James. And with you."

When you have nothing to say, say nothing.

"And you, Ben? Well, I know what you will do."

She could always surprise me.

"You do?"

"You will pursue Venetia. Bring her here to me, so that I can tell her about you."

I said, "I don't know. I'm not sure."

"You should," she said. "It's what life wants you to do. My garden—I will begin it soon. We will both be gardening at the same time. In a manner of speaking."

How old was Miss Fay? I think in her seventies, but passing for sixty; and when she eventually died I found three birth certificates, all showing different ages.

After dinner, she led me into the drawing room. She had set up the long dining table to its full, extended length. White sheets concealed piles of objects. She loaded a Chopin nocturne onto her gramophone. No. 19. Peaceful as deep snow. She laid a finger on her lips. As the first breaths of the E Minor moved across the room, she beckoned. Together we lifted and folded the white sheets.

In sectors along the table, she had laid out James's possessions. First, his shirts, all white, all collarless; the starched collars lay folded beside them. Next to them, laid to their full length, lay James's one dozen black ties.

She pointed. Across the room, on a coat stand from the hall, hung his four black suits. Draped across an armchair lay his famous long black coat, empty now, and hollow with missing him.

Next to the shirts sat his tobacco pipes, and his two pouches, one in soft black leather, one in brown. All the accoutrements lay there, too: his cigarette lighters, the pipe-cleaning tools, a little brass tamp he had like a tiny barbell.

James used this to punctuate his stories as he told them; just at the moment of greatest suspense he would finger the barbell, turn it over in his fingers like a magician doing a coin trick, and pause in his telling as he tamped down the tobacco. Sometimes he made it worse; he allowed the pipe to go out, and then, with short, grunting pauses in his tale, he'd relight it and tamp down the tobacco. Maddening, but I now recognized where he had learned it.

From looking at the pipes and the tobacco equipment I understood that two versions of James had been on this earth: the James who traveled the roads and the James who had maintained an identical life in this house for much of his adult life. And he'd kept this side of him a secret from most people.

We moved along the table to a series of boxes—ebony, sandalwood, mahogany, some with inlay, all about the size of an average book. Miss Fay opened each box like an Egyptologist and displayed the contents: pens and nibs, some as old-fashioned as quills, some fountain pens with shiny black or marbled barrels and gold bands, more than one of which bore the initials J.A.C. I hadn't even known of a middle initial. "Abraham," she told me; even at christening his life had been unusual.

I stroked the boxes; I handled the pens; I fingered the gold bands with the initials. Beside me, Miss Fay leaned across the table and pulled the boxes toward us. With a sweep of the hand, but not a word from her lips, she gave me the boxes; I have them still; you have seen them, children, and handled them. I cherish them; in fact, as you know, I mention them specifically in my Will.

By now I understood that I was being led through James's life, and being asked without words what possessions of his I would like to have. James's books had long been merged with Miss Fay's, and in time, when she left the planet, all of those came to me. They are full of annotations, those books, some in James's handwriting, some in Miss Fay's. Often I come across a notation from one or the other of them, and for that moment they're standing beside me again.

The next group made me smile. James had a passion for small, useful tools—screwdrivers, pocketknives, bottle openers, and, as he used to say, "things for taking stones out of horses' hooves." Some had metal handles and casings, some bone, some mother-of-pearl, and when Miss Fay saw my smile she swept them, too, toward me.

Now we came to an attaché case, again with the initials J.A.C. About the size of a deep modern briefcase, it had a new leather smell, and the central brass catch also looked undisturbed—no scratches, no wear and tear. This case had scarcely been out-of-doors.

Miss Fay clicked open the brass lock and then pushed the attaché case to me. I took hold of it, felt its significant weight. She made an "open it" gesture. When I eased back the lid, I saw a card lying on a green felt cloth: James's handwriting: "For Ben: a legacy of sorts."

Beneath the green cloth lay packet after packet of banknotes, each denomination a hundred pounds, each packet containing a hundred bills—ten thousand per packet, and the case contained twenty packets.

I recoiled. Too much, too much—both the size of the gift and the intent behind it. I already knew, though, that I had no way of refusing it; and Miss Fay—as she had often made clear—had deep financial security (all of which she bequeathed to me).

Later that night she would tell me that James had had a "saving demon" in him, and every Monday he'd put aside what he had not spent of his previous week's allotted budget. When it reached a hundred pounds, he went to a bank and translated the smaller bills into a one-hundred-pound note. From time to time he took the older notes to the bank and refreshed them with new issues.

My arithmetic raced. How could he have saved that much money? Not on government pay. The full story didn't come from Miss Fay. In the following months and years, out in the country, I learned that James had been a card player—who always won. Miss Fay never told me that. Nor did she confirm it when I found out. It was probably the only time I ever saw her defensive.

The last pile of possessions on the table lay under a brocade tablecloth of blue and gold. Miss Fay hesitated for a moment, slipped a hand under the cloth, and pulled forth a card much like the one I'd found with the money. James had written, "Ben's true legacy."

As tenderly as nurses, we removed the tablecloth—and exposed neat piles of black notebooks. I counted them: eighty-two; I opened one— and learned that every notebook had been numbered, and that these contained everything private that James had taken down in his life of collecting folklore, and that each of these unofficial notebooks covered approximately six months at a time.

I said to Miss Fay, "This is—" and got no further. Tears took over.

"He admired you so much, Ben."

She left the room. While she was gone, I turned to the notebooks, and at great speed, I found the summer of 1932. That was when I had introduced him to Venetia.

Easy to find: James had written, "Ben's young lady, Venetia, is tender and lovely. She is so kind to him. He is mature in her company, and gentle."

Miss Fay returned, lugging a suitcase. In silence she laid it on the floor: more notebooks, different in size and texture—James's official notebooks, his own daily journals.

"They'll have to go to the Commission archives," she said, "but you should trawl through them first. I'll hold them for a year."

We had almost finished. Miss Fay pointed to the suits. I shook my head—but I picked up the long black coat. First I draped it over my shoulders. Then I put my arms in the sleeves. Finally, I wore it.

The mood snapped. Miss Fay stared. Then she turned away and with the vigor of a woman half her age began to hammer on the wall. And howl.

I reached for her, but she rejected my hand. Thinking of last straws and the backs of camels, I began to take off the coat.

"No, no, no, no, no!" she screamed. "Leave it on. Go away. Go!"

46

Where could I go after all that emotion? How could I come down from those heights? I waited in the hallway. Miss Fay wept for long minutes. In due course she allowed me to lead her to another room and an armchair. Brandy? She nodded; I took none. By now we had come close to midnight, and she looked exhausted.

The weeping stopped. She asked me, "Can you stay?"

"Of course."

I said that I felt uneasy about the private notebooks.

"Shouldn't they go to you?"

She said, "No!"

"Why so vehement?"

"He said they'd be a fuel source for you."

"Do you know what he meant?"

"Open one."

I went to the other room, took a notebook at random, brought it back, and handed it to Miss Fay.

She thumbed and mused: "At the end of each notebook James kept some spare pages for what he called short jottings. He used to read them to me. Look."

I read, "Irish legends state that a king will always be a king. Not even a wizard can bring him down."

"Few characters in mythology gain as much respect as the hero or champion, i.e., the man who shows determination no matter what challenges he faces."

"The beauty of women in mythology doesn't always denote beauty of spirit."

"In legends, the hero always knows his destiny, even if he refuses to face it."

Miss Fay, detached as a clerk, said, "That was his favorite quotation. That's what James lived by. See what I mean?"

47

The next day, I should have climbed into my safe car and gone back to the countryside. Why didn't I? Pusillanimity again. It even trumped my passion for fields, lakes, and stories told by the fire.

Unease nagged, too. The joust with Man One and Man Two had disturbed me. On two counts: they might set out after me, and I hadn't freed myself from the guns nonsense. In broad daylight I couldn't believe that I had come so close to such events. Or that they'd happened.

On impulse, as I walked past a police station near the Commission offices, I went in. Might I find a superior officer? Someone with a broader view? No thugs to manhandle me?

Naturally, my mind was asking, *What would James say? Meet it head-on.* Or would he again say, *Never trouble trouble until trouble troubles you?*

I waited. For two hours. First, the desk sergeant asked if I had a complaint to make. *No, no complaint.* He asked the nature of my business.

Important. And confidential. About what, like? *This is serious.* He asked how serious was serious. *Gun serious. IRA serious.* He asked my employer's name, and when I said, *A government department,* he grabbed a notepad and pencil and disappeared. When he came back, many minutes later, he took me to a small room and locked the door behind me. And there I waited. For two more hours.

A superior officer did indeed appear—accompanied by Man Two. *Not good,* said my mind. *This is not the result I wanted.*

Man Two said, "Heh, Little Boy, I thought it was you." I presumed that the sergeant at the desk had made a phone call.

James, where are you? In legends, the hero always knows his destiny, even if he refuses to face it. But what the hell is my destiny in this stuff? Another mistake, eh, Ben?

The senior man, not quite as old as my father, and with a cyst on his forehead, held out a handshake.

"I knew James Clare. I hear 'twas a great funeral." *James, you're still here, thank you.*

I said, "He was very well known."

"Now, was James your boss?"

"He was indeed."

"Well, you must be all right." He smiled. "What's the trouble?" He offered a cigarette—to me but not to Man Two, who stood behind him and glowered. "Larry here tells me that you've met some undesirables."

I said, "It's complicated."

"Ah, sure nothing is simple," said the Man with the Cyst. "How complicated?"

"Very."

"Now, are you frightened or something? People who volunteer to see us are usually lunatics or frightened, and I don't think you're a lunatic."

Oh, Christ! I haven't thought this through. I don't know where it could go.

"Now, what do you want to tell me, Ben?"

I said, "I don't know."

"Well, in my department we always say, We can't torture you for facts, but we can hang you for them."

He chuckled, and Man Two snorted.

I said, "Suppose I did meet some 'undesirables,' as you call them, and suppose they were running guns, and suppose one of them told me in detail about an attempted murder or about a military-style operation outside of this—" I hesitated.

"Jurisdiction?" he asked.

"Jurisdiction, yes." I reached for some steam. "And suppose, say, just for the sake of argument, suppose I had ferried weapons here and there, and suppose I'd even handled a gun—even if I hadn't taken part in anything?"

Behind the other man's back, Man Two mimed a hanging. Hands around his neck, he rolled his eyes. Made silent, gagging faces. Tongue far out.

His superior remained kindly. "The burden of proof is always on us, Ben. But now there are ways of handling everything."

Why does he say "now" so often?

"Such as?"

Oh, great, rampaged my mind, *terrific. At one leap you wind up in something so deep and dangerous that you get yourself caught every which way.*

The Man with the Cyst took his time, looking at the floor and dragging on his cigarette.

"Hmm. Now—the best way, and in fact the only way—" He paused, contemplating every word. "In fact, yes, the only way—if what you're describing—for the sake of argument—if it had, say, already happened." He looked up at me quickly. "The only way you could cope with that would be, well, you'd have, so to speak, to become one of us."

"But—how would that work?"

Yes, yes, yes. Caught. Comprehensively snagged and snared. Breathing in and breathing out. Would Jimmy B. put a bullet in my head? You bet he would. What did Randall call him? That little narcissist. Didn't somebody— my father—call Al Capone a narcissist? Or was that Pretty Boy Floyd? My father and his books and magazines about gangsters. No use to me now.

"You'd work with Larry here. Tell him where you were going. Who you'd be with."

"At all times?"

"Well, if there was something undesirable going on. Or about to go on. That's how it would work."

I looked at Man Two—"Larry," as I now knew. He winked at me. Not a nice wink, not a friendly wink, not a decent wink, but a wink that said, "I'll cut off your private parts"—which he would, one day, actually say to me. "And feed them to my greyhounds, only they'd probably choke."

Violence everywhere. Everywhere. Oh, God, how I needed Venetia. Or James. Or any kind of kindness.

"So—I need to get this clear. If I knew of anything that was 'undesirable' as you say—"

The Man with the Cyst interrupted me. "We're not talking about a fellow who hasn't put up the tax disc on his car or anything like that. Or hasn't paid his income tax. Do you get that, Ben?"

I looked at the floor. And took a pause. Which they didn't interrupt.

"Is this," I asked, "what they call 'turning' somebody?"

The Man with the Cyst smiled. "You must have read a lot of spy books."

I said, with a touch of rue, "My father."

"And your next question will be," said the Man with the Cyst, "what would happen to you if those you turned against found out?"

"I'm not with anyone," I said, "so you can't say I'm against anyone."

"Well, you bloody well should be," said Larry (who, by the way, went on to become a leading figure in Irish security matters). "Enemies of the state."

"Larry, you sound like a Communist," chuckled the Man with the Cyst. "Now, Ben." He sat on the edge of the banged-up table, his cigarette almost down to the butt. "Do we have some kind of understanding here?"

I said, "I'll have to think about it."

To my surprise, he shook his head. "Too late for that, I'm afraid."

"But I didn't say a thing."

He smiled—sympathy, compassion, regret. "My job is to address any implications that these recent activities north of the border have for us." He became official. "The government has made it clear that it will seek the death penalty for any such killings committed down here. Killers and associates. If and when convicted. And it will extradite to Britain anyone wanted there."

I said, "Hold on, hold on. I've said nothing about anything."

The Man with the Cyst said, "I could have you in jail within minutes—and for years." He snapped his fingers at me. "Fix it. Stay on the right side."

I backed away. "But either way—"

Larry drew his hand across his throat. "Either way a man could have his neck damaged," Larry said.

The Man with the Cyst headed for the door. "My advice would be: do the right thing."

He went. And Larry said, "If I don't hear from you, Little Boy—I'll come looking." He winked again.

48

Thanks to that delay button in my emotional metabolism, I don't respond fast to dramatic moments. Whether through paralysis, fear, or a wish to postpone delight, I store them until I can control them. How else could I have not shrunk into drink after such a meeting?

And what, children, happened next that day of the Man with the Cyst? I met Jimmy Bermingham again—the man upon whom I was supposed to inform. At the funeral party he had asked me to come and meet his "heart's delight."

"If she's that important to you, Jimmy, why do you keep calling her 'Dirty' Marian?"

"Ah, you'll see, Ben, you'll see."

"I bet she doesn't like being called that."

"What she likes, Ben, is a tongue sandwich." He came close to embarrassing me with his roughness. "D'you know what, Ben? I'm always wanting to feel her."

His cackle defined the word "lewd."

We met inside the General Post Office on O'Connell Street, the iconic locus of the 1916 rebellion. He wore a brand-new coat, identical to the one wrecked by Elma Sloane's father, including the brown velvet collar tabs. Hopped up with excitement, he said to me, "Any minute now, Ben. Any shaggin' minute." He waxed dramatic. "She's going to walk through that door, and she'll have a basket on her arm, and it'll be full of letters."

"What's her name?"

"She's a Killeen, Ben, from Mayo. 'Mayo, God help us'—isn't that the old saying?"

We stood there, looking all around for a girl with a basket. We saw girls with handbags. We saw girls with parcels. We saw girls with dogs on leashes. My guess is that we stood there for at least an hour.

"Maybe," I suggested, "she's coming on another day. Or maybe she's gone to a different post office."

My patience drifted—and then Jimmy jerked his head.

"Hey, Ben, look."

A tall girl, with, indeed, a basket of letters, walked to a window and spoke to the person behind the brass grille. "Dirty" Marian? No. Not in any way. Nothing low-grade or lewd here. Graciousness, yes, and reserve. A swan's neck. An aloof head. A walk so poised that she might have trained as a dancer.

"Go over and say hello."

Jimmy said, "No, no, we mustn't do that, Ben, that's the last thing we must do." He saw me puzzle at this. "Give it a minute, Ben; we'll see what she does." He began to babble. "I don't want to interrupt her, like, when she's in the middle of her tasks. She's very efficient, and she doesn't appreciate it if you don't let her do things the way she wants to."

I watched her transact her basket of mail. Handed a form to sign, she took off her right glove and reached into her purse for a green fountain pen. When she had signed, she restored the glove.

"Listen." I grabbed Jimmy Bermingham's arm and gripped. "You have to tell me now, Jimmy, this instant. Why do you call her 'Dirty' Marian?"

"Kind of a joke, Ben."

"But it misrepresents her completely."

"Isn't that the joke?"

I asked, "And she's in on this joke?"

"Jesus, no. She'd kill me if she knew."

"Then stop using that name to describe her."

Marian Killeen. Actually, Marian Bernadette Killeen. How important she would become to me. We watched her at the window. She unloaded her basket, piece by steady piece. When I changed positions to view the clerk behind the brass grille, I saw the deference in his face.

Marian Killeen turned away from the window and headed for one of the main doors. Jimmy darted after her; I followed.

"Hello, Marian," Jimmy said, full of hope and charm. "This is my great friend, Ben, who works for the Folklore Commission. Howya doin', Marian?"

She paused, and looked at us as at drunks or beggars. But she had good manners and gave me the respect due to a stranger. With a gloved hand extended to me, she said, "How are you, I'm Marian Killeen." She had an unlined face, a complexion of cream linen. Eyes clear as day.

"Would you like a bit of lunch, Marian?" Jimmy's voice had gone higher. He was perspiring, his eyebrows angled high in anxiety.

Ice seeped into her eyes. "I have to go shopping."

"But sure we'll help you," said Jimmy.

"There's really no need."

"It'll be no bother."

Marian Killeen said, "Actually, I have to do some personal shopping, and I like to do that alone."

She nodded at me and said, "Nice to meet you, Ben." *Are her eyes saying, What are you doing with this worm?*

"So it'll be all right if we follow you?" Jimmy had descended to pleading.

Speaking as though to a disliked child, Marian Killeen said, "I can't stop you, of course." Her eyes registered my embarrassment; I knew it.

During this exchange, I had become aware of a tall man, thin as a flagpole. He stood by, ten feet away, watching and waiting; I'd seen him come into the post office behind us.

"Off you go so, Marian," said Jimmy. "We'll be right behind you to carry the parcels."

Marian Killeen pushed through the heavy doors. The flagpole man approached us.

"Jimmy, c'mere to me. How many?"

"Oh, howya, Paddy?"

"And where are they?"

"Paddy, it's a bit complicated."

"Have you them or haven't you?" He had a rough voice, thin with edge.

"Paddy, listen, I have to go. Why don't I see you at Neary's this evening?"

"What's wrong with now?"

"Paddy, this is my friend Ben, and he's the one in charge of them."

With a stride of rage, I headed for the doors. On the street outside, Jimmy Bermingham caught up to me and picked up on my anger.

"What was that?" I demanded. "Was that about—?"

"Shh, Ben, Jesus, don't say anything out loud; you don't know who'd be listening." He changed tack. "Where is she—can you see her?" He pointed and said, "Quick. Cross over here. She's heading for Clerys."

Yet again I failed to refuse him.

We followed Marian Killeen into Clerys, one of Ireland's few department stores. And then we followed her around. In today's terms, we stalked her. Never once did she look up or back to see us; she didn't care.

"Where does she live?"

Jimmy whispered back, "Rathmines. Eighteen Grove Road."

They'd known each other for several years. As a student, he'd worked in the grocery store around the corner. She lived alone, both parents dead.

"Big house, Ben. She's worth a stack."

Marian Killeen's phrase "personal shopping" translated itself. She made ladies' underwear her first port of call. Jimmy nudged me and cackled. In my annoyance, I came close to lifting him off the ground by his shiny black hair. She stayed fifteen minutes and more, sifting and handling. We lurked in the distance, behind a pillar.

When she moved, we moved. In the name of God, how did it look? This respectable young woman striding from department to department and being stalked, several aisles away, by two fools who walked in her parallel. We stopped when she stopped. We waited as long as she waited. We moved again when she moved again.

At any moment I expected the store detectives to intercept us. What a spectacle! This dapper, dark-eyed, dark-haired little chancer might have come from a card game. And this tall, awkward man in his forties, in his long black coat and big boots—mightn't he have just walked in off the fields?

Shoes, millinery, frocks—Marian Killeen stopped at every department. *This is no love affair; this is the worst possible mismatch. Perfectly civil to me. But she thinks Jimmy's a maggot.*

Since we learn fastest about people by the reactions of others to them, I studied those who served her. She made sure to thank each one, apologized if she didn't make a purchase. They smiled back. They deferred to her. They tried to please her, give her every help she wanted. *There's no way Jimmy Bermingham can close this gap.*

For most of an hour we pursued her. We watched her down the gun barrel of every aisle. Never once did she look at us, whether with a smile or a frown.

Her final stop took her to a florist's booth. She bought assorted flowers, which the woman arranged into a pleasant bouquet. Marian Killeen babied it in her arms.

I nudged Jimmy. "Go and pay for the flowers."

"With what?"

In those early days, I handed over the money.

He ran up that aisle. I followed, watching. She retreated, wished to refuse his offer. His words reached my ears:

"Show me where it's been recorded in history that a woman didn't let a man buy her flowers."

Close to blushing, she looked at me. Behind Jimmy's back, I nodded.

"I accept," she said. "And thank you." As Jimmy settled with the florist (using my money), Marian Killeen stepped toward me.

"This is your doing?" she asked.

"He has to learn," I said, low enough for Jimmy not to hear.

"And you've given yourself the role of teacher?"

"When the student is ready, the teacher appears."

"We don't get many Buddhists in Dublin," she said.

I replied, "Oh, he's just a handsome young tear-about."

She raised an eyebrow at me, then walked away. Jimmy turned and grabbed my arm.

"Stop her, Ben. Will you?"

I strode after her. "Listen."

She didn't break stride, so I edged ahead and began to walk backward. At this she laughed—and stopped.

"What is it?"

"He's very funny," I said, "And he's very good company. And—and—"

"Next you'll be telling me he's a patriot."

"That, too," I said. "In fact—"

"Don't tell me," she said, acid dripping from her voice. "Perhaps I already know."

I walked back to Jimmy, who stood there on that famed bridge between hope and despair. "No dice, Jimmy."

"Shag it," he said, as profound in two words as Dante in thousands. "Try again."

"Yeh," he said. "And I might hit her a belt or two if she's still as cold as that."

"Not while I know you," I said.

He picked up my sudden force. "Ah, Ben. I mean—Jesus! Take a joke."

I watched him as he watched her walk away. He looked miserable. The façade seemed to work no more; the new coat looked cheap. His shoes scuffed, his tie shiny, he seemed like a man too young and too lowlife for the image he was building, and too far out of his depth to bring off such a face to the world.

How did she perceive him? Her face said it: *This scrawny, would-be-posh layabout with ambitions—what is he? A bookie's runner? A failed gambler? A poolroom lizard?*

As we stood there, a sandwich man walked by. His boards, front and back, carried an advertisement for the Olympia Theatre: "ALL WEEK! THE SENSATIONAL GENTLEMAN JACK & HIS FRIEND. YOU WILL NOT BELIEVE YOUR EYES."

49

My ticket, one of the few left, gave me a seat to the side of the stalls. I could see into the orchestra pit; I could see the faces of the performers; I could even see the stagehands in the wings. Best of all, I could look along the rows of spectators and observe their reactions.

Most Irish theaters in the midfifties survived on a mixed diet. The Olympia in Dublin put on some Shakespeare, some international plays, and a few works, new and old, by Irish playwrights. When it could, it booked visiting stars from overseas, big marquee names who could carry an entire show.

Often the management had a variety card, a mixed bag of all kinds of acts, with something of a sensational nature to top the bill. Such as *Gentleman Jack and His Friend*—"his friend" being Venetia Kelly, now Venetia Stirling. *Jesus!*

In the mangy red plush of the seats, I sat patiently through the first few acts. Not fidgeting. Scarcely looking around. Deep in thought. *What will I feel? Will it hurt? Should I go now?* People drifted in, some merry with pretheater booze, and there sat I, dry as a bone with terror, torn open by homage to a long gone past.

A comedian—though he laughed more at his jokes than the audience did—held the program together. He introduced an Irish tenor, nasal, sad, and often flat. A nun played a harp. Six girls in a troupe, their skirts armor-plated with medals, danced high Irish reels. The biggest of them, square, blond, and intent, had medals on her shirt, too. She looked like Göring.

The comedian returned. "Lay-dees 'n' genn'lmen, you will not believe your eyes. The management of the Olympia Theatre proudly presents to you. Ably aided and abetted by his lovely and mysterious assistant. See this miraculous, astounding, dazzling sleight of hand. Put your hands together, for the first time to the Olympia Theatre—Gentleman Jack and his friend!"

The bastard doesn't even allow her to have her name. Be fair. All you have against him is that he married Venetia. And raised my children. No! He hits her. But that's gossip. Don't listen to gossip. But gossip is what I listen to for a living. What else is legend but the gossip of the ages? Have I calmed down too much? Avoidance again?

And so the curtain began to part, to a black stage and a drum roll.

She wore blue shoes. Blue satin. With heels high as heaven. She wore a boudoir version of a swimsuit, all black and red lace and flesh colors. She wore fishnets on those endless legs. *This isn't my beautiful, modest Venetia.* I didn't see him for the first few minutes—in fact, I didn't see much at all, because of the bulging tears in my eyes.

So you were right, Ben. It wasn't all a long time ago. No, it wasn't long ago at all. Our little lives are rounded by a sleep. Well, then, in a little life it was only a moment ago. And James is dead, James, my teacher, my mentor, the man who could have told me how to handle this, the man who, unasked and uninvited but unstoppable, took responsibility for my growing up, for the half-healing of my heart—James is dead. The mythmaking of his life and mine—that's over. You're on your own, Ben, you have to make your own myths. Why not begin here and now?

I knew I had a decision to make, but that night I didn't have the stuff in me to make any decisions, and I knew it the moment I saw Venetia's face.

Let me calm down.

Gentleman Jack and His Friend. Note: the pronoun was also given a capital letter, yet he couldn't give your mother her own lovely name. But that doesn't surprise me—people by and large are what they do, and what did Gentleman Jack do? Gentleman Jack was a pickpocket and a mass hypnotist. He took things from people without them knowing it, and he mesmerized them into thinking they were what they could never be. As he did with your mother.

Skill? He had it in abundance; those weren't hands at the ends of his arms, those were dancers, and those weren't fingers on his hands, they were sorcerers. In tall, tight black pants and a billowing white shirt and shiny patent leather shoes winking in the lights of the stage, he was Mephistopheles, and his pencil of a black mustache juiced up the impression.

He began his act by calling attention to the body of his "friend." He had festooned your mother: three necklaces of pearls, one a choker; a watch on one wrist, a tight bracelet on the other. Bangles climbed up her arms, colored and jangling, gaudy as a gypsy camp. Above one knee she wore a twinkling garter, and on each high-heeled blue satin shoe she wore a large bow.

And yet, and yet—when I could bring myself to look closer, his vulgarization of her couldn't take away her essential dignity, just as the violence I saw every day didn't spoil the beauty of my landscapes. She was still Venetia. She was still the thirty-two-year-old woman who rose from a sea of cushions and silk bedspreads on her sultana's couch in a little south of Ireland town in the summer of 1932 to hold in her arms that red-haired boy of eighteen. She was still the creature of the ocean whom I watched as she swam, whom I followed down that long, serene, and deserted Atlantic beach in Florida, and from whom I then retreated in dudgeon and pain. She was still everything I had held in my heart and my mind and my soul ever since, and I could see it now, here, in her eyes, and she wasn't even looking at me. *Ben, you were right all along.*

With flamboyant announcements to the audience, Gentleman Jack announced what he was going to do.

"The quickness of the hand deceives the eye. My lovely friend here—she will be the first whom I bamboozle. You will not believe your eyes. Nor should you—because your eyes will have let you down. Your eyes will have failed to tell you what they are seeing—because your eyes will never be as quick as my fingers."

Venetia was now standing center stage, arms by her sides. Gentleman Jack walked quickly around her and downstage, where he held up a hand like a victor. In it flashed the watch he had just taken from Venetia's wrist, and he'd done it so quickly that I'd never spotted it. I, who was watching every fiber of her body, never saw her arm move, not a flinch, not a flicker.

I have trained myself to control my reactions in general—and yet I couldn't stop a gasp.

Item by item, Gentleman Jack removed the festoonery from Venetia. He even took the two voluptuous bows from her high-heeled blue shoes, and I swear that I never even saw him stoop down to do so. Perhaps I was so mesmerized by looking at her.

My rage simmered—had it begun to blind me? Like any vulgar performer, Gentleman Jack played to the lowest common denominator. As he removed yet another trinket from Venetia's arm, he leered at the audience and winked. *I know what you want us to think, you lout. I know you want us to ask ourselves, "What's he going to strip off her next? Or what'll be the last item he'll remove?" I know how you're using her, you bastard.*

"Well, lay-dees and genn'lmen, let me assure you I could remove everything—everything—without her—or you—even knowing it, even the small tattoo on her lovely bottom that says, 'I love Gentleman Jack.' The quickness of the hand deceives the eye."

He patted Venetia on the behind.

After all these years, was my proprietariness also political? We Irish don't let go. For centuries we wrote of our country as a woman who had been taken from us and whom we wanted back, whom we had never stopped loving. Too preposterous? Well, maybe not.

When the last bangle and the last bow had been removed, Jack Stirling led Venetia forward to the footlights and asked her to take a bow.

"Round of applause, please, lay-dees and genn'lmen, for my lovely friend."

Venetia, trouper that she always was, bowed low and smiled as sweet a smile as she had ever given me. Or—was there yearning in it now? She'd never been wistful, not even when playing Juliet, a role to which she'd brought more muscle than we usually see. Now, though—or was it my imagination?—her smile never reached the limits of its curve.

Gentleman Jack led her back to center stage and declared that his act had now truly begun. I noted that he had never given her a name—he didn't say "my lovely assistant, Venetia"—nor did he have any other showbiz name for her, "Anthea" or "Cordelia" or "the beautiful Miranda" or any of the names within that old convention. No: Venetia's anonymity had been deliberately created and maintained.

For the core of his act he called for volunteers from the audience. They lined up, laughing, giggling, shoving one another, taunting, teasing. A bulky girl in a fluttering white dress—she looked like a wedding cake—lost her shoes without knowing how. Her swain lost his necktie and his watch, and then his vest—from beneath his jacket. His pal lost the laces from his shoes but not the shoes. A game elderly woman lost a wristwatch and her earrings, Gentleman Jack again holding them up to the audience in triumph before handing them back to the astonished old dear.

His tour de force came when, after some swift passes over and around a girl's head, he held up her brassiere and waved it like flag. The girl, fortunately, laughed in what seemed like genuine mirth, and I watched Venetia. She laughed professionally—but she didn't laugh. I knew her laughter; when truly amused, she belly-laughed. Not here, not now.

50

Much had been made in Ireland of "The Risen People," the brave generations who, in the deep darkness of cultural and educational deprivation, had held on to our old traditions of sainthood and our instincts for scholarship. Was this vulgar display what The Risen People had risen for? I thought not.

And there was one more patriot to come and warm himself at this low fire. I should have known; why hadn't I anticipated it?

He had changed his clothes. No longer the elegant dark, striped suit; now he wore a Prince of Wales check with a burgundy waistcoat, and he had draped a silver pocket-watch chain across the stomach. His shoes had points that could have taken a snail from its shell, and he wore yellow socks with red diamonds on them; he looked like a singer from a shoddy band.

"What's your name, my friend?" asked Gentleman Jack.

"James, but you can call me Jimmy."

"Very good, James. Is this yours?" Jack held up the pocket watch and chain. Jimmy patted his stomach, then looked down, then looked up and shook his head.

"How did you do it?"

"Trade secrets, James, trade secrets. And is this yours, dear boy?" He handed Jimmy his necktie.

"Do it slowly," said Jimmy. "We'd all like to learn."

The audience loved this. Jack, however, flinched; was this man going to upstage him? He was. Jack now waved Jimmy's burgundy vest. Remember: I watched all of this but couldn't see it actually happen; it was like lightning. I saw as far as the flash of the hand, and then the object would appear in that same hand—but how or in what fashion he got the vest out from underneath the coat sleeves I have no earthly idea. After the vest came the wallet from Jimmy's inside pocket and a pen. And then came the upstaging.

When Jimmy saw the vest, then the wallet, and then the pen, he stepped back in mock alarm and pretended to try to escape from Jack, heading to the rear of the stage. Then, ten feet from the action, he turned.

"All right, all right. I know when I'm beaten." He made a gesture of surrender, hands out, palms flat—and began to unbuckle his belt and take off his pants. The audience cheered and cheered. Jack didn't look pleased. Jimmy had gotten his waistband down as far as his knees when Jack called a halt—and I left my seat. I did so without any real thought other than to avoid meeting Jimmy outside after the show.

The audience wanted more—and more, and more. I stopped in the aisle to look back as Venetia bowed beside Jack. We had once upon a time anticipated that audiences would do exactly this for Venetia—but it was to have been Shakespeare, and the Greeks, and the best of Shaw and Wilde, in different theaters all around Ireland. Neither of us would ever have meant for this talented, distinguished, and dignified classical actress to be propping up the butt of a coarse trickster show.

Do you remember it, children? Your mother's shows in Dublin? Not her first ever, of course, because she had been part of the Abbey Theatre all those years before, but this was her first time in Dublin as the "Friend" of Gentleman Jack. Perhaps you do recall it—because you were there; I saw you both.

It had begun to rain, not heavily, just a pretense at a drizzle. My exit took me through a side door into an alley lit by the "Stage Door" sign, a rectangle of white light with the words in red letters. For a moment it felt almost as a lighthouse to a mariner—and then I remembered that light-houses stand there to remind sailors of the rocks beneath.

Just as I thought of leaving the shadows and heading for the dry safety of Dora Fay's house, I heard voices. You emerged from the door beneath the lighthouse sign, you first, Louise, then you, Ben, and you fell into step side by side. Even in that dim light, and even had I been a stranger, I'd have known that you were twins. Not that you looked alike; you felt alike, and that's a very different thing.

I turned back toward the exit door, pretending to light a cigarette, and I know that you didn't even see me, my face close to the old, dirty brick. As you walked past, how did you not smell the fatherhood off me? But no: you walked on. I heard you speak; you were discussing the fact that the show had three matinees a week and hoping that "Mom won't be too tired." The Americanness of your voices carried in the night.

And then I followed you. In a father's life, nothing is so poignant as the backs of his children's heads as they walk away from him. I didn't walk fast after you; I made no attempt to stay within earshot—I just wanted to see you. In Florida, on that terrible day less than a decade earlier, when I'd first learned of your existence, I didn't ask what you looked like, whether you'd been born free of blemish. Worse, and it was my crime, my awful crime—I didn't ask whether I might meet the pair of you. So I didn't know what you looked like. But I knew it was you.

I followed you along Dame Street, toward Trinity College. You were twenty-three years old and, as I now know, on your first visit to Ireland.

You came level with Foster Place, and then the Bank of Ireland. You crossed in front of Trinity College. You headed for Nassau Street, or perhaps Grafton Street. I say "perhaps" because I gave up following you at that moment.

Too painful. You were deep in a conversation I could never have with you, and there was I—back in the throes of loss again, this time in a misery I had never anticipated, not even once.

My mind went to a place I know in the Knockmealdown Mountains, where, in a pocket of rocks by the lake, I have spent many a bleak night. Too far away to get there now.

PART THREE

❊ ❊ ❊

A Kind of Salvation

51

Do you think it strange that a stony mountain fastness can be comforting? Believe me: it can. Such places have embraced and saved me. Not that night.

I should have gone to Miss Fay's and tried to sleep. Instead I walked. As your two shadows disappeared under the weak yellow of the streetlamps, your heads close together and both of you deep in talk, I watched you slip out of sight. Can I recall what I was thinking? No.

Remember, I had no means to measure what kind of feelings I had for you; I didn't know how a father of children was supposed to feel. Ask me now, and I'll keep you here all night.

Dublin in those days had locales to suit any dank and feeble mood. Behind the Olympia Theatre spread a web of narrow little streets. Cobbled and inward-looking. Shabby as shame. Just as I felt.

I retraced my steps, past the stage door, to the rear of the building, where I waited—and waited. For what? I was summoning up the courage to intercept your mother.

The courage didn't come—surprise, surprise—and when I heard the applause, filtered like far-off machine-gun fire through the dense brick of the high walls, I walked away.

A vague river mist floated at knee height. These lanes had few lamps, and most houses had succumbed to the dark. Here and there, a window glowed. Through one, I saw a man sitting by the fire, fast asleep, his legs stretched out. The almost-closed lace curtains of another revealed an elderly woman with a shawl draped over a nightgown. Her gray hair fell down to witch length; from a black, steaming kettle she mixed something in a mug. I stood and watched. Wished that I could knock on the glass. Be taken into her house. Comforted.

I heard a footstep. Or thought I did. Behind me. Close behind me.

Looking back, I saw nobody. But how could I tell? In that gloom everything had a shadow. A bicycle here, a tall old crate there—they seemed like creatures.

I stepped forward again, trying to soft-foot it on the cobbles. After five paces I halted. Yes, a footstep. I spun around. Did I see a figure step back into a doorway?

"Who's there?"

No answer. I couldn't be sure. *What do I do now?*

I waited. Stood still. Didn't move. For how long? It felt like ages, but had I timed it, it would probably have not amounted to a minute. I pulled my coat tighter, my long black coat, James's coat. My bladder pressed. My breath came up short.

Move on. Set a strong pace. Begin as you mean to continue. I looked as though I intended a destination; I picked up a firm walking style—not too fast, just that of a man who knows where he is going. (Dry chuckle at that thought, as I write it down.) I measured twenty of these strides, stopped dead, whirled around.

Nobody. Wrong. Somebody. Where? In the shadows. By the wall. An old warehouse. Do I wait? Tried that: nothing happened. Do I walk back? What if he's dangerous? What if he has accomplices?

Already I had assumed that somebody had been following me. I froze. From my pocket I took one of James's lighters and held up the little flame. I saw nothing, and it sputtered out. *Is that a shoe? At the edge of the shadows? A toe cap reflecting the light? Do I go back?*

What do you think I did? Well, being me, as I then was, I ran. I didn't even shout—I ran. On slippery cobbles. I took no thought of direction, just raced through those lanes, those mean little alleyways, and eventually, through an arch, I burst out on the river. And paused to take a breath. And listen.

Somewhere a song floated, followed by lazy cheers. I walked across a high-curved metal bridge, stopped, and looked down into the water. Sneaked glances back behind me.

More light here. Nobody could stalk or pursue without being seen. A face briefly appeared under the arch, then ducked back again. A mild sense of comedy relieved me for a moment, but the river offered no support. Dark, silent waters, swirling wildly to no apparent purpose—did everything around mimic my state?

My boots clanging with false bravery on the metal of the bridge, I walked on. When I looked back I saw not a soul.

52

For ten, maybe fifteen more minutes, I roamed the old and dilapidated streets just north of the river: Capel Street, Chancery Street, Smithfield, where a light or two attracted me, but their rooms seemed to contain no people. I was alone in the city and the night. When I found myself again on Church Street, the wind must have changed, because for the first time my nose warmed to the most famous of all Dublin odors: the Guinness smell of the brewer's malt from across the river. Just ahead of me a door opened outward, and a man lurched into the street.

"Give it a minute, Joey, and knock twice," he told me, even though I hadn't asked and my name wasn't Joey. "Two big, slow knocks. Hard knocks, Joey. Life is the school of hard knocks. Yep. Hard knocks, sure enough." He sauntered away, saying aloud, "Hard knocks, Joey, oh, aye, hard knocks." He would surely sing ere long.

When the night had taken him, I knocked. Twice. A tall man in a brown mackintosh raincoat opened the door, jerked an invitation with his head, and closed the door behind me.

Back then, closing time didn't stop people from drinking. Yes, we had raids, but not if the police sat in the pub; in fact, the raiding officers usually joined them. I counted seven cops that night, caps off, tunics open. And I listened. They chatted about overtime pay, patrol duty, studying for the sergeant's exam. Not about guns. Not about me.

In a gap at the bar I ordered a whiskey. A mistake; whiskey never let me drink slowly. I took it like a shot, up and down, then called for another. Always got up to three or four too fast.

"Hard at it?" asked a man beside me.

"Ah, and why wouldn't you?" said his friend. "Isn't the night young?" If Greece may be considered the birthplace of the rhetorical question, call Ireland the country that robbed it of all meaning.

As the harshness of the whiskey kicked in, I felt eyes on me. Hard, keen, focused eyes. As though they knew me. Which they did. Long afterward, I grasped that they had been staring at me for some time.

He'd banked on the fact that I wouldn't see him in the crowd. When I'd first eased my way forward to ask for a drink at the mile-long bar, he'd stepped back. Hid behind the heads at the far end.

He waited. Cat with mouse. On my fourth whiskey, he moved. Sidling through the throng of men. No women to be seen; maybe they had taken over the snug. I downed the shot. He tapped me on the shoulder.

"Well, hello, Little Boy."

I turned, belligerent with the liquor. "So it was you?"

"And whatcha doin' here, Little Boy?"

"Was it you?"

"Aren't these waters too deep for a little fella?" he said, laughing. Actually laughing.

"Come on, was it?" I asked. "Was it you following me? Or are you ashamed to say?"

"It'll always be me, Little Boy." He stood maybe six inches shorter than me but weighed heavier, a chunk of a man. "I told you that, didn't I? Where you go, there I'll be. You don't listen, Little Boy, do you? Shake yourself. Take the wax out of your ears."

"Go away and leave me alone."

I turned back to the counter, held up my glass, handed over the cash.

"Did you enjoy the show, did you?"

Ignore him. Look straight ahead. Go slowly on this. Wait. Hold it before drinking. Must gather myself. Clear the head.

He leaned in close. "She looks good, doesn't she? Great tits on her. Shame you'll never get your hands on 'em again."

Pretending to lift my drink, I swung my elbow in a wide arc and caught him, not hard enough, on the cheekbone. Spilled his drink.

The man beside me, who got jostled a little, said, "Hey, lads, go easy there."

"Little Boy" jerked his head, and two of the uniformed drinkers rose as one.

"Well now, Little Boy," said Little Boy, and stepped aside.

The first uniformed man grabbed my hair, the second my collar. No resistance from me. They marched me to the door, which the man in the brown mackintosh opened wide. As they pushed me into the street, Little Boy stepped after me.

"See? See what it's going to be like?"

He slapped me across the face twice, as though I were a girl. I can remember the rending split between a surge of rage at being humiliated and a leap of anxiety to get away. I lunged at Little Boy but drew back when the uniformed men stepped forward.

"Nighty-night, my little patriot," said Little Boy. "Don't let the bugs bite. Except that we will."

The closing door swallowed them.

53

Let me rest a moment, after the violence of that memory. Across the bay I can see Howth Head, a slumbering beast. There's a particular time of day, around four o'clock in the afternoon, when an angle of sunlight falls exactly on the little hill cemetery where we buried James. Nearer to me, the windows in the houses on the top of my hill shine like diamonds.

When the weather gets fine again, I'll see the children who live up there come out to play. Pleasantly for me, they appear in the midafternoon, home from school. I've seen a lot of them lately, because I've been here, at my desk, for such long hours. Trying to get it all down. Trying to make sense of it.

I believe that I now have a clear understanding of how it all finally resolved itself. So unpredictable it was, with so much of it so harsh and unexpected.

If you'd asked me before I began to make the notes for this account of things, *Why do you need to do this? Why recapture all that pain?*, I'd have said, *Look, I loved Venetia from that day we first kissed under the trees at Goldenfields; I've already told you that. And I never, never ceased loving her, not for a moment, in all the years apart.* And I'd have clinched my argument with *Who has that happen in their lives? Who gets to experience that drama, that power of feeling?*

I'd even have admitted what a fool I'd been in Florida.

Love, though, isn't strength. That was my greatest error, just as it's a mistake to confuse kindness with weakness. And it was never enough, children, to mope about your mother. Never enough to say to myself, *But you love her*—and then do less than nothing about it. That was another definition of "weak." In those days, though, that's how I was. Like bad music, I seemed to have only two speeds, fast and slow: sudden rage or sad cowardice.

54

My head hurt where they'd grabbed my hair. My arm throbbed from their grip. My heart cringed at the humiliation. Kicked out into the street.

At about three o'clock in the morning, I got to Miss Fay's house, a long trudge. Light showed around the kitchen door, and from the hallway I caught the smell of baking: Miss Fay's insomnia again. If she didn't sleep, I ate the next day—glorious apple pies, raisin scones, fruitcakes.

She didn't wish to talk; I knew from her glance.

"If you want to take a bath," she said, "you won't wake anybody."

I soaked for an hour, lost in black, painful thoughts. But I forced them out and made it to the other side and a brighter mood. I decided to get myself right again; in other words, to go back to the place I knew best, the open road.

In the morning, Miss Fay had returned to work. The housekeeper, May, made my breakfast. *Little Boy might not necessarily be following me.*

He'd have been watching the theater because he expected that I might have gone there. Simple as that.

Into my thoughts broke May, polishing my boots and making non-stop commentary.

"Your feet must be only like an elephant," she said. "You should be paying rent, boots the size of them. If you ever need to walk on the water, you've a right pair of canoes here; they'll think you're Jesus all over again, and all you'll need is a couple of loaves of bread, and was it five fishes he had? You'll be able to feed the city on that, although nobody in Dublin likes fish. How many holes for your bootlaces, is it ten on each side? You must have rheumatism from bending down to tie them. Isn't it a good job you went to school and learned the black knot, or you'd be walking around, your laces flapping, and they wrapping theirselves around the ankles of passing strangers and tripping them up, and you'd be getting sued for malicious injury and broken bones."

James used to call them "May's monologues," and we had debated whether we should be noting them down as genuine vernacular.

I sat on after breakfast, planning my next weeks. The Folklore Commission had some cures they wanted me to collect. I wanted to interview a woman near Galway who had been wooed by three brothers. The ghost of a Spanish sailor had been appearing in North Clare. There was a healing stone somewhere in the same area.

By noon I had rearranged all my schedules. I repacked my bags and my car. Several weeks on the road faced me—such a delight, and I would end with John Jacob O'Neill. Perhaps we might reconstruct a week, or at least a few days, of his past life on the road.

But the newspaper arrived, with a headline shouting, "THREE MEN KILLED IN BORDER ATTACK." In an instant, not quite knowing why, I altered my plans.

55

The director of the Folklore Commission knew how much I liked the road. I think he liked me, too; he had paid me some compliments. My report "Matchmaking in Rural Ireland" had gone down well, which had helped his annual budget deal with the government. And I was James's protégé.

After the necessary conversation—the funeral, the obituaries, James's history in the field—the director sat back and listened. He had boot-brush eyebrows and smoked a pipe big as a toilet, incongruous for a man so small. Without filling in too many details—such as the presence in my life of Little Boy—I outlined the idea that had sent me hot-footed to him. He listened—that was his greatest asset; he made one feel well regarded. And then he summarized:

"I agree with you that what's happening has an element of interest for us. But it's awkward. I think you should take your planned trip now. But if you bumped into one of the two funerals—I see from the newspapers that they're being held tomorrow—that'd be fine. We might not need these records to appear for years. In fact, we won't ask for any reports from you on this topic. Don't break the law. I can't give you any official papers—by which I mean I can't give you a letter saying, 'Ben MacCarthy is covering this campaign of violence along the border on behalf of the Irish Folklore Commission,' can I?" He smiled at his own irony.

He counted on his fingers. "Read every newspaper report. Make your own assessments as to what you can and cannot research. Note down what's safe to observe. Be more discreet than you ever imagined possible. And keep us out of it."

As I left, I asked him, "What would James say?"

He laughed. "James could be a bit nefarious himself when he wanted to be."

And so I changed course. I went back to Miss Fay's with as many different newspapers as I could find. All day long I read. Measuring what was happening. Trying to see where I could work. I told myself, *If you can prove that your interests are objective, you'll keep yourself from harm.* And now I had something powerful that I needed: the moral backing of my own job.

I'll summarize it for you. "Three Men Killed in Border Attack" rescued me. I saw a way out. Make official a record of this new political violence. Somebody should do it. Excellent alibi; I felt that I had hit something of a jackpot.

First, it kept me safe. From all sides. To the police I had an official role, like a journalist, and to the activists I was recording their effort. Second, I placed a prime value on the idea of "records": notated observations of the life of my country as seen from the fireside, from the kitchen chair. That's where you discerned the shape of a nation, the history and the dreams. Now I had made it the instrument of my safety. Or so I hoped.

56

The three deaths took place on the night of New Year's Day 1957. One man was a police officer, and two came from the south, both of them Irish republican activists carrying guns. A raid on a police barracks in County Fermanagh collapsed. Doorstep bombs didn't explode. Police opened unexpected fire and hampered the attackers' escape.

The two IRA men became heroes and martyrs. In front of its own eyes, the country's emotions changed. This had happened before. When the rebellion of Easter 1916 broke out, the public jeered the insurgents and threw cabbages at their marching columns in Dublin. But some weeks later, when fifteen of the leaders were summarily executed, opinion swung one hundred and eighty degrees, and thus did the Easter Rising become Ireland's most iconic moment of history.

One headline said, "TWO DEAD RAIDERS IDENTIFIED," and reported them as "Feargal O'Hanlon of Park St., Monaghan, and Sean South, Henry St., Limerick. Yesterday their bodies lay in the Royal Ulster Constabulary barracks in Enniskillen."

On the next page, the fashion reporters of the wire services listed "eight of the world's best-dressed women according to the New York Dress Institute. Heading the poll was Mrs. William Paley; the Duchess of Windsor second, Princess Grace of Monaco, third." Also-rans included Marlene Dietrich and Audrey Hepburn.

Such was the life of the moment.

The newspapers were forecasting huge attendances at the funerals of O'Hanlon, aged twenty, from Ballybay, County Monaghan, and South, aged twenty-eight, from Garryowen, in Limerick.

And then I tightened my focus to a paragraph lower down. *What?!*

Alongside a speech condemning the IRA action by the Irish premier, Mr. Costello, ran a report stating that "several men, believed to have been involved in the raid, had been treated for injuries in the Mater Hospital, Dublin. One of them had discharged himself, although rumors that he had disguised himself as a woman in order to leave the hospital could not be confirmed. The police continued to question the others."

Of course it's Jimmy. Must be! Who else would do it? I can see Jimmy in a skirt; he certainly has the figure for it. Won't Randall chuckle? And don't I need to record this?

57

Here, from 7 January 1957, is one newspaper report:

FUNERAL OF LIMERICK MAN KILLED IN RAID

The funeral of Sean South (28) . . . took place in Mount St. Lawrence Cemetery, Limerick, after a Solemn Requiem Mass in St. Michael's Church.

The celebrant of the Mass was Rev. P. Lyons, C.C.; Rev.

T. Lyons, C.C., was deacon, and Rev. P. O'Donnell, C.C., subdeacon. *[Note: "C.C." indicated "curate," the lowest level of ordained priest; did nobody of seniority in the church wish to be associated with the event?]*

Thousands of people lined the footpath as the funeral procession, led by the Cork Volunteer Pipe Band, moved through the streets. The tricolor-draped coffin was carried from the church to the house by young men wearing black berets and black armlets with tricolor ribbons. Other young men formed a guard of honor flanking the hearse, which was followed by groups of people from Dublin, Galway, Mayo, Roscommon, Clare, Kerry, Cork, Limerick, Tipperary, and other counties. Tricolors, some with black drapes, hung from the windows of a number of business premises.

My instincts felt right. Something was again happening down among the people: note the "business premises" draped with black. Maisie had said it. It wasn't over. For many people, especially in the southern counties, the War of Independence had never ended.

Their long memories still held fast to the dispossessions and humiliations of occupation, the loss of land, the servile roles. They, too, were the people who had believed in rejecting a border; they, more than most, had said, "Fight on."

And if those passions had subsided a little, these two deaths in this new campaign gave a mighty scratch to the surface of that culture.

I saw all that subliminal remembrance played out in Limerick. How many people at Sean South's funeral? "Thousands," said the newspaper—and it's true that I had never seen a larger crowd, except inside a stadium at a sporting event. Here are the notes I made:

First the cortege: These are the men whom I meet in their own homes. But their faces have a somber darkness here, and they frown. They range across all ages, grandfathers and grandsons, the storytellers I meet, and their families of listeners. Many have formed up into loose honor guards, attempting marching formations. Nobody looks wealthy. All seem committed, though, and they share an intensity of purpose. I see no grief on their faces, nothing personal; I see a kind of pride, an air of being where they feel they should be, solidarity.

In the crowds along the streets I perceive less of that. Curiosity dominates, and I see a smattering of sentimentality, women blowing noses and wiping away tears, and a respect shown by the bowing of heads as the cortege passes. Most impressive of all is the silence. I can hear the footsteps of the marchers, the swish of the hearse's tires. Even when the cortege had long passed I could hear the barked orders of the commands—in Irish—far ahead.

From the beginning of the procession, the people waiting in the streets swung in behind the marchers; only a few people didn't follow. By the time the hearse reached the cemetery, the wide streets had filled. Two funerals in a week with thousands following the coffin: are we once more the Land of the Glorious Dead?

Unlike James Clare's funeral, they didn't wait for everybody to get to the graveyard. Half a mile from the gates I heard the three volleys of shots, then the trumpets and drums playing "Last Post" and "Reveille."

By the time I got there, the oration had long ended. Some newspapers, mostly local, reported the speaker's words: "He died for my freedom; for my sake, for your sake, for the sake of the generations that are to come. Let his life and death be a lesson and a guide to us all, as his deeds and the honor he earned were a cause of joy and pride. His sacrifice on the altar of freedom encourages us."

58

Contradictory details emerged of how Feargal O'Hanlon and Sean South had died. That's always dangerous in Ireland, where suspicion makes its living from embroidery. Some facts went uncontested, which is to say that both sides gave out the same version. Then they diverged.

The Royal Ulster Constabulary spokesman said that both men had been killed at the scene, and their bodies carried by their comrades on a truck to a distant barn. The rest of the rebels had then escaped across the border.

An Irish Republican Army version said that both men had been hit in the first phase of the action. Their comrades carried them to the barn as a firefight followed all of them. While conducting a rearguard action, the active members hid the injured men until nothing more could be done for them. As the survivors headed out in the dark, said the IRA, the police found the two men and killed them.

Well, Ben and Louise, you know what they say: Truth is the first casualty of war. And I surmise that in your professions you know that more than most. And truth lurched about a bit after that incident. The Irish Republican Publicity Bureau issued a statement saying that "an Irish resistance fighter" had been killed in an attack on the police station and that "later, a second fighter died after being captured by the enemy." That's the view that stuck all over the south, and among the north's Catholics.

The Northern Ireland police put out their version. It was fully reported by all the newspapers. And backed by medical evidence given at the inquests on the two dead men. The police resisted accusations that they had "finished off" the two wounded men in the old byre.

Few believed them—especially as the dreaded name "B Specials" came up. However, from all I have been able to determine, Sean South had indeed died on the truck, and Feargal O'Hanlon had lost too much blood to survive. (I made extensive notes; you can find them in the commission archives.)

The men who got back across the border that night went to the houses of friends. Who took them to Monaghan Hospital. Where they were arrested by the southern police. Who took those needing greater treatment to the Mater Hospital in Dublin. Whence one escaped dressed as a woman.

59

After the funeral in Limerick, I tried to get back to normal. The crowds dispersed. Somberness remained. Rain still fell. I went to see my "Occasion Merchant"—his name for himself, not mine; that's what the signboard outside his door called him. He rented and sold goods for every possibility; I'd met him with somebody who'd hired dentures from him to go on a date.

I liked Mr. MacManus, a big bear of a man, with his heavy breathing, and his own black-and-white teeth like piano keys, and his habit of speaking in paragraphs. He always had news for me of some erratic kind: some unusual emigrant returned from "the New World," as he persisted in calling the United States; a new cache of bizarre goods he had found; a family row out in the country. To this last sort of account, no matter what the details, he habitually added the same final remark: "And I'd bet there was a bit of incest there, too."

He didn't disappoint me; he had just purchased a stock of chamber pots from a hardware store in County Waterford that was closing down.

"Come here till I show you," he said, heaving himself along the crammed passageways of his storerooms. "You're the one man now that'd be interested in this. It'd never strike anybody that the humble chamber pot, in its willing existence under the beds of the world, would supply historical commentary or social observation. You're familiar with it, I know, because you grew up in the countryside with the chamber pot in all its forms, white enamel with a blue rim, or china in decent house-holds, and flowers everywhere, including on the bottom, which always struck me as odd and superfluous, given what has to land on them same flowers. But here's something you never saw. This hardware merchant supplied Lord Waterford and a great number of other Protestant gentle-men with household goods, and he had one pot left from a stock that was popular with them gentry in the last century. Look at it."

He pulled the china pot from a long, high drawer. For a handle it had a grotesque human ear. Around the side were pictures of dozens of Irish peasant children, romping and disheveled, and on the base of the interior the portrait of a whiskered man. Above him ran a curved caption: "Daniel O'Connell, the Liberator." The line below said, in a wide curve, "Do Your Duty."

Mr. MacManus said, "Isn't that a treasure? If proof were needed of how they feared O'Connell, there you have it, as round as a hoop. I like to think of the gentry who opposed Mr. O'Connell as being unable to combat him with ingenuity and wit in the departments of debate, rheto-ric, and logical assumption, they being reduced to bodily functions of the basest and most private kind to express their indignation and frustrated sense of contentiousness."

How does a man with such short breathing run off such long sentences?

The chamber pot helped me. Further validated the link between folklore and history. People knew of O'Connell like they knew of Finn Mac-Cool. Years later, maybe prompted by Mr. MacManus, I researched O'Connell. His body may have expired in 1847, but he never died; heroes don't. And he had the essential legendary status—of outwitting the British Parliament. And fathering dozens of children. Both sides of the blanket.

I asked John Jacob O'Neill one day if it was valid to count a figure such as O'Connell as myth. His answer clinched it for me:

"Did he earn his legends?"

So the stories of O'Connell will have to wait for another day. If you remind me, children, some night here around my own fireplace I'll tell them to you. And we'll be up until dawn.

From Mr. MacManus, I headed out to the Atlantic, to a house just south of Doolin, in Clare, where an old woman told me of her marriage. When young and pretty, and evidently mischievous, she had been wooed by three brothers. Each of their names began with the letter *P*—Peter, Paul, and Patrick.

They didn't know about the others' courtship. Hannah never told them. Not only that—Peter and Paul were twins.

"I kept them all dancing on strings," she said. "Because I found that very enjoyable."

"You did?" I prodded.

"They each had their different nights of the week. That was the only way I could manage them. Because they all sounded the very same, they all spoke alike, and in the dark of the night I didn't want to make a mistake when I went out to meet them."

"What would have happened," I asked, "if they had switched places one night?"

Hannah laughed as openly as a rogue. "I'd have known from the kissing," she said.

"The kissing?"

"They were all different. Peter never shaved himself right. Paul was always trying to get the tongue working. And Patrick would keep his lips pressed on your mouth even if a crowd formed and told him to stop."

"Which of them did you marry?" I said.

"None of them." She giggled, eighty and naughty.

"None of them?" I could hear my surprise in my own echo.

"No." She paused. "What happened was—didn't they all find out. A jealous girl at the creamery, and I thought she was my friend, she told them. And without any of them telling the other, they all emigrated."

"Where did they go, Hannah?"

She held up three fingers and took them down one by one.

"Peter went to Canada. Paul went to San Francisco. And Patrick went to Brisbane in Australia."

"And who did you end up marrying?"

"A nice man. He was an only child, and my grandmother said that a girl should always marry an only child, because they were always looking for love, and if they found it with you, they'd look after you very well."

"And what happened to Peter, Paul, and Patrick?"

"They came home for my wedding. Would you believe that? They got over all their bitterness, and each of them danced with me, and we laughed and laughed about the three years they courted me. I said, If you added it all up didn't I give each of them a year of my life. We had a great time."

Her name was Mrs. Hogan, originally Hannah Prendergast; she's long dead, but you never saw such a twinkle.

60

The next tale I gathered that week—I'd been told it was a ghost story. A man in North Clare, on the edges of Galway Bay, had always boasted that he possessed a complete Spanish Armada uniform: "Haven't I the tunic, the breastplate, the silver helmet, and the long sword?" Nobody believed him, because nobody had seen it. And he, a bachelor and a suspicious man, wouldn't let anybody into his house.

One winter he'd been saying that he hadn't been well. Then came a time when nobody had seen him in Ballyvaughan for weeks. They went out to the house, broke down his door, and found him dead—but prepared for death: he'd arrayed himself on his bed in the silver uniform he'd always insisted he owned, all the parts of which had been maintained in museum condition.

My informant said, "He told me one night, with drink on him, that he dreamed of being a Spanish conquistador because his family came from out there on the coast near Black Head, where some of the Armada ships foundered in 1588. The helmet was shining in the dark when we found him, and I knew how he died, and it probably answers a puzzle. He probably caught a chill."

I asked, "What's the connection between the uniform, the puzzle, and the chill?"

My narrator answered, "For years local people said they saw a ghost out there, the ghost of a Spanish soldier, walking the cliffs at night, with his helmet gleaming in the moonlight. Now I know who it was; it was our man. I bet he used to put on the uniform and go for a stroll when he thought nobody would see him. That's how he caught his chill. So 'twas his dream that killed him."

61

The following day I went east, inland by many miles. At dusk, I parked my car at a gate. This farm, half a mile from the road, never had an avenue. James used to say that the people who lived there didn't want anyone to know they were alive.

A shopping bag flapped from the gatepost. I snooped; it contained a note. I took the bag back to the car, where I could read the paper with some light. It was a letter two weeks old from the local health authority: one of the people in the house had contracted polio. "Accordingly," it said, "these premises must now be considered quarantine."

I drove into the nearby town. It shall remain nameless; its people lacked decency in this case. At the grocery, I asked about the farm I'd wanted to visit. As excited as gossips, they told me that yes, it was true, the house had polio. A child might have died; they weren't sure. Had anybody gone up there? Oh, God, no. Was anything confirmed? Listen, they said, even the police aren't going in. Nor the doctors themselves.

I said, "But how is the family managing for food?"

Somebody answered, "Aren't we all asking that question?" And then they looked awkward and began to resume their prior conversations, shutting me out.

I loaded up: bacon, eggs, bread, butter, anything that seemed viable and convenient. If the people inside that house had serious illness, they surely had low morale. When I asked for milk, the owner, who hadn't spoken a word, said, "They have their own cows; they'll be milking every day."

I asked him to tally up my items. Maybe I expected him to say that they were free. Or that he'd give a discount. No such thing. I paid him, and as he gave me back the change, I said, "Maybe some sweets or something? For the children?" When he turned to fetch something, I planted the knife. "Do those people shop here? I mean when things are normal?"

The blow landed. Embarrassment set in. He didn't meet my eye.

"That's for the youngsters," he said, and handed over a solitary chocolate bar.

I took the risk of driving across the fields, a slow, careful journey, avoiding ruts. Gravel around a house is a good watchdog. Curtains twitched; I saw a face caught in the headlights. It disappeared when I climbed out of the car. From directly inside the door a man answered my knock.

"Sir, we have polio here."

"I know that."

"We can't mix with anyone for another three weeks."

"How are you fixed for food?" I called back. "I'm Ben MacCarthy, from the Folklore Commission. James Clare used to be my boss."

The voice spoke again: "Sir, we've no food, only boiled potatoes and milk; we ran out of tea yesterday."

I said, "I have food here for you. Let me in."

"Mr. MacCarthy, you might catch the polio."

"I might and I might not."

Why do misery and dignity so often go hand in hand? I could see that these were decent people, that this was a good farmhouse, on forty-five acres, enough to make a living in those days. Of late they'd been leading a shattered life. All day every day, and sometimes all night, each watched the others, they told me: father, mother, two sisters, three brothers.

"Sir, we don't even know what polio might look like."

"You seem healthy to me."

The boys unloaded the car. Their energy notwithstanding, a pall hung like a fog over the house and the yard. Their father, as strong a man as I have ever met, said, "How much do we owe you?"

Dilemma: if I don't let him pay, it will seem like charity; if I do let him pay, I can do it again. And the house feels as though they can well afford it.

I said, "I'll tell you how much because you're not charity people. But on the condition that you let me do this again."

We agreed on the money. The family fell upon the parcels. I had included shop bread, even though I'd guessed that this woman did her own baking, like every other farmwife in the country—and, indeed, I'd also included flour and baking powder. They had no electricity yet—too remote—so the girls set to making toast on forks in front of the fire.

Their father poured me a whiskey. He hadn't known that James had died. We mourned with raised glasses.

Then I asked about the polio. In school, their youngest child went sick: sore throat, stiff neck, and so on. A young doctor, new to the locality, called for an ambulance. He sent the other siblings home and quarantined the house. Since then they'd seen nobody. Nor had they heard from any hospital or doctor anywhere. No, there was nothing they could do about it.

When I had shared their supper I left, promising to return. At the door, the wife, a handsome, quiet woman, thanked me again.

"It'll be a lucky woman that gets you, sir."

What is it I used to hear you say, children? *Tell that to the marines.*

62

Now the texture of my life changed again. I found myself on the banks of the River Shannon, near Limerick, alarmed and jarred. With flood warnings everywhere, and the river looking as threatening as a war, I did not want to be there. But in Adare the previous night a woman had given me a note. I don't have the piece of paper; it was destroyed the next day. I can remember, though, what it said: *Name: Kilconnell House. Address: You know where it is—on the riverbank below O'Brien's Bridge. When: To-morrow noon. Why: Urgent.*

Nothing more. I looked at the note again in the daylight. Did it offer anything else? No. The wind blew a hint of rain in my face. I looked at the house. Uneasy.

Shouldn't have come. Something's up. Something's amiss. That woman had bad air around her head. And how did she know me, how did she find me? Had somebody seen me, written the note? Given it to her to give to me? Are there people watching me and I not knowing it? Not seeing them? Not sensing them? Not good. And how did whoever they are know that I knew the house? Did "they" assume that I knew every prominent house in the country?

Architecturally, I would love to have owned the place, a Georgian manor with a hint of Palladio. Not as grand as Randall's and his floor-to-ceiling windows, it yet had a greater delicacy. Double pillars flanked the recessed front door, which somebody in love a long time ago had painted yellow. The fanlight above had ornate bones.

Nobody answered the clanging bellpull. Four times I tugged it, shivering in that cold east wind. Thirty yards away from my legs, the Shannon flowed fast as a millrace. *This is dangerous.* She'd already flooded the land upriver: hundreds of acres under water, a shed swept away in the flood plains near Athlone, a man plucked off a riverside path and drowned. *More and worse floods,* said the news.

When the bellbull produced nothing, I turned the giant brass door-knob, in the shape of a pentagon. It yielded, and the door swung aside as easily as a curtain. Either the original craftsmen had built superb hinges or, contrary to appearances, somebody was keeping the place oiled.

The hallway echoed. Behind me, the door, when I released it, swung closed with a deep and secure *click!* When my eyes bested the gloom I could see the marks on the floors where furniture had once stood. *Gold-enfields will soon be like this. Empty and hollow. Our porch. My room. The parlor. Marks on the floors, the tracks of my life.*

To my left stood a door that had also been yellow. I tried it: locked so tight I couldn't budge it. To my right rose the wide stairs. On the walls of the hall and up along the staircase, vacant rectangles showed where huge paintings had hung. They had taken the stair carpet when they left. And the lightbulbs.

Which way? And if I move, won't my footsteps be heard? Wait. Do nothing. See what happens. Whoever is here will have heard the bell but may not have heard my footsteps.

Getting colder, I waited. One hand, deep in my pockets, touched my notebook; the other, my pen and pencil: comfort. And still I waited. All along the walls at hip height ran a mysterious heavy line. It looked as though somebody had thought to paint or apply wallpaper, and had then abandoned the decision. The floor planks had massive stains and blotches. In a corner, moss grew, a tiny, incongruous oasis.

The sounds of the house came to me and, soon, the sights, like a photograph developing. I heard a windowpane rattling somewhere and a regular creaking, as of something oppressed by the wind. And I saw the corridor leading off the long hallway, and the doors in between. I heard the hoot of a gale down a chimney somewhere, and with the sun outside escaping the clouds briefly, I saw other doors off the hall, two of them, left and right.

Guessing: the one on the right, that's under the stairs; the one on the left, that's perhaps a dining room. This locked door here beside me in the hall; that's a parlor or a drawing room. I bet that was nice paint once.

The creaking came from the end of the corridor. A door down there had a top panel that opened like a stable door. It creaked because it tried to do its job and let in the sunlight. *How far away? Fifty feet?*

And still I waited. Patient though I am, my limits do make themselves felt. *What to do? Stay or go? Maybe they haven't heard me. Maybe they've yet to arrive. Maybe they know this place is vacant and they've squirreled the key from somebody, been here earlier and left the door unlocked for me. Maybe they're somewhere else in the house and can't hear the doorbell; these old houses have very thick walls. Let me test the place.*

I stepped forward, soft as a cat—not easy to do with hobnailed boots. A second step, wobbling a little as I tried to stand on one foot. *Why so cautious? Because there's something not good here.* A third step, steadier. I picked up speed. Three, four, five more steps; silent and striding now, I reached the first door, the one on the right, under the staircase, the door that, I felt sure, led to the cellar. I tried its handle: no yield.

By now I was two or three strides from the door on the left, which I had guessed to be the dining room. Ahead of me I could clearly see the top panel of the stable-style back door. *If I lived here, I'd put on new hinges.*

As I reached for the porcelain-egg doorknob at my left hand I heard a noise, an echo with a metal heart. Today I know what it was; back then I didn't: the safety catch on a gun. I stopped, looked around.

Two things happened at once, and fast. From the doorway behind me that I had found solidly locked, a man stepped into the hall, aiming a gun at my head. And the doorknob in my hand was wrenched from inside by another man with a gun.

I recognized both of them. They had been pallbearers in the Limerick funeral. Now, with their weapons and their eyes, they gave me no choice. I stepped into the room. Which contained two surprises: a long dining table—and Jimmy Bermingham. Sitting on a chair, eating a sandwich, he looked as though he dined at this table every day of his life.

"Well, now, Captain, howya doin'? I hear you were looking for me."

Think, don't feel; play it cool. Smile. And keep it natural.

"I wasn't, Jimmy."

"Well, now you've found me."

"Looks like that, Jimmy."

"Why weren't you looking for me, Ben?"

"I was busy, Jimmy."

"Yeh, we guessed."

Different clothes today: a natty suit, Prince of Wales check; a white shirt; a navy paisley tie. He wore a black coat, again draped over his shoulders like a cloak, his hands and arms free.

"Sit, Ben."

I perched a haunch on the edge of the long, solid table.

"What have you been up to, Jimmy?" I asked.

"You'll have to tell me what you want to know, Ben."

"I saw a report in the papers that a man had discharged himself from the Mater Hospital dressed as a woman."

"And you thought it was me, Ben."

Jimmy laughed, and I laughed.

"I owe you some money," said Jimmy, and he reached into an inside pocket and handed over cash. "All there. Count it."

"There's no need."

"For the flowers, right? With Marian."

He looked executive, and he smiled at me, open and friendly, and in some ways more reliable than my memory of him. A man in a tweed coat from a better past now moved into full view. He laid a handgun on the table. I tried not to look at it. Eight more men came in, at ten-second intervals, making ten in all. They all saluted Jimmy.

It felt rehearsed. I pocketed Jimmy's money, saying, "I was glad to help." Then I asked, "So, yes or no: was it you?" He began to laugh. Nobody could resist that laugh, so infectious was it. "I thought so."

"Did you ever try to put on a pair of women's knickers, Ben?"

"Where did you get them?"

"They were a nun's. I found a locker in the hospital when I was looking for a smoke. That's where I got the idea."

I said, "And the rest of the clothes?"

"Another locker. A nurse's." I raised an eyebrow, and Jimmy reacted. "Hey, hold on, Ben, I didn't go the full whack. I mean I didn't go for the—" He made a gesture with cupped hands, miming bosoms. "The engineering would have been too much for me. I know how to take one off, but I'd never have managed to put one on." By now we had all decided to laugh. "And I nearly broke my leg in the high heels."

"You see, Jimmy? I was right."

He sobered up. "Well, Ben," he said, "that was then, and this is now. And I'm a little bit sad. We got word, like, that you were talking to people."

Men of charisma, I have found, have a useful gift that we often don't notice: they know how to create silence. James Clare had it. John Jacob O'Neill did it when telling a tale. I've seen the same control in leaders.

Jimmy, believe it or not, scrawny Jimmy, thin, often uncertain, petulant, sulky Jimmy—he had it that day. Perhaps it came from the circumstances, his position of command in a group of several men. Or perhaps he also felt more empowered by their presence. Or both.

I looked over my shoulder, took a moment to scan the other faces. Most of the men hadn't shaved for some days, some had red blotches on their skin, one had a heavy blue bruise on his cheekbone. None seemed as fresh as Jimmy; all seemed exhausted and sullen. A few of them fiddled with weapons; three had handguns, one a rifle with a wonderful stock of shiny oak.

When I looked at them, they tightened their faces—frowns, a scowl, anxiety. Some moved along the table and stood behind Jimmy's chair. One, who wore gloves and caressed his revolver over and over, stood directly across from me and never ceased to stare at my face.

And still the silence held. Was I inspired? How was I able to resist breaking it? I looked all around me again—and found that I generated a curious effect. The men behind me, as though wishing to be seen, came forward, until they all stood within my full field of vision.

Did I feel menaced? Yes—and no. Yes, because if surly armed men are staring at you with a layer of suspicion fifty inches thick, you have reason to worry. And no, because their faces had such warm connection to me. Beyond all the tiredness and latent anger I had seen these faces, too, glowing by firesides. These were the shy men who made sure that my glass was never empty, or who led me back up to the main road late at night with an awkward torch, or who played a tune on a tin whistle in their mother's kitchen. They had no good reason for standing so menacingly in front of me, but my knowledge of them—and my affection— enabled me to keep cool.

Jimmy broke the silence.

"So, Ben? What have you been saying about us?"

A man on his right, the heaviest of them and the darkest in spirit, cut in.

"We know why you're here."

I said, "Tell me, then."

Jimmy looked, for the first time, a little nervous.

"I want to hear Ben talk," he said. "I know what Ben is like."

The words came out of me clear and calm, unplanned and open:

"I was asked to spy on you. By the police."

"We know—" The dark-spirited man blurted, but Jimmy held up a hand.

"Let Ben tell it."

"Harcourt Terrace police station," I said. "Not the first contact, either. And they're following me."

The room stiffened. Weapons rattled and moved. Jimmy sat straighter. Behind him, one man spoke to another in Irish, assuming that I wouldn't understand. He was wrong; my mind translated in an instant: "Do him now, the river's high."

Jimmy, still calm, and wiping a crumb from his lips, said, "*Ciunas*"— the Irish word for "silence"—and for an awful instant I thought he was starting the word "queue"; in other words, "Queue up to kill him."

"Why are you telling us, Ben?"

"So that you know."

"Did they follow you here today?"

"Who knows? Are they outside?" This caused further unease.

One of the men said, in Irish, "There's nobody out there; we can see for miles."

I asked, "What did he just say?"

Jimmy lied: "He wants to know if we can trust you."

I said, "How many people have told you something like I've just told you? That I'm being followed. Why would I tell you that, Jimmy?"

One of the men whispered in Jimmy's ear. I was in an old black-and-white gangster film, and any moment now a fat man would come through the door with a mournful face and a gun.

"Ben, what's your reason? Come on."

"Simple, Jimmy," I said, and it was, at last, simple and clear. "I don't want to be caught in the middle, and yet I want to record what happens."

He was so quick. "But if they find your notes?"

"They won't find them."

"How do you know?"

"Jimmy, I have more hiding places on this island than you fellows." This brought a general smile.

One of the men, the most senior, said, again in Irish, "Ask him how he's going to do this and not get caught."

"So how will this work? How come they won't catch you with a note-book? You wrote down a lot of stuff when I was with you, and there were other people around."

I said, "The funerals last week. I was at one of them. As you know. When I leave here now, I'll go somewhere quiet, and I'll make sure that nobody has followed me. And I'll write down everything I saw and heard here, and I'll hide that notebook immediately. Nobody will be identified by name. In the years ahead, when it's safe, when this is all over, I'll re-trieve the notebooks and write it all up fully."

Everybody considered this. And the most senior man said, "I don't believe you."

Three things happened at once, in a frantic outbreak of anger and catastrophe.

"I don't believe him, either," said another. And a third. And a fourth.

The senior man slipped the safety on his weapon and, in Irish, gave an order to the two men beside him:

"Take him out. You know what to do."

Marvelously, I didn't sweat. Nor did I move. I pretended not to un-derstand. But when somebody hammered on the front door I, like every-body else, jumped. And then came the chaos.

63

The door to our room burst open. But nobody stood there—it had been forced in by a savage swirl of water. That hammering from outside had been a lookout telling us a flash flood had hit the river.

The first wave struck that old dining room like a swirling liquid tor-nado. I remember the noise—a gigantic, spurling *splash!* as though a giant single tide had slapped tons of water against a seawall.

The long, massive table heaved, floated for a moment, and spun up-ward in a slow, wet whirl; then it crashed down and was dragged along the room. Chairs tumbled after it, higgledy-piggledy, bouncing off walls, vanishing beneath eddies and rolls. A gulp of cold water hit me in the fork of my legs.

A second wave, a brown and dirty wash speckled with twigs and leaves, hit the far wall and rebounded at head height. The men who had remained in a group were spun like dolls. They crashed into one another and got struck by chairs or the edges of the table as they fought to keep some kind of footing. And failed.

Water hit them everywhere. I saw men clawing at their own faces. Going down. Coming back up again, terror in their eyes. No comprehension of what might happen to them.

A third surge devoured Jimmy Bermingham. The men nearest to him fought to get to the door. Sheets of water blew them back in. They plowed out again, arms flailing, trying to keep their guns above the water, which had now reached shoulder height and was climbing fast. This wave looked big enough for surfing, and it lashed in with a deep rolling, punching splash. From the fireplace came a sucking noise, as the water tried to climb up the chimney.

Jimmy went under like a twig. Behind where he'd sat, the water ripped a shutter from the windows. Trying to stay tall, I glanced out. As far as I could see, roaring waters raced around every square foot of open ground near the house. It was as restless and as mad as the worst form of anger. The road had disappeared.

I had a leaf in my mouth. Something else, something slimy, slapped across my eyes. I clawed my face, too, trying to think, trying to reason. Jimmy Bermingham's head came up at my knee, and the heavy shutter cracked him across the skull; he couldn't have stayed conscious. I recall having the thought *Live by violence, die by violence.*

His head came up once more. Even in the water I could see the darkness of his blood. With some skull injuries, we scarcely bleed; with others, we gush like a stuck pig. Jimmy's scalp poured—and down he went again. The water hit me in the chest and sent me flying backward.

By now I had nothing left to do but survive. I went under, and took in a mouthful of watery grit. My head hit something—a dining room chair, submerged by the wet weight of its heavy cushion. One of the legs stabbed me in the cheek, another caught me in the chest; I fought off this octopus, and then used it to lever myself upright.

In a momentary lull I got my head and shoulders up, blubbered the filthy water from my mouth, and stood on my feet. The furniture washed here and there, in savage, rolling motions. Some of the table had come apart; as it swung past me, the edge caught me in the crotch.

I grabbed the table and held on. But I might as well have been holding a rope in a high wave; the table pitched me here and there and up and down—I had to let go.

To my right, the door began to bend off its hinges. The water now came in like a tide, a few low waves and then a spasm as high as the transom. Something crash-tangled into my legs, and I reached down to free myself. I caught cloth. A person. Jimmy B. I grabbed him, hauled him up. Unconscious.

Keeping his head above water, I waited until the great burst had passed. Then, in waters still chest-high, I hauled him to the door. A nasty stinger of a wave hit us so hard that it washed his head clean, and for a moment I saw the gashed whiteness of his wound.

Outside the wrecked dining room, the long, narrow hallway had become a funnel, a tunnel, a crazy tube of rushing water. Though I kept my feet, my head was under, then above, then under again, then above again. Lugging Jimmy, I tried to walk and managed to take a step at a time and hold it.

After three such steps I found handholds, the lowest reaches of the staircase. I caught the banister. My hand slid from the foot of a wet upright. I fought to get another grip. Made it to the foot of the staircase before the next big surge. And it was the biggest of all.

But it washed us up the stairs, and deposited us almost on the landing. Then it ebbed fast. I hauled Jimmy up another flight. And then another. The waters slammed up the stairs again and snarled at our feet.

64

The infamous Shannon flood of 1957 rose to twenty-five feet high inside Kilconnell House and more or less did for the place. Later reports spoke of "a wall of water that raced down the Shannon and wrecked everything it reached," including one and a half floors of that great old manor.

Will you be surprised if I report elation? We were high and dry. Is that what people feel after surviving water? I have no comparisons to make, have never known anybody who beat a flood. Genuine, bulging elation, a huge and immediate reward—that's what it was.

It didn't last long—a flash, perhaps: I had work to do. Jimmy's face was blue; blood poured from his head. I laid him flat on his back and began the procedures I had learned in school. *Is he drowning?* I wondered. *Has he drowned? Is he unconscious? That's some wound.* I was able to move his head sideways, as though it were a marionette's.

Water spurted from his mouth and nose. *Jesus, turn him over—it'd be quicker; it'd all pour out.* A rhythm began in my head, in tempo with my thrusts on his chest. *Jimm-mee. Jimm-mee. Jimm-mee. Jimm-mee.* And still the water blurted from his mouth. Now flecks of blood began to appear. *Oh, my Christ! Keep the rhythm going. Jimm-mee. Jimm-mee. Jimm-mee.* I checked his tongue again, found a twig in his throat, tugged it free. Pressed even harder. *Jimm-mee. Jimm-mee. Jimm-mee. Jimm-mee.* From his hair some mud fell on his eyes. With my icy, wet sleeve I wiped it away, wiped his forehead. He twitched. I grabbed his hair, lifted his head, and with my free hand pressed his chest. *Jimm-mee. Come ON! Is he breathing?* Are you breathing? *JIMMY!*

He didn't recover enough to speak. I kept wiping his face, kept clearing his airways, made him belch, stood him up, supported his head, walked him up and down. Every step I took squelched. Every breath rasped. Those waters had hammered me, too—but not as badly as Jimmy Bermingham. The blue color faded and a gray took over, an awful pallor.

I don't know how long I walked Jimmy that day, up and down, up and down that sodden, freezing upstairs hallway. It could have been ten minutes, it could have been an hour. I failed to make him conscious. The nearest I got was a kind of half moan, a grunt. Below us, the waters raged and boiled like a mad, vengeful herd. Those vicious surges—they hungered for destruction, and they lashed the downstairs rooms again and again.

And then suddenly they stopped. Subsided to a calm and orderly receding flow, slipping backward gentle and slurping out of the house. With Jimmy's head a ton weight on my shoulder, I looked out the window at the end of the corridor. The waters outside, though still trying to hold on to the land, searching for claw handholds here and there, like a man slipping down the face of a cliff, had begun to slide back to the river.

My car appeared above the flood. *That engine will be useless. There's the roadway. I can follow its track.* Soon all the mad tides had returned whence they had come, the great flood bore died, and the river slid back within the boundaries of its own banks. The Shannon family of water devils calmed down.

Not a human being to be seen—nothing but large gray-brown pools and puddles. I eased Jimmy downstairs. The flood had claimed one man inside the house, a thin fellow whom I had seen among the group but whose voice I hadn't heard. From the angle of his head I guessed that his neck was broken. I stopped, tried to manage his body with my foot, a gentle probe. When he flopped over, I saw that his face had been smashed in like a pug dog's; blood leaked everywhere. His fingers had broken and meshed in the trigger guard of his rifle.

I got Jimmy to the road. Following the sun, which had begun to appear, I hauled him along. To my right, the river beside us kept up its fast gurgle. Not a house in sight; now I knew why, and wondered who had been so foolish as to build a house so low beside such a volatile, whimsically violent creature.

Exhaustion arrived. I could feel the blood drain from my face. Then, in a high field on my left, I heard our saviors. They had bunched together, making an untypical collective *Moooo!* Cattle, still venting their alarm. *If there are cattle, there must be a farm; if there's a farm, there must be people; somebody will come.*

"Somebody" arrived on a tractor, with hay piled on the trailer. He saw us, a man named Lane, a gentleman. Down the hill of the field he came, having dumped the hay faster than I know he wanted to, and got us onto the trailer. How Mr. Lane did it, I don't know; I was no help to him.

Jimmy almost died. He had multiple problems: hypothermia, a fast-moving respiratory infection, and, not least, a crazed split in his skull.

"You'd think he'd been attacked by a crooked carving knife," the surgeon in Barringtons Hospital told me.

I had no such injury. When my exhaustion had passed, and I showed no infectious symptoms, I did my own examination. A cut in my thigh;

a scrotum swollen to plum-purple; a hip bruised to look like a map of Italy. And no warm or dry clothes.

The hospital kept Jimmy for seven weeks. I stayed two days; through Mr. Lane and his excellent wife, a woman of immediate and strong capabilities, I organized clothes, and then my car. It needed a new battery, a new alternator, a new floor on the passenger side, where the river had hammered in a rock like a nail.

I took the train to Dublin and recuperated with Miss Fay, who was so pleased to have my company that it almost made the entire river fracas worth it. When all became settled once more, I confined my travels to within a forty-mile radius of Jimmy in his hospital bed.

A life of some normality returned, with little pressure and less fear, as I prepared myself for the Goldenfields auction and the pain of losing my home.

65

Goldenfields: from the moment I'd known the auction date I'd "planned" my feelings. I described to myself what would have to happen, and then asked myself what I might feel. And with no chance of enjoying what I expected, I tried to prepare myself.

I had, for instance, to find storage for what I wished to keep. My parents wouldn't have room in their new home for all their furniture. They needed to sell things for convenience, not for financial reasons, and in any case, since I would be their sole heir and legatee, the proceeds of everything would eventually come to me.

Best to go home several days in advance. As well as my own boyhood things—my room had remained the same since 1932, the year I married Venetia—I felt attachment to many other items scattered throughout the house and gardens.

A furniture warehouse in Cashel offered storage facilities. I had no idea where to live. For three or four days I trucked to the warehouse the pianola, still in excellent condition, with dozens of music rolls; our din-

ing room table and our breakfast room table; my bed and the two dressers that went with it; the large, long, yellow bookshelves and all my
books; the two armchairs from either side of the fire in the parlor, in one
of which I had sat with Venetia leaning against my knees the first time
we had ever been alone.

I kept many of the pictures, including the four Stubbs, and of course
you know how valuable they proved. They bought houses for both of
you, and added to my pension. And we'll still have enough for you to live
on for the rest of your lives. When I told my father how much they'd
yielded, he whistled.

"Do-do-do you know how much I paid for them?" he said.

We all knew; he told us every week of our lives.

"Yes, Harry," said Mother.

"I-I-I p-paid three hundred, seventy-five each." And away he wandered, singing, "Kay-said-off, said-off"; no matter who told him, or how
often, that Doris Day was actually singing *Que sera sera, whatever will be
will be,* he sang what he heard. He had picked up a few of the other hits
too, and mangled them likewise. How did Pat Boone, Perry Como, and
Frank Sinatra sleep easy in their beds at night?

Mother surprised me. I had expected melancholy to match my own.
No. Skittish and excited, she trotted here and there: "I wonder what we'll
make on the auction?" "Do you want this?" "Ben, who should I give this
to?" "That awful vase, your father must have hidden it."

From cupboards and the tops of closets, we retrieved. Things she'd
forgotten she owned. Ancient wedding gifts she'd never used. Useless
objects bought by mail. She had a memory for everything and one hundred percent accurate recall. Every item had a story.

As I watched and listened, I felt cheered. I was seeing a woman glad
to get away from a farm that had been hard work for many years, and
had had one patch of indescribable terror and pain when she'd lost everything. Now I saw a woman fulfilled, and as happy as she might ever have
expected to be.

As a teenager, your grandmother drove a neighbor's cows to be milked.
She got to know each cow on a personal basis and spoke to them more
than to any humans. That was how she managed her own red-hot shyness.

Harry, my father, your grandfather—he, on the other hand, became opaque as the sale drew near. Today, long years after his death, I know what that signified: intense depression and disappointment.

In some ways, he had done it again—he had leaped before he looked. Now that all had been settled, he wished he hadn't. I'm certain that he'd felt the same about Venetia after he spent some weeks on the road with the show—but he couldn't find a way out of it, no way home.

Oddly, though, he had it right this time. He mightn't have liked it, but neither he nor she had been cut out for dying in harness. If they'd gone on living there and trying to farm, using as much local hire as they could, their frustrations would have mounted. Perfectionists both, they'd have been distressed beyond endurance by any increasing slowness or infirmity that prevented them from doing the chores they'd always done. Both controlled their own domains and could never have given them over to anybody else.

The morning of the auction dawned clear. On the auctioneer's instructions, we had closed and locked the eternally open front gate the night before. Yet at half past six, as dawn broke, three men in suits and rich coats stood on our lawn. They'd parked down on the main road and trudged up through the river fields, past the well and by the woodlands.

All English, they made gracious and humorous apologies—and then tried to cut deals for individual items. Their offers, they said, wouldn't be bested when the sale began. (They lied.) Mother, knowing Father's propensity for being sold to, took over. She invited them in, and sat them to an early breakfast—in the kitchen, because I had taken so many tables to storage.

Mother made it clear: "No deals; everything goes under the hammer." The "Three Wise Men," as they called themselves, relaxed and sang for their breakfast. They vied with great tales: eccentric owners, dream finds—including, they said, a Vermeer in a County Wicklow cottage and a Stradivarius cello in Belfast.

66

Just before nine o'clock, the auctioneers arrived. An hour later, scores of people surged through the opened gate.

"Gawk-gawk-gawkers," declared my father, "burn-burn-burning with curiosity to see what we have." He appointed himself patrolman for the day. "They-they-they'd take the milk out of your tea and come back for the sugar," he said. And he said it often.

My spirits must have been improving. I must have been getting stronger. Maybe my adventures in the Shannon flood strengthened me. Why do I say this? Because without angst or mood, I emptied my own bedroom bare. Down to the boards. Even unhooked the curtains. So that no feet could trample through, I then locked the door, hid the key, and stuck up a notice: "This room is empty and is closed off to protect it." Did that mean my old room or my own soul?

We had a day of amazement. So much went for six, ten, or fourteen times above appraisal or expectation. Everybody was bidding. As the crowds grew, it got ridiculous—heated escalations for a wallplate, a pitcher, a watering can.

Mother, nervous and astonished, presided over the day. She walked here, halted there, greeted old friends, recalled past acquaintances, bent to small children like a queen at an orphanage. Which is how she used to inspect her flowers in the garden. The distress I feared never surfaced. Rather, she kept an eye on my father, as though he might be the one who combusted.

Harry, though, held himself together. I watched him, too, and when, late in the afternoon, he wandered off in the direction of the kitchen garden, I followed him at a distance.

I'd been a child spy; I still knew all the places to hide. Where ivy congealed on the walls, some bricks had long broken loose. Through these I could peer into the garden and not be seen. My father went down the seed beds, looking at earth in which he would never again dig.

I gave him several minutes. The wooden garden door had a noisy hinge. He waved and beckoned. His face seemed both strained and flushed.

"Do you think-think-think the new crowd will till it as well as we did, Ben?" he said.

"Are they gardeners?" I hadn't met them—a family from Carlow, with a horde of children.

"They'll be able to teach the little ones how to grow radishes," he said. "Do you re-re-remember?"

I smiled. "And lettuce. And onions."

"And-and-and you even managed to grow carrots," he said.

We paused. "Do you see that spot over there?" I pointed. "That's where you knocked down Mr. Kane."

"God above! How do you know that?"

I said, "I was hiding up there, behind those black-currant bushes."

"What? Why?"

I said, "I was afraid you'd get hurt, and I wanted to be ready to run for help—I was too small to attack him."

He laughed. "I-I-I got him a good one, didn't I?"

We walked on. Saying nothing. Multiple feelings never to be spoken.

The lower gate led to the meadow adjoining Mr. Treacy's field.

"Will-will-will you be all right, Ben?"

"I'll be all right."

"You're sure?"

"I'm sure."

"Are-are-are you—I mean, will things change for you?"

"Dad, things are always changing."

He knew what I meant. I knew what he meant. And there we left it.

67

Back at the auction, Goldenfields was closing down in front of my eyes. People I had never seen before bustled away hugging intimacies from my life. The large copper pan—how often had I stirred plum jam or apple jelly? Two men carried the mangle. I'd built my childish biceps turning that handle to squeeze the water from the towels, with our housekeeper Large Lily telling me, "That'll put hairs on your chest."

Her husband, Billy Moloney, who ran our farmyard, and who couldn't speak without profanity, came over to where I was standing. I would report to Mother later what he said, and I would make sure to use the euphemism we had long, long ago agreed on.

"The whole thing's flocked, Ben. And I'm flocked with it. Nothin'll ever be as flockin' good again."

Even though she laughed and laughed—how it touched her.

That night they drove away, Harry MacCarthy and his wife, Louise; they drove all of eight miles to Goold's Cross, but it might have been to Moscow or Atlanta or Cádiz.

And I? I stayed in a bed-and-breakfast place in Mitchelstown, the first place I'd ever stayed away from home, where I'd lodged when I went looking to bring my father home the day after he ran away with Venetia.

68

Broken ribs, broken ankle, fractured skull, severe lung infection—did he look shaken? But he still had the seducer's grin.

"They're saying to me here, Captain, How did you survive at all? And I says to them, Ah, I have good friends, I have a guardian angel." He looked at me with his usual cheek. "And I've learned how to answer to 'Liam.'"

"I bet that confused you for a while."

"It wasn't till someone called me 'Mr. MacCarthy' that I figured it out."

"I said you were my cousin. Our car went into the river."

"Actually, Ben, it was the river went into our car."

"You're in good form—'Liam,'" I said.

"The fellow in the next bed keeps telling me jokes all day."

"You like jokes."

"I do, Ben. But his jokes are very bad."

"What does a bad joke sound like?"

"No. I'm not telling you. It'd make me worse."

"So—tell me a good joke." I sat down, put the bunch of grapes I'd brought on his nightstand.

He reflected for a moment, a lock of his black hair making a fat comma on his forehead.

"Okay. I have one. There's an old farmer. He's out in his field looking at his cattle, he's smoking his pipe leaning on a gate, and he hears a little voice saying, 'Help me. Sir! Please help me.' " I laughed; Jimmy mimicking a small voice was, in itself, sidesplitting. "The farmer looks everywhere and finally, as the voice keeps calling, he looks down and he sees this frog on a clump of grass near his feet. And sure enough, 'tis the frog that's talking.

"So he bends down and he picks it up and the frog says, 'Sir! Kiss me and you'll discover wonders. I'm actually a beautiful young girl who was trapped in a spell by my cruel and jealous stepmother. In true life I am tall and slender and eternally loyal, and if you kiss me and restore me to human form I will be your loyal and loving and very beautiful companion for life.'

"So the farmer takes the pipe out his mouth and says, 'Would you mind repeating all that?' And the frog says, 'One kiss. That's all it'll take, and I'll be your adoring love, always young, to take care of you forever.'

"The farmer says, 'One kiss?' The frog says, 'One kiss,' its little eyes bulging, its little green chest heaving. And the farmer says, 'And that's all?' And the frog says, 'That's all.' So the farmer thinks for a minute and then says, 'D'you know what? At this age of my life I'd rather have a talking frog.' And he puts the frog in his pocket and goes on smoking his pipe."

A nurse came by and said, "Shush!" When I'd stopped laughing, I had an idea.

"What are you going to do when you get out of here—'Liam'?"

He said, "I was hoping you'd drive me to Marian's. But maybe I can stay with you?"

I said, "My parents have just sold up. I'm homeless."

We sat quietly for a while.

"Thanks for the grapes," he said. "I knew you'd come in."

"Any other visitors?"

"No. I'm sure everybody thinks I got swept away. Which I nearly did."

"You nearly did."

"Any idea what happened to the others?"

"I wasn't exactly looking out for them," I said.

"Why did you look after me?" Jimmy asked. "Especially after we all threatened you?"

I shrugged. "That's a stupid question."

"Well, thanks anyway."

"Now," I said, "you have to make your life a good one."

"Listen to Bishop Ben."

In acting mode, I pretended to start, as though with a sudden thought. "I have an idea. Randall is very fond of you. And nobody will know you're there. If you go to Marian's, you'll be in Dublin. All those cops."

I swear that I actually saw his mind working, *click-click-click!,* like the tumblers on a safe being burgled, a lock being picked.

He said again, "Thanks for the grapes." Jimmy repeated himself when he was thinking. I didn't draw attention to it. "Will you drive me there? When they let me out?"

I nodded and said, "I have a question."

He looked at me. "I think I know what it is."

"What is it?"

"No, Ben, you have to ask it."

I took a deep breath. "That day, the day of the flood. Would they have killed me?"

He looked away. "No, Ben. They wouldn't." But I sensed that he hadn't finished. And he hadn't. He said, slow as a funeral, "They wouldn't have killed you—I would."

I said nothing. What was there to say?

69

Did John Jacob O'Neill understand that he'd told me two tales and each had foreshadowed events of which I had later heard? A few moments after I arrived, he decided to bake.

He cleared a quarter of the long table, rapped it with his knuckles, declared it "the Territory," and laughed. "Now the Right Order." He assembled his ingredients, one above the other: flour, baking soda, sour milk in a blue-and-white pitcher, eggs, salt, and sugar. "The Weaponry," he said, and another laugh: sieve, wooden spoon, an old-fashioned scale, a knife, and a large yellow bowl. He fetched an apron, long, wide, and blue, and tied it at his waist in front with the awkward commitment of a little boy tying a shoelace. Into the apron's cord he stuck a clean dishcloth. "Let Life Commence," he said and smiled at me.

Before he began to mix he paused and, with fingers touching each item, checked to see that he had everything: the eggs, the flour, the baking soda, the salt cellar, the little sugar bowl ("A Souvenir of Galway"), the sour milk, on which curds floated like tiny blue-white ice floes. Satisfied, he weighed the flour, tipped it into the bowl, and shook the bowl, from side to side. Then he sifted, letting it flow like powdered fog through his fingers. The afternoon light through the window turned the flour to magic dust; he might have been caressing a beloved woman's long hair.

He made a well in the flour, a deep socket, and lowered in some of the sour milk. Then he cracked the three eggs and dropped them into the milk in the well, and began to mix with the wooden spoon. It looked like a tiny canoe paddle in his large, boyish hands.

Is this why he has no age spots, no liver marks? Because he bakes? And has his hands stuck in ingredients all the time? Children, do you know how unusual it was in those days to find a countryman in Ireland who cooked and baked?

Only when he had the process under way did he speak again.

"I hear James's funeral was a grand business."

"So you didn't get there yourself?"

"No. I had a Japanese visitor, and he's afraid of crowds and doesn't speak English."

"Most of the government turned out."

"Was that such a good thing?" said John Jacob O'Neill, and laughed. He concentrated again.

"Now," he said, "why did you ask me such a question?"

I told him my second experience: first, Ballyneety, followed by the raid on the British convoy at Larne. He went on mixing. I sat, expecting a pronouncement. None came.

When he had mixed and melded and molded, he had created a loose egg of dough. With both hands he raised it from the large yellow bowl and rested it like a patient on a patch of flour that he had sprinkled on the table. There he shaped the dough into a pale flying saucer.

He went to the fireplace and brought to the table a large black pot with three short legs and a long iron handle.

"Did you ever see one of these, Ben?"

I said, "Is it a bastible oven?"

"The very thing." He lowered the dough cake into the pot, which he then took to the fire. A hook swung from an arm that looked like a little black crane. He suspended the pot from the hook, and satisfied himself that the pot hung at the most suitable height. From beneath the burning logs he then plucked, with a long pair of tongs, several glowing embers, which he distributed all over the lid of the pot. He would do that many times, as they burned out.

"It's not true," he said eventually, "that a watched pot never boils. It certainly bakes." And then he told me a new story, quite short, about a haunting, but of a kind I had never heard before.

70

I was in Macao. Have you ever been to China, Ben? Macao is a tough old town. It gets all the flotsam and jetsam, all the dross of the South China Sea, and therefore it's a great place for sailors and their stories and people who get lost. There's a quarter of a million people packed tight into that old town. It's a place of shadows and knives and people who weep.

My story is about a woman who called me from a doorway as I walked by. The time was two o'clock in the afternoon. I was wearing a white suit and a Panama hat.

She said to me, "Come here, stranger, come over here."

I walked to her door, and she said, "Come in, stranger, come in here." In I went, and she said, "Sit down, stranger, sit down here." And I sat down.

"Did you see a man up there on the street," she said, "a sad man, with a long mustache drooping down?"

I had seen such a man, so I said, yes, I saw him, and yes, he did indeed look sad.

"That man," she said, "is haunted by a ghost. A ghost that comes to him every night."

She said to me, "Move closer. Not everybody's ears are pure enough to receive what I'm about to tell you."

Truth be known, my own ears struggled a little. Her dialect lacked the music that had helped me learn the easier ways of Mandarin, and a few more of the Chinese languages. There are three hundred of them, but don't we all have to smile and frown, language or no language?

So I moved closer, because she also directed me; she had fingers of ivory, long and tapering, and her fingernails curved a little in their length, and she had rubbed a kind of rosewood paint on them, so that they seemed like little flowers on long stems.

As I looked at her, I began to perceive that whatever her age—and it's difficult to tell with some Chinese people; she could have been sixty or ninety—she had retained a remarkable beauty. Imagine a small face, of a *kind you might see painted on a jar from a faraway dynasty, or on a doll for an emperor's daughter.*

In truth, she might have been Japanese, though when I later asked her if that was possible, she gave me an answer as blunt as it was brief, I can tell you. And she wore her hair in a great, thick cascade around her head and neck, to her cheeks on both sides.

I complimented her on her beauty, and she looked at me as though I suffered from fits of idiocy. As calm as candlelight she pursued her theme, and told me the story of the haunting. I believe I have remembered it much as she told me, although you, Ben, must, of course, suffer my translation. I'll speak now as she spoke. Am I going too fast for your notes?

I shook my head; I wanted to say that the translation didn't matter, since I spoke none of the three hundred languages of China and thought that the word "mandarin" signified either a dignitary or an orange—but I would have cut out my tongue rather than interrupt him.

Here she is speaking: We have had pirates for centuries in the South China Sea. Macao being a port, they come ashore here when the fruits of the shipping fail, as they do from time to time. One year, when all the big vessels and the rich cargo freighters were keeping away from the South China Sea, a pirate named Wong Kiu came ashore [I asked him to spell it]. *Wong Kiu had so much power and seemed so frightening that not even the dogs would bark at him.*

From his ship, he swaggered along the quays as you'd expect a pirate to swagger, with his drooping mustache and a black bandanna around his head, his knife in his belt. Behind him walked his pirate crew, the cutthroats everybody imagines pirates to be. They commandeered provisions here, liquor there, tobacco and cigarettes somewhere else, grabbed girls and kissed them, and when they had supervised the carrying of all their contraband goods back to their ship, Wong Kiu decided to give his men a drink.

Down on the port there was an old tavern whose name when translated from the Chinese means "Time to Rest from the Sea," and they made for this place. Now, the tavern was closed for business that day because the owner was giving his daughter her wedding party. Wong Kiu and his pirates knocked on the door and were waved away, like everybody else who tried to get in. The pirates, though, unlike everybody else, kicked down the door.

A hundred and one people, the luckiest number, were attending the wedding, and most of them knew who Wong Kiu was: the most feared buccaneer on the sea, whose ships came like arrows out of Bias Bay. The owner, a decent man, and prudent, explained that it was his daughter's wedding, but that the pirates were welcome to stay and have a drink. Instead, Wong Kiu saw, over the owner's shoulder, the bride. She had flowers in her hair and looked as pretty as the summer.

Wong Kiu walked over to the girl, took her by the wrist, and dragged her from the wedding. His pirate gang followed. Not one man, not a single one, of all the men there that day attempted to stop him, not even the bridegroom, a big, hefty fellow. He just stood there, weeping.

They took the bride to the pirate ship, and they sailed away with her. Her husband languished ashore. Oh, yes, he went to the authorities, but they told him that they could do nothing, and that unless he were to charter a shipload of even more bloodthirsty pirates, there was no chance that they could see of him ever getting back his bride.

A few days later, a messenger came to the bridegroom's door. He gave the weak fellow a package. It contained the left ear of his bride, with a note from Wong Kiu: "You need not mourn. Now she is not so beautiful anymore. She will be my servant for the rest of her life."

Again the authorities said they couldn't help. And again the bridegroom, who could well have afforded it, did nothing—he didn't charter a ship and muster his own pirate gang. And his bride, the prettiest girl on the coast of the South China Sea, was never again seen in the port of Macao.

Or was she? The bridegroom grew old and sad, as weak and indecisive men do. As his energies declined, so did his industries. He took to sitting on the street corner, hoping to see his bride one day, hoping that she would come back to find him.

Did she? He said she did; he said that she had begun to haunt him, that every night she came to him in dreams, that she stood across the street from him and called to him, but that he could never hear what she was saying. And so he sits where you saw him, sad and despondent, and I expect that you will now go and look at him again, now that you know his story.

71

Throughout his telling, John Jacob tended his baking. He refurbished the fire, and heaped its new embers on the lid of the bastible pot. More than once he took his great watch from his vest pocket and checked the time.

Again my eyes devoured him. He had indeed lost no height on account of age; my first impression had remained accurate. And the quality of his clothes: certainly he dressed like an Irish countryman, as did my father, in tweeds and brogues, but not even Harry MacCarthy, who believed, he said, "in put-put-putting money on my back," had as good a tailor. Or taste; this man dressed like an aristocrat.

That day, he wore a three-piece suit of brown herringbone tweed, a silver watch chain, a shirt of soft gray wool, and a cream tie with brown pheasants. In his breast pocket he wore a great gray handkerchief with white polka dots. And, over thick-knit gray socks, brown brogue shoes with enough strength to march him to Antarctica.

"The funny thing is," he said, as he sat down one last time, "I have a story that was told to me in North Clare, up near Ballyvaughan, that has all the echoes of that story. About a woman who was kidnapped the week after her own wedding and taken out to sea, where she lived on a fishing boat for the rest of her life. Never came ashore. Never wanted to come ashore. And when she was an old woman and they brought her to the hospital in Galway, and the nurses got to talking to her and one nurse began to realize who the woman was, she asked her about having been kidnapped and why she didn't ever want to come ashore, and the woman said that she'd always been waiting for her bridegroom to come and get her.

"And you find that kind of motif in stories all over the world. Although the other one is the more common—the girl being married against her will, and her true love gallops into the church or the castle and whips her up onto his saddle and they ride away, happy ever after. I have dozens of those stories. And I was in a village in Sweden one year where they assured me that the very same thing had happened there the year before."

72

Those bushy white eyebrows—he looked like a cartoon professor.

"Mr. O'Neill, why did you select that tale now? Out of all the stories you could have told me?"

"Didn't James teach you? 'Never ask the poet, always ask the poem. Never ask the painter, always ask the picture. Never ask the storyteller, always ask the story.' " He rose from his chair. "I think our staff of life is ready."

He took the bread from the oven, stuck a knife in it, peered at the blade, and smiled. Then he turned to me and said, "The Macao story didn't end there."

I had put away my notebook; I retrieved it.

"Was there a ghost?" I asked.

"I'm glad you believe in them." He shook his head. "I can't say. Tell me what you think." He smiled at the puzzled look on my face and completed his story:

I thanked her for her tale and rose to take my leave. There was a red sun going down into the water. She said to me, "Will you?" I looked as though I didn't know what she was talking about, and I said, "Will I what?" She said, "Will you now go and look at the sad man?" and I said that I didn't see how my curiosity could be stopped. She held up a hand to halt me, she leaned forward into the fullness of the light, and she pushed her hair to one side to show where she had lost an ear.

We ate the bread, with butter and honey melting on it. I complimented him—and tried to drag him back to the Macao story and his reason for telling me.

"James didn't tell me," he said, "about your tenacity."

"You find me tenacious, Mr. O'Neill?"

"I think you should now begin calling me 'John Jacob,' " he said. "After all, we're not going to fall out."

I wanted to say "Thank you" but couldn't find the words. So I ate some more bread.

"This is delicious."

"Good," he said.

We cleared the dishes from the long table in the kitchen. In the renovation of the house he had kept the more aggressively modern sights away from the traditional. The sink, the electric stove, and all other such conveniences lived in a scullery, what he called "the back kitchen." Together we washed and dried cups and plates and knives with butter and honey on them, and I felt so comfortable beside him.

"Macao," I said, thinking aloud. "And you speak Chinese. And I don't."

"But you know a special language," he said.

"English. Like everyone. And I still have a lot of my Irish."

"No," he said. "Always look to the words. And the great language that you know is *seanchas*." He pronounced it twice; the second time he dragged it out: shan-a-kuss. "It means 'knowledge of the old ways.' That's a language unto itself."

"Hence, naturally," I offered. "*Seanchai*—shan-a-key. One who knows the old ways."

He laughed. "Others give it different nuances."

73

Controls fail. Even my delay mechanism crashes. And then I drink. Hard. Unless I can grab myself in time. I came away from his house with two reactions: annoyance and fear. The old sorcerer—he had bamboozled me again. How did he know the life I was living?

When good advice makes you afraid, you're in trouble. James's mantra came hurtling back: *Stories are where you go to look for the truth of your own life.*

The tale of Macao had splayed me. John Jacob O'Neill had just told me a story about a weak man who wouldn't or couldn't reclaim the woman he loved. I needed help. But from whom? Following a blind instinct, I drove to Dublin and knocked on a door.

"Have you been expecting me?"

She said, "No," but the word had some room in it.

"Meaning?"

"You didn't ask me if I'm surprised," she said.

"All right. Are you surprised?"

She laughed. "That's better. And the answer is 'Not at all.' Does that surprise you?"

"So you were expecting me?"

"Oh, stop fencing and come in," she said.

Jimmy had said that she lived alone. And I had seen her forthrightness. She could afford to be direct; Jimmy had said that she had been left comfortably off by her parents. She had stayed so well in my mind that it made emotional sense to meet her again.

"You haven't asked me," she said, as she led me to her kitchen, "whether I'm pleased to see you."

"I haven't."

"Tea or a drink?"

"Whatever you're having."

"Is that what your problem is?" she said. "That you can't ask for what you want?"

I didn't answer, just stood there, large as a lump in her kitchen. She filled a kettle, plugged it into a hefty black outlet, and threw a switch big enough to inaugurate a dam. And then I said, "Everything in me is blocked. I don't even know why I'm here."

"Give me your coat." *Does nothing faze her?* "My God! The weight of this thing," she exclaimed, and she hung it on the newel post of the staircase. The coat's folds sank to the floor like a tired widow.

"Now." She stood with her back to the stove, waiting for the kettle. "Let's clear this up. Do you understand the difference between not expecting you and not being surprised?"

"Of course."

"There's no 'of course' about it. What puzzles me is that you aren't pressing me on the point."

"I don't know what to say."

"Try something," she said. "Anything. We're neither of us fools."

"All right. So why aren't you surprised?"

"That's better," she said. "I thought you had some guts in you."

"Why did you think that?"

"It's what people say about you."

"Now I'm the one who's surprised."

"The only one," she said. "Remember I said I wasn't surprised."

We both laughed; I could hear the ice breaking and the floes drifting away. She held her arms out wide, as a sign of peace. "Relax, Ben Mac-Carthy."

"Is that an order or a project?" I said.

"Dora Fay is an old family friend," she said. "Now will you relax?"

I gaped at her. "What?!"

The kettle began to sing its little song; she let it grow shrill. With her back to me she prepared everything, then sat at the table.

"By the way, where did you pick up that worm Bermingham?"

"Dora Fay baked this cake," I said.

Marian Killeen nodded. "I can't bake. Simply unable to. I can cook, though."

"I met him in a pub in Urlingford. He had been following me, looking for me. And we got dragged into a strange kind of fiasco." I told her the story, including the legend of Malachi MacCool.

"Dora says that you're a man to whom things happen," Marian Killeen said. "And not all of them good."

"A long time ago, Miss Fay kind of saved me," I said.

"I know. And she wants me to do it now."

"Dear God!"

"All right," she said. "Full confession. I was intrigued by you when I met you with Bermingham. I had already seen you."

"Where?"

"Beside Dora. At James's funeral. And at the party that night."

"How come," I said, edging toward being irked, "I didn't see you?"

"You don't notice women," she said. "That's what Dora says." To stop my protest she put a hand on the back of mine, an electric touch. "It's all right. I know why. I know a great deal about you. In fact, Dora admits that she kept you and me from meeting all these years."

"I didn't know a word of this."

"Of course you don't. Women have so little influence in the world that they have to invent secret powers. And you're a man around whom that kind of thing happens."

"Am I?"

"I believe in things getting paid back," said Marian Killeen. "I believe that if you trust it, that life will give you what you want, provided it's healthy and good and does the opposite of harm."

"Whew! That's some faith."

"Now." She leaned forward, her eyes flowing into mine. "Can you do this? Can you figure out why you're here? And can you also determine what it is you'll take from me? What it is I can give you and what you can give me?" She had the clear punctuation and emphasis of the very assured. "While you're thinking about it, let me tell you about the belief that life will give you what you want."

I said, "Hold on, hold on. Go back to Miss Fay. Not wanting us to meet and now wanting us to meet."

"Don't interfere with my stride when I hit it."

I leaned back to listen. "Fine. Go ahead."

I should feel bewildered, but I have no right to be. After all, I'm the one who came here. Just listen now, see what she has to say. For once in your life, flow with the stream.

"You have to know what you want. The Chinese have a proverb: 'There are two things in life that are difficult—knowing what you want and getting it. And of these, the former is the more difficult.' Ever hear that? No? Well, you have now." She had a good, strong grin that puckered her nose.

I have heard it, but I don't want to complicate things. Is this going too fast for me?

She held her hands out flat on the table and drew a deep breath.

"For reasons that will become plain to you"—she glanced up at the clock—"in half an hour or so, you'll know that I'm going to keep no secrets from you. I'll answer any question you ask me. If I can."

"I don't know what to ask," I said.

"Very well. I'm in charge." She settled into her command. "My beliefs first. Payback and how it happens. And how to get what you want. I have a good life, as you can tell. I'm more or less my own boss, I love my work, and I have this house and enough money for the rest of my life. My first twenty-eight years, though, were rotten. My father and my mother fought all the time and they used me as a go-between and a punching bag. How I survived I don't know. You're looking at a miracle."

I said, indicating the house and its comforts, "So this is your payback?"

"They died," she said. "In a car crash. Both drinking. My guess is that they had a fight and that she wrenched the wheel. I saw her do it many times. Terrifying."

"Did they die at the same time?"

"Instantly," she said. "Ask me what I felt."

"What did you feel?"

"Relief."

She wore no rings but had perfect fingernails, painted a strong pink. Her eye contact never wavered: straight into mine, almost defying me to look away. Now and again her gaze flickered down toward my mouth.

"Did that make you feel guilty?"

"Not many men would ask that question," she said. "Dora Fay said you were smart." I raised a querying eyebrow, and she continued: "Dora says that she kept you from me for years because she thought I would get hurt."

I sat up. "Why did she think that?"

"Calm down, Ben MacCarthy, no need to get het up. She meant that I might want to get involved with you, but that you never had any intention of looking at any woman other than the wife you lost."

"She told you that?"

Marian Killeen nodded. "Loud and clear."

"But if that's the case—"

She finished the question for me, as she often would. "If that's the case, why does she want us to be in contact now?" And she paused, her gray eyes searching me.

"Exactly. Why now?"

"I can only repeat her words. She wants me to 'take you in hand'— that's the phrase she used."

"Take me in hand?"

She nodded. "Yep."

"Did you ask her what she meant by that?"

"I did."

"And?"

"And what?"

"What did she say?"

Marian Killeen sat back and measured me with her eyes. For a moment or two she said nothing, and then she nodded her head slowly.

"She said that was up to me. And she said that I'd know what to do. And she was right."

74

When I awoke, I knew at once where I was. The day had long ended. In the window I could see a streetlamp's yellow glow. Light danced on the ceiling from a fire, lit while I was asleep. She saw me raise my head.

"What time is it?"

"You don't need to know."

"I mean, how long did I sleep?"

She said, "Five hours. Give or take a few minutes."

"Jesus."

"You slept like the dead. I watched you."

"Have you been here all the time?"

"Apart," she said, "from tending the fire."

She added, "We have to have rules."

I said, "Fine by me."

"There's only one rule," she said. "Nothing but kindness."

"I can do that."

"Oh, I know," she said.

We rose and went downstairs, each proclaiming ravenous hunger. She cooked omelettes with bacon and cheese and made mugs of strong tea. I found my courage and told her the Macao story.

"Am I that sad and dreary man? That's what I ask myself."

A silence fell; Marian broke it.

"Ask it."

"What?"

"Ask the question you're wanting to ask. Which is, why did you come here?"

Conceding with my palms turned up, I said, "Very well. Why?"

"You should be able to answer your own question."

I took my time. Then I said, "I think I know."

She looked at me, her gaze level and intelligent, and still with the blush of the bedroom on her cheeks.

"Go on."

I said, "But it's corny."

"No, it isn't."

"Is there something in there about making—" I paused. "Don't know how to put this."

"Try. I won't laugh."

So I said, "Is it—was it—is it—" I stopped, half-laughing.

"Don't be embarrassed," she said, reaching across and taking my hand.

"Is it about making me a man?"

"No. You have two children. It's about reminding you."

"Of what?"

Now she took her time. "I know your story," she said. "I know it in detail from Dora. She has talked to me about you so often. She says you're impossible to care for. That you won't allow it. And that you've forgotten what care feels like on the receiving end."

I said, "I certainly recognize the word as she uses it."

Marian continued, "If you've been unable to care for the people you love most, you need to be reminded what care feels like. And you have probably never been cared for like this in all those years."

I said, "There's some truth in that."

"But I know," she went on, "that you devoted several years of your life, back there during the war, to somebody."

"Her name was Kate Begley. She was a matchmaker."

"And from what I hear, you didn't get much out of that."

"I learned a lot."

Marian said, "That's generous of you."

I said, "It's true." Then I asked, "Is there more?"

"That I want to say to you? Oh God, yes. But it will wait till the morning."

We went back to bed, leaving the kitchen immaculate again. I damped down the fire, did some small domestic chores. She watched me all the time.

At breakfast she asked, "Now do you know why you came here?"

"Instinct."

"Good."

"But this has been all about me."

"No, it hasn't."

"What have you got out of it?"

She said, "A lot. But I'll be specific. I've just had the experience of losing my virginity to a wonderful man. Who will now do me a great favor."

"If I can." Not for a second did I feel wary.

"Keep Jimmy Bermingham away from me."

I said, "I can do that."

"And," she said, and to my astonishment she became upset. It happened at the speed of light. She sat back, her face crumpled, and she covered her eyes with one hand.

"And what?" I asked, as carefully as I could.

Pulling herself back together, she said, "And I get to tell somebody a secret he will never tell. Because he's that kind of man."

"I know many secrets," I said.

"James said you were the most trustworthy man he ever knew." She stopped, reconsidered. "Ben, look at us, look at the two of us in this country that pretends hour by hour, day by day, not to be corrupt and it's a cesspool of violence and hypocrisy. Somebody has to find a way forward," she said, "and it has to be people like us."

I nodded. "I see it every day." And I waited.

"Here's my secret," she said. "I discovered when my parents died that they were not husband and wife but brother and sister. That's probably why they fought so bitterly and took so much out on me. I can never marry, because I could breed idiots. In fact, I had my womb removed. I went to England, got it done there."

I rose from my chair, walked around to her side of the table, and held her head in my arms.

To this day, I have difficulty reaching for the appropriate image to describe that extraordinary moment in my life. Years later she said to me, "You called me your tanker that lovely night. Do you remember?"

"Tanker?"

"You said that I refueled you."

"Well, you did."

It was the first time we had ever talked about that night. I asked her, "Did you think about it much?"

"Every day. Still do."

"And what do you think?"

"Not enough words in the dictionary," she said. She smiled. "So it comes down to a single phrase: 'My one and only.' "

At that meeting, Marian Killeen also told me that she had known what would happen next.

"I saw it in your face."

"I did it because of you," I said.

"No, Ben. You just needed someone who would know that you were doing the right thing."

75

Sooner rather than later (as you'll well recall), Gentleman Jack took over every bill on which he appeared. That was the kind of force he had. Pickpocketing before the intermission, hypnotism in the second half, and he sold out every night. The next day I waited for hours to be the first in line.

In an aisle seat, I sat through the disappearing neckties, wallets, shoelaces, belts, scarves, jackets. This time, with more presence of mind, I looked closer.

He was not as tall as me; I already knew that. Much thinner, too; he had no flesh on him. He prowled like a cat, light on his feet in his shiny patent leather shoes. The black line of mustache curled when his lip did. He had a forced, insincere laugh. Unbiased of me, eh?

When not picking a pocket, he held his hands out from his body. Like blades, ready and poised. Rarely motionless, he ran a ceaseless patter. His lean face showed no feeling.

The act consisted of Jack and only Jack. Venetia had no task and a minimal presence; he had reduced to a cipher this talented woman who used to dominate every board she trod. She handed him things or, hands held high, walked around and led the applause for him.

How rarely she smiled. And then only a pasted-on stage smile. No more the warm, wide heart-stoppers. I'm sure you knew those smiles, children. First thing in the morning I saw them, or when she kissed me good night, or hugged somebody she loved, such as her nurse-housekeeper, Mrs. Haas, another casualty of those awful old family events.

Yet, now and then I could see some of the Venetia I had known and remembered. A flick to the hair. A folding of the hands. A way of standing. When I saw such a moment, I could actually hear the crack spreading across my heart.

The hypnotism began just after the intermission. Jack walked from the stage down the steps to the front row. One, three, five, seven, nine, eleven, thirteen—he asked every alternate person to stand. Before each one he paused for a moment and said, "Open your eyes wide and look at me."

Then he passed his fingers before their faces and said, "Now close your eyes, and you will feel a wonderful cloud descend on you."

They seem to have done exactly as he said—though from six rows behind I couldn't see their faces. As he finished with each one he said, "You will now rock a little on your feet," and each audience member did indeed rock a little, back and forth, and then stopped when he said, "Stop."

When he had assembled the five women and two men, and the last one had ceased rocking, he ran back up the little steps and commanded the front of the stage above the footlights. Lit from underneath, his face shone dark as a vampire's.

"When I snap my fingers," he said, "all of you on your soft clouds will become my seven-piece band." He moved to stand before the first person. "You," he said, "will be the first violin."

He snapped his fingers. The woman, a frizzy blonde in a cheap lavender blouse, began to saw at an imaginary fiddle. The next, an older woman, began to play an imaginary trombone. Number three began to pound an imaginary piano. The fourth puffed his cheeks blue blowing a trumpet that didn't exist. The fifth sawed at another invisible fiddle, the sixth, a shy and remarkably pretty girl, played a harp with dreamy hands, and the seventh hammered at the drums until his glasses almost fell from his face.

The imaginary musicians reached full tilt. Gentleman Jack walked across the stage to the conductor of the real orchestra down in the pit and cued him. "Music, Maestro, please!"

The conductor did his count: "A-one, a-two, a-three, a-four." From the pit came a quickstep, a tempo to fit the hypnotized "musicians."

Gentleman Jack then walked across to Venetia, bowed deep, and said, "May I have the pleasure of this dance, my dear?" When he swung her into the quickstep, the audience cheered.

He danced with her for perhaps thirty or forty seconds, then relinquished her. Abandoning Venetia center stage, he ran down the little steps again and along the hypnotized row. Each time he snapped his fingers next to someone, that person ceased playing their instrument and came back to life and, with a sheepish face, sat down beside their laughing friends.

Jack climbed back onstage and took his bow, but he didn't include Venetia. She stood alongside him, smiling a professional half smile. Tonight she wore ruby red with black fishnet tights, and high-heeled crimson shoes with gleaming buckles. I tried hard to make her glance at me, but Venetia was focusing nowhere.

When the applause died down, Jack stepped forward to the footlights again. Shading his eyes with one hand, he peered dramatically into the audience.

"I'm selecting volunteers," he said. "If you refuse, I will compel you to come up here by mesmerizing you."

The audience laughed, a nervous and half-whooping sound, and then fuller cheers broke out as he chose his first "volunteer." He pointed to her—an obesely large woman, probably in her fifties, but the wobbling red-blue jowls made her age difficult to assess. Her friends cheered as Jack walked down the steps to meet her and helped her onto the stage. Venetia wheeled forward a plush sofa and patted one cushion, inviting the woman to sit.

Next, Jack went down into the audience and made hay of choosing a handsome young man with slicked hair. He delivered him onstage to Venetia, who took the young man's hand and seated him on the sofa beside the oversized woman.

Jack had one last choice to make: an elderly woman, chosen for her granny looks. He escorted her onstage arm in arm, handing her carefully up the steps, whence Venetia led her to a simple kitchen chair some distance behind the sofa.

Now Jack took up his position—at an angle to all three "volunteers" but able to take in the audience, too.

"This is our little play," he announced. "Grandma here"—he walked over to her—"is the chaperone, the gooseberry, but she will fall asleep." He went across to her, murmured something, passed his fingers before her eyes—and her chin fell onto her chest. "However," Jack continued, "she might wake up. And if she does, she will be angry. Why? Because she will see the lovers here—I will call them Romeo and Juliet—making mad, passionate love."

The couple on the sofa giggled nervously. Jack addressed them from the side, standing where the audience could see his every move.

"Romeo, when I snap my fingers, you will make very, very amorous advances to Juliet. And Juliet, when I snap my fingers, you will kiss Romeo as ardently as in your wildest dreams."

Bending to each, he murmured. He made passes with his fingers. When each seemed to have drifted into an altered state, he stepped back. Holding up one hand, he winked at the audience and gave a wide-eyed, eyebrows-raised leer, then snapped his fingers hard and fast, once, then again.

On the first snap, Romeo lunged at Juliet, pawing her face and her stringy hair. On the second click, Juliet heaved herself across at Romeo and began to kiss his mouth. She overwhelmed him; it was a pillow covering a mouse. Half-lifting herself from the battered velvet, she launched herself at the boy, not so much kissing as eating, chewing.

He fought back—insofar as he could. For one brief sally he managed to get his mouth onto her face, and he stuck there for a moment, like a limpet on a ship. It didn't last. Juliet surged again, and eventually he disappeared under her bulk and we saw little more than his flailing young legs.

Jack prowled during all of this and then, casting a leer as wide as a wall, snapped his fingers at Grandma and said to her, "My word! Aren't you supposed to be chaperoning your pretty young daughter?"

The old lady woke up—except that she didn't. Gentleman Jack held his hand out to Venetia, who handed him a rolled umbrella, which he gave to the old lady. She rose from her chair and began to lay about the lovers on the couch. Before any damage could be done, Gentleman Jack woke all of them with the double snap of his fingers in their three faces. He raised their hands and presented them to the audience, joined in the applause, and then took his bow.

They returned to their seats. With the applause subsiding, Jack began his next announcement.

"Now, ladies and gentlemen, before I hypnotize all of you—and I do mean each and every one of you." He pointed dramatically to individual members at random. "You. And you. And you. And you."

People went, "Oooooh!" in that pleased-to-be-scared way children have.

"Before I put you all under my spell, I want you to see just how great are my powers. I want you to see what I can make somebody—anybody—do."

He strode upstage and held his hand out to Venetia. She laid her hand in his. Jack led her downstage, close to the footlights.

"This lovely lady—she is as modest as she is beautiful. She is as shy as she is statuesque. This is no burlesque actress; this is a lady who wears a swimsuit taking a bath—that's how respectable she is."

The seat around my body grew warm. I pressed my hands together, like a man in prayer.

Gentleman Jack said, "But when I place her under my spell—" He paused, dropped Venetia's hand, stepped forward a pace, and peered into the audience.

"Are there any policemen here?"

He waited; someone shouted, "No!"

Jack replied, "Good. Then we can have some fun."

On the word "fun," I slid from my seat. I sprinted the ten yards. Sprang up the little steps. I rushed the stage, grabbed Venetia by the hand, tugged her back down the steps, and raced her with me up the aisle.

The audience gasped. They thought it all part of the act. I'd wagered on that in my planning. Jack convinced them when he shouted, "Stop them!"

Nobody made a move. We burst out to the street.

Raining. Again. In those days, nobody had any difficulty parking in Dublin. Around the nearest corner within seconds, Venetia and I climbed into the car, and I drove helter-skelter down a steep cobbled street with not a soul in sight.

PART FOUR

❋ ❋ ❋

The Pursuit of the Past

76

We got clean away. *Old joke about a dog chasing a car: What does he do with it when he catches it? How long has he been treating her like that? So lewd. Bastard. Ask her. The utter, utter bastard. First question.*

"Has he been doing that to you for years?"

"I don't know where to begin."

All the old power of her lovely voice had dwindled, faded even since I'd met her in Florida. Hands pressed between tightly closed knees, she began to shiver. I stopped on some empty street, climbed out, took off my coat, ran around to her side, and managed to get the coat wrapped around her shoulders. She began to cry, crumpled as a hurt child.

As I climbed back in, she said something. I didn't catch it and leaned over to hear; she repeated it.

"All the years I've waited for this."

I grabbed her face and pulled it to mine. We sat clamped cheek to cheek.

Which is the child, which the adult? Think, don't feel. Logical next step? Safest move? We need to be where nobody can find her. Or me.

The police knew that I stayed at Miss Fay's; therefore, we couldn't go there. Goldenfields was unoccupied—the new owners wouldn't arrive for many weeks—but it was too far away, and too empty. No hotel would take us at that hour of the night—we looked suspect.

James said to me once, "Often when only one remedy presents itself, it's the best way. That's why it seems the only one." I knew what to do.

77

She hadn't yet gone to bed. Had there been no light, would I have rung the bell? In my new frame of mind, yes. She opened the door in pajamas with little bears on them. At one glance she took it all in. She stepped back, beckoned us in, closed and bolted the door.

"Good man!" she whispered to me. "Well done!" To Venetia she said, "Hello, I'm Marian—I'm delighted to meet you. Stay right where you are, and I'll get you something warm."

She raced upstairs and returned with a tartan robe. In the hallway of 18 Grove Road, I slipped my coat from Venetia's shoulders. She stood there for a moment in her ruby-red-and-black-lace, sleazy, décolleté stage costume, with the tawdry fishnet tights and the ribald garters, and we helped her into the robe.

"Tea," pronounced Marian Killeen, and we went into the kitchen. The fire hadn't quite gone down. Marian's eyes told me to load it up again. Within minutes, the coal and the kindling together gave us a flame.

She didn't fuss over your mother. As I handled the fire, she sat Venetia at the kitchen table and began the arrangements for tea.

"Toast, I think?" she said to me, in not much above a whisper, as Venetia sat there, huddled and still, her head lowered a little.

Is my heart going to break? Did I cause all this? Sins of omission? This is agony.

The fire billowed; the warmth would follow. I sat across the table from Venetia and took her hands.

"Venetia. My love. Look at me. Are you all right?"

She didn't look at me. She didn't answer my question. She had a question of her own.

"Why didn't you come sooner?" she asked.

"Venetia, they're all dead now," I said. "Your grandfather. Your mother. My father has retired, and my mother has him under control. We're safe."

She shook her head. "We're not. Jack will kill you. Or his friends will."

"His friends?" Marian Killeen and I spoke together.

"He gets his money from bad people. That's how he has so many shows in big theaters."

"But not here in Ireland?" I asked.

"We met some of them yesterday. From London. They'll find us."

Oh, Jesus. How many ways are there to feel fear? Make it numb. Don't listen to it. Eyes on the prize. Sitting in front of you. Keep with it.

Venetia nibbled at the toast and drank the tea. Marian whispered to me, "I'll fill the bathtub, and I'll leave out some things. We'll get clothes fixed tomorrow."

She could have shouted at the top of her voice and I don't think Venetia would have registered it. I wondered whether she had made a decision to collapse.

Upstairs, Venetia, silent throughout, offered each arm and each leg. As a child does when being undressed. But she stumbled like an old lady as she tried to climb into the high-sided old tub. I lifted her off the ground, placed her feet in the water. Then helped her to lie back. When I had raised her hair out of the way and placed a towel cushion under her head, she seemed to relax.

"What happens now?" she asked after some minutes.

"You take some rest."

"Ben, why didn't you come for me sooner? Why? Why?"

"Shhh. We'll talk about all that. But I'm here now, and I'm staying here."

She calmed down further. With a washcloth I patted the stage makeup from her face. I held a warm towel to her dear neck. I bathed her as I'd have bathed you, children, had I been there when you were infants. I wrapped her in towels and took her to bed, on fresh sheets in Marian Killeen's guest room. And there I held her until she fell asleep.

I wish I could sing to you, but my voice would croak. I wish I could sail with you on the wrinkled sea. I wish I could grant you the fullest joy of life.

The bedroom fire, lit by Marian while we were in the bathroom, needed stoking; I kept it going all night as Venetia slept. *Now only death will part us.* I had expected her to have a restless, tossing sleep; instead, she never moved. As dawn came, I slept, too.

78

Waking before her, I stacked the fire with coal and some logs. Through a crack in the curtains I could see sunshine.

I daren't think. I mustn't think. I must control the speed at which I absorb what has happened. I must delay my reaction to the deed I've done, to the fact of who lies in that bed. This is the dream come true, this is what I've thought about for twenty-five years. Is she the same Venetia? Not yet, not outwardly. But I see glimpses. There's so much that I have to find out. Have I done the right thing? Have I merely held on to some kind of dream because it was a dream? Wasn't the young man of twenty-five years ago very different in his needs and desires from the man I am now? What was that old saying: Be careful what you wish for? What would James advise? James would tell me to "get the practicals done."

And so many of them to be done. A doctor first: Venetia's upper arms and shoulders had bruises under the stage makeup; I had to stamp on my anger as I'd have stamped on an ember about to flame. *Where to live. How to hide. If we need to.*

I slipped back into bed, and Venetia began to wake. No smile yet; no smiles last night either.

"Good morning," she said, and she let me hold her again. After a few minutes, I said, "The bathroom is through there."

As she climbed out of bed, she realized that she was naked, held the sheet to herself, and found last night's towels—Venetia, who, all those years ago, had been an unabashed nature child. I located the tartan robe and left it at the bathroom door, dressed quickly, and said, "I'll be down-stairs."

Marian Killeen had left a note in a sealed envelope.

Dear Ben,
I'll be at work until six o'clock. My advice is to stay here for a few more days at least—and of course you're welcome to stay as long as

you like. She's a lovely woman, though not in good shape. In case you don't know any doctors, I'll make an appointment with mine for today at four o'clock. I know he'll make room to see you both, and I'll telephone you at noon to make sure that's all right. Take it very easy—and I know you will; you're doing all the right things.

Love, M.K.

I heard Venetia's footsteps on the stairs and went to the kitchen doorway to meet her. She moved like a ghost, frail and slow. *Get everything as pleasant as possible. Warm fires. Comforting food. No strain, no pressure, just peace and quiet and comfort and warmth.*

Do you remember, children, how I described for you the moment I first saw Venetia? She was Portia, in that goofy extract from *The Merchant of Venice,* Shakespeare in an Irish country town. I can recall phrases from my account:

"What is it about what we call today a star? What quality, what dimension? Is it an inner burn? . . . Venetia Kelly made no dramatic stride into the center of the stage; she didn't leap or pounce. She kind of slouched on, a slow walk, shoulders taut, like somebody wondering whether to be wary . . ."

Now I could see that slouch again. When she needed to, of course, she could pull herself up to her full height, be regal, statuesque. I can recall, too, what she wore that night. A black gown of light velvet brocade, throat to ankle. Small black velvet shoes with pointed toes. Not a hint of jewelry, no ornament. She didn't need it. And everywhere she looked people sat up, giving her their full, riveted attention. She was thirty-two, with the innocence of a girl and the fiber of a queen.

And then when I met her in the flesh—remember that? She was getting ready for bed, in that house in Charleville to which we have all returned for a visit. Part of putting the story of our lives together. And she was wearing a mask of white night cream all over her face, and a long blue robe with a hood. I remember reflecting on the bizarre combination of presence and absence, because she had disappeared beneath the hood and behind the death-white mask. And she never said a word. All I saw was the pair of eyes and the expressive finger pointing to the ceiling to indicate that she was retiring for the night.

79

Now I stood by the open door, waiting to greet her. She glanced at me and looked away, to the floor at her feet. No smile, no connection. With slow steps and her shoulders down, she walked past me into the kitchen, her face as white as an altar. I thought her a woman in shock. She sat at the place I had set for her breakfast. The fire glowed; the kettle sang.

Randall and his fish. The image rubbed and rubbed until it almost wasn't there. Life has rubbed at her, and rubbed and rubbed. Is there no blood left in her? Can I give her mine?

When she had settled in her chair, I put a hand on her shoulder.

"Would you like breakfast?" Venetia nodded. "A boiled egg? Some toast?" She nodded again.

Take this very slowly. Very slowly indeed. This may not be what you expected, but it is what you've got. So—go easy.

I made tea, let it steep for five minutes. She used to love boiled eggs, during those few short months we had together. And toast "soldiers"—fingers of toast cut so slender that she could dip them into the soft-boiled egg. And strong tea. All of these I took to the table, contriving to place myself where I could see whether she remembered. No recognition.

From the chair opposite her I could watch every movement. Twice she sighed, her hands resting in her lap, before she even made a gesture toward the meal. Then she sat up a little and began to take her food. Her hands moved like tortoises—to the toast, the butter, the egg. Low on one forearm I saw a deep bruise I had missed last night, as though she had been gripped there by a handcuff.

"What happened to your wrist?" I said, my first attempt to address the general matter of the bruising.

She looked at me and held eye contact, her most direct gaze yet. Airing the bruised wrist with a little wave, she said, "I call it 'life,' Ben."

Easy. Easy, Ben. Slow down. Don't rush your fences. Take it slowly.

"Marian—whom you met last night. This is her house. She thinks—

and I agree with her—that maybe you're a little pale. And she has a friend who's a doctor. Who could, if you so wished, see you today."

"If you think so," she said.

"They're keeping an appointment open for you at four o'clock. I think Marian left out some clothes, too."

Venetia didn't answer. She followed each piece of toast with a swig of tea, as careful at the table as an old nun. Her melancholy, her downbeat bearing suggested a woman aged beyond her years. Indeed, the woman I'd met in Florida seemed like a young athlete compared to the person who sat opposite me now.

Somehow I held on to myself and demanded nothing of her. I prattled a little, told her the story of Jimmy Bermingham and Dirty Marian, felt that I had made it amusing—but Venetia didn't smile. She drained her teacup, rose to her feet, and said, "I'm going to be sick."

In the hallway, I opened the door to the downstairs lavatory. She slid in there and pulled the door closed behind her. She retched and retched. A noise like a machine with dry cogs.

Should I help? No. If she'd felt that need, she'd have kept the door open.

Back in the kitchen, I cleaned and tidied; at least she had made the effort to eat breakfast. When she emerged she didn't come to find me; she climbed the stairs. I listened to each step, heavy and slow as leaden boots. She went back to bed.

I gave it a few minutes and followed. She lay on her side, facing the door. I sat in the chair.

"Are you all right?"

"I'd like to sleep."

"Of course. Do you need—I mean, would you like me to lie with you?"

"If I'm alone I'll be no trouble to you."

"But it would be no trouble."

"I think I need to sleep, Ben."

And she turned away.

80

As you both know, I've never raised a child. Which makes me sad. But if I'd been there when you were ill, I'd have sat with you, or looked in on you every few minutes. At two o'clock, after my umpteenth silent inspection, I decided to wake Venetia. We had two hours before the doctor's appointment. Given the pace of her movements, she'd need every minute.

I filled the bathtub, and she closed the door behind herself. When she emerged, I led her to the clothes Marian had set out. My memories of my time with her were of intimacy beyond closeness—no secrets other than deliberate surprises, no doors closed except for fastidiousness. And Venetia—an actress, after all—had long experience of relaxed dressing rooms. But now her body language said, "Privacy, please." I left the room.

In the car, she didn't speak. At the doctor's, she went into his inner room without a word. She emerged—it took almost an hour—with eyes red from weeping. The doctor, in Venetia's presence, told me, "She's a bit run-down. But in good organic shape. She has a scrip for a tonic. We'll see her again in a couple of days."

Venetia, with the piece of white paper tight in her hand, left the surgery ahead of me and walked to the car. At the chemist, she insisted on taking in the prescription to be filled. I pointed out that I had to follow and pay.

So did our first reunited day run its course. In the car on the way back to Marian's, she said, out of the blue, "In good organic shape. In good organic shape."

Back at the house, she went to bed again and was fast asleep when Marian came home at a quarter past six.

"I hear you were at the doctor's."

"You talked to him?"

"He said she's a bit melancholy. Noel is very understated, so that means a lot more than he's saying."

"She hasn't spoken a word all day. Nothing."

"Did she eat?"

"Threw it all up."

"When my parents were killed, I vomited for a month."

"And apart from Dr. Brady, she's been asleep all the time."

Marian offered, "I think you should wake her."

In a heated linen closet at the top of the stairs, Marian found a different robe, gave it to me, and I walked into the room. The curtains had remained open, and the streetlight haloed Venetia's hair in the shadows.

"Are you awake?" I whispered.

She raised her head as though it bore a weight, then subsided again. I sat in the chair.

"I've been thinking, Venetia. How do we contact the, can we—" I paused.

Don't know what to call them? The children. The twins? My children? I remembered what she'd said on the Atlantic shore at Jacksonville: "There were—are—twins. Do you want to know their names?"

I found the best words: "I mean, where are Louise and Ben staying? Can we find them?"

She rose, still in the tartan robe. I gave her the fresh dressing gown Marian had chosen.

"We're downstairs."

"I have none of my clothes," Venetia said. "Does the telephone work here?"

Good sign. Talking about clothes. Good.

We waited for her in the drawing room; I had lit a fire. Somehow those early moments of being with Venetia again seem to have so much fire in them—logs burning, coal piled on, keeping the fire going overnight. Today, of course, I look back and recognize what it was: I was trying to give her twenty-five years of comfort.

Marian poured sherry. And received a smile. Plus some words.

"Sherry? Goodness. Haven't tasted it in years. My mother's favorite tipple at the end of the day."

Progress. Maybe the drink will loosen her.

Marian asked, "How are you feeling?"

Venetia smiled. "Ben's father, if someone asked him that, used to say, 'Medium.' Do you remember, Ben?"

"Actually, he used to say, 'Med-med-medium,' didn't he?"

She laughed. Not long or loud, but a laugh. "How is he?" she said to me.

"They sold Goldenfields."

Venetia put a hand to her mouth. "Oh, no! What will we all—" She stopped, and changed her words: "Where will they live?"

"They bought a house eight miles away. Between the woods and the lake."

"But—what about you? Where will you live?" She assumed me single and alone.

"I'm on the road a lot. D'you remember James Clare?"

Venetia grew the most animated I'd seen her. "The old folklore man. With the beautiful long hands?"

I said, "He died. I got his job."

Marian said, "I feel like cooking."

"Don't go," said Venetia; actually, she gasped it, in a kind of desperation, but with such force that Marian sat down again. All three of us fell silent.

Marian broke the hush. "Ben told me about the twins. Do you want to contact them?"

"I have a telephone number." She rattled it out: "Six-seven-zero-six-seven-nine. They're staying there."

"Would you like one of us to call them?" Marian said.

"If you'd be so kind," said Venetia. "I don't want them alarmed."

Her accent had a slight American overlay, and she spoke as she had always done, with great, slow clarity. While Marian remained outside the room, Venetia gazed into the fire, her face closed to all approaches.

81

Not that you need the details—but I can remember what I was wearing next day, where I stood, the expression on my face when I first met the pair of you. That evening outside the Olympia Theatre doesn't count; in the dark and the mist, I didn't quite see your faces. Now the resemblance between you left me short of words. And your hair, Louise, cut as short as Ben's, and how much like my mother you both looked.

I, who prepared every thought in my head lest I be open to the dangers of spontaneity, I had not prepared for seeing you. Oh, yes, I had flirted with the idea, made up little speeches to you both, even practiced smiles and handshakes. But remember: I'd never really allowed myself to believe that a day would come when I would know you both. And I had no idea how you would greet me.

We've talked about this moment, all three of us, many, many times, and I think that you were as mystified and bewildered by your feelings as I was by mine. Let me put on the record here and now, for you and your children, and your eventual grandchildren, my account of the meeting.

In my black suit, my white shirt, my black tie, and my big black boots, I stood in the doorway of Marian Killeen's kitchen as she and Venetia answered the door knocker. I heard no squeals or shouts, just murmurs of concern, safety, and introduction. Each of you embraced your mother, and then shook hands with Marian and thanked her.

And then each of you looked over the shoulders of Venetia and Marian and saw me. The women parted to let you through, and you stepped forward. You reached me first, Louise; you said, without a smile, "I believe that I know who you are," and you put your arms around my neck and clung to me as though you or I might die.

You had no reason to do so; I was a perfect stranger to you, and you might even have had reason to resent me. Yet there you stood, holding on to me as though you had just found the most important and precious person you had ever known.

Then, Ben, my dear namesake, you came forward, and you said, "We have the same name," and as your sister moved aside a little, you hugged me from the other side. And with just as much ardor. And with just as much freedom.

As for me—I had no words, none at all. Do you recall how tongue-tied I was? I think I managed to squeeze out a "Well, well." And then I repeated it: "Well, well." And then I said, "Here we are." I was forty-two, and I had not known the emotion of such parental contact before, and in my many imaginings I hadn't even come close to anticipating the feelings of that moment.

You must take full credit, both of you—but I've told you that so often. You were so kind to me. So interested in me. So careful with me. I believe the word "delicate" applies.

And of course I knew—and this was hard to cope with—where your attitudes had been nurtured. How did you manage—it still mystifies me—to express yourselves like that when you met me? I know, I know—you've told me often that your mother spoke of me in the dearest and gentlest and kindest of ways.

And she, Venetia? She stood there and watched and fought back tears. She said nothing. She took the hand Marian Killeen offered.

Together they simply observed us, and how we looked at one another. I don't know if I remembered to tell you this, but Marian said to me, late that night, "You all looked as though you'd won prizes."

82

We had drinks, just the four of us, our first time together as a family. Marian stayed a long time in the kitchen, preparing food—chicken and ham and hot soda-bread scones and tea, the inevitable Irish tea, and I saw that both of you had my hungry habits.

You know, to this day (how many years later?) I remain astonished at the same thing that astonished me then: that in an instant we became as close as though I had raised you in the warmest intimacy. We began to chat like old friends. I asked how you liked Ireland, and you used words that made me smile; you said, for instance, that Dublin was "neat" and that the Irish people were "cute." You meant that the city was exciting and engaging, whereas in my terms, "neat" meant clean and tidy, which was decidedly not Dublin; she was, in those days, a filthy and unkempt city. As for "cute": you used the word to denote handsome or pretty; with us, it has always meant ratlike cunning.

The meeting rattled along with a brisk and enjoyable air. I found your openness disconcerting at first—no hanging back with you. Louise, it was you, I think, who went straight in and asked, "Have you kidnapped Mom?" And you, Ben, followed up with "Jack is like a raging beast." And you both essentially implied the main questions: "What's happening?" and "What's going to happen next?"

I felt a strong sense that the two of you had somehow taken over your mother's life a long time earlier, and that you had a vision of her, and an understanding of her needs and difficulties. All of that now became clear.

Whatever your loyalties—and how strong they were, and how gracious—it became ever clearer that her life had not been easy. As our general bewilderment with one another settled down, a picture of Jack emerged: a quick-tempered cliché of a man, prone to swift violence and then binge drinking. Followed by more violence. It still mystifies me that he took no violence out on the pair of you—yet did, repeatedly and perennially, on your darling mother.

Was that the reason for her almost catatonic state with me? Did she equate me with him and his viciousness? Or was she so unforgiving of my failure to rescue her that she couldn't speak to me? I never found out.

We began making tentative plans. Both of you seemed certain that a continuing life with Jack Stirling had moved beyond the limits of Venetia's safety. Your mother shook her head—but said nothing.

All three of us agreed that for the moment Venetia should not go near him. Again she shook her head. And again said nothing. I put forward my ideas: that I would soon have a permanent place to live; that for the present she could travel with me. Marian, naturally, offered us her house anytime we needed it, and I said, "And there's Miss Fay's, where I usually stay when I'm in Dublin."

To all this Venetia neither shook her head nor said anything.

When she did at last speak, she said, "I have to see him, though. No matter what happens."

Ben, you were the one who said, "Not right now, Mom," and Louise, you elaborated: "He's going a little crazy. Drinking and shouting, you know—the usual. And wild fits of weeping."

I remain fascinated by the way your sentences often end in an inflection, like a query.

Louise, you said, "I'll smuggle some clothes to you."

Marian chimed in: "We should at least have some idea of the next steps."

Which is when, Louise, you said, "My next step is leaving now—I'm standing in for you, Mom, in the show."

My stomach turned a little.

83

Dr. Brady spent longer this time with Venetia. Again she looked as though she had been crying. As we were leaving, he called me over and spoke in that quick and vital way by which so much crucial information gets transferred—in a few seconds, in a whisper:

"She's not being dramatic when she says she's afraid for her life."

We drove back to Grove Road. I stopped to buy some newspapers and some milk. When I climbed back into the car, I found Venetia trembling and hunched. She kept looking behind her.

I knew little about nervous states or emotional crises. In Ireland we didn't allow the existence of such things; prayer solved all. I didn't need special knowledge to see the grip of this paroxysm—she almost had to be carried from the car. Inside the house, however, she calmed. And addressed a question to me for the first time:

"What did you think of the children?"

"Wonderful. I loved them."

"So you should."

"How could I not, Venetia?"

"They've been on this earth since 1933, Ben."

Her words lashed me. All her power as an actress came across. She played bitterness. Deep and true. And she didn't look at me. Indeed, she had scarcely made eye contact in the four days we had been together.

Once again she went to bed. I sat downstairs. And found new discomfort. The newspapers carried a report that an IRA apartment had been raided. A stash of documents had been found—"a revealing cache," said the report. It listed the names of "hundreds of activists and a large number of sympathizers, including doctors, lawyers, priests, and civil servants."

Then came a stinging line: "One employee of a government department, whose job takes him around the country, is believed to carry guns for active service units. A police source would not confirm, however, whether the information that led them to the cache of papers and weaponry in Dublin's Baggot Street came from this public servant."

No sleep that night. With Venetia in the same bed but as far away as an island, I had a new kind of "alone" in my life.

84

Miss Fay spoke the words I needed to hear: "Get out of Dublin." Followed by "Has she been silent since you found her?" Followed by "Silent and cold when you need communication and warmth? Sounds just like our own beloved country." She concluded with "Ben, dear, none of this is good."

I watched their meeting with great attention. Dora Fay now had a telephone, and I called from Marian Killeen's house to ask for a good visiting time. She invited us for an evening meal—which she always called "supper." How many legends tell of two women who love the same man not liking each other? I have to say, they looked mutually wary.

In her grave and gracious way, Miss Fay said, "I feel I know you, Ben has told us so much about you."

Still using "us"—as she would for years; in her soul, James never died. She took Venetia's hands and said, "We've longed to see you in this house. For years and years you've been a great topic of our conversation."

I could see both of their faces clearly. Miss Fay, wearing not black but purple ("the color of emperors for James," she told me later), struggled with warmth. Later she confided that somehow, and foolishly, she had been expecting a lissome young woman.

Venetia registered shock.

"A great topic?" she asked.

What's surprising her? Doesn't she know that I've thought of nothing and nobody since the day we parted? But we'd never even said "goodbye," never had the chance.

I had been at Goldenfields. We had won a resounding victory. My parents were coming back to the farm they thought they'd lost. Swindled from them by Venetia's filthy old grandfather, King Kelly.

That drive from Goldenfields—I recall it so well. On a night when the moon was clear-faced and innocent. I remember thinking, *My friend the moon. And tomorrow my friend the kind old sun.*

What did I find in the street outside our house? Venetia's great prop, the ventriloquy doll Blarney, who topped her bill in the road show, had been decapitated by the kidnappers, and I accidentally kicked his head as I walked to the front door. Venetia knew none of this, knew none of my aftermath—so much to tell her.

Miss Fay began the process that night, filling in for Venetia the blanks of my life. We heard a great deal about James, and how I now wore James's coat.

"Literally and metaphorically," said Miss Fay. "James was a major man," she said. "So is Ben. But how could you know that, my dear? And I can see so clearly the beauty of which Ben spoke. When you met most recently in America, Ben came home saying that if Venetia returned to Ireland, people would think she was Grace Kelly—didn't you, Ben? And all of Ireland loves Grace Kelly."

Venetia smiled, actually gave a little giggle.

Had we found a way through? I wondered, I hoped so—although I knew, actress or not, that she wasn't vain. Not with the mother she'd had, your other grandmother, who used to introduce herself with the words "I'm Sarah Kelly, the great actress."

85

The evening went not badly—I'll put it no higher than that. Venetia thawed, in part because of May, who kept looking at her and then saying, "Oh, missus, I shouldn't be gawking at you, but I can't take my eyes off you."

May, however, also overheard our conversation about the show.

"*Gentleman Jack and His Friend.* Oh, I know you now, miss, you're the friend. Wasn't I there last week, my pal Nancy, she had the head hippomatized off of her, and she playing a fiddle, her that hasn't a note to throw to a dog."

I felt my gut tighten. Telephone, telegraph, tell May—that was Dublin, where, as in any small city, information, gossip, and talk constituted powerful currency.

Before we left, Venetia excused herself to the bathroom, and Miss Fay grabbed the moment.

"Ben! What is the matter with her?"

"I'm baffled. She doesn't say a word to me; there's no connection."

Miss Fay put a hand on my cheek. "Oh, Ben. I'm so sorry. So different from what you expected."

"But the children are terrific," I said.

"Why wouldn't they be?" I looked at her, puzzled by her now. "Well, they're your children too, my dear. What's bred in the bone comes out in the blood." As we heard Venetia approach, she muttered, "Go and start the car; give me a few minutes alone with her."

When Venetia emerged, huddled again, and hunched against the world, I opened the door, installed her in her seat, and went back to thank Miss Fay.

"Get out of Dublin," she repeated. "As soon as you can. Change her scene. Get her away. Out on the road that you both used to love. Oh, by the way, a friend of yours called—he's ready to leave hospital."

"Any idea what ails her?" I asked.

"Impossible to tell." She paused. "Ben, it is twenty-five years; people change. But she is frightened."

As would Miss Fay herself soon be; Gentleman Jack Stirling showed up at her house and beat her senseless with his fists.

86

Some brief notes: Marian took Venetia shopping the next day. She reported some liveliness, but a desire in Venetia to be furtive and quick. "She asked more than once if anyone was following us," Marian said. Venetia showed some animation during actual purchases. "But," Marian noted, "not perhaps enough."

You, my lovely twins, came around late that night and said that Jack hadn't subsided. I told you of our plan to drive to Limerick the next morning, if your mother felt fearful. I knew every hotel and boarding-house in the country and would choose the best. I telephoned the hospital to tell Jimmy Bermingham that I'd collect him.

We had one of those days when spring peeps in at us, weeks ahead of time. Venetia reacted to it with smiles—how could she not? The early daffodils, the primroses on the grassy verges, the buds, the lambs, all the lovely clichés came to meet us.

Never have I observed a human being so closely. I managed to angle the rearview mirror so I could see most of the road and much of her face. In those days the journey took between three and four hours; twenty miles out of Dublin, Venetia finally sat back and released her shoulders into the seat.

Though now lacking sleep over several nights, I had massive energy. In my insomniac mind I'd planned every mile of this road. As a man trying to recapture a wonderful past, I had much to help me.

Venetia had loved the road. In this dwelt an irony, because she'd been forced to build the road show when her famed but jealous mother elbowed Venetia out of a star place in the Abbey Theatre. Sarah had once triumphed in all the roles that went on to showcase Venetia, and people with long memories—meaning, in Ireland, everybody—never felt shy of saying that the daughter was outshining the mother.

Once Venetia had taken to the road, though—with as rag, tag, and bobtail a company as was ever assembled—she loved it. And every town and village held some kind of likable memory for her. Indeed, in the weeks before she was kidnapped, we'd been planning a new kind of company, an upgraded, less rackety show.

"More Shakespeare than shaky," she called it. She had a passion to introduce the best of classical theater to the worst venues. Meaning she wanted to play the places least likely ever to see such drama. We couldn't afford to visit town and city theaters, and Venetia believed that Shakespeare's groundlings were alive and well in the Irish provinces.

In the car on that glorious sunny day, the Venetia I had known began to return. We drove through the village of Rathcoole.

"Remember?" I said to her.

"Wasn't this the place where Peter came onstage blind drunk? And forgot he was supposed to be in character?"

She began to laugh.

"And he made a speech." I could see it clear as day. "He said that the Irish loved Shakespeare because Shakespeare was a Catholic."

"Not just a Catholic," Venetia said, and did a perfect impersonation of Peter slurring his words: "A secret Catholic."

It happened so fast. Children, I'm sure you must have seen those short pieces of film where they speed up a flower unfolding. That's how I remember that morning: your mother came racing out of that tight bud, that emotional bandage. And soon, sitting beside me, I found the sweet, dancing girl I had missed for so long.

I wrote in my journal that night:

A memory—from today; every time I read this entry I will savor it. We reached Kildare sometime before noon. Not a cloud in the sky. Venetia looked all around her, in every direction, like a child.

Venetia asked, "Is this the town where you told me a legend about a saint?"

I repeated it: Brigid, a holy woman, wanted to found a convent; she asked a rich pagan man for some of his land. He scoffed, told her that she could have as much land as her cloak would cover. Brigid lowered the heavy cloak from her shoulders, laid it on the ground, "and it spread and it spread and it spread, for acres and acres and acres."

Back then, Venetia had clapped her hands in delight.

"That's a perfect image for loving," she'd exclaimed. "It just spreads and spreads and spreads." Today she said, "Lovely metaphor." She didn't say for what. But this was the old Venetia. Who came forth even more. As we passed an old ruin, she asked, "Weren't our lives filled with castles, Ben?"

87

We halted for lunch in Mountrath. Venetia took my arm as we crossed the street. In the absence of a worthwhile hotel, I chose a bed-and-breakfast that also served meals, run by a Mrs. Dennehy, who had the gift of tact.

We ate well, the standard Irish lunch of meat and potatoes, followed by a deep apple tart. Farmers came here, and commercial travelers, and one or two schoolchildren. As we finished, something pleasing happened.

A woman in her forties, dressed like a farmwife who was spending the day in town, had been trying not to stare at us. She had a daughter with her, aged twelve or so, in a school uniform. The mother, with a huge mop of hair, came by our table and, shy as a panda, said to Venetia, "Excuse me, but didn't I see you in plays, in a show, here in Mountrath a long time ago?"

Venetia looked at me and looked at the woman. "You might have."

The woman said, "Oh, you were marvelous. I hope you'll come round again—I never forgot you, you were so lovely and clear. We were doing that old Shakespeare in school, and I never understood a word of it until I heard you say it." And then, in the manner of all shy people who have suddenly spoken in a burst, she ran off. The daughter, not at all as withdrawn, said, "Will you be doing it again here soon? 'Cause we'll all buy tickets." Then she thrust forth a school jotter she'd hauled from her satchel and asked, "Can I have your autograph, please?"

Venetia smiled and signed, "Best wishes, Venetia Kelly." And she did it in long, clearly legible letters, not her usual scrawl; the old kindnesses hadn't deserted her.

88

Jimmy Bermingham could not have been coarser.

"Shite's sake, Ben, is this her? I was expecting a young one."

Venetia looked at him, her face shrieking disgust. He was waiting in the hallway of the hospital, wearing a mauve shirt, nylon and cheap, and a tie with red clocks on it: What was Jimmy's obsession with clocks? Did he use them to make bombs? I should have asked him.

Trying to get over his gaffe, he said to Venetia, "This man here, he saved my life, my actual life, and nearly got himself drowned doing it—isn't that right, Ben?"

"How are you feeling?" I asked.

"I had pneumonia," he said. "On the double. And I got pleurisy. And every shaggin' disease from here to Timbuktu. I had the shakes for three weeks, and I have enough penicillin in me to feed a greyhound." Jimmy's similes and metaphors didn't always mesh. He turned his attention to Venetia. "D'you know what, girl? This fella here, he's only mad about you; he talks about you as if the sun was shining out of your you-know-where." The trouble with this remark was its ambiguity.

I said, "Jimmy, where are we going?"

After he'd directed me, he sat in the back of the car and talked nonstop. From time to time he leaned forward and asked Venetia a question. She never answered. She had disappeared again; I could have throttled Jimmy in his cheap brown striped suit, with his nonstop chatter.

Near Birdhill, we turned left and the Shannon hove into view beneath us. Jimmy fell silent, looking at the river that had come close to taking his life. And mine. Eventually he said, "Christ Almighty."

I said, "Is that a prayer or a swear?"

He patted me on the shoulder. "Ben, you're some man, d'you know that?"

Venetia might not have been in the car.

He directed me to a cottage and told me, "We'll say goodbye here."

Venetia neither spoke nor looked at him as he wished her well. Standing in the road beside me, he said, "Well, Ben, your life is fixed and mine isn't."

"Yours can be fixed," I said.

"How so?"

"Go and stay in Randall's house." I meant it well; I meant it for him—but my vile ulterior motive must have been lurking somewhere.

89

As I traveled the countryside, I'd always had a significant advantage: extra money. I'd never had to depend on the government salary. Just as well; my life would have been much more miserable. It's easy to see why James had needed to gamble.

My financial independence began the night they kidnapped Venetia. They left behind a suitcase of her cash, probably in some half-baked attempt to appease me. Or, more likely, they meant to come back for it. With this money Venetia and I had intended to form our new, more powerful, much classier touring show. I hid the cash and then invested it.

Later, when my life settled and I took to the road as a collector, I used my investment as the compensation it felt like. It afforded me access to every hotel in the country, in case I hit nightfall with no bed for the night. I'd had enough of the barns, the sheds, the damp itinerant-workers' mattresses that I'd known in those self-imposed bad years of my twenties.

With Jimmy Bermingham gone, we went to Cruise's Hotel in Limerick. I knew it well. So many Irish hostelries had twilight lives—wee-small-hours drinkers, all-night card games, nervy local whores.

Cruise's had none of that, but it did have tourists coming in off late flights into Rineanna (now Shannon) and, therefore, night porters. All of whom I knew. We got a room without difficulty.

Two quiet, awkward days we stayed there, leavened only by the fact that Venetia's appetite for food hadn't diminished, and that she felt easy enough for me to take her shopping.

Of the more relaxed woman in the car on the drive down—no trace. We did talk, though. We had difficult talks that followed a distressing pattern. Here's a sample:

"Ben, when you didn't come to look for me—that was irresponsible. Uncaring."

"Venetia, I thought you were dead."

"How could you think I was dead? I sent you five telegrams. And letters and cards."

"I never got them."

True; and when eventually, one day, I asked my parents, Mother quit the room without a word.

And so, round and round and round Venetia and I went, in the same circle of accusation and defense.

"But I would have walked away from that beach in Florida that day with you—I'd long planned it; I'd have managed to get the twins later— that's what I had always hoped for."

"Venetia, I was too immature."

90

Children, here's an official statement—from your father, Ben MacCarthy. Looking Back on His Life. I was now sick of myself and my past. All that moping, all that self-pity, that hesitancy, that indecisiveness, that talent for being led around the world by the nose, that failure—no, that refusal; call it what it is—to stand up for myself, that moral and emotional cowardice: how I must have bored the world to tears. And by now

I've probably bored you with it, too. I doubt that there could have been a more unattractive or stupidly pitiable man on the planet earth.

There are times when, in all the English language, the word I most appreciate is "but." Here it comes: But—I was improving. And I knew it. I ran through my mind a quick list of my "accomplishments."

Worked at a job I loved; survived a war's deep horrors; and in the deep snow of that war killed a man trying to kill me and the person I was protecting; found a matchmaker her dear match; and, most recently, saw my beloved friend, James Clare, into his Valhalla—wherever it was—with no panic or collapse from me. Plus: saved a dubious friend from drowning. (Well, anyone would save anybody else, wouldn't they?) And then essentially kidnapped, rescued from her cruel world, the love of my life. All that must count for something. So I said to Venetia, "From now on it will get better. Watch. And believe."

"How?" she asked, sad, afraid, and acerbic.

I said, "We're going to see a truly wonderful man."

91

Unlike most people—put off from the medium by the fear of bad news—John Jacob O'Neill liked to receive telegrams.

"I enjoy their vitality," he told me. "It would be a poor world if we shunned urgency."

And so, when I wished to visit him, I usually sent a telegram, a day or two in advance. Our relationship had become relaxed. If I called and he didn't answer the door and couldn't be seen in the garden or strolling his lane, which he so loved—he called it his "entry point into the wide world"—I came back later. Or the next day. Or dropped a note through the neat brass slot in his door, saying I'd be back soon.

Now, from the Limerick post office, I telegraphed, "Would Thursday suit? May I bring my wife?"

Although I loved using the term, it still felt hollow—a shallow ownership, something to which I was holding on for grim life. Indeed, it had crossed my mind that, when matters had settled, Venetia and I should undertake a new marriage ceremony to give ourselves fresh emotional muscle. We could do so in a Catholic church, since her divorce from me in Reno and her marriage to Jack Stirling, in an American registry office, would not be recognized as legal in Ireland. Technically, the church saw her as never having been married to him.

In the hours that I lay awake beside her (she, miraculously to me, slept soundly every night), I planned every mile of the journey to John Jacob's strong farmer's house. In Limerick, we were within twenty miles or so of Charleville, the town where we'd met, and whose surrounding woodland and countryside I had searched with spade and shovel for years.

Though it was still a place of great pain for me, might I not now anneal that anguish? After all, she and I had spent formative days and weeks in that area, talking to horses across fences, dawdling on the banks of small rivers, gathering armfuls of meadow flowers in those idyllic married months of 1932.

What were the risks? She had been taken from there with force—she hadn't yet given me the details—but we'd had such glorious days in that peerless land of milk and honey. All her troubles had begun and congealed there; but she'd conceived you, her twins, there and had been loved, according to her own admission, as she'd always hoped to be.

"It's astounding," she'd said to me once, "that a boy of eighteen who has never had a girlfriend, never even kissed a girl, could arrive as so complete a lover."

I'd joked about reincarnation, and she'd agreed.

When I surveyed and balanced every thought, I came down on the side of touring the old haunts. I could always quit them in a hurry should their memories prove too stressful, and then I could take some time to calm Venetia again.

92

We left Limerick in midmorning, and the hope in my heart shone as bright as the sun. She saw the road signs and made no comment, and I felt that she sat up a little straighter in the seat beside me. At breakfast she'd again had little to say, had made almost no response to my various attempts at conversation. One piece of communication worked: when I pressed a hand to her cheek, she caught my hand and held it there.

We drove past a sign for the road to Lough Gur, and to my astonishment, she looked across at me, sharp and expectant.

"Don't you want to take me down there?"

I shook my head. "But how do you know about it?"

She took a moment before replying, then said, "It was part of my imprisonment."

It was my turn to look at her in anticipation. "Now, that is something you'll have to explain."

Again she unfolded at her own slow pace. "Sarah told me a story. About her father, my grandfather. I'm sure you remember him."

I nodded. *Who could forget him?*

"He was once suspected of killing somebody. Of course he denied it, but Sarah said it was true, and he had dumped her body in that lake and moved it later. If I came back to Ireland, I'd have been in danger of a police investigation. They'd have interrogated me if they thought I knew about it."

This is not the moment to tell her that the murderee was Venetia's own grandmother, little Sarah's frail mother. And that I had sat there and watched the police drag the lake for, possibly, Venetia's own body. That, in part, was the official response to my reporting her as a missing person.

I said, "Nobody would have asked you any such questions. That was a bit far-fetched."

"Not if you were afraid of your own shadow."

Ha! A twitch of the veil, a glimpse into what her life then had been like.
Fear all the way.

"Was that how it was?" I asked.

She didn't answer; she took a pace back into her shell.

How can I keep her from retreating, how can I keep her out and bright?
If Jack Stirling didn't exist any longer, would her life be better?

Some minutes later, I turned off the Charleville road, and then turned
again, down a lane that became a cart track that became a field.

Under a great tree, I stopped and looked at her.

"You fell asleep here," I said, and climbed out of the car. She followed
me and we walked to the tree, not yet in leaf, and stood looking up at it.

"Do you remember?" I wanted to gauge how much she—and her
memory of me—had been damaged.

She thought about it. "You told me that it was an old copper beech.
That it had been an ornamental tree in a great estate. And when the new
Irish government came in and the old estates were broken up and the
land divided, this was the only part of the estate left intact. I remember
everything about it." She'd become animated, full of her old self. "It's like
Russia, it's like Chekhov—wasn't there a great house here somewhere?"

"And not a trace of it left," I said. "I've seen the sepia photographs. It
was magnificent."

She looked up at the heavy branches, some low enough for grasping
and swinging. "But the tree is still here. And, look—the buds will soon
swell." She walked all around it, circled to where I stood, and leaned
back against the tree trunk. "And I can tell you something about this tree
that you don't know. When I woke up here that afternoon," she said, "I
guessed that I was pregnant. I remember the feeling so well. Slightly
dizzy in my head, my eyes full of magic dust, and I could just sense the
beginnings of a feeling of warmth, and delight and safety. You had a
striped shirt, green and white stripes. And white pants. You had taken off
your shoes to go barefoot on the grass."

Too cold that morning to stand for long in the shade; but we did
linger in the car. Venetia huddled deep into her coat—a heavy navy
tweed we had just purchased for her in Limerick. She pulled a scarf
around her neck, reached for my hand, and pressed it to her cheek.

"We both went through bad times," she said.

"I didn't know how to handle it," I said, and I thought, *You have a better chance now; you know more, you're more mature. So take your own advice. Don't rush it. Take it easy. Give her her own time. Don't make the mistake of driving a conversation about the future. Let her wounds cool. Let John Jacob heal her.*

93

Such healing. Such balm. I want to tell you now the story of our day and our night with John Jacob, because for a time, for a crucial, magical few hours, your mother became once more the complete Venetia.

We came away from the great copper beech more relaxed than at any time since the night we ran from the Olympia Theatre. In Charleville, Venetia said, "Stop the car. I want to see the house." We stood on the high sidewalk across the street. Did somebody live there now?

For twenty-five years I had avoided this stretch of the town, unable to look. *Shall I point out to her where I found the head of Blarney, her ventriloquy doll? Over there, in front of the little gate. On the cobbles. Midnight. The witching hour. I kicked his head. By accident. Shall I tell her how I found that front door open, how I ran screaming around the house, up and down the stairs several times? Looking for her. But knowing she was gone.*

I said nothing. Nothing about my wild panic. My fierce certainty. Something awful had happened. Nothing about my dread to look to the floor lest I see bloodstains. It all came back—and I said nothing.

Perhaps I should have spoken and let her know my truth. But I didn't, and now I'm telling you, her children. Not for the first time, as you know, but, I hope, for the last.

We stood side by side, not touching. This was the house where I'd first met Venetia. Where we'd shared a bed so often, so thrillingly. I think it must have been Charleville's weekly half-day holiday, because not a soul did we see. We climbed back into the car.

Venetia's mood subsided again, but not in that same shocking fashion. However, the moment we reached the top of John Jacob's lane, she emerged from her hiding place, looked all around, at the dense and benign trees, and the high, grassy bank of the lane ahead of us, and said, "Stop the car!"

She jumped out and walked ahead of where I'd parked, her arms outflung, her head thrown back. I walked after her, and when she heard my footsteps she spun around.

"This is a fairy-tale place," she said. "Look!" She pointed to the plume of smoke from the chimney.

I said, "It'll be wood smoke."

"Can we walk down? Will the car be in anybody's way if you leave it here?"

She took my arm and set the pace, strolling with slow, thoughtful steps, marveling all the way.

"Oh! Can you imagine what these hedges will be like in spring and summer?!" And "Look! Are those wild apple trees?" And "We have to come back for midsummer's day." She began to recite: "I know a bank whereon the wild thyme blows, / Where oxlips and the nodding violet grows, / Quite over-canopied with luscious woodbine, / With sweet musk-roses, and with eglantine."

She clapped her hands and spun ahead of me, once again the girl I'd first seen onstage, in that damp, raggedy hall in Cashel, with my father close to swooning beside me.

These changes in her, these highs and lows of moods, these sudden "appearances" and then cold "disappearances"—is that a sign of damage?

I halted us, wrinkled my nose. "Sniff," I said. "Can you get it?"

She made herself look like a dog, a setter's nose to the blue, cold air.

"I'll never forget this." She returned to the canine pose, comically this time, and raised a hand like a pointer's paw. "What wood is it?"

"I'll let him tell you."

When we reached his gate she said, "Let's stop for a moment. I want my eyes to photograph this."

We didn't stop for long, because John Jacob O'Neill opened his front door and stepped out to meet us. In Ireland, we didn't hug when we met; we didn't demonstrate affection. Unlike the two of you, Ben and Louise: I'm so grateful for your embraces, with which you are both so generous to me.

And men of John Jacob's age—for whom reticence was a way of

life—they, especially, didn't show affection in public. But he had traveled the world and had learned other ways, and so he walked across to us, and held his arms out to Venetia as though she were his long-lost daughter.

"How are you, girl?" he said. "A lot of good people have been waiting for you."

94

Venetia fell into his arms. Like father and daughter, they stood for a moment as she admired the house, the neatness of the garden. Proud as a parent, he showed her the apple trees, the garden bench he'd made with his own hands, the thickness of the walls, told her about the cherry wood on the fire. Inside he gave her the same tour he had given me. I followed, keeping a short distance away; I wanted her to have the same full experience of his welcome I'd had.

John Jacob must have thought me out of earshot, because he began to speak of me.

"This man of yours," he said. "He's a remarkable fellow." I couldn't see them, but she must have been listening attentively, because he continued: "Some people I know—or, I should say, knew; his late boss was my dear friend—they thought the world of him. And from everything I've seen, he's a steady and loving fellow. If he has a fault, it's that he's a bit too conscientious. But if you were looking for a man with whom to grow old, and who will look after you—that's Ben."

Venetia said something I couldn't hear, and John Jacob replied, "Let life do it. We're always pushing rivers, and it doesn't make them flow faster or better."

They emerged from the rooms at the back, hand in hand. When they came toward me, John Jacob said, "I'm keeping her here forever. Is that all right?"

To which Venetia said, "And I'm staying. I'm never ever going anywhere else."

95

Naturally, John Jacob made tea—it's impossible to sit and talk in an Irish countryside house without tea. He produced a pie he had made, telling us, "I store my own apples in hay. It keeps them very fresh. I picked these back in September, and so I always have an apple something-or-other for Christmas Day. Maybe applesauce with goose."

When he'd finished his pottering and served us, and while Venetia ate her way through most of the apple pie, he plied her with questions about the stage.

"How much do you have to project your voice?"

"Is there a trick to projecting it?"

"How do you project without your voice going harsh?"

"What's the best register, do you find, for projecting? Is it soprano or contralto? I'd say contralto wouldn't be as hard on the voice, although people complain that my voice is sometimes too deep for them to hear everything."

I watched her, while pretending otherwise. She answered every question with a smile. By the time she'd mopped up her giant segments of pie, she'd engaged as much as I'd ever seen her.

"There are tricks," she said, "techniques. I'm sure you have them, too, Mr. O'Neill. Inflection. Timing your breathing. I used to take singing lessons."

"Oh, I took singing lessons from a lady in Valparaiso," he said, excited by the memory.

"Valparaiso?" Her enchantment with him grew—and he was off.

"I was walking down Serrano Street one morning, I was going out to visit friends in Viña del Mar, I was wearing a white suit, and I heard this wonderful man singing from a window above my head. I looked up, and there he was in full voice, glorious. He had a fat belly, a white shirt, and red suspenders.

"So I stepped back and listened to him, and when he had finished I applauded him, and he bowed down to me. I called up to him, 'Sir, where did you learn to sing like that?' and he said, 'Right here in Valpo, and not only that, I learned in that house there behind you. See that big doorbell? Push it hard and you'll find somebody who'll teach you to sing like me.'

"So I pushed the doorbell, and a lady opened it. She was a maid, and she showed me in, and I met this other lady, her employer, and I said to her, 'Senora, can you teach me to sing like the gentleman across the street?' And she said, 'He sings to me every day as payment for his lessons.' And then she asked me, 'Sir, have you any money? Because that's how I make my living.' And I said, 'How much money do you need?' And she said, 'Sir, I won't charge you anything because you said "need" and not "want."'

"And she taught me to sing; her name was Rosa-Rosa Pionara. Of course I fell for her—she was sixty-six and I was thirty-three."

Was he telling us the truth? Did it matter?

Venetia, her eyes shining, said, "Will you sing for us now?"

John Jacob O'Neill said, "I'll sing you a snatch of a song I'm fond of, because when I heard it, out west in America, I knew that it had come from County Armagh." He sang, "As I walked out in the streets of Laredo, / As I walked out in Laredo one day; / I spied a young cowboy wrapped up in white linen, / Wrapped up in white linen as cold as the clay."

Venetia took over: "Oh, beat the drum slowly, play the pipes lowly, / Play the dead march as you bear me along." And, with her harmonizing, they joined forces on the last lines: "Take me to the green valley and lay the sod o'er me; / For I'm a young cowboy who knows he's done wrong."

When they finished I stood and applauded, and they both performed little mock bows.

"A standing ovation," said John Jacob. "My first." He turned to Venetia. "But not your first, I daresay. Now it's your turn."

She said, "Who's your favorite character in Shakespeare?"

"Oh," he said, "I had a lady friend once who used to tell me I was Prospero. Now, was that a compliment or not?" He reflected for a moment. "Hamlet, of course. Though sometimes we take much of our learning from the minor characters, and I'm very fond of poor Ophelia."

By now we had all sat down. Venetia clapped her hands, and with that single gesture she commanded our attention.

"Ophelia?" she said, in an inflection that signified something interesting to her. "Well, in that case."

She closed her eyes, and then, as though holding a veil, covered her face with her hands and lowered her head. John Jacob looked at me wide-eyed, and we both sat back. Not breathing.

Venetia raised her head as though lifting a great weight, took her hands from her face, and, crazy of eye, looked from one to the other of us.

John Jacob said, as though nervous of frightening her, "How now, Ophelia, what's the matter?"

A lesser person might have halted in surprise at his acuity and his knowledge, but Venetia stayed in character.

"O, my lord, my lord! I have been so affrighted!"

Again, John Jacob rose to it and gave her Shakespeare's next line: "With what, in the name of God?"

Venetia went into the speech as though she had been in a castle outside Copenhagen centuries earlier:

"My lord, as I was sewing in my closet,
Lord Hamlet, with his doublet all unbraced;
No hat upon his head; his stockings fouled,
Ungartered, and down-gyvèd to his ankle;
Pale as his shirt; his knees knocking each other;
And with a look so piteous in purport
As if he had been loosèd out of hell
To speak of horrors—he comes before me."

She paused, and John Jacob picked up his cue like a pro: "Mad for thy love?"

Venetia looked at him in a way that would have told any audience how to feel in the same circumstances. Miming all the actions, the hand-wringing, the trembling, she continued, "My lord, I do not know. But truly, I do fear it."

Did John Jacob see some discomfort cross my face? He clapped his hands and said, "Very good. I'm afraid my old head can't remember the rest."

Venetia turned to me. "Did you enjoy it?"

"Do you remember when I first saw you do that?"

"Ballyconnell," she said, "on an August night. With the rain lashing down outside in the middle of a heat wave."

"Do Portia," I said. And I went on, for the next hour: "Give us Titania. Do Cleopatra. Miranda." When I asked for Desdemona, for the beggarly divorcement speech, she began, "What shall I do to win my lord again," then said, "Oh, I don't remember this fully."

I said, "What about Juliet?"

She looked at me and replied, so that I alone could hear, "No." Then she turned to John Jacob and said, "It's your turn."

96

Logs on the fire. More wood ready nearby. Adjusting his place on the hearth. Arranging his pipe. Preparing his tobacco. And then, when all was ready and we had settled ourselves, as expectant and excited an audience as he might ever have known, he launched.

"This comes from the long, long ago," he said, "and it has gone through many mutations. But my version, I believe, has the virtue of ancient truth, because the feelings that we'll hear and see are the same to this very day all over the world. I took the versions of similar tales that I've heard all over the globe, I combined them, and settled them into a story that anyone can recognize."

The skin on the back of my neck began to tingle. I ran my tongue across the ridge of my teeth. Venetia kicked off her shoes and curled her feet under herself in the chair. I organized my notebook.

"Ben," said John Jacob, "you'll recognize the names. And you, girl, may not, so I'll pronounce them first for you. The names of the lovers. The man's name is Diarmuid."

"Deer-mid," she said. "Deer-mid. What does it mean?"

"You'll find it in many forms," he replied. "I'm sure you know some-body named of 'Dermot.' It means a friend to all or a man loved by ev-eryone."

Venetia smiled.

"And his Juliet's name was Grainne."

"Graw-nyeh," said Venetia, working hard to get astride all the refer-ences. "Grawn-yeh?"

"That's it," he said. "It means 'love you' or 'love for all time.' An Irish-man will say, *'Mo gra thu'* when he wants to say, 'I love you.' Note the root word for 'love,' *'g-r-a'*—which we pronounce 'graw.' "

I had an impulse to leave. An urgent feeling. My shoulders tightened. But I could do nothing. Mustn't cause offense.

So I sat back, and John Jacob O'Neill launched into one of our most famous legends, "The Pursuit of Diarmuid and Grainne." He told it in a surprisingly brief version; I've collected it a number of times, and one telling (in County Waterford) took six hours.

97

The old warrior Finn MacCool sat weeping and lonely in his summerhouse overlooking the sea. His beloved wife had died and left Finn alone. Upon her death, he had bound himself to the Irish tradition of mourning for a year and a day. The year had passed, and in keeping with tradition, he stayed up all the night before the single day, thinking memories of his wife, and waiting until he saw the next twilight. And down, down, down went the globe of golden flame, and Finn's mourning was doused in the sea alongside the fire of the sun.

The next night, his warriors came to see him with the news they'd been waiting months to bring: they knew of a new wife for him. Finn, they said, knew her too—Grainne, the daughter of the king, a girl of great beauty with magical powers.

Finn, who had magic of his own, liked their choice. He ordered his war-riors to kill a boar, his servants to prepare it, and his riders to take the animal

to the king for a feast. By such a rite would the king know that Finn wished
to be a suitor for the princess.

The king accepted the boar, and his guests ate it for dinner. They praised
it, and they hailed the man who had sent it, and the king was well pleased.
Now it was his turn to sample the animal. The guests included Finn's riders,
and they all watched the king eat. So did his daughter. And when they saw
the king devour the slices of wild boar, they knew that the suit had been accepted. The next day Finn would be received.

When, in the regalia of a great warrior, Finn MacCool arrived at court,
he had as his bodyguard his finest, bravest, and most handsome warriors in
the wide, rolling world. They rode beside him into the castle yard, they dismounted when Finn did, and they flanked him as he strode into the castle
throne room. There sat the king and his wife, the queen, and between them
their exquisite daughter, Grainne.

Now, one of the warriors flanking Finn stood taller and more handsome
than any man in the world. His name was Diarmuid, and the princess's eyes
alighted on him. As did the queen's, and the eyes of every other woman in
that court that day.

Diarmuid's reputation preceded him. He could jump over the back of a
running deer. He could dive off a cliff by the sea and soar like an eagle on his
way down. He could sing a song sweeter than that of the nightingales in the
woods or the dawn larks in the fields.

Grainne looked at Diarmuid and saw this embodiment of many gifts.
Then she looked at Finn and saw an old and angry man, one whose sorcery
had begun to fade. She made her decision.

One of Grainne's magic powers resided in speech. From her throne between her father and her mother, she began to speak a poem. The rhythm of
her words rose and fell. One by one, she looked at every person in that court,
and they began to fall asleep where they stood. Slowly, one by one as she
looked at them, each person tumbled to the ground, so gently that no injuries
were caused. And soon everyone there, including Finn himself and his warriors, had slumped to the floor in a deep sleep.

Except one. Throughout her recital Grainne had not once looked at Diarmuid. Even as she spoke the most beautiful words in her long poem about
how flowers eventually become the gemstones we wear as jewels, she didn't
look at Diarmuid. Even as she described how, during certain times of the
night, we leave our beds and lie on the clouds and that is where we receive

our dreams, and that is why we must never lie on a black cloud, she didn't look at Diarmuid. Even as she told the court how every man, woman, and child will leave the solid earth and in time become a wave of the sea, she didn't look at Diarmuid.

When her story ended, and all but Diarmuid had fallen asleep, she climbed down from the place of thrones, walked to Diarmuid, and took his hand. Stepping between the sleeping people, they left the palace. In the court-yard they mounted two white horses and rode out across the countryside, singing and laughing as the sun shone in their eyes.

Every spell has to wear off, and the courtiers and visitors in the room of thrones began to wake up. Finn saw that Grainne had gone. Soon his men found the courage to tell him that Diarmuid had gone too, and the fur began to fly. Finn ordered his warriors to horse, and so, for seven days and seven nights, ran the famous and tragic pursuit of Diarmuid and Grainne.

The clouds parted so that the gods could look down on the drama unfold-ing below. And maybe direct it, because that's what gods seek to do. They sent the lovers to spend their first night in the cave of a bear high in the mountains above the sea in County Down. The bear welcomed them and then stood guard outside the cave, while inside the lovers ate berries and drank clear water from the crystal spring in the cave's floor.

And when they lay down to embrace each other and then fell asleep, the bear tiptoed into the cave and covered them with great warm bearskins that had been worn by his ancestors. The next day, the lovers bowed to the bear, who returned the compliment and waved as they rode away. Half a day later, Finn and his warriors rode up to the cave, found the lovers' traces, and killed the bear.

The lovers spent their second night in the lair of a wolf deep in the plains of County Meath, not far from the high hill of Royal Tara. As they rode into sight, the wolf and his mate took their cubs by the neck and moved them to a quieter place nearby, so that Diarmuid and Grainne could spend an undis-turbed night.

But the lovers, when they had supped and dined, and before they lay down in each other's arms for the night, played with the wolf cubs, who then slept curled up with them as the wolf and his wife sat guard outside the cave.

The next day, the lovers thanked the wolf and rode away. Ten hours later, Finn and his warriors galloped across the plains of Royal Meath, found the lovers' traces in the lair, and killed the wolf, his mate, and their cubs.

The lovers spent their third night on the shores of the lakes in Westmeath. There they found an empty castle that seemed to have been vacated especially for them. Fires blazed in the courtyard and in the dining hall and in the bedchamber. When they sat in wonder on two great chairs at the head of the empty table, birds and squirrels and other woodland creatures, badgers and weasels, and great, happy, and fat smiling toads appeared and began to serve them rich food—berries, nuts, fruits, and mead.

And when they retired for the night, the woodland creatures sent to them, as a living blanket, a thousand tiny and warm bodies of baby squirrels and rabbits and badgers.

The next day, the lovers said farewell to the woodland creatures and rode away. Eight hours later, Finn and his warriors galloped along the shores of the lakes of Westmeath, found the lovers' traces in the empty castle, and set fire to the place, killing every squirrel and badger and fox and all their little ones.

98

John Jacob said later that we were the best audience he had ever found. I, already captive, took notes at the speed of light. Whenever I glanced at Venetia, her eyes had grown round as moons, and her face as flushed as fire. Her mouth almost moved in time with his, as she repeated phrases that he had just spoken.

On the fourth night, he told us, the lovers came to the stone lair of an eagle in the mountains of Munster. The eagle had made courteous inquiries as to their health and their future, as he gave them the hospitality of his aerie. The next morning, Finn himself slew the eagle with one launch of his spear high into the blue air.

They rode the sands of Kerry on the fifth night, and a great sea creature of the Atlantic, glassy of eye and booming of voice—"he sounded," said John Jacob, "like the waves in the caverns of the deep"—gave them a welcome in seaweed halls, with a feast of lobster and salmon served by seals and dolphins. This time, Finn and his warriors put out to sea and with wide harpoons killed them all.

On the sixth night, they rode north to Galway, and out there on the white rocks of the Burren, the place on earth that looks most like the moon, because a piece of the moon fell off one day and landed there, they met foxes, of all colors—red and silver and gray.

And the foxes, creatures accustomed to pursuit, told them that Finn and his warriors were a matter of hours behind them. The foxes took them down into the underground, down a rich maze of burrows and coverts and into their own homes, those wide, low palaces beneath the earth, where fires blaze and food abounds, and there the foxes cared for the lovers because they recognized a princess when they saw one, and in Diarmuid they perceived a warrior who was kind as well as strong.

By now, as the sun rolled around the sky to meet the moon, the lovers had fallen under each other's spells. They saw little but each other's eyes. They heard little but each other's silver speech. They felt little but each other's velvet skin. When not asleep, being watched over by the citizens of the natural world, they talked to each other all the time—of their plans, of their future home, of their life ahead.

And all the while, Finn and his warriors grew ever closer. So close that the badgers and the rabbits and the foxes along the route wondered why the lovers couldn't hear the hooves of their pursuers drumming along behind them. Or feel the hot breath of Finn's anger, which had grown ever wilder as his pursuit drew ever closer. Or recoil from the growls of mounting rage that emerged from his throat.

At noon on the seventh day, the lovers reached the foothills of the magic plateau, Ben Bulben, that stands high above Sligo Bay. Here, for the first time, they fell among humans—a chieftain and his family, who claimed to have magic powers that would protect them from Finn. Grainne, of course, had her own magic powers, but she wasn't sure that they would be equal to the ancient ungodly powers of the great warrior-god himself.

Diarmuid had made up his mind that they should stand up and confront Finn and declare their love for each other. So sure were they of this love that they felt it would quell all hostility.

On the side of the mountain, the lovers made their stand. High above them, the clouds parted so that the gods could lean on their elbows, look down, and watch. From far away, Diarmuid and Grainne saw the warrior band riding hard for them. The riders drew nearer and nearer. Finn seemed to have gathered a number of supporters on his wild pursuit. What had left the palace of Ulster as a party of not more than twenty men had now swelled to more than two hundred.

Because the gods had parted the clouds, the day grew glorious. You could hear the stones splitting with the heat on Ben Bulben. Flanked by the chieftain and his warriors, the lovers sat on their horses to face the oncoming riders. In war, in peace, and in hunting, Finn always led his warriors from the front. And he did so now, astride a great black horse, his faithful dogs loping along beside him.

Up the foothills of the mountain they came, thundering with urgency, and yet the lovers felt not a qualm of fear. Diarmuid, after all, had been the greatest of Finn's warriors, capable of defeating any number of men in battle, and Grainne had magic powers, the strength of which she did not fully comprehend.

Finn reined in his horse, and his warriors drew up in ranks on either side of him. They outnumbered the lovers, the chieftain, and his warriors by ten to one. Nobody spoke. Finn looked at Grainne, the woman who had left him, and Diarmuid, the warrior who had betrayed him, whom he had once loved as his own son. Across his face traveled first disappointment, then rage, and then cunning. When Diarmuid saw the last emotion, he felt fear for the first time—because nobody could outsmart Finn, nobody could outguess or outthink him.

Finn spoke: "My beloved son, we have come to this."

Neither of the lovers replied; nor did anyone on their side.

Finn spoke again: "And since we have come to this, let it be decided not by bloodshed but by a trial of strength and skill. I am an old man, you are young; therefore, the odds are on your side. As you know, you have come to the side of a mountain wherein dwells a magic boar. Together, Diarmuid, we will hunt this boar, and whoever slays the animal shall be the rightful lover of the Princess Grainne."

Grainne had long heard the stories of Finn MacCool's cunning, and she felt no reason to trust him. She spoke up.

"I fear this plan," she said. "I fear that during the hunt you will find a means of wounding my beloved man, and then come back and tell us that he was gored by the wild boar. How may we have a means of trusting that this will not happen?"

Finn rode forward. "You have your magic powers, and they should be proof enough against any disaster. But as a token of my trust, I will give you this ring, and as long as you keep it, all whom you love will be safe from injury or death."

Grainne accepted the ring, which would have fitted around three of her fingers. It sat on the palm of her hand as she watched Diarmuid and Finn ride off together up the mountain to hunt the boar. What she did not know was that Finn, being a god, was untrustworthy, as are all gods, and that his ring had its own magic, which canceled all the magic powers of anybody who held it.

From the moment Grainne closed her hand around the ring, her magic began to wane. So powerful was the ring that she was unable to speak and protest, and she sat there on the horse with tears rolling down her cheeks, fearing the worst.

The two riders reached the top of the mountain, and the dogs began to bark. Soon they had flushed the wild boar from its cave, and Diarmuid, the best horseman in Ireland, took off in wild pursuit. Within minutes he caught up with the boar, dismounted, and cornered the snarling beast in a hollow in the rocks.

Finn arrived and surveyed the scene. He called out words of congratulation to Diarmuid. But his call distracted Diarmuid, and the boar charged. A tusk caught Diarmuid in the side, just above the hip, and almost went right through him. Diarmuid jumped back, dislodging the tusk, and the boar escaped. Diarmuid fell to the ground, blood pouring from his wound.

As everybody knows, the top of Ben Bulben mountain is inhabited by magic people. Across the valley stands the grave of Queen Maeve, the ruler of all invisible people everywhere, and the countryside is protected by her people. The very heathers and grasses contain cures and healing powers, and the waters in the springs and streams can fix all ailments. One hundred paces away, the most potent of these waters bubbled from the ground. Finn knew this, and so did Diarmuid, and he sent Finn to fetch a drink for him.

At first, Finn protested. He said, "I have no vessel in which to carry the water."

Diarmuid prevailed upon Finn to dip his hands into the cold spring and bring back the water. Finn went to the spring and dipped his hands, but as he reached Diarmuid one hundred paces later, the water slipped through his fingers.

Finn went back to the spring and dipped his hands again, and this time he brought a full handful, but he spilled the water so close to Diarmuid that he only splashed him.

Diarmuid was slipping away, and Finn went back to the spring a third time. He dipped his cupped hands deep into the freezing waters and scooped up a big handful. But as he stood above Diarmuid, he let the water trickle through his fingers, and Diarmuid, the most handsome and most brave warrior in the land, died on the side of the mountain.

Finn gathered Diarmuid's body in his arms, and when he appeared at the top of the mountain, holding the body of his beloved warrior, Grainne, waiting below, let out a scream and expired.

To this day, that same scream is heard near households and on farms and by lakeshores when a beloved person dies. It is the voice of the banshee, the woman fairy, and it haunts all those who have ever heard it.

And that is my story tonight, and I am glad to have told it to you, because it will now make room in my heart for the next story that wants to be told.

99

Children, by working diligently, by concentrating on my rewarding life collecting folklore all over the Irish countryside, I managed long ago to give myself tremendous purpose, and I absorbed the most useful material you could imagine.

Every day I collected some kind of story, song, or tradition that gave extra meaning to me, that helped to guide me, to steer me. When I'd first begun to look at this material with the help of my beloved friend and mentor James Clare, I'd seen a pathway stretching out ahead of me. This road, should I take it, would surely lead me to a higher place, a plateau upon which, when I'd reached it, put me above the places through which I had toiled. Now, I'd said to myself, the snarling tendrils of the past can no longer entwine around my legs and pull me down.

I loved those stories; I still do. Their vigor, their relentless optimism, their trust in nature and humanity—they told me to look at my own life in a different way. I wasn't able to achieve that immediately, but in time I came around to it, and I was able to see that moping on a day-to-day basis, which is what I had been doing, was absolutely no good for me.

Yes, I know, I know—it took me years to overcome the deep and morbid depression after my great loss. For more than a decade I endured constant self-blame for not having protected your mother. But once I got hold of the fact that I could learn from these legends, I slowly began to absorb the possibility. And one by one I saw the steps being cut into the rock of the mountain ahead of me, the steps I would climb to reach that high and sunny plateau.

When Jimmy Bermingham came into the pub that afternoon in County Kilkenny, I was at last a sunny person. My parents—your grandparents—might have told you how morose I used to be, how I used to mope each dawn, day, and nightfall, with not a word to throw to a dog. At last, though, by constant and consistent self-exhortation, by constant and consistent self-improvement, by constant and consistent self-awareness, I had taken myself up onto a place where the sun shone until it was time for the night to arrive.

When the night did arrive, it wasn't always cold, chilly night anymore, like all those darknesses I'd lived through; it was a night bathed by the moon and the stars. Benign winds blew.

I had put so much behind me, so many bad character traits, so many ill-informed tendencies—I had even allowed myself to be dragged through that pit of hell we call World War II, because I hadn't yet come into my full emotional domain. Well, by that afternoon at John Jacob's with Venetia I had surely arrived in the place I considered mine, the place of my very best self.

In myself, nothing much disturbed me. I had perspective; I had calm; I had good judgment. Not for me anymore those days of irrational behavior, of wild mood swings, of punches thrown in bars; of savage depressions, and money spent like water; of morbid sulking and dramatic self-pity. I had determined my way forward. And now that Venetia had returned, whatever her difficulties, I was about to be complete. Or so I told myself.

100

We slept soundly that night, in the lovely loft room of John Jacob's house. Before falling asleep, Venetia turned to me and put her head on my chest, her first overt movement of affection since our reuniting.

"Thank you for all this magic," she said. "My soul is on fire." Then, as she always did, she fell asleep in an instant.

The next morning, we both sprang awake at the same time—because we heard a noise. With our heads still full of John Jacob's wonderful story, we thought it an enchanting sound. I opened the door a little to hear it better.

John Jacob was singing. He was practicing scales. When he had run up and down the scale many times he launched into an exercise practiced by professional singers—no more than two words, "Bella Signora," but with the "Signora" drawn out into many, many notes. It had been designed, I assume, for coloratura sopranos, but he made a good job of it. At breakfast I said to him, "I didn't know there was such a thing as a coloratura baritone."

Venetia delighted him. He served her almost as a butler, quelling efforts by her to help, even to pour milk into her own tea. They began a long conversation about performance, about the need to identify what he called "the sagging pockets" in an audience. I listened, happy to see her so nearly returned to the woman of twenty-five years ago.

We stayed until eleven o'clock or so, and left with slow footsteps and many last moments of "Oh, I forgot to tell you . . ." and "Next time you come, remind me to tell you . . ." and so on.

She took my arm as we walked up that lane, a place I so often visit in my memory. Her deepest interests had been reignited. The Venetia I had first known wanted more than anything else to share the joys she had discovered with an audience.

I looked ahead to where I had parked the car by the roadside at the mouth of the lane. And I knew, in the part of my soul that's as deep as a mine to this day, the part whence all good and bad comes, the cavern where all prophecy, good and bad, is born, that fear had returned. And I recalled—again—the dangers of hearing a legend from John Jacob O'Neill. And the values.

PART FIVE

❄ ❄ ❄

A Carelessness with Death

101

Let me draw you, children, into the story at this point. I want to remind you of the parts you played, how kind you were and how compassionate— to all parties. For a moment it will feel like leaping ahead, but please bear with me.

On the evening of the day we left John Jacob O'Neill's house, I telephoned Marian Killeen from Limerick. I'd had time to think. I knew that we faced serious problems, and I'd made sure that we lost ourselves in the city, the first place where we tried to hide (of which more in a moment).

Marian told me that you'd visited her a second time. And she told me of her own visit to Miss Fay. In the hospital. Jack Stirling had broken one of Miss Fay's fine cheekbones with a punch.

In the theater he'd heard the gossip from the housekeeper May's friend, or her cousin, or some connection or other (Dublin is a village) and had ascertained the address where we'd been visiting. Miss Fay, telling the truth, said she didn't know where we were or where we'd gone. Drunk as a skunk, he hit her anyway. Repeatedly. Left her lying in her own blood on the floor of her tiled kitchen.

When you visited Marian's that second time, you knew what had happened—that I had taken Venetia away. Insofar as you could, you took over. Marian had found out about Miss Fay, had organized doctors, hospital care, and so on. And the two of you, abject with apology, visited Miss Fay. A long time afterward, she told me that this had brought her great comfort, especially when you reassured her that Jack wouldn't return. She even made jokes with you, I gather, regarding "Gentleman" Jack.

By now his stint at the Olympia had ended, and he told you two things: That he'd cancel his upcoming shows at different venues. And that he'd devote all his time to pursuing your mother. You feared murderous intent. How did you keep calm? Or did you?

And you knew nothing of the other characters in this lethal farce. It had all become much worse than you could imagine. The word "ludicrous" would have leapt to mind if it hadn't all been so frightening. D'you remember that I mentioned earlier how violence hung in the very atmosphere of the country?

102

At the top of the lane, the mist of the night had clouded the windows of the car. By the hedge, a red-haired boy waited. He handed me a letter and fled on his bicycle.

They think you gave the cops names and addresses. Go. Get out of the country. J.B.

The boy disappeared, hell for leather, up a track on which I could never drive—gone before I could get hold of him. Venetia stared after him. At that exact moment another car arrived and blocked the lane. Out climbed Little Boy and a uniformed policeman.

"Well, now. Thanks for waiting." He grinned with sarcasm.

"What do you want?"

"You, Little Boy."

How do I play this? Don't fight him. Use cunning. If you can find some.

"Where do you want us to go?"

He looked at me, daring to believe that I'd comply. "So what you gonna do, make a statement?"

I nodded.

"Name names?"

I nodded again.

"Times and places?"

I nodded once more. "Sure."

"Gerry," he said to the uniformed man, "get in there beside him and don't take your eye offa him."

I said, "No room. Look." On the back seat lay our luggage, as untidy as Venetia had ever been. "I'll follow you," I said. "I'm sick of all this."

"Any tricks," he warned, "and you'll be singing high notes." He looked at Venetia. "We want to talk to you, too, miss."

They climbed into their car, moved up the road a little, and waited.

I knew every stick and stone of that countryside. You can guess what happened next. Little Boy had his car pointed in one direction, and I took off in the other. We raced away from him. Two steep dips on that crooked old road helped.

To my left ran an old cart track that connected to another road through woods. I turned at a sharp angle. Steamed the hundred yards into the trees. Hidden from the road. Stopped and waited. Opened my door. Heard Little Boy's car roar past the entrance to the cart track. He hasn't seen us. Climbed back in and began to move forward. Slow, even, and steady across rough ground. I found the old track, in better condition than I might have expected, protected by the woodland.

By now Venetia had begun to weep.

I've slept in this wood. At least twice. Over there, I think. Can I see it? Yes. An old limekiln. Like a large, unfinished igloo. Made of stone. Cold as snow. Slept there in bad times. But is this time any better? Jesus!

Venetia began to rock back and forth.

Stop the car. Attend to her. You're clear for the moment. Stop the car. Get out. Go around to her door, open it, and squat there. Talk to her. Stop the car!

"What's the matter, my love?" *Why won't she answer?* "Venetia, come on, tell me." *What does that shake of the head mean?* "Are you all right?" *Face streaked with tears. She's trembling. Is she well or unwell?* "We'll be safe soon. I promise." *There it goes again, that silent shake of the head, like a grieving child. In a woman her age.* "Venetia. Please tell me!"

She leaned back, head on the seat, eyes closed, tears streaming down.

"You're wanted by the police. Oh, God. You're some kind of awful criminal. I can't handle this."

Nothing but tears have I seen. Since I found her. Crying more than not. Why? What am I doing wrong? These events, they're not my fault. Is this all going wrong, was this all wrong to begin with? Has the dream fallen apart? But I still love her. I love her more than ever.

In failure I stood back, stepped away from the car, leaned against a tree, and closed my eyes. I waited some moments for the ruckus inside my head to calm down. The sounds of the woods took over—leaves, birds, a distant cow, rustles at my feet—and murmurs in my mind. The hard cylinder of the tree began to assail my shoulders. And then matters changed again. Without as much as the noise of a footfall, Venetia crossed the few paces—the hundred miles—between us and laid her head on my shoulder.

"I'm sorry," she said. "I don't recognize this dreadful world of yours."

"Neither do I."

"I think we must be under some old curse," she said. "Probably from the evil in my family."

We stood without moving, my arms around her shoulders. Her shaking stopped. *What is the way back to her, the way in? What have I done wrong? Twenty-five years of longing and wanting and yearning, and now that she's back again, now that the long dream has been realized, why and how am I wrecking it?*

A sardonic voice in me took over. *Because, you idiot, you do nothing but whine. You're hesitant, indecisive. And when you try to be decisive, you make bad choices. You consort with risky and ruthless people. This is no way to build a new world. With the love of your life? No, not at all. Stop thinking about yourself, you donkey. Get some practical steps going. Look at yourself. Why are two, maybe three, lethal groups of people now pursuing you? You must have some responsibility in this. And you have no way of coping with it.*

We shook ourselves loose and walked back to the car.

"Let me try to make us safe," I said.

"Please," said Venetia, and in the car she fell asleep.

In that part of Ireland, there's a handsome peak—they call it a mountain, but it's more of a modest hill. Forest stretches on the generally bare ground like whiskers on a face most of the way up, and a forestry trail climbs through it. I knew the views from the highest point, three hun-

dred and sixty degrees; and I needed half of that to see where our pursuers might be. (You can grasp how few cars we had in the Irish countryside
during the 1950s!)

With Venetia still asleep, I reached the top of the trail. From the edge
of the trees I could look back at where we'd been. Not a car in sight.
Some farm machinery. Fields here and there, dotted with animals. A
river. We could stay here all day.

And we did. She remained asleep, and in the late afternoon, when she
woke up, declared hunger.

103

A day of hard thinking produced this notion: we need to lie low until we
get to a port. And by my reckoning, we couldn't hide in small places
where the jungle drums beat; they'd find us, any of them, within hours.

*Food and seclusion? Where can we have both? Not a village. Not even a
town. Try a city. Where I know a good man.*

I had never seen Mr. MacManus in his bearskin coat—although I had
seen the coat. It was impossible to avoid; it hung like a live thing on the
back of his front door. The "occasion merchant" told me the story:

"Didn't I find it at an estate sale? One of the rooms had been locked
off for years. Nobody had a key."

Since Mr. MacManus had agreed to buy the entire contents of the
house, they'd allowed him to break the lock.

He found a room that, he said "was as fabulous as the Arabian night-
shirts." (I never interrupted him when he flowed like that: too many
gems would have fallen loose.) "There was jewels the size of your knuckles, and a big bowl for washing your behind, a French thing, I think they
call it a 'be-there'; a woman from North Cork bought it from me—
they're very clean down that way."

The "jewels" proved less than authentic, costume jewelry from an
ancient music hall act. However, he also turned up an early Winchester

rifle, a cache of antique maps, and half a dozen bottles of homemade hooch, or "poteen," made from potatoes.

"It'd put hairs on your chest," said Mr. MacManus, "whether you wanted them or not." And hanging there, too, he found the massive coat.

The sign on his door said, "Back in Five Minutes." Venetia asked, with calm logic, "How do we know when the five minutes began?"

We waited half an hour. As we were talking about driving away, I saw the great figure lumbering along a narrow lane off Catherine Street. He looked like a creature from one of those films of grizzlies in the wild, his arms out from his body, akimbo and relaxed. His hat had a homburg shape, but made of the same ursine fur? Impossible. No: when Venetia later complimented him on the hat, he told us that his wife had made it for him. The coat had been tailored for a man of about six feet, seven inches tall.

"A giant altogether," said Mr. MacManus. "So Mamie cut off the hem, and she draped and glued the bear's fur to an old homburg that had belonged to a priest, and that's my hat."

I, who had years of practice in asking for a bed for the night, had no problem in approaching Mr. MacManus.

"It'd be an honor," he said, bowing to Venetia. "And we have new sanitation." (I almost asked him if it included a "be-there.")

She thanked him, and something in the way she spoke made him spin around and stare at her. He clasped his hands in front of him like a man meeting a bishop and said, "Oh, Holy God, tell me it is and tell me it isn't." His eyes shone like a child's. "Didn't I see you, weren't you in a show or something?" He wrestled with his memory. "Isn't your name Alicia Kelly?" (Given his verbal erratics, we were lucky he didn't say "Alopecia.")

"Venetia," we both said together.

"D'you remember—of course you do." He took her hand and chanted, " 'O, young Lochinvar is come out of the west, / Through all the wide border his steed was the best.' I used to follow your show across the country. And you're not dead at all—I heard you were killed in an accident at sea. 'Lochinvar' was my favorite poem ever, and nobody ever recited it as well as yourself."

To my great surprise, Mr. MacManus had surrounded himself with luxury. No hotel I knew could offer the same level of comfort: rich, deep beds, superb bathrooms, sumptuous towels.

"The two of you are the first people to use one of my guest rooms," he said.

"How many guest rooms do you have?" Venetia asked. *Good. She's engaging again.*

"I've six," he said.

"You must have a lot of guests."

"Oh, not really, Alicia, but the way I look at it, you never know who'll show up, and I always like to be prepared."

We ate that evening with Mr. MacManus—sandwiches as high as bricks. Venetia managed by breaking off chunks and gathering such contents—ham, onion, chicken, cheese—as fell to her plate. Mamie never appeared, though Mr. MacManus spoke of her all the time.

Some years later, I discovered that Mamie had been dead for more than three years before our stay there. He simply needed to keep her alive—and that is something I so profoundly understand.

104

We stayed in warm comfort for two days and two nights. I had the crude idea that the longer we stayed, the more Venetia would forget that we had problems. Each morning we rose to the sound of talk coming from below. Too early for Mr. MacManus to have customers—so who's down there? At breakfast he said, "I was just talking to Mamie. She's gone out to get some messages." The second morning he said, "You just missed Mamie; she's gone over to her mother's. The mother isn't at all well."

Mr. MacManus, in his shirtsleeves (and amazing primrose suspenders), had one of those stomachs that seems unconnected to the rest of the body. It wobbled like a great, separate egg when he walked. I saw Venetia looking at it, transfixed.

I had some thinking to do. As I often did, I worked out my thought process on paper. I still have those notes, and here they are: *Dilemma:*

unreal. Being pursued by IRA fellows who think I mocked them. Also pur-
sued by thuggish detective who believes by now that I must be a member of
the IRA. What to do? First thought remains unchanged: Get to a port with a
ferry. Or an airport. Only two on the island: Shannon, Dublin. Get to
France. Or Spain, for the sun. No extradition.

Other dilemma: puzzling and upsetting—Venetia's state of mind. Yet I
glimpse her in there. Can I get her out of there? If we go abroad, will she be
different? She thinks there's a third possibility—that J. Stirling is also follow-
ing us.

First option therefore—the major priority: buy time to think and orga-
nize. Then choose airport. Arrange money. Make schedule. Explain to Vene-
tia. Contact twins.

At this stage I knew nothing of Miss Fay and her injuries. Or of Jack's
ranting.

I decided that we would travel the longer distances by night and the
shorter stages by day, to try to keep Venetia's mood light. With a map
from the car, I worked out a schedule that would take us by quiet roads,
never seeming hurried, to each best next place. An irony surfaced: our
safest point of departure, least scrutinized by those searching for us,
would be a place I hadn't thought of; the forbidden territory of north
Belfast had an airport.

On that first morning I read in Mr. MacManus's newspaper, "ALL
BORDER POINTS CLOSED FOLLOWING BOMBING." A "fierce outbreak of
violence" near the town of Newry had activated "the greatest security
operations since the war." Not a problem for us, with my knowledge of
all the many roads. Besides, no general alert had been issued, and I had
no sense from any of the reports that the police north or south were stopping people and asking questions. Their searches seemed specific.

As ever in Ireland, most lives remained normal: no war zones, no
emergency measures, no martial law. Indeed, if we hadn't had newspaper
reports, nobody would have known that a new guerrilla campaign had
broken out. In general, the country seemed to show no visible support
for the IRA—except at an occasion that called for a rekindling of ancient
emotions, such as the two funerals.

I read down the page. No great depth of reporting had yet begun.
Given the official disapproval and condemnation, I wondered whether it

ever might. We had a degree of self-censorship; the politicians and the church spoke, and the newspapers barked their echoes. Thus did the country build some kind of ill-defined moral antagonism to the men who called themselves "freedom fighters."

Nobody tried for balance. Not a reporter or columnist addressed the discrimination in Northern Ireland—no jobs for Catholic men, bad housing for Catholic families, who were always subject to police harassment. In the south we knew so little of what went on in the place that we dismissed with the vague term "up there."

105

We left Limerick by quiet roads. *Can we learn to tolerate any of this nonsense? And for how long? Get out. Let it die down. Find a safe town somewhere in Europe. Germany, maybe one of those villages I saw during the war. Settle down. New life. You have enough money.*

Did the same thoughts course through Venetia's mind? I had no idea. She wanted to get out of this stupidity; of that I felt sure. But to settle with me again? From her demeanor, I couldn't begin to guess.

Unclear and confused, I tried to buy time. Once we were clear of the city, I drove down a small country lane, looking for quiet, linking roads. It led nowhere. I turned the car in the tightest of spaces and headed back the way we'd come.

"Where are we going?"

I didn't answer, and I didn't look at her. Some miles later, I turned right. The previous foray had been a left turn. This road led only to a farm lane with a lone white house in the distance. I knew the place, had visited there once, hadn't stayed.

"Is this the place you're looking for?"

"No, not really."

I retraced our route. Out on the road again, I looked for signposts. It seemed that there was nobody in Ireland that day—which is to say that every road and every yard and every village seemed empty. Far away, I saw a man in a hill field with a black-and-white dog—and nothing and nobody else.

"Do you know where we're going?" Venetia sat up straight. "You don't, do you?"

I said, "We're going down here onto another main road." True, but I hadn't planned it.

"Shouldn't you be avoiding main roads?"

I said, "That's what I've been trying to do."

As though I'd had a plan. As though I hadn't been screaming at myself inside my head: *You imbecile! How did you let your life come to this? What kind of fool are you? Where are you going?*

She said, "Are you as frightened as I am?"

"Venetia, I don't know what to do about you."

For a moment it looked as though I might have made a breakthrough. It didn't happen. She caught her breath, sat forward, braced herself—but then sagged and sat back. She closed her eyes. Catatonic again. Unreachable.

See if you can shake her out of it. Ask her. Go on, ask her the crucial question. Say to her, "Have I got this all wrong? Did I completely do the wrong thing? I'd hoped that you had continued to feel the same about me as I did about you. Was I—am I—wrong in that?"

James had a good friend who lived in a woodland thirty miles from Limerick. We now sat within his radius. I had been there twice, one time with James, once alone. The man, George Williamson, had married an Irish traveler girl, a "tinker," to use the term they didn't like. He interested me because he collected stories of the Gypsies and knew some of their old dialects, including Shelta, the Romany-sounding tongue in which some of them traded horses.

I admired his house, which faced south in a clearing of the woods; a member of the Guinness family had built it as a love nest for a nineteenth-century mistress. It had oriel windows hanging out over a quiet garden. Bookshelved walls swung open to reveal secret rooms. The main fireplace had been carved in white marble and had birds on branches, warbling etched notes by a vivacious fountain.

We drove the mile-long avenue through the forest that George Williamson maintained with love and passion. A self-educated arborist, he knew how to graft, to bud. "I like trees to marry," he said over and over, and on any walk near his house you'd find interesting and cultivated hybrids. Half apple–half pear was the least of it.

He held to the same principles of hospitality as Randall: turn up any time, stay as long as you like. George had a quiet army of servants—"the H. H." he called them, the "hired help," and in his deep seclusion he lived the life of a Renaissance prince. He even dressed for dinner each evening, typically in a brocade smoking jacket with a stiff dress shirt, white bow tie, and monogrammed slippers that had belonged to his grandfather.

Under the arch, past the peacocks on the acre of lawn, the house glowed in the sun. The crenellations around the windows looked like the lacework of a giant seamstress. George's butler stepped from the great doorway, immaculate in a black suit.

"Good afternoon, madam, sir. How nice to see you. Mr. Williamson will be so pleased."

Such an intriguing house—such excellent taste. A Parisian hostess might have created it. Not for the first time did I wonder about Mare, his dark-eyed tinker wife, whom I'd met briefly on my two previous visits. True, she had been dressed exquisitely, but that didn't answer the question of where and how she'd acquired her dazzling sensibility.

George knew that we all had such questions. Mare said nothing; I had never heard her utter a word. James, who had spoken to her, said that she had the same fast, undulating accent of her people, whom he knew on the road in their bright horse-drawn caravans.

"Ben!" George Williamson had a handshake of oak. "How. Welcome. You. Are." He spoke every word one at a time, as though sentences hadn't yet been invented. I introduced Venetia; she didn't flinch when I said, "My wife."

George took her hands in his. "Such. A. Delight."

Within minutes, a tray of drinks had appeared in the hall. Whiskey. Nothing else. With six glasses. He drank as I'd always seen him do: one, two, three, and then he relaxed with the fourth glass. As I'd often done myself.

"How long can you stay?" Before I could answer, he turned to Venetia and said, "My wife died last month."

We both gasped. I said, "George, I'm very sorry."

"She walked across this floor, I was watching her, she went to fix some branches that she had arranged in that tall pot over there. I heard her grunt. She put a hand to her head. Swayed. Side to side. Fell. Dead when she hit the floor. Brain. Hemorrhage."

His eyes shone. Tears? I thought so. Later I wasn't so sure.

A maid showed us to a room. Venetia made for the window seat and looked down at the garden. I bounced on the four-poster bed. A large engraving of Napoleon hung above the fireplace.

"What a strange man," Venetia said. "Hidden in the woods."

"He doesn't allow photographs," I said. "People have wanted to write books about this place."

"I can see why."

I said, "Not just the architecture. During the building, a feud broke out between two local families—stonemasons and carpenters. Each killed members of the other family."

"Look!" Venetia pointed.

Across the grass, behind tall hedges, two maids in full uniforms of black dress and starched white cap and apron were leading—I counted—four, five, six small children to a perfect stable block.

"Whose are they?" I mused.

At dinner we asked. "We saw some children," Venetia said.

"My. Dear. You must have been mistaken. When the shadows fall here, the light does. Strange. Dances." He knew how to close down a topic.

Three of us sat around the end of a long table, Venetia on George Williamson's right. We finished a starter course of piquant smoked trout with lime jelly. When the three manservants had taken our plates away, George stretched out his right hand and caressed Venetia's breasts. Casual. Relaxed. Interested.

What do you do? Venetia did nothing. I did nothing. George said, "Very beautiful."

The next course came, potato and onion soup. Repeat performance. This time Venetia, more prepared, caught George's hand. She pushed it away.

"Don't you like me touching you?"

I said, "Venetia hasn't been well."

"So. Tactful." George beamed at me. "Not many guests know that you don't insult your host."

And not many hosts know that you don't insult your guests. Try it one more time and I'll break every bone in your face.

But I smiled, and we all dined on.

After dinner, we walked to a drawing room—big house, long walk. George put his hand on Venetia's backside. I didn't see it, but I guessed it from her little forward trot away from him. I made sure to sit beside her for the last hour of the night.

Back in the four-poster Napoleon room, Venetia lay down at once. She fell into a sleep so deep that I was able to pull the bedding out from underneath her and cover her without waking her. All night she remained immobile. I sat on the window seat for hours, looking at the starlight and the shadowed garden below. From time to time I checked that Venetia breathed.

Somewhere around one o'clock in the morning, I heard a noise in the passageway outside our room. When I eased open our door, I saw one of the aproned maids leave a doorway and walk in the opposite direction. The next morning, as we walked down to breakfast, George Williamson came from the same doorway.

106

The lovers spent their third night on the shores of the lakes in Westmeath. There they found an empty castle . . .

Though far from Westmeath, I knew a castle. Within a few hours' drive.

When Venetia woke the next morning, she sat up and grabbed her hair with both hands.

"Easy, easy," I said.

"Oh, my God. Oh, my God."

"You're fine, you're with me, I'm here." The ironic voice in my head added, *If that's what you think of as "fine."*

Like a cat with quick paws, she ran her hands around her face. She made little whimpering sounds, scarcely audible. And then made hand-washing gestures. *Don't rub off your skin.*

I knew these symptoms: habits of fear. This woman woke up every morning afraid. It would take me years to heal her. If I got the chance. I knew enough to understand that keeping her from returning to Jack Stirling, no matter how illogical that action would be, might be the battle I'd have to fight.

"There's a place we can go," I said.

"Well, we've stayed with the bear. And we met the wolf last night," said Venetia. *Good. Touch of her old humor.*

"How about an empty castle?"

She said, "I thought that's what you were doing. Does this mean that you die when all this is over?"

"Think of it as a play," I said. "How would Shakespeare have written it?"

This engaged her. She half-smiled. "By now he'd have poisoned somebody. And stabbed somebody else."

"We can change the ending of the legend," I said.

She sighed and yawned. "Take me to your castle, Sir Ben."

More humor? This might be good. Don't push your luck; keep it light.

The hours of wakefulness had given me my plans for the next three days. My confusion had abated. At last I knew where I was going and at what pace.

We stopped at a village shop for supplies, enough to keep us going for a night.

107

The gate to the castle estate stood open.

"What's the name of this place?" Venetia asked.

"Kilshane," I answered, and I told her the story—the not unusual family argument, with one member of the family keeping the place in some kind of order and the others fighting over who should pay for it and, ultimately, inherit it.

"None of them wants to give it up, but they refuse to meet the full upkeep. It has a hundred and thirty acres, though most of it needs to be cleared."

At the steps to the terrace, two bicycles stood together, interlinked like lovers.

"Wait here," I said, and parked at the edge of the overgrown lawn. I tiptoed up the high steps to the open front door. In the hallway stood two teenagers kissing. I coughed, and they jumped.

Neither tried to run away; both came forward. Fifteen, I guessed, and tall for their ages, she dark-haired, he with fair curls and green eyes.

"Hallo," he said. Local accent, but well-spoken. "Are you lost?"

"Are you staying here?"

The girl blushed, and the boy answered: "No, this is where we meet. To be private."

I said, "I understand."

The boy said, "Do you know this place? It used to belong to the O'Connor family. They were descended from the high kings."

"I've stayed here once or twice."

"The roof is all caved in." He beckoned me, and I followed them. The pair had impressive composure. "Look," he said. "Isn't that awful?"

Most of the roof's rear slope had collapsed. We looked up through the jagged rafters at the clear blue sky. "It has affected the whole house," he said.

"What did it?"

She answered: "We'd like to think it was a mighty creature. But it was a huge branch that fell in a storm."

The boy said, "Well, that was a kind of a mighty creature, in a way."

I said, "Where are you from?"

She answered for both: "I'm from the town; he's from over the hill."

He added, "That's right. I'm the boy from over the hill."

The girl asked, "Are you by yourself?"

"No, the car is over there at the top of the avenue."

She darted away, and in a moment I heard voices.

"I'd be getting lonely out there if it was me," said the girl returning.

Venetia followed the girl to where we stood in the desolate rear of the building. Part of a bird's nest from last year lay on the floor. The main shank of the fallen branch stuck up outside the door like a broken limb.

Venetia said to me, "You found your woodland creatures."

The boy, quick and bright, said, "That's what we are, Bea, isn't it?"

"We wear clothes made from leaves," she said, and they laughed. Impossible not to laugh with them.

"So you're escaping," I said.

"From prying eyes," said the girl.

"We're allowing ourselves to flourish," said the boy.

"And we're intruding," said Venetia.

I couldn't resist the tease. "They were kissing," I told Venetia.

She defended them: "I hope so."

The girl blushed, but the boy, self-possessed and relaxed, said, "It was practicing, really. We both want to get good at it."

Venetia laughed—my heart strengthened.

We said goodbye to them. The boy apologized.

"I'm sorry you can't stay here," he said, as though he owned the place. "But it'd be uncomfortable for your wife."

As we drove away Venetia said, "What charming children." After a moment, she added, "Are you sorry that we won't have birds and squirrels and badgers serve us berries, nuts, fruits, and mead?"

108

Padlocks on the front gate kept us out. But I had read someplace that bringing a distressed person face-to-face with a deep and important memory can help. Time to try it. We drove through Mr. Treacy's gateway and down his farm lane to the front of the house.

With all the windows shuttered, Goldenfields looked like a huge blind person, its face turned to the sun. Someone had been cutting the grass under the great beech tree. The irrelevant white fence that runs up through the field had a new coat of paint. Maybe the new owners had already retained Billy Moloney?

Venetia sat up, alert. "You and I—we came up that way." She pointed. "From the well and the trees, from Miss Fay's cottage. Has that been sold, too?" When I nodded, she said, "And didn't we sit in that room?" She pointed to a window.

We'd always had a hiding place for the key, under a slate outside the back door. No reason to think the new owners might not have followed suit—and they weren't expected to move in for another two months.

It has an echo! The house in which I grew up has an echo. Am I charmed or hurt? Both.

Nothing in the kitchen—no cups on the hooks, no plates flashing from the shelves, no great black pots on the stove, no smell of what my father called "You-you-your mother's eternal soup."

In the hallway, Venetia paused and pointed to one of the central motifs of my life: the colored leaves thrown onto the floor of the porch by the sun through the stained glass.

"If I'd grown up in this house," she said, "I'd have that picture in my head every day."

Children, the two of you never have to stop and think about your closeness to each other. You were born with it. I had by now been validating, over and over, my feelings toward your mother. Looking for confirmation. Waiting for proof that my choice had ever been accurate. That I had been right to have let nobody else into my soul.

She hadn't affirmed it, and my need for her to do something, say something was getting more frantic. She had looked, as you know, like a different person. But that moment, that remark about the porch—it washed over me like a healing tide. A small thing, yes. But I clutched at it. I had little else.

And she went on to make similar connecting remarks. In the drawing room, she stood before the dank and empty fireplace.

"Now. Let me think." Hand to chin. "Your chair was there." She pointed. "Which means that I sat here. With my head against your legs. Stand over here."

She's retelling herself the story. She's rebuilding the story of Ben and Venetia.

I stood. She dropped to the floor and arranged herself against my legs. "And I sat like this, didn't I?"

"You told me the story of my father and you," I said.

Silence.

"I had gone down to the cottage by the river. You walked up to meet me in the wood and you kissed me," I said.

Silence.

"I had never been kissed before," I said.

Silence.

"You told me that you wouldn't let me down," I said.

Silence.

We remained like that until I said, "I'm sorry, but I have to move; my leg is gone dead."

Venetia leaned forward to let me ease away. She put her hands on the floor to either side of herself and stared into the empty fireplace.

We couldn't stay at Goldenfields. Too painful. Too empty now, and nowhere to lay our heads and not a warm scrap of cloth to cover us. I'd have managed—God knows I had enough experience of rough nights—but I wouldn't have put Venetia through it. And, an hour or so distant, we had options. Or so I thought.

109

As we left from Mr. Treacy's farmyard gate, I looked back down the road. A black car sat outside Goldenfields. Facing away from us. Never saw us—whoever they were. I drove off in low gear so as not to rev the engine, and I had a blinding, tear-making a fit of coughing. When I had finished, Venetia spoke. "Do you know why I allowed your father to get close to me?"

I said, "You told me that it was because he spoke so lovingly of me."

"He had red hair," she said. "When I was a little girl I had a toy called—you won't believe this—'Harry.' It was a stuffed fox with a bushy tail. I believed it was real, that it chatted to me. Then I lost it. I suspect that my mother stole it. Because I was so attached to it. And I believed that one day the fox would come back. And he did."

After that, the silence of the house took over the car.

I reviewed the day. I'd done the right thing by getting Venetia out of George Williamson's clutches—literally. She'd gone to sleep at ten o'clock, so I'd felt it all right to wake her at seven. I'd found a way of easing her up from these deep, buried slumbers: I sat on the edge of the bed, foraged with a cat's-paw touch until I found one of her hands, held it and stroked it. Sometimes it took five minutes; sometimes she awoke at once.

As she'd done that morning. Which surprised me. Her waking had deep absence in it; her eyes held a generation of troubled feelings. And the repeated "Oh, my God." And the fear. But no sign that George's attentions might have hurt her spirit somewhere.

On the road we'd made poor time. Stopped twice for Venetia to be ill. Stopped a third time for her to get out and walk into a field and sit on the grass. Stopped for lunch, which she ate. Stopped after lunch for her to throw it all up.

110

Does it always rain at Randall's? Tell Venetia about the lily pads on Randall's lake.

"In August one year, hundreds of lily pads. I wanted to think of them as stepping-stones."

No reaction. And in Randall's house, no lights anywhere. *That's strange.*

I walked around the side, through the doorway that led to the almost secret backyard. The studio blazed with lights from the big windows. I rapped on the glass. Not a person could I see—and then Randall appeared, his great head angled, his beak nose shadowed, shading his eyes with his hand to look out into the dark.

"Randall, it's me, Ben. I have Venetia with me."

He heard me. I knew it. He turned his back and walked away, back to the part of the studio I couldn't see. I rapped again. And again.

Randall didn't appear that night. Nor did anybody—not Annette, or Elma, or Jimmy. I tried the front door, hauled on that bellpull. We know, don't we, when we're not wanted somewhere. We drove away and we drove through the night, skirting Dublin, heading north. I knew more than one road across the border. Venetia slept again. No surprise.

111

We stopped at Jonesborough. I knew a house where we could get a late meal. Its anomalies also made me feel that we had some protection, because Jonesborough didn't know on which side of the Irish border it stood, and the police on both sides liked to stay uncertain about it.

Venetia ate: no matter what her emotional state, she always ate. I tried to entertain her by describing how ludicrous the border could be.

"The preacher is in the north, and his congregation is in the south. The border runs just underneath the pulpit."

"You told me that years ago," she said, in a voice so neutral that I couldn't judge her thoughts.

Conversation didn't take place, not even chatter. There did come a moment when she seemed apologetic.

"I think I must be very tired," she said.

"We'll rest when we get there." I took her hand, but she didn't respond. "Not long now. I'm sorry about all this; I never expected any of it. It's not how I live."

She took back her hand, though not in a harsh way.

"We both need sleep."

I said, "Let me get us close to the airport."

Which didn't happen. The woman of the house came to the table and said, "If youse are going to Belfast, the airport's closed."

As she walked away, Venetia looked at me, her eyes asking, "Now what?"

I said, "We're as near to Dublin Airport as to Belfast."

"But I thought you said they'd be watching for us."

"I know. We'll have to take a chance."

She pursed her lips and looked away. "This is ridiculous. And, any-way, I'm an American citizen."

"Won't make much difference."

We drove back the way we'd come. In an even deeper silence. After midnight, I pulled off the road and drove to the beach. I knew every lane around here; some outstanding storytellers lived north of Dublin, and I'd visited all their houses.

"We're half an hour from the airport," I said. "We'll take the first flight to anywhere. But now we'll sleep."

From the back seat I took the heavy Foxford rug, climbed out of the car, went around to the passenger side, and tucked Venetia in. To the murmur of the sea, fifty yards away, we fell asleep, both exhausted.

Dawn's rosy fingers woke me. It takes a few seconds, doesn't it, to wake up in strange surroundings? But—I was alone in the car.

The shot of panic stopped, though—because I saw, far, far away, a distant figure in a dark coat on the beach, near the water.

Such a benign morning. I eased myself into the world, strolled toward the shoreline. *History's repeating itself,* I thought, *and this time I won't get it wrong, like I did on the beach in Florida. Don't rush her. Give her some space. Let her enjoy the water, the air, the sky.*

A freighter inched across the horizon. Nearer, a dredger hauled mud up into its huge mouth. Indignant gulls scrawed and cawked. The water lapped my shoes, and I pranced back. *Too cold.*

Taking my own sweet time, I began to saunter in the opposite direc-tion. After a few hundred yards I turned back.

Still there. Far distant. Standing. Looking out to sea. What's she thinking? Leave her alone.

I turned again, the same exercise, and when I turned back she had begun to walk in the opposite direction. The distance shrank her almost out of sight. *Soon I'll have to remind her that we have a plane to catch.*

As slow as Jimmy Bermingham's encyclopedia-salesman snail, I began to follow. She continued to walk. I hustled a little. *She's not looking back, so I can walk faster.* And still she walked. *I'm not closing the gap. Better hurry it up.*

I stepped out, long strides. The distance grew tighter.

We pass each other face-to-face at the sum of our speeds; we overtake at the difference between them. In this case, what? Two miles per hour. Go faster.

Instinct. Dreaded, bloody instinct. She continued to walk—so why my panic? She was walking normally; this wasn't someone trying to get away from me. I ran.

"Venetia!" *Okay. Take it easy. Don't show her any agitation.* "We should go."

I sprinted, and called again, a lower shout.

"Venetia!"

Fifty yards from me she turned—a wrinkled woman, puzzled. *What's happened to her?*

"Oh, I'm sorry. I thought you were someone else." The woman showed no anxiety. "Did you see anybody—" I began. "You didn't by any chance see somebody wearing a navy blue coat like yours, ma'am?"

"I've this old coat thirty years," she said in a surging local accent. "My daughter's always at me to get a new one, sure isn't this fine? I'll get a few more years out if it yet."

"Sorry to trouble you," I said. "You didn't see anyone, did you? I mean, earlier?"

"There was a car up there," she said, pointing.

"Up where?" I turned to find her direction. Two hundred yards down the beach from where we'd parked.

She got into a car? With a stranger? She wouldn't have done that; she must have known him. Christ! No! But how? How? He can't have followed us, can he? No. He'd have had to have been to the border and back. Unless she'd had some contact—but no, that's ridiculous and impossible. But she's gone.

I thanked the woman and raced back, going first to where she said the car had been. Sure enough—fresh tire tracks on the sand. And, a few yards in, wet tracks on the lane: he had driven close to the waves across this firm shore, and he must have done so before I woke up.

Two cottages sat side by side, shuttered and curtained—summer places. Along the lane a small farmhouse: no sign of life yet. I walked and half-ran to the main road but found not a trace. From there I cut back to the mouth of the lane where I had parked—in case she had chosen to stroll. I saw nothing more than a derelict house to my left, my own car just ahead, and beyond that the endless sea.

A thought—awful of me—took me to the water's edge. *Filled her pockets with stones and just walked?* Call it an exaggerated response. Who knew, though, how Venetia's mind was changing? I scanned the waves. Nothing.

Time to think. Get a handle on the timing. Does she have any money? Is she now at the airport?

I drove two miles each way, up and down the road, hoping maybe she had simply decided to go for a walk. No trace. My focus changed. To her state of mind. Not good. And, of course, it hadn't been. Only in flashes had I seen the old Venetia, the laughing and thoughtful young woman of the carefree past. Accusation seemed her strongest suit: I hadn't come to find her; I had now brought her into dangerous living; I had misjudged her needs; I had never considered what had happened to her.

Guilty as charged? Or not? I couldn't make sense anymore. How ludicrous could it all get? Police and gunmen on my trail, and I, now, on Venetia's. It had to stop. But first I had to find her.

No police at the airport. You can't visualize how different air travel was in those days. We even had a classy restaurant, from whose windows you could watch the planes take off and land. People came there for a day out. As to a resort.

I had the presence of mind to use the washroom and eat breakfast. Watching everything that moved. From a table in the corner. Behind a newspaper.

I can cut this short by telling you what you already know: I didn't find her, not at Dublin Airport nor in Dublin, not at all.

And I never found her. I gave up looking for her. What was the point? Where could she have been? Once I had established later that day that you, Ben and Louise, hadn't heard from her, what else could I have done?

All kinds of possibilities crossed my mind, from doom to deliberate. Death or abduction? Not death, no; she still had that life force. Abduction? In which case I knew whom to blame.

From this moment you can track my thoughts. You knew Jack Stirling better than I did; you lived with him for all of your formative years. Did he have enough cunning to find us and take Venetia? Yes, he did. And didn't he have friends who looked less than sanitary? Yes, he did. And didn't he have a motive? Yes, he did. I had humiliated him, and so had Venetia—at least I bet he thought so. So I called you—remember?

"How's Mom?" you asked, and I knew that you didn't know.

You told me long afterward how he raged after that snatch from the Olympia stage. I'd have raged, too, in his shoes. Trouble was: if, while so motivated and furious, he had found Venetia and taken her—what would he now do to her?

Hello, obsession, my old friend. Here we go again. Don't look for her; look for him. And we hadn't even "completed" John Jacob's legend.

112

If I had known the truth, would I have behaved differently? No. Hatred had set in. My spirit fed off it. That's an admission of baseness—that I should harbor such a feeling. I tried to justify it to myself by saying, *Big tree, big shadow; big love, big hate.* It gave me temporary ease.

Jealousy drove it. And a sense of inferiority. Venetia had gone back to him because he had come and found her. Enticed her away. And I hadn't done that—at least, not soon enough. Worse, she preferred the urgency of his violent attention to the quiet of my peaceful care.

So I sat alone in Miss Fay's house and brooded and plotted. I didn't let myself do much else all day. When, two days later, the pair of you didn't return my calls or reply to my notes, and when I couldn't find you because you had moved from your digs—that confirmed my fear. And my fury. The "family" had come back together again. My search began—for him, not for her.

If he wasn't working Dublin, where was he? He had canceled, you said. But somehow I knew that he hadn't gone back to the States. You might have done; that was possible—but I felt that he hadn't. And I gambled on that.

The National Library took in all the Irish provincial newspapers, most of them weekly. I began to trawl them, working in that benign room with the green lampshades on each small table.

Week after week, nothing. The *Westmeath Examiner,* the *Kerryman,* the *Connacht Tribune,* the *Anglo-Celt*—every Monday I flipped through more than a dozen newspapers. North, south, east, and west. Some appeared on Thursdays, some on Fridays, typically in time for the advertisers to hit Saturday shoppers. All carried notices of entertainments in towns, cities, villages.

It looked as though Jack had stopped working. Then I changed my mind and assumed that he had returned to the United States. With Venetia. With all of you. Then I changed back again, and kept searching. Partly because of my obsessive nature (well honed, you might say, in the years of holding your mother in my heart!) and partly because of a hunch. He had to eat. He liked to perform. He had an independent air, and enough aggression to carry on his life.

I found him. A pub conversation, overheard late at night, near Dublin, alerted me. Two men had come back from a soccer game in Liverpool, but the night before they'd also gone to a variety show there, and Jack had topped the bill. I muscled in by saying with enthusiasm that I had seen that show.

They'd loved it, and people like to share unusual delights. Did he have that gorgeous assistant? No, they replied, but he'd apologized and said she'd soon be back with him. When I asked whether he was returning to Ireland, they said that he had a week to play in Liverpool and was then playing in Cork sometime soon. Two days later, I headed south, giving myself plenty of time. My tool kit in the car contained a hammer as well as a tire iron and a large screwdriver.

The soccer men had the dates wrong; he didn't appear for a further month—but, in the uncertain and casual way of things in Ireland, he was "expected any day." He had booked gigs in some halls, one theater, and one pub. I prowled the shores of the south coast, beachcombing, watching the seabirds, making tracks in the sand, and waiting for the tide to erase them.

And then I began to consider his arrival in Ireland. Would he be with Venetia? Would he cross to Dublin? Or would he take a ship directly from Liverpool to Cork? Freighters still offered passenger berths on such routes. Convinced that one day I'd see both of them step onto the docks somewhere, I haunted the Cork quayside.

Days and nights of watching arrivals according to shipping schedules, the damp, the cold, the gloomy half-light, the little whores soliciting me, their attempted finery making them look like birds with ragged

plumage—I lived a twilit life, fueled by hate and revenge. Whether this
would bring Venetia back, I didn't care. Whether I wanted her back, I
didn't know.

The changeable weather of the south coast made life at least interesting. I visited old haunts, found ancient battlefields I'd always wanted to
inspect, met one or two of my old storytelling friends. I always asked if
any of them had ever met or heard John Jacob O'Neill. None had,
though all said the name sounded familiar; some reported hearing of
him from a friend of a friend of a friend. I had no thought of visiting
him, no thought of shedding this obsession. In my pocket I kept a newspaper cutting that said, "GENTLEMAN JACK COMING TO CORK." That piece
of newsprint fell apart from being opened and folded again.

One evening around six o'clock, with a strong wind whipping up the
waters of the River Lee, and Patrick Street crowded with home-going
workers, I saw him. In a crowd ahead of me I recognized the thin shoulders in the white raincoat he had worn in Templemore. Him. No doubt
of it. Gentleman Jack Stirling.

Was he alone? I couldn't see. I crossed the street and hurried, got parallel, then ahead, then far ahead. When I got to Grand Parade, I turned
back to make sure. No doubt of it. Him.

Now the stalking began in earnest, and it went on for days. I discovered where he was lodging: a small, musty hotel on South Main Street
near French's Quay. He went there that evening, his head bent against
the wind, and closed the glass door behind him. I watched from across
the street, like a spy, but saw no upstairs light; he must have had a room
at the back—probably wouldn't or couldn't pay for anything better.

He didn't appear again that evening. At midnight I searched the area
for a suitable, unnoticeable place from which to observe the hotel. The
next morning I returned, to the inside of a deserted warehouse, where I
could move boards from a window on the upper floor.

At noon he emerged, alone. He walked no more than a few yards, to
a pub along the street. I sat back and waited. At half past four he reappeared and set out in the opposite direction. I followed, and for the next
hour he walked across Cork, always choosing crowded places. An ob-
server who knew nothing of the story would have said that he seemed to
be looking for somebody. He examined every person who walked near

him; from the far side of the street I couldn't tell whether he scrutinized men more than women.

When the workers petered out, he turned back. I followed him all the way to his seedy hotel. He didn't reemerge that night.

The pattern I've just described continued for one week. Eight days, to be exact. He walked. I followed. He returned. I watched. How fortunate that I needed so little sleep. And as my surveillance continued, I became ever more persuaded that he, too, might be looking for somebody.

No trace of Venetia. I tried not to include that fact in my plans. Nor did I worry that something might be amiss. Whatever her emotional volatility with me, and however meekly she had submitted to his abuses, her life force had remained intact. I'd seen that, and I felt that I knew her life force better than anybody.

Except, of course, the two of you, her children. Yet children don't always know the essence of their parents. It took me decades to establish anything like a true knowledge of my mother and father.

I must point out to you that in all this stalking I never wavered. In my mellow older age now, I feel appalled at myself for this, but I've enjoyed my guilty pleasure in the moments when this plan worked—the surprise on his face, the anger, the embarrassment. (As to whether I've forgiven myself for other things—we shall come to that.)

Here's how it played out, and I'll conceal nothing, not even the parts that do me no credit. I scoured the Cork newspapers, especially the *Echo,* which carried even the most local of entertainments. At last the announcement appeared: "Direct from His Resounding Success in London and Liverpool: The Sensational Gentleman Jack. Come and Be Mesmerized." In the Father Mathew Hall on a Sunday night. I bought a ticket that day. It sold out two days later.

Now I could open the special valise I had packed so carefully in Dublin. Heavy spectacles, gabardine raincoat, a tweed hat: nothing in my appearance would connect me to the man he'd seen in Templemore or on the stage of the Olympia Theatre. He wouldn't be expecting somebody so old. The cotton wool I'd stuffed into my cheeks changed my appearance so much that my landlady in Cork passed me in the street without acknowledgment.

113

How carefully I had planned.

Don't be the first to sit in the hall. Move in with the main body of the crowd. Just in case he's around the place. Or looking from behind the curtain. Seats are first come, first served. Which is good. Keep calm. Remember why you're here. Remember the tactic. Don't touch the hammer until you're about to use it.

I sound deranged, don't I? Psychopathic. If you think so, I can't blame you. But remember what I was doing and you may feel better about it. I wasn't simply scoring revenge for myself—consider the mistreatment of your mother. Excessive of me? Perhaps. But what is it you used to say, Louise, that made me laugh? *You ain't see nuthin' yet.*

Around me, the chairs filled. The singsong of the Cork accent rang like the bells of Shandon. Does everybody in this city know everybody else?

In a sequined jacket, and pants with a wide red stripe down the side of the leg, he bounded out. Bowing and smiling. The bastard.

Some patter: "I hear you have a newspaper here called the *Cork Examiner.* Is it for the drink trade?" Yeah, yeah, the old jokes are best. I tried to stop myself from grinding my teeth, a habit of tension and fear. "What do you call a Corkman who hangs from the ceiling? Sean Doleer." They loved it. "I knew a Corkman once who used to bounce off the walls. His name was Rick O'Shea." Some jeers. But overwhelmingly cheers. We'll soon change that.

He began with the pickpocket routine, and I have to admit that it dazzled me. Neckties, shoelaces, purses from within handbags, wallets from inside pockets—how did he do it? Coins, even, from deep in pants pockets, and a bunch of keys from a jacket; I watched like a hawk, but I never saw. No wonder he kept repeating his main tagline, "The quickness of the hand deceives the eye."

Talk, though, helped him most. He pattered and chattered, usually with a personal remark at the moment of striking. As he distracted a woman with a comment about her "lovely hands," he lifted her necklace. As he asked a man about the fear of going bald, he took his belt.

Who can resist brilliance? And your stepfather, the late Gentleman Jack Stirling, was brilliant. The audience knew it, too, and ate him up. Lines formed in the aisles; after the first ten minutes he didn't have to call for volunteers anymore.

No intermission—which surprised me; he went straight into the hypnotism routine with an overt change of gear.

"Now, ladies and gentlemen, did you ever hear of a man named Dr. Mesmer? No? But you have heard of people being mesmerized? Well, tonight I'm going to be your Dr. Mesmer, He's the man who invented it; I'm going to mesmerize you—in fact, I'm going to mesmerize all of you. The entire audience."

They hooted. And then they laughed, because next he said, "And while you are in a hypnotic trance and under my influence, each and every one of you will get up, go out, cross the street to that pub over there, and buy a drink for yourself. And bring one back for me."

As they finished laughing he said, "Only joking, ladies and gentlemen. But you will see some remarkable things. And I have to warn you: if you suffer from a heart complaint—other than love, of course—or are of a nervous disposition; don't come up here. But if you're a bank manager, come up right away   I need the money. Now, who's going to be first? No takers, no? Very well."

I knew what would happen next. Selecting seven people from the front rows, he stood them all up and soon had them sawing instruments while he sang, "On the Street Where You Live" from *My Fair Lady*. He conducted the imaginary instruments in perfect time.

When the applause ended he called for a volunteer. I waited. A young woman, pushed by her giggling friends, ran up.

Gentleman Jack said, "You look like a lamb to me. Are you a lamb?" She shook her head, still in the giggles. "No, sir."

"I think you are." She had bobbly blond hair. "Ladies and gentlemen, doesn't she look like a lamb? Yes, she does."

Taking her chin, he tipped up her face and looked long and deep, forcing the hall into silence, and said, "You are a little lamb. You will gambol and play and make lamb sounds." When he stepped back, the girl began to prance around the stage. She dropped to her hands and knees, kicked up her heels, and cried, "Baaaaa! Baaaaa!"

The audience went wild.

When she had "gamboled" for several minutes, he followed her, stood her up, snapped his fingers—and she smiled like a waking child.

His next volunteer, again a girl, became a monkey. She made "Unh-huh" sounds over and over, and scratched herself, and grunted.

"Now peel your fruit, there's a good monkey," he ordered, and she peeled an imaginary banana. "Now walk over and look at the nice people." Knuckles to the floor of the stage, she came to the edge and frowned out at us. She will never live it down.

Next Jack dealt me my hand of cards.

"So far it's only the ladies who've shown any courage. What's wrong with you, chaps? Don't the men of Cork have any gumption? If we were in England, the stage would be crowded with men."

I rose. With ostentation. Put up my hand. The crowd cheered.

"That's right, sir. Bit of gumption's what we need. Come on." I stepped into the aisle and headed for the stage. "Give him a big hand, ladies and gentlemen."

Did he look at me extra closely? I'm not sure. If I had to swear, I'd say he was too distracted—exactly what I was hoping for.

"What's your name, sir?"

"Eddie."

"Is that Edwin, Edmund, or Edward?"

"Eddie. 'Tis Eddie, like." I can do a Cork accent.

"Very well, Eddie. Now I want you to relax. Would you like to take off your hat?"

"No, thanks, I'm fond of it."

The audience suspected something; they had long experience of outsiders being guyed and made foolish. They got it right, but for the wrong reasons. How could they have known?

Jack clapped his hands and turned to the audience.

"Now, ladies and gentlemen, Eddie doesn't look like a lady, does he? But in a moment he will take off his coat and put it back on like a lady puts on a dress."

He stood in front of me and stared into my eyes, the eyes I'd been unable to look at in Templemore, the eyes I'd avoided on the stage of the Olympia, the eyes whose vile light I was about to extinguish. He passed his hands in front of my face, and I, with full resistance closed my eyelids. When he snapped his fingers I gave myself a little jolt and stayed locked, seemingly, inside his trance.

"Now, then, Eddie, I want to you take off your coat and put it back on just as you've seen your wife put on her frock. You know—tug all your underwear into place, pat it and pull it, and then put on your dress, because you're going out shopping and you don't want all the other ladies in Cork to see you looking dowdy."

I could tell that he was leering at the audience; I heard their chuckles.

Behaving at first as though a little sleepy, I took off my gabardine coat. For extra effect I tipped forward the tweed hat. I trailed the coat a little, then picked it up again and inspected it, peering as though myopic. Some belly laughs rose, and a heckler shouted, "Edwina!"

For a moment or two I patted my shoulders and my chest, and then I opened out the coat, took it by the collar, and whirled it high above my head in a mad circle. I danced a little jig.

The audience roared and Jack went along with it, but through my half-closed eyelids I could see the irked query on his face: *What's this fellow up to?*

I let the coat fall to my side, holding it still by the collar.

"Well, I must say, Edwina"—he turned and winked to the crowd—"I don't know where you take off and put on your dresses, do I? Now be a good girl and put your clothes on; there are people watching."

Whirling the coat, I set off on a gallop around the stage, whinnying like a horse. Now the audience felt the prank, and like all local communities they liked nothing better than seeing a smooth-tongued outsider being bested—especially in Cork, and especially an Englishman.

I finished my gallop, came to a halt in front of Jack, pawed the ground, shook my head with a flurry, and went still again.

He didn't know what to do—which surprised me; I'd have thought he must have been guyed before. Evidently not. He took my face in his hands, not kindly, and I had to suppress my revolted shudder. Hard hands; and I imagined them hitting Venetia.

"Well, Edwina, we have a misunderstanding here, haven't we? But that's all right. All wives need to be taught how to obey their husbands—isn't that right, ladies and gentlemen?" To this he received a mixed cheer. "But Edwina is at last going to put on her dress and act like a lady." To me he hissed, "Do as I say. You are under my command."

Idiot. That was my first thought. Next thought? *This is all going exactly to plan.* And it was, and continued to do so—for the next few moments.

I took the coat, opened it out, began to slip it on in an exaggeratedly female fashion, and then, when I had secured a button or two in what I thought passed for a ladylike way, I put out my hands like a boxer, closed my fists, and began to spar with Jack.

He didn't know what to do. He was, as you know, shorter than me and a great deal thinner, he didn't have my reach, and he couldn't stop my hands from tapping his face. I crowded him and danced away, moved in again, huffing and puffing, dancing on the balls of my feet, feinting and jabbing.

Trying to go along with it, he turned his back on me and walked to the front of the stage.

"Ladies and gentlemen," he began.

From behind, I grabbed him by the collar and shook him like a dog.

"This fellow—" I shouted. "No gentleman. Let me tell you about him. He beats the shit out of women. Want proof? I have plenty. I've seen the bruises."

After a stunned gasp, some shouts floated up:

"Get off."

"Get out of here."

"Go on with the show."

Jack wriggled, but he couldn't wrench himself out of my grip. I needed only one hand to hold him by the scruff of the neck, turn him around, and run him off backstage. As we ran I could feel the hammer jolting in my pocket.

The next part had to work fast—because I had to get away. I had parked the car two streets from the hall, and I calculated that the shock of the incident, and his fallen body, would delay any pursuit. But I knew I had to be quick.

It didn't happen. Backstage stood two men, hefty and louche. They knew Jack had nothing like this in his act.

"Grab him!" Jack shouted, and they did, and ran me to the street door.

For the next three or four minutes they held me splayed and wide as Jack kicked me, pummeled me, blackened my eyes, broke several teeth. He used his elbow first to hit me where I wore the glasses. For weeks, the rings around my eyes made me look like a blue raccoon. He broke my nose and two ribs, and only his henchmen stopped him from kicking in my head.

They threw me into the street with a flurry of kicks. My haunches still feel their boots when frost descends. I never got to throw a punch; that fact hurt most of all.

114

Confession is its own engine, an unstoppable impetus: tell one sin and you want to tell all. Especially if that sin was committed in cold blood. It took some time for my blood to cool—and then it went icy. I knew exactly what I wanted done and how to make it happen; I was prepared to take my time; I merely needed to do the planning, nothing more. My country's history helped. I visited a hero.

When I fear the final ravages of age, I think of Dan Barry. I found him at home, reduced to a hank of bones, imprisoned in his bed by a fierce housekeeper. She allowed me to see him for five minutes, then told me to scram. More or less. But his eyes said something else; his eyes said, *I'm more alert than I seem.* We shared a silent nod. My unspoken message: *I understand. And I'll be back.*

Learning had authority back then. A college degree had a pride of place. Add medicine and you faced no challenge, not even from a savage housekeeper who was trying to bully an old man into changing his will.

The world gives us two kinds of magic, hard and soft. Hard takes your breath away—John Jacob met his only and long lost brother in Vienna when he dropped his matches on the floor of a bus: that's "hard" magic. Usually, though, I think of coincidence as "soft" magic.

I didn't know any doctors near Dan Barry's house, so I asked in a pub. (Where else?) The drinkers directed me to the "new fellow, but he's green; he's only just out of college."

He weighed a ton and a half; his neck bulged from his collar like two rolls of sausage. Most usefully, though, he had the small, piggy eyes of a bully.

"Where were you before here?" I asked him—and, soft magic, I knew the answer. When he told me I said, to make him my slave, "They had polio over there, didn't they? Were you involved in that?" He grunted, and I took him captive. As we drove I said, "I came to you because this needs a man with authority. You'll see what I mean."

Of course, like all bullies when you give them a free hand, he almost overdid it. By the time we left he had taken down the housekeeper's home particulars, interrogated her about her nursing experience, asked for references, and told her he was sending in a nurse. I saw him as an advance squad—clearing the ground. He terrified her: you can always bully a bully: they live on fear.

The next day I came back, to assess what had to be done. Mr. Barry had to be fed, but with care. The nurse we'd found arrived an hour after I did, and together we drew up a menu and directed the housekeeper to go shopping. We changed his room—from the dark little closet over-hung by trees at the back of the house to a wide-windowed, sunny room at the front.

"This is my own room again," he said.

The nurse mouthed to me, "That bitch."

Who soon returned. When I saw the car, I let the nurse loose. "Say what you like," I told her. "Make sure there are no witnesses."

Ten minutes later, she came back smiling. "She thinks she's going to jail."

We searched his closets, his dressers. He had clothes he'd never worn, pajamas, shirts, underwear still in their shop wrappings. I paid the nurse, who said she'd stay the night. The housekeeper not only held the front door open as I left the house, she darted ahead of me and opened the car door, too. The first part of the plan had clicked firmly into place.

Sunlight picked out Phase Two. She wore red; he, a white shirt. Even at several hundred yards I could see how their relationship had waxed. To a full moon. They heard the car, turned around, waved—and leaned against each other.

Take it easy. Slow walk. Watch them. Yes, no question. James Bermingham has been staking a claim. Planting a flag. Is this going to work? Second part, yes. Phase Three? I hope so; I just flocking hope so.

"What are you doing?"

"Hiya, Ben!" She ran across the grass barefoot and threw her arms around me; her hair smelled of lemon.

"Stranger," said Jimmy Bermingham. "The man. How's she cuttin'?"

"In little slices," I said. We had so many of those meaningless banter phrases, those icebreakers. And each had a variety of answers. To "How's she cuttin'?" I might have said, "Up the middle and down the sides" or "Around the front and across the back" or "Round as a hoop and you'd roll it."

Everybody in the country had them. My father said to people, "Where-where-where are you goin' with no bell on your bike?" Large Lily said to all and sundry, "Well, look what happens when you're not lookin'." Billy Moloney, her husband, seemed to have an anthology of them: "The river's flockin' risin' and it's not flockin' full." And "Up and down like a hoor's drawers." And "Wherever you see a fox, there's always a flockin' hen."

As I say, they were meaningless—but without malice or harm, and they helped awkward people get over their embarrassment at being alive.

Jimmy looked me up and down. "You're as healthy as a brown dog," he said.

"Are you fully recovered?" I asked.

Elma answered, addressing first me, then Jimmy: "He's still coughing up marbles—aren't you?"

Behind them on the ground sat a bucket of walnut-sized stones.

"What were you doing?" I asked.

"Jimmy's improving my aim."

In the next few minutes I understood why Jimmy got paid for his patriotism. Along the fence he had set out five old blue tin mugs. One or two bore dent marks.

"He's trying to get me to hit them mugs," said Elma Sloane, "and sure the fence won't let me hit them, and anyway, amn't I as left-handed as a duck."

In fact she was right-handed, but with poor aim. I tried, and hit not a mug.

"We'll go closer," I suggested, and Elma said, "No, let Jimmy have a go."

Thirty yards, I'd say—and he knocked every mug. When he saw my eyebrow raised he nodded, and he was saying to me, *Yes. With a gun, too.*

We sat on the vanquished fence. No wrinkles of fear threatened Elma's forehead; the sun landed on her hair like a butterfly; the world around her sang and danced.

"How's Randall?" I asked.

They looked at each other.

"He's as cross as a bag of cats," said Elma.

"Artistic temperament," suggested Jimmy.

"He's out with me," said Elma. Translation: "He's not speaking to me."

"When did this happen?"

Jimmy said, "He was bilious the day after I came here."

"But you're still all right to stay?"

Elma nodded. "I'm still posing for him."

Jimmy cut in: "Yeh, you're still stripping off your clothes for him."

"But wasn't that the arrangement? That Elma would be safe here and learn to pose for Randall."

"He hates me," said Jimmy. "But he's afraid to throw me out."

So that's why Randall didn't acknowledge me at the studio window that bad night. I controlled my rising excitement.

"Let me go and talk to him."

I drove the final stretch of avenue. And saw how Randall got inspired. The lake, gray and long, dull under the cloud cover, yet had a shimmer. Like one of his fish.

He heard the door close behind me and shouted. I followed the yell down the same corridor.

"We're in here."

In a new work space, opened beneath a long window, Annette lay on her side, facing Randall. Naked, of course. And unaffected by my arrival. I peered around his shoulder at the canvas: would this be another voluptuous fish?

He looked grumpy. I asked, "How are you, Randall?"

"Can you get that fellow out of here?" He didn't say it; he shouted it. Annette would have shrugged if she could have raised a shoulder.

Done. My task complete. I needed to tie the ends, but I saw it all. And it played out as simply as I had hoped. That afternoon I joined all the dots. The next day I completed the picture.

Mr. Barry welcomed every move. Jimmy Bermingham loved it. Elma saw the sense. Saw the future. As to her old fears—no worry necessary. I said to her, "You know Jimmy's connections, don't you?"

"The things he told me," she said.

Randall's mood improved at dinner. "But you'll still come and pose for me."

"If he'll let me," said Elma.

I said, "He will."

We went out in the night, Jimmy and I, and when our eyes made the darkness brighter, we looked at the lake.

"What about Marian, though?"

I said, "She has a boyfriend. Longtime. He's a big cop."

"Ah," said Jimmy. "That's why she couldn't accommodate me. Opposite sides of the fence."

Letting him have his justification, I said, "Are you done with all that?"

"I can go back anytime I like. But the flood scared me, to tell you the truth."

"This is a better deal, Jimmy. He doesn't have long to live, he'll leave everything to Elma, and you'll marry her."

Jimmy said, "I might have to, anyway."

"I thought as much. Is that why Randall was furious?"

Jimmy said, "Ah, there was a bit of stuff about Annette, too."

"Jimmy, you're a goat."

"I owe you," he said to me. "If there's ever anything I can do."

Oh, there is, Jimmy, oh, there is. And another piece of the jigsaw slipped into place. Or, should I say, a bolt slid home. Was there a moment in which I hated myself for the coldness of my long-term scheming? Not then.

115

The next day, I drove to Mr. Barry's house—twice. First, to reconnoiter. And, indeed, the nurse had taken control.

"The bitch won't stay long."

"But she doesn't bully him anymore?"

"Put money on that. She knows I'd wring her neck."

"How is he?"

The nurse said, "D'you know what? I never met a nicer man. He's great company. I could listen to him all day. The books that man has read." She folded another towel. "But he hasn't long left."

"Did he say anything about a girl?"

The nurse gave me her complete attention. "D'you know what? I think she should be here."

"How much of the story has he told you?"

She said, "D'you know what? I know the Sloanes. Elma is over in England." She winked at me. "Or so everyone says."

"In Ireland," I sighed, "a secret is something everyone else knows about you."

"She's a very nice girl," said the nurse, "and she has a very nice mother. And an animal for a father."

"Wave a magic wand," I said, needing confirmation. "What do you think should happen?"

"If there was some way that girl could live here. All he wants to do is look at her and talk to her. He's not able to do much more than that, anyway."

"Could he live long?"

She grimaced. "He's going down the home straight. The body is weak, and that bitch downstairs wore him down."

"Let me try something on you. If there was a way of fixing it so that Elma could live here—would it work?"

"She'd need protection. From that bloody housekeeper. And I can't be here all day, every day. But he's stone mad about Elma."

"Make sure he looks his best in about two hours," I said.

She grinned and winked.

Jimmy took his brief with great attention. He looked at me from time to time with surprise. I told him not to interrupt me.

"He will leave Elma everything. I don't know how much money he has, but I'd say it's a lot. And the place is top-notch. You just have to be patient. You can't marry her till he's dead. He'll love you anyway—he'll love your involvement with what you call 'the cause' and he calls 'the movement.' He can never know that there's anything between you and Elma. You have to be discreet. He won't be leaving that room often. But just be careful. And leave it to me—I'll build the bridge. You'll never have to do a day's work for the rest of your life."

I finished. Jimmy looked at me, mouth open, eyes wide.

"I didn't know you were a wizard. Ben the magic man."

I said, "But it's good magic. We're going to do it in stages."

The nurse announced us: "Mr. Barry, you have visitors."

I could see him in the distance across his wide room. *My God, he's even frailer today. I forget how ancient he is. This is like looking into the past. Did he suddenly let go of his defenses with the new nurse? But he's lucid, that's for sure.*

"How are you?" I said, as I walked toward his bed. "Look who's here."

Elma, as instructed, had slipped in behind me so that I masked her. When I stepped aside, he gasped. At the other side of the bed, the nurse helped him sit up.

"Now, Mr. Barry, isn't that a nice visitor to get? Hallo, Elma."

"Howya, Irene. Hello, Dan." Elma handled it with warmth and grace. She reached for Mr. Barry's hand, then leaned in and kissed him on the forehead.

"Are you back or am I dreaming?"

"This is me, Dan, in all my little glory," she said. "How are you at all?"

"But—but, I mean—are you really back? For good?"

"For good and bad," she said, and laughed.

"Will you come here to stay with me?"

She said, "I will, that's why I'm here, Dan. To look after you."

Malachi MacCool took one look at the girl and reeled back. . . . His heart's desire. . . . A flash of forked lightning . . .

"I knew it'd happen one day," he said. "I had faith." And he leaned back on his pillows.

Elma stood by the bed, not relinquishing his hand.

"Didn't I always say I was the bad penny, Dan? That I'd always turn up?"

When he opened his eyes, the girl hadn't gone away. . . . A pillar of the gentle light. . . . Sweet as cane sugar, thoughtful and serene . . . of a fond nature.

"And you'll be here with me?"

She squeezed his hand. "For ever and a day, Dan."

My head began to spin.

What am I doing? What have I done? Played games with an old heart? Or looked to the future? What ethics? Where is this ethical? Do the emotions have their own ethical compass? Then the ice in me set again, and I didn't care about ethics.

Dan Barry, barely able to speak, asked, "Elma, will you marry me?"

She looked around the room. "You'll all have to go out for a minute; I'll call you all back."

Nurse Irene and I walked—and waited. Within minutes Elma called. We went back in as soft-footed as though going to a wake.

Elma said, "Dan has proposed to me, and I've accepted."

Mal couldn't speak, except in his head, where he kept saying, "Oh." At last he took the girl's hand and welcomed her.

Irene hugged her. I said, "Another good man gone. There's only a few of us bachelors left." Dan Barry wept.

"This," he said, eventually, "is the happiest day of my life."

My father's voice in my head. Machiavelli was Irish, Ben. His-his-his name was actually Mac Hiavelli. Like MacMahon. Or MacCormack. Or MacCarthy. We-we-we're the same Mac as Machiavelli. Didn't you know that? Ask-ask-ask your mother. She'll tell you.

When the excitement settled down, Irene took Elma downstairs. To bring back a bottle of something. Glasses should be raised. While they were gone, I settled by the bed.

"Did you do all this?"

I said, "No. But I know the man who did."

In clear but brief detail, I told him about Jimmy Bermingham. My summary: "He's a crack shot, a marksman, and a great strategist. He's injured at the moment and on the run."

"Bring him here," said Dan Barry. "I was a wanted man myself."

And I did. To this day I cannot say whether I did right or wrong in respect to that dear old man and Elma Sloane. But in the paying back of the favor that I asked of Jimmy Bermingham, I have no doubt of the wrong I did. I've lived with it ever since. Or tried to.

116

I mean to tell it all. Nothing held back. Think of it as the higher purpose for this family memoir. If that's what we're calling it. Some memoir. In which your father seems, with icy calculation, either to have lost his mind or abandoned his principles. Or both. Let me begin with the planning.

I scrutinized the newspapers every day. Every bomb, every bullet, every court hearing, every flake of political fallout—I almost memorized them. The closer I could get to this issue, this "action," the more I could interpret and use it. Did I feel shame? Not yet. Obsession doesn't let shame get near the obsessed.

In March 1957, a general election in the Irish republic produced a change of government. Not much else altered, in terms of rebel violence. The IRA leaders blamed the Irish and British governments for having divided the island in the first place and called a plague on all their houses. I needed a change of mood for my best result.

The coming to power of the former rebel leader Eamon de Valera helped. He cracked down on his old sympathizers harder than anyone else. In relation to the Border Campaign, the country's mood swung all that spring and summer.

Where there had been violence I raced to the scene. As discreetly as I could I attempted to establish what had happened. The nearer an incident happened to the border, the more useful to me. In high summer, for instance, a gunfight broke out a handful of miles inside the north. From behind a ditch, a dozen and more IRA fellows opened fire on a truck carrying a dozen police. One officer died; another took terrible wounds. In Dublin the government decided to round up far more than the usual suspects and then launched internment—a policy of imprisonment with no trial, and no prospect thereof.

Later that month, de Valera sent almost two thousand troops from the south to positions along the border to see whether he could snuff out any forays. I traveled from post to post, chatting with soldiers, pretending I was visiting relatives nearby. In cold blood I was gauging, measuring, checking every option.

During August I managed to inspect a body shot by the northern police, and view a house near Coalisland where a booby-trap explosion killed a northern police officer.

The next month I sat drinking with two northerners who had lured two young southern men into a trap. And shot them both. You could call that the coldest of cold blood.

What was I thinking? I was learning. And I wanted to view this upheaval from all possible angles to see how I could use it. No visibility. Nothing to connect me with anything. Everything as smooth as silk. To maximum effect. I toiled for months, talking to people I'd never met before. And would never want to meet again.

117

From a last reconnaissance along the border, in which I checked again every detail—dates, times, addresses—I drove back down the country. In beautiful early sunshine I strolled to Mr. Barry's door, a cheerful and warm midmorning visitor, bringing a bottle of whiskey. I found a serene household. Mr. Barry, ailing faster now, sat up a little.

"There you are. My great benefactor," he said.

"How are you?"

"As happy as a man can ever be. I'll never be able to thank you enough."

"She's a nice girl," I said.

He smiled that innocent smile of eternal love that men smile only once in their lives. If they're fortunate . . .

Beside me, the same nice girl grinned. "Marriage improves a man—isn't that what they say, Dan?"

Burgeoning in his spirit, a gentleman respected and admired . . .

He sipped at his whiskey. I licked mine; clear head needed.

"Walk me through your fields," I told Jimmy Bermingham.

"Hold on, Ben; they're not my fields."

"Not yet," I said. "But I'm sure you'll see to all the legal work." He laughed.

We spent the next hour together. I discovered why he had been so valued. He took a brief with accuracy and speed. Superb questions. On the point. Across the references. He knew everything I was talking about. And he knew everything I wanted.

He asked me one last question: "How near will you be?"

"I'll follow the action beforehand. I'll look at the results. But I'll witness nothing."

And I had one last question: "How much?"

He pondered. "I won't be doing it myself. The word is that everybody's looking for me."

I said, "We'll talk again."

"No. I need a postal address for you. Where I can send a telegram." He checked. "And you're sure you want to paint the placard yourself?"

"Without question."

"And you're sure of your numbers?"

I nodded. "Certain. But take no chances."

118

A Sunday night proved ideal. All week, in various ways, in various guises, I had prowled and surveyed. Local newspapers gave me the first reach of information. Friendly chat confirmed it. And some gossip.

On the Saturday morning, out by a remote lake, I met Jimmy's two men. All three of us concealed our faces. We stood in a grove, the water lapping at the high sedges behind us. No handshakes. No greeting.

I said, "We know who we are."

One of them answered, "And we know why we're here."

"Do you want a briefing from me or are you sure of your ground?"

The second man said, "No harm to tell us again."

I briefed them. When I had finished, the second man said, "Best reason I know. And you have something to give us?"

Money in a small, tight packet. The placard in a large envelope. Job done. Not yet, though.

"Confirm the timing."

They looked at each other. "Half past ten, right? Tomorrow night?"

"Good," I said, and I left them.

Could I have stopped them? Not then. Should I have stopped them? Of course. And if I hadn't been there and hadn't insisted on seeing what they did—would my life have been different? Would I now have this compulsion to tell you? Would I have taken the track of life that I followed? Who knows? Not me, that's for sure.

I'm so old now, older than Dan Barry was when he died, and—I've just decided—these various accounts of my life will be sealed until long after my death. You may publish them if you wish, but all the sealing and all the publishing, all the open confession, and all my breast-beating—none of that will undo anything.

The day had some drizzle. A wet Sunday in Cavan in 1957 didn't attract many people out-of-doors. Once the last Mass had ended, the women and children trickled home, while the men found the pubs. I had a vantage point—a bed-and-breakfast just down the street. By twisting my body tight, I could gaze along a narrow compass. But I could see enough. Not that I expected to see anything until that evening.

No disappointments. Everything went as planned. The same hour that I expected. The same pace that I predicted. I saw every move. Heard the satisfaction in my own inner voice.

Half past eight. Soft rain. Lemon light from the streetlamp, weak and thin. I heard their voices first, their laughter. Then I saw them scurrying toward where I stood, then into the pub. One held a newspaper above his head. They jostled, they jeered. Lively as monkeys.

Ten o'clock. Pub begins to empty. Drinkers reluctant to leave. One or two parting remarks on the street. No sign yet.

Ten minutes after ten o'clock. Two more drinkers. Quick goodbye.

Twenty minutes past. Holding brown paper bags of clinking bottles, they appear. Still laughing. I can hear them—the jokes, the happy jeers. They reach their own front door, he can't find the key, he fumbles, they're in, the door closes, they're gone.

I wait. On the second of eleven o'clock, the car arrives, slows to a long, coasting, silent halt down the slope of the street. Out of the car step my two men from the lake. I can't see what they're carrying; they knock on the door, they bundle through. I hear the shots. Then the silence.

Nobody else seems to have heard them. The men from the lake emerge, close the door behind them, and drive away. Nothing else moves on that street. I wait. And wait. Nothing, not a sound not a sight.

The night closed down, and I slept like a child.

Early the next morning, I woke and went to the window. The street remained as empty as a hole. I stood for perhaps fifteen minutes. One man rode by on a bicycle, his cap down low on his forehead, his collar hunched up against the rain. For the next half hour I watched and saw not another being, not even a cat slinking home.

I shaved, washed, got my bag ready, ate breakfast, paid my bill. The rain began to lift. I walked to my car, which was parked around the corner, and drove away. By another road, I drove back to the edge of town and parked where nobody could see, under trees, off a lane. On pathways that I had mapped and measured days before, I reached the back of the house. Couldn't get in. The men from the lake had forgotten to open it for me. I got away from there, but not so fast that I'd draw attention to myself.

If I had calculated accurately, nothing would be found until evening. By now I knew every street, every house, every laneway, every rear wall, every back door. I could lurk near the cathedral and ramble back down toward the post office and the friary; if I timed it well, I'd be on hand when the commotion broke.

It worked. I saw the youngster arrive and hammer on the door. He got no reply. The woman next door put out her head.

"They were there last night," she said.

The youngster hammered again.

"I have a key," said the woman next door. "Mrs. Mitchell always gives me a key when she's leasing out the house."

At which moment I crossed the street, minding my own business. And ran back when I heard the screams.

The woman from next door came hurtling out, shrieking "Mother of God, Mother of *God!*" and the youngster, white as a sheet, crouched toward the street, looking to retch.

"What's wrong, what's wrong?" I asked, the concerned citizen.

The woman from next door, her hand to her mouth like a victim, pointed.

Nothing neat in there; the men from the lake hadn't bothered with tidiness. One lay sprawled facedown on the stairs, blood congealing on the steps and in the hallway at his askew shoes. Another lay faceup in the doorway to the shoddy kitchen; they'd blown away most of his face and head.

Neither being what I wished to see, I searched. In the tiny sitting room I saw what I'd come for: the black mustache was accented now by a line of thickened blood. They'd shot him in the right eye and in the chest. His white shirt had turned mainly dark, and his mouth hung open in a rictus; dentures half-protruded.

Even in death he seemed loathsome. I looked at the hands by which he'd made his living. One had a bullet wound—he must have raised it to try to stop a shot. The other had the fingers curled round a gun. Did the men from the lake put it there? On his chest sat my placard: "Shot as British spies." I knew my history.

I stood and surveyed. *Three lumps of dead human flesh. Odd how they're bent out of shape. How will they straighten them for burial? Who will do that? This is like* Life *magazine in Chicago. I'm seeing it in black and white. Like the gangster movies. What's that odor? Toilets and sweetness? But beginning to be overpowering. No, I'm not gagging. One last look. Blood is blacker than I thought.*

The man who had beaten Venetia savagely and, as I suspected from her veiled remarks, raped her often wouldn't do it again. Nor would he mock and leave open to humiliation innocent people who merely wanted an evening's entertainment. Never again would his henchmen taunt me and hold me helpless as he punched me and kicked me, and then throw me out onto the street.

I took my time, savoring—if that's not too appalling a word—the sight of the three bodies. Especially that of Jack Stirling, Gentleman Jack, the man who raised you, my children, who violated your mother in so many ways, who forced his way time and again into her body. I told you I would pull no punches.

Then, as the wailing continued outside, I left, drawing the door closed.

"Go into your own house," I told the woman from next door. "Take him with you." The youngster had now turned green and was clinging to her. "I'll tell the authorities."

PART SIX

The Passing of the Torch

119

What is our most interesting emotion? The most compelling? Love? Jealousy? I'll put a bid in for remorse. Better still, let me describe to you what happened that night and how remorse can strike.

That youngster who found the bodies, as I expect you've guessed, had come from the local hall. Jack had a second week's booking starting that night; the management had found him the rented house.

Late on the Saturday night, as the hall was closing, and Jack and his pals had left—I'd watched them go to the pub—I'd easily learned where Jack was staying. I knew that they wouldn't be able to tell him until Monday that somebody had asked about him. He was too suspicious not to be alert.

By now the disappearance of Venetia, though a puzzle, didn't deter or deflect me. I didn't care whether Jack had hidden her away somewhere or sent her back to Florida. She had moved from the front of my mind. Too much pain from that quarter. Too much hurt. Had to postpone even thinking of her. I dreaded what would happen when my feelings for her bloomed again. If they ever did.

While Jack and his pals were in the pub, I checked the house. Front and back. Opened the unlocked back door. They were living like pigs. Clothes everywhere, clean or soiled. Old newspapers that had held food packets. Empty beer bottles. Pigs. To be slaughtered.

Later, from my window, I watched them come home. Playing like puppies. Half drunk. Singing. Mocking. Taunting each other. Their ac-

cents so different in the echoes of this small town. Soon never to gibe
again.

On Monday, when I left the woman from next door and the
green-faced youngster, I quit town. Found my car and drove away. In a
neighboring village I found a telephone kiosk, spoke to the operator (no
automatic telephones yet in the Irish countryside), and convinced her of
my northern accent and rebel status.

"Shot as spies," she repeated. "Oh Jesus in heaven."

That night, I made it down to Mullingar. Ate and slept well. The next
day I took the road to Lough Ennell and tried to keep my appointment
with Rex Beaumont, the flamboyant ex-actor who lived in Belvedere
Lodge. He had the full, accurate story of the Jealous Wall, a ruin in his
gardens.

Local chatter said it had been built to stop a neighbor from eyeing
another man's wife. Not so. It had been built to prevent one man from
seeing what a fine house his brother owned.

No Rex. I'd catch him again. The lake stretched like glass. Over there,
on the left-hand shore, Jonathan Swift stayed. Same family as the Jealous
Wall. And when Swift saw the tiny figures on the far, far bank of the lake,
in a place named Lilliput, he had his Lilliputians. Lovely thought, delicious piece of lore. I drove out of Belvedere and turned right. I'd spend
the night in Tullamore, where I knew of a music session with a fiddler
home from New York. And wherever there's a fiddler, there's a story.

Not more than three miles farther, a girl of about twelve years old,
lanky and shy, drove a small herd of cows along the road. *Ah. Mother used
to do this.* I waited as she angled the animals into a field; they would
spend the day there, until she fetched them again for the evening milking.

I opened the window when I reached her.

"Did you milk them all yourself?"

She blushed and trotted away.

I drove on. A mile later, a sledgehammer slammed into my heart,
stomach, and chest. Actual pain. I stuck the brake to the floor and pulled
to one side. As though hit by a sudden squall, my face became a panel of
cold sweat. My bowels exploded. No control. Instant and foul mire beneath me, and I began to wet myself as freely as a faucet.

An anguish, in the form of a stabbing pain, entered my heart through my face, and left indelible wrinkles. People have laugh lines: do we also have pain lines? I do; I got them that day. My hands hadn't left the steering wheel. I didn't think I could detach them. The car sat on a fortunately wide verge. Condensation whitened the windows.

I couldn't lean back; my body refused it. It would be years before I ceased sitting tensely. And my mind replayed that gaping "Chicago" scene, that black-and-white film. Gentleman Jack. And his friends. Is blood so black only when it's old? The foulness congealing beneath me began to leak and forced action.

I heaved myself from the car, clambered over the ditch, lurched into the fields like a drunk, like a man shot, like a man with serious motor disability, and threw myself to the ground. The only action I could take.

Facedown I lay. I clawed at the ground, I scrabbled, I grabbed tufts and they came away in my frantic hands. My face merged with the earth. I think I was trying to burrow down into hell.

Then I heard the noise. Distinct and distinctive. From somewhere nearby. A moaning. Some poor soul in dreadful pain. I raised my head—I was listening to my own howling. For so many years that disconsolate sound echoed inside me, like the voice of a lacerated and outcast wolf. And nobody heard it but me.

I stayed in the fields all day. Anybody could have broken into or stolen the car. When I first rose to my feet I lurched off, away from the road, over a hill, into unknown territory. I saw nobody. Even the birds went quiet when I approached their trees.

What an awful thing it is to have taken human life. And in revenge. What could be worse? Remorse is a man staggering across fields he has never seen before, pitching himself face-first to the ground now and then, rolling every part of him into the earth, getting up, staggering some more, doing the same thing all over again.

Isn't hell a place echoing to "weeping and gnashing of teeth"? I didn't know how to gnash. But I wept. And how can you beg for forgiveness when there is nobody from whom to beg?

Somehow, time passed. Believe it or not, I saw a fox and her cubs in a hollow not far away.

The foxes took them down into the underground, down a rich maze of

burrows and coverts and into their own homes, those wide, low palaces be-
neath the earth, where fires blaze and food abounds, and there the foxes cared
for the lovers . . ."

Not for me such comfort. Not for many, many years.

When evening came, and the dank filth of my own condition began
to overwhelm me, I found a small river. It probably flowed into the lake
that had been my last lovely sight of that day or many days to come. I
stripped. In fact, I rended my garments. I know, children, that biblical
references didn't come with your cornflakes; Venetia and I shared paganism. The rending of garments signifies deep mourning of the most personal kind. And that is my definition of remorse: a mourning that is out
of control and never ends, that can strike out of the bluest of skies, across
the softest of snows.

Here endeth the lesson on remorse. I rolled in the little river and
made myself wash my filthy body with my hands. Freezing water caught
my breath, and my howling abated to a kind of nasal whimpering. How
could I have done such a thing? How could anyone?

I retrieved essentials from my pockets and discarded my torn and
ruined clothes, gave them to the gods of the stream. Naked, a white pillar
moving in the dusk, I went back to the car. Trying not to shuffle, trying
to stride. By now I had begun to mutter, and when I listened I heard
myself giving me instructions: *The news will break in the morning. Front*
pages. Find the twins. Not Tullamore tonight. Dublin. Miss Fay, not Mar-
ian. No body contact allowed. From this day forth I am unclean.

I always traveled with spare clothes; now I dressed by the roadside.
Not a soul saw me. This indeed was a quiet land. The car stank. I opened
all the windows and doors, lit matches. The sulfur smell of hell. I stood
back and tried to think.

Is this a dream? Did this happen? Had I hired so-called freedom fighters to kill someone for me? If for a moment I were to stop and imagine
it a dream, the justification laid that low.

But he was scum. Look what he did to Venetia. Who never harmed any-
one. Who spread nothing but goodness and delight. And what he did to me.
Above all to dear Miss Fay.

No good. Nothing worked. The emotional pain settled in my chest
and interfered with my breathing. I tried the accepted methods: sit back,

close eyes, breathe deep through the nose, hands open and simple. Didn't work.

I walked up and down the road, in the dark, feeling the silent hugeness of the empty countryside. A hundred slow paces; turn. A hundred slow paces; turn. Make the car the middle point. Fifty paces either side. Turn. All car doors and windows open. Still the faint odor. Of my own shame. Some more matches added sulfur, burned off some more methane. I braved the car.

For as long as I was on the road I always knew two things: the time of the day and the points of the compass. I knew how to get to Dublin by the smallest roads. Why didn't I go directly? Safety: the major routes might have police roadblocks. And shame: I was fit only for hidden places. From now on I would have to slink about the world.

120

Miss Fay's house had no lights. She was still, I would discover, living in a nursing home. Six months rehabilitating. I had a key, of course, and found no trace of recent life. The broken chair still sat propped against the kitchen table from Stirling's brutal visit.

Yet even that vile recollection didn't ease my pain. In that remorse I learned so much: That any attempt to ease guilt by justification is false. That the crimes of another appease none of one's own offenses. That, if one is being truthful, the greater pain is that of the offender. I know now that I would much rather be a victim of violence than a perpetrator.

Nonetheless I tried, for the first time, to find traces of the assault on Miss Fay—which had long been cleared up by May, the housekeeper. Why hadn't I done this before, when I'd stayed here after Venetia went from the seashore? Like a mad person, I now scoured the floor on my hands and knees. Shattered spectacles? Traces of blood? I found none, and the broken chair became the poem.

Little sleep came that night, and then only a troubled rest. My limbs ached, I might have caught a cold, I heaved and twitched. Went downstairs, made cocoa, no milk. And nothing to eat, none of Miss Fay's baked comfort. Sat and struggled. For an hour. Back to bed and woke at seven, after two hours of drunken slumber.

The newsagent at the corner of Brighton Road had the earliest opening hours in the district. A distance to walk, but it'd do me good. Had the shootings made the pages? I bought all the daily newspapers; only one ran the story, in a "Late News" column on the right-hand side of the front page:

IRA SHOOTINGS

> Three Englishmen found shot dead in Cavan house. Police found a placard round the neck of one: "Shot as British spies." The popular touring entertainer Mr. Jack Stirling, "Gentleman Jack," is believed to be among them. Other identities withheld pending the informing of relations.

Back at the house, I made tea. And more tea. And yet more tea. At half past eight, and knowing that it was futile, I again telephoned the old number I had for you, children—well, you know this anyway. Nobody answered. I know now that the two of you had long ago left. By boat to London, you told me years afterward, then trains to Southampton, where you boarded SS *United States* and crossed the Atlantic, and I lost you for the second time. And I knew it. Osmosis or something, or instinct.

Never again, I swore. *If I can find a way into your lives, I will. And stay there. But how can I, being as sullied as I am? What right do I have to share anyone's life, except in fleeting tangents?*

The next day, May, the housekeeper, appeared. She looked at me wide-eyed, in shock.

"Oh, sir, is it you? Did you hear the news on the wireless—that fella was killed? God, I hope you killed him, God, that's a terrible thing to say, but you shoulda seen what he did to Miss Fay, broke her bottom teeth and all. She'll have to get new ones and they only a new set from last year; I found the old spares and took them into her—she was bleeding here on the floor, right over there, and that chair bursted when I came in that very morning, and she still crying. Oh, I hope you killed him, he deserved it."

With no unease I said, "I wish I had."

That morning, under May's directions, I at last went to Miss Fay's nursing home. Beforehand, I managed to find irises, her favorite flower.

She knew, she said, my step in the corridor. "But I was waiting for it."

"I'm sorry I've been missing for so long. Are you all right?"

"They tell me I went fifteen rounds, but I say no, that it was a technical knockout in the first round."

I'd forgotten her fandom of boxing. "How bad—I mean—what was damaged?"

"The arm's the most troublesome. They're still trying to knit it." It lay alongside her like the corpse of a doll, swathed in white. "I don't mind if you punch him, Ben."

I said, "Haven't you heard?" I showed her the newspaper. "The funeral is in a few days."

Miss Fay looked at the paper, paused, looked at me.

"He shook me like a rag," she said, "nearly choked me." She pawed at her throat. "Then he threw a few hooks. Got me with an uppercut. There was a weight difference. And he had the reach. I was blue from here to here." She drew a line from her left eyebrow to her jaw. "James would have said I had the blues."

"I am so sorry. I am so sorry."

"He's dead now," she said. "Good riddance to bad rubbish." She paused. "You know, Ben." When she used my name, she usually had something portentous to say. "It's the only time that I've been glad James was dead. If he'd seen all this"—she fluttered a hand to her face—"he'd have asked you to kill him."

"Well, someone else did."

She looked at me, and I saw the query travel across her mind. Or did I imagine it?

"How is Venetia? Is she any better? I thought her lovely but very reduced. Now we know why."

I told her. The whole story. And I lied: "That's why I've been away so long. Looking for her."

"Another disappearance. Dear God. Poor you. I wonder if she's so damaged that she can't be herself anymore. She needs to go into a convent or something."

"If she's still alive."

"Well, at least," said Miss Fay, "that fellow can't get at her anymore."

I muttered, "I wonder if he already had."

"Oh, my God," she said, and we left it at that.

It was the first time I'd allowed the thought to have free rein. And yet—did I believe that Stirling had killed Venetia? I feared it—but I didn't believe it, and I hope that you can understand that.

We made our arrangements. I would visit every day. Stay in the house. Endure May, maybe even note down some of what she said. And then bridge Miss Fay's homecoming until she was ready to go back to her Civil Service office.

"Don't tell your mother," she said. "Say I fell. I had a letter from her—you haven't seen them lately?"

"I owe them a visit." In truth, I hadn't been able to face their new house. Or the idea of them having such a small place, so little to do.

121

They couldn't have been expecting me, could they? Their appearances and demeanor said otherwise. So ready did they seem, and so excited, that I came to believe Miss Fay had sent them a telegram.

What had I anticipated? A dreary cottage, a small house with cramped space around it, too close to neighbors, no style. Do we ever look closely enough at our parents? How could I have imagined that either of your grandparents would have settled for something low and cheap?

They had bought what they called a "bungalow"—which it was, if the definition of a bungalow is "built on one level only." This was no bungalow; this was a Georgian villa, from around 1730, with decorations at the windows as fond and delicate as lace. Somebody had later added a frieze under the roofline, with carved shamrocks and four-leaved clovers; it should have looked hokey but instead gave an unexpected elegance. Between two pillars the white front door stood as framed as a girl in a ball gown.

Your grandparents looked ten, twenty years younger. They had a fresh joy—in their new home, in their refurbished selves. The house had first attracted them because it had a three-acre garden; as Mother said, "I can be at one end and your father at the other." She didn't add—but she might have done; I saw the idea in her face—"And I can still keep an eye on him."

Each cultivated a separate herbaceous border. "Women only like fussy flowers," my father said, "and men-men-men like strong, muscular stuff."

Mother said, "But isn't the point at least to have flowers and color? And not just green and gray shrubs? That's not a herbaceous border, that's a funeral."

Harry had brought to new heights his pastime of writing to newspapers and politicians. "The-the-the *Irish Times* published two of my letters in the last month," he said. "About the first cuckoo."

And he was off. For as long as I could recall he had spent the early days of summer standing by fences listening with his ear cocked. That night, he'd say, "I think I heard it, but we'll know tomorrow." When tomorrow arrived, everything would repeat itself—until the day he came running to find us.

"He's here, he's here. He's up in Treacy's paddock. All the way from Africa to us, eh?" Or "He's ba-ba-back, he's down by the well, I knew he'd come here first," and he'd juke for joy and delight around the kitchen on one leg. It mattered not a whit to him that letters had already appeared in the *Irish Times* from people in Longford and Carlow and Galway saying they had not only heard but seen the first cuckoo of summer. "Bloody liars," he'd scoff. "Fabulists. Inventors."

In idle moments I often wonder about Harry and the cuckoo. If you think about it, I was his cuckoo; his own son turned him out of his nest with Venetia. I've never succeeded in getting my mind around that. Best, after all these years, to leave it.

They had settled to their new life so fast. Mother had begun something she'd longed to do: serious, time-consuming cooking. My father said she was "fattening him up like a gamecock. Any-any-any day now I'll be ready for the table, but you'll have to do the carving, Ben."

She cooked pheasant for lunch, astringent with lemon and rich with peppered cream. The diced potatoes had been first pan-fried, then finished off in the oven; the turnips came from the fields across the road. My father said, "I-I-I steal them for her; she's turning me into a thief."

They asked little about my life—and never would again. Perhaps they felt their own existence too special and even fragile; they wanted that glass never to break. And in this I found the first mild abatement—only temporary, of course—of my appalled state, because they looked content. By the time I left, Mother had begun to search for her glasses in that concentrated way that said the crossword loomed.

On my way back to Dublin, I stopped at the storage warehouse. Perhaps if I touched my own things I would see a future for them and for me, too. Their abundance took me by surprise—both in number and depth. I had more possessions than I'd realized, and they had more grace than I'd remembered.

As I drifted among them in the late shadows of the day (the warehouse had no electric light), touching this, stroking that, I began to see that someone had added things.

The buhl cabinet; that small Hepplewhite chair—I hadn't taken those. A sideboard just inside the door (I'd missed it on the way in) gave me my answer. On it sat a little boy's cowboy hat—black, and the white braid all around the crown descended into a cord that I used to tie around my neck. Pinned to it a note: "Remember this? You used to wear it to bed. I kept it where I could always find it. Much love, Mother."

James Clare had had a saying: "No matter how bad things are, the universe has a way of healing. All you have to do is watch out for it." At that moment, though, I couldn't see the universe's smaller fingers at work—I couldn't see at all for the tears in my eyes and the hatred in my heart. Of myself. The next day, I received confirmation of that opinion.

122

"Weird." How I loved that you used that word. I had only heard it as an adjective in gothic tales. Both of you employed it back then to describe anything out of the ordinary. Here I bring it into play because, for the second day in succession, I felt that people had been waiting for me. Weird.

My intention had been to file some overdue reports at the Folklore Commission. I also wanted to check the appropriateness of having written up the polio-quarantine experience; we had rules about collectors breaching family privacy. An account of it (more or less what you've read earlier) lay in my bag anyway, though I had, of course, excluded my own involvement, and my bullying of the health authority official to change the doctor's verdict.

Valerie, the girl who supervised the typing up of every field report and expense account, looked embarrassed when she saw me and stood from her desk. I couldn't imagine why; by now I had cleaned up to my former appearance, and had also managed my facial expression better. Whatever lay inside did not, I felt sure, show to the world.

"You've to go upstairs," she said. Normally she overused my name: I was "Ben" this, that, and the other—"from Easter to Christmas and the whole way back again," as John Jacob used to say. Today, she didn't say "Ben" once and she shifted on her feet, a sure sign of awkwardness.

"Upstairs" meant the director's office. "I'll tell them you're on your way," she said and picked up the office telephone.

"Them?"

She didn't answer.

"Them"—two senior officials—sat in front of the director, who sat behind his desk. A third chair waited, at an angle whereby all could see me. How long ago had this been planned and how quickly set up? Nobody had known I was coming in that day.

The director hid behind a cloud of smoke from his vast pipe. In Irish he told one of the two men, "You're the one who wants to do this."

I'd never liked this other man. He had a ferocious adherence to the Irish language, and had repeatedly castigated James and myself for not submitting our reports in the native tongue. James argued that we hadn't heard it in Gaelic, and that had we translated, we'd have lost a great deal of nuance and color.

That argument didn't wash. As James said, "Well, some folk are more folk than other folk." Nor did I like the man's sloppy mouth and his wet lips.

He addressed me using the formal Irish: "*A chara.*" Pronounced "a-korra," it means "my friend"; every official communication in Gaelic began with it. Impersonal, not friendly, it meant nothing. He launched, in Irish, into his complaint and was interrupted by the director.

"We're not all as fluent as you," he said, and who could say whether he meant it kindly. I braced myself; the "foreigner's tongue" would embitter the official's delivery.

"We at the Commission have been concerned for some time now about the sporadic nature of your work. Reports come in at irregular intervals. Your monthly administration sheets do not arrive on time—as of today, you are four months behind. An impression has grown that you have allowed factors in your private life to interfere with the pace and method of your collecting work."

I began to speak: "There are things I can say—"

He held up a hand. "You will be given an opportunity to defend yourself. If you can."

The other man, whom I only knew by sight, and with whom I had never conversed, took over. A thin fellow with dandruff, he spoke in a voice with a creaky edge.

"I'm going to make it much more personal. It never seemed to me that you were right for this job. You're not one of the people. You're pompous and arrogant, and you have a decided air of self-interest. There's no humility in you that I can see, and so how in the name of God can you understand the ordinary people of our country? You give the impression that you're above us all, that only your own private concerns are important, that only you matter."

Wet Lips cut in: "And you go about the place as though you were thinking important thoughts. One colleague here described you as lofty and moping, interested only in yourself, and that's not the humble spirit we look for in our collectors."

Dandruff came back: "I can't think what kind of training you got from the late Mr. Clare." He dragged the word: "Miss-ter."

Aha. So this is the picture. James is dead. He had no time for these uninspiring officials. "Petty clerks," he called them. This is their payback. They'll now knife all of us who loved him.

Wet Lips confirmed it for me: "Clare never counted as a serious collector, in my book. Too self-indulgent. As for his morals—" He let the sentence hang, as though to finish it would put too great and awful a strain on his soul. What was it that Marian had said? *Ben, look at us, look at the two of us in this country that pretends hour by hour, day by day, not to be corrupt and it's a cesspool of violence and hypocrisy . . .*

I had nothing to say. Nor had the director.

Wet Lips said, "Any money owing to you will, of course, be paid. I believe that you are due some annual leave. As soon as you bring your administration sheets up to date, the commission will tie up the loose ends."

It gives me some satisfaction that he never became director. Indeed, he left the Commission the following year, took a job in his brother-in-law's company, and made a whole new slew of lives miserable.

123

Ineluctably, I met Marian again. Was it bound to happen, given that I had been recalling her "cesspool" speech? Can you see how James's idea of the universe and its gifts and its synchronicities had rubbed off on me?

She gasped when she saw the huge bouquet of flowers Mother had given me for Miss Fay. We left the nursing home together, and I drove her home.

How many hours did we talk? At last I went to bed in her guest room. We didn't even discuss whether we'd share a bed; no need. That was over, and anyway I was now, in my own terms, unclean, unfit to be loved. Even for a night.

Obviously, I can't reproduce the entire conversation, but I can give you—because I noted them down—the three major points to emerge from our talk. The best parliamentarians will tell you never to make more than two points in a speech, no matter what its length. To recall three makes me feel privileged.

First of all, she quizzed me about the death of Gentleman Jack. "I know he was a bad lot, but was he a spy?"

"Who can say?" was my answer—but it didn't shrug her off.

"When I saw it in the newspapers," she said, "you were my first thought. I wouldn't have blamed you if you had killed him."

"I certainly didn't like him."

"And I said to myself, 'Ben didn't want to soil his own hands with that vandal's blood, so he got his republican friends to do an assassination. And covered it up with the history of what Collins's men did when they shot English spies.' See how clever I think you are?"

I kept it light. "And if I had?"

Marian said, "I'd have told nobody. See why I told you my secret? Incest is the biggest taboo we have. I'd never be able to show my face in this country again. So if I told you my secret, you could tell me anything. And you've never had someone like that in your life."

I nodded. Didn't say anything. And wouldn't. For two reasons: I didn't want to burden her with my guilt; and I didn't trust life enough, because it contained such things as liquor and, perhaps in her future somewhere, pillow talk. There truly is no such thing as a secret.

As our second item, obviously we discussed Venetia. Here, I gained freedom; Marian released me. When I think of Jimmy Bermingham calling her "Dirty Marian," I fume; she was so above reproach.

"Isn't it clear where Venetia has gone?" she said. Not giving my surprise time to mature, she continued: "She's gone into herself. She may not even know Jack Stirling is dead. And she may not care."

"You don't think he killed her?"

"It crossed my mind—but she's alive. My bones tell me."

"What should I do?"

"Leave it. She's gone, Ben. Far away. I saw it in her eyes. And it's a long way off in there. Move on."

I shook my head. "Is there anything left in me for her? Don't know. Can't look. Or can't see—which is it? I'd like to get close to the twins."

"They're wonderful," she said. "So open. And those terrific teeth. And they could be a pathway for you. Maybe Venetia had enough force left in her to forge a life away from everyone. But she won't live without them." Marian stretched her long legs and fetched whiskey.

And so we came to our third point—which made sense, though in that state of mind I'd never have thought of it myself. It happened in one short sentence. From Marian.

"You need to buy a house, Ben. Your own home."

124

In essence, I needed more than that: I needed care of myself; I needed belief. In the telling of my own story to myself I looked back and examined where I had been in the worst of times. And what I had learned. From that blurred picture, the road gleamed brightest, the road around Ireland—as much an idea as a fact. It shone as a ribbon winding through my disheveled life. Which meant that it still exercised remarkable power over me.

And the power went deeper than I had understood. The road had given me much more than I had realized. In my years as a silent workman on a farm, and then when all those random farmers had given me jobs, I had acquired all manner of useful knowledge. When I took Marian Killeen's advice to the letter, I had the practical skills to do whatever was needed.

On this hill, where I sit now, writing my testament for my children, I found my house. The word "dilapidated" would have praised it. An absent inheritor had neglected it, and for years it had sat, unknown, a hundred yards from the road, behind a high, crumbling wall. Weeds grew head-high, and the tentacles of brambles smothered its windows. Ancient but powerful rosebushes obscured the front door.

I saw it from above, from the hill, and even though it looked about to expire, something about it caught my heart—the vulnerable and brave chimney, perhaps, above all the rampant growth, not to mention the view if somebody would only cut back the garden.

The legatee lived in London; he had no interest in the place. It took three weeks to get the contract done. On the day I received the key I went to work—seven solid hours of getting rusty hinges free, the gates moving again, the plumbing fixed. For a week I scarcely went into the house; I cleared the garden, chopped down tall weeds, released old and lovely shrubs, including a wisteria that must have been there for a hundred years. Then I found the gravel path that ran all around the house and freed a gazebo from years of savage ivy. Dawn to dark I worked, arriving with flasks of tea and slabs of sandwiches, made in Miss Fay's kitchen.

My skills returned. All day, every day, I hammered, hacked, chopped, and cut. I painted, I papered, I routed, I repaired. What the original advertisement had called "a good villa, Victorian brick, merchant class" began to reappear. As the house recovered, so would my soul. Or so I hoped.

125

One morning, as I struggled with the leaden flashing on one of the chimneys, I heard a car engine. Nobody came up that road, except to look at the view. The sea gleamed, and the bay's horseshoe shone like beaten silver, but sightseeing cars move slowly, stopping here and there, seeking a better vantage. This driver knew where he was headed.

The car turned in at the gateway, blocking mine. Indeed, it nudged the rear bumper. *Well, that's aggressive.* Four men climbed out, in suits. They looked up, and I had to shade my eyes against the sun to see them. No formalities; no courtesies.

"Come down here."

At the foot of the ladder they grabbed me. Bundled me into the car. Said not a word. Backed out. Drove down the hill.

"I haven't locked my door."

Not a word.

"Where are we going?"

Not a word.

"Who the hell are you?"

Not a word.

I sat in the middle of the back seat, wedged between the two largest. Never saw them before. Any of them. We didn't head into the city. By back roads, and a lane or two, we went across the hills south of Dublin. Nobody spoke.

I tried to judge their intention from the road signs. Brittas didn't help; and what were we doing in Ballymore-Eustace?

Half an hour later, I knew. As his response to the outbreak of violence—the IRA called it Operation Harvest; the country called it the Border Trouble—Mr. de Valera, now the leader of the government, had opened an internment camp that became known as Tintown, a collection of steel huts behind barbed wire in the lovely Curragh of Kildare, a wide open plain famous for ballads and racehorses.

We drove through the gate of Tintown, swung open by a soldier. Just inside, the car stopped and all four men climbed out. I stayed where I was, until a hand reached in, grabbed me by the hair, and began to haul. One of the other men said, "Stop, stop, don't do that—you know what we were told."

The hair puller let go. I stood in the sunshine alone, while they huddled and whispered. Two of them led me to a long, low building; a third followed; the driver stayed by the car, smoking a cigarette. Inside, we walked down a long, wooden, paint-peeling corridor to a green door. My escorts opened the door and led me in. Inside sat two men, more disheveled than me, and I still wore my roofing dungarees.

"Here's your pal," one of the suited men said to the shabby pair. Neither man answered. Not sullen. Not withdrawn. Just—didn't answer.

"You know these two fellas," said one of my escorts. A statement, not a question.

"No. I don't."

But I did.

"They know you."

"I can't speak for them."

"How much did he pay you, lads, eh?"

Neither of the lakeside men spoke. They looked without feeling at my captors. Never said a word. It would have unnerved me had I been trying to get information. Nor did they look at me. Which I thought an error.

They corrected it, though, because one of the men in the suits said to them, "I notice you're not looking at him. Are you afraid you'll give yourself away?"

Both of the lakeside men now swung their heads and looked at me. And I at them. None of us was going to squeal. And we each knew it.

The captors had none of the modern techniques. No room from which they could spy on us, no two-way mirror. This was 1957. No eavesdropping microphones, no lie detectors, no truth drugs, nothing. Nothing but suspicion and psychology. Their suspicion drove them; but their psychology failed them. As though we had worked it out between us, the lakeside men and I drifted into a tactic. I answered every question; they answered none.

"So when did you first meet?"

"Who?"

"You and your two pals here."

"I don't know these men. I told you that."

"How did he bring you the money, fellas? In a brown paper bag? Or did he give you a leather wallet each? A souvenir?"

The lakeside men didn't answer. I looked at them when they weren't looking at me. Younger than I had thought—each below twenty-five. Fresh faces, too, an innocence. How could that be? I had seen what they'd done.

You can guess, though, the big questions that coursed through my head: How did this leak out? Who talked?

Both of those lakeside men died a long time ago—one in that Border Campaign, the other in the Troubles, which broke out in the late 1960s and lasted for three decades across Ireland and Britain. Years later I discovered how my involvement came under scrutiny.

They'd had a jealous platoon leader; he believed they hadn't handed over to the movement all the money I'd paid them, that they'd skimmed some. He tipped off the police. No evidence. My bank account didn't help them, because I kept most of James's bequest as cash. Nothing connected us.

Thus, the captors had no idea what to do next. As an interrogation, it grew even more pathetic, and it didn't even have the delight of farce. At one stage I expected them to say, "Well, if you don't know each other, you don't know each other."

A moment came when they began to flail about. We three "prisoners" stayed as we were. Doing nothing and saying less. The captors went into a corner and whispered. When they emerged they said to me, "Right. Come on."

Back along the shaky wooden corridor. Into the car. Away. They dropped me out in the country, a few miles from Tintown. Without a word. It took me most of the day to get home. A van here, a silent motorist there, and eventually a long, long walk because I had no money in my pockets.

The house welcomed me. Nobody had taken advantage of the unlocked doors, my car, or the tools left out in the open air.

My mood surprised me; I had stayed calm. Fury hadn't come along to help. Nor did relief that I hadn't been charged. But I'm not surprised; you see, by now I had no rights, in my own estimation. And yet—and yet: some kind of obstinacy, some stubborn form of self-preservation kept me from admitting my guilt.

The next morning I returned to my roofing. At about noon I heard an engine. Determined. Not a sightseer. Not again! A different car stopped on the road outside, and another man in a suit came and stood in my gateway. He looked up at me, watched me for several minutes, then went and sat on the fence across the road, where he lit a cigarette and observed my work.

When I needed to come down, I walked across the road to him.

"May I help you?" He dragged on another cigarette, his third, and looked at me, then looked away. "Is there something I can do for you?"

He didn't even bother to glance at me again.

All day he sat there, until long after darkness had fallen. Then I heard his engine roar into life, and he drove away—to be replaced minutes later by a different car. It sat outside the house all night. Last thing before I went to bed I saw the glow of the cigarette behind his window. In the morning, with the car still in place, a man walked up and down outside the gate. At eight o'clock he drove away, as another car arrived.

Two hours later, I went to get the newspaper and some groceries. As

I drove from the house, the car followed me. When I reached the shops, the car stopped behind me. In the shop, the car driver stood behind me. When I drove back, I saw him in my rearview mirror. He, too, stayed until night had fallen, and he, too, was replaced.

This procedure lasted three weeks. Wherever I went, they went. To the hospital to see Miss Fay. To the builders' supply yard to buy planks and cement. To the newspaper shop every day. Did I panic? No. I saw this as part of my punishment, and I accepted it.

126

It all twisted again. At the evening changeover, the new car brought three men, none of whom I had seen before. Different, tougher fellows. They grabbed me in a way the others hadn't. Had fewer compunctions. And a new plan.

They blindfolded me. I had no idea where they meant to take me, and I never found out. The journey lasted under an hour, ended in a tall, anonymous old room.

They sat me on a bench in the angle of two walls, and they set three chairs in a semicircle in front of me. Cornered, so to speak. They had no routine of any kind that I could detect—no kindly face to generate trust, no savagery to create fear. Fact. That's what they relied on. Straightforward fact.

"This is what we know. You met two fellas out by a lake near Cavan. You gave them five thousand to kill a man called Jack Stirling. Who'd run away with your wife. And who'd kicked the shit out of you in Cork. Kill his pals, too, is what you asked for, because his two pals held you while he hammered you. You were in Cavan all the week before, wandering here and there. And you stayed in a B and B where you could see the job being done. The fellows you hired struck a bargain with us. They'll get off and you won't. And we'll keep you in this room until you confirm all this."

They made two errors—one they should have known about, and one they couldn't have known about. When they said, "They'll get off and you won't"—not possible. And certainly not in the climate of the times. Had I been arrested, and had the case come to court, the heavier weight would have fallen on the men who'd done the deed. So I knew they were bluffing to some degree.

And the error of which they had no knowledge? My conscience welcomed their attentions. Every accusation they hurled at me, every scowl, every glance, every scrap of contempt—these affirmed my sin, they became part of my penance.

I sat in that corner for hours, maybe days. Men came, men went, the same men, different men—it all blurred. They didn't let me sleep—or tried to stop me. But if you wanted to bet, and if you knew about me what I know, you'd have put your money on me beating them. As I did. When they jostled me awake for the hundredth time, shook me by the head for the thousandth, and yelled in my face for the millionth, I finally spoke.

"Everything you're doing is wrong." And I said no more.

Since those amounted to the only words I had said in their custody, they had to consider them. Some of the men seemed as exhausted as me. I saw them retreat. Heads together, they whispered. And I knew they were saying, "What did he mean?" When they asked me, I wouldn't answer them.

My next tactic finished them off; I went "senseless." No feeling. No buoyancy. No nothing. They shook me. No resistance. They stood me up. I fell. As boneless as a rag doll. There was nothing more they could do.

They left. Someone brought a basin of water, food, a towel. In an hour or so, one of the men came back. He beckoned. I followed. Pitch-black and I could scarcely see. I fell asleep in the car—and was awakened at my own gate.

The next morning a new car sat outside my gate.

127

No matter which way I turn—blocked. A vise. I'm jammed in. Unfree. Getting frantic. No power in myself. No greater power to whom I can turn. No power to think. Not enough power to feel better. A time to listen. For instinct's voice.

I was down to that bedrock.

Although they followed me everywhere for weeks and weeks, I knew that I could shake them off on the back roads of the countryside. It took me that long, anyway, to think through the gamble I had in mind. I was wagering on the past, looking to myth, seeking lessons in legend.

You see how my mind had begun to work? You see how myth and its principles had worked in me? Any other man might have considered the stories that John Jacob O'Neill had told me no more than legend. Interestingly coincidental. Slightly magical. My configuration, though, and my daily intake of tales had led me to think otherwise. I trusted in them as I trusted in maps. Was there a risk that I might see things that weren't there? Not at all.

I didn't send him a telegram. That could have been traced. It didn't matter. This time John Jacob had a warmer welcome, if that were possible.

He said, "But you can drop in anytime."

"Intruding always concerns me."

"You don't know how to intrude," he said. "That's part of your problem."

We sat outdoors, on his garden bench. Afraid to ask for help or guidance, I tried to frame a question—about the general principle of myth as teacher. No need; without comment or introduction, he began to speak; he gave no reason.

This is a Persian story. A woman from the mountains came down one day onto the plain to visit her married sister. She looked haggard and broken. Her sister took her to see a wizard who lived on the edge of town.

When the sister had gone, the wizard said to the haggard woman, "You have two men desiring you, am I right?"

The haggard woman said, "You're right."

The wizard said, "And you don't know what to do, and they're both violent men, am I right?"

The haggard woman said, "You're right."

The wizard said, "And either man might kill you if you go with the other, am I right?"

The haggard woman said, "You're right."

The wizard said, "Well, I have powers greater than either of those two men, and I will use those powers on your behalf."

He knelt on the ground, and, as the woman watched, he drew two circles in the dirt as a child might draw a pair of primitive eyes. He stood up and he did a little dance in which his feet erased the first circle. A wind came whipping in, and with it came rain, sharp as knives. In five seconds the wind and rain went away and the sun shone.

With his feet in another little dance, the wizard erased the second circle. This time, a new wind came whipping in, carrying snow, huge and soft. In five seconds it had gone away, and the sun shone. The wizard stood with his head bowed, and as far as the haggard woman could see, he was muttering some incantation.

Then he turned to her and said, "I have done this for you because you are a good woman and I know that. Go back to your mountain. Be safe. You will never see either of those men again."

And that's the story of the haggard woman.

I didn't stay much longer. John Jacob seemed especially fatigued. With his great courtesy, he declined my invitation to eat at a nearby hotel.

This time, no car waited for me at the top of his lane. Nobody knew where I was.

Within days I identified my wizard. Three days later, after a long drive, I called on him, unannounced. I didn't know him, and he didn't know me: perfect.

He had much to say. A learned man. And lonely. He wore darkish glasses indoors, as though light hurt him. On his feet he wore striped red-and-green socks that looked like slippers, and he peeled them back to show me his corns and bunions.

"Can you imagine," he said, and it was a genuine question, "how difficult is my journey through life on these feet?"

I nodded in sympathy. "Have you seen anybody for them?"

"There's a chiropodist in Ballylooby, but she always puts her hand on my knee, and to tell you the truth, I'd prefer that she didn't. She has a very handsome husband."

Within a short time it became clear that he didn't subscribe to the sequential rules of conversation.

"What's it like to be tall?" he asked me. "I've been five feet two and a quarter inches high since I was seventeen, and I'm sick of it. The shoes don't help. Would you inspect them and tell me what you think, a big, good-looking man like you?"

He contorted, reached under his chair (from which his feet didn't touch the carpet), and pulled out a pair of shiny, buttoned boots. They had lifts built onto the soles and heels.

I turned them over in my hands—a child's shoes with wooden platforms. "Isn't this what's hurting your feet?"

"Oh, I have urine problems, too. And I've done a translation of the Apocrypha. Full of bloody heresy. Do you understand this fellow Einstein? I think he gets a lot of things wrong. Are you a chess player at all? No? Pity. But you read, don't you, you have the eyes of a reader, haven't you? I was looking at Kipling this morning—imperialist old bugger but a good poet." He began a quotation: "You can go where you please, you can skid up the trees—"

I finished it for him: "But you don't get away from the guns."

Thank you, Harry MacCarthy, for your love of Rudyard Kipling, and for passing it on to me.

Thus did my wizard warm to me. I had scored high on his tests—not shocked by feet or bladders, or possible mathematical genius, and well-read.

He was an ambitious man, hence my choosing him, and he went on to fulfill his drive. At that time, though, he'd been content to advise those higher than him: his local bishop, his archbishop, the cardinal in Armagh. Since they knew him to be clever above their reach, and shrewd beyond what his personality suggested, they had no difficulty accepting what he suggested. And he even did a two-year stint in the Vatican, where they prize shrewdness above sanctity.

He saw my strategy. In an instant. He might even have seen the innate hypocrisy of it, the end justifying the means. But he nodded.

"Good boy, good boy."

I don't think he believed me—but he recognized a sly thought process when he saw one. When I asked him his opinion, he nodded slowly. Thought some more. Then blinked.

"I suppose you know that I have a major building project under way; a smart man like yourself would have figured out that it needs donations. For the greater glory of Almighty God, of course."

"Of course," I said.

Here's what I told him: I could deal with the gunmen. Their ire would cool, they had other problems, and they owed me favors, because I had rescued one of them from a life threat. But I had no way of handling the forces of government, who chose to misinterpret me. They had disrupted my reuniting with my wife, who had been through an American divorce and remarried. I had persuaded her to leave that man, on the grounds that we didn't, in Ireland, recognize divorce. We had meant it when we said, "Till death us do part."

Canon Sheridan bought the story. Or at least he entered the deal. He warned me that it would take some weeks:

"Big wheels move slowly. But we know a lot of things about people in power."

A month later, on a fine morning, while one car sat outside my house, another arrived. They conferred, the men in the cheap suits. When they left, one after the other, I knew that they had gone forever.

We met, my wizard and I, many years later, when the canon had become a bishop. After our first greeting he whispered to me, "Wasn't that good business we did?"

I said, "God has the power."

"I prayed hard," he said.

"Did you also rub out circles on the ground?" I asked him and, when I saw his bemused look, added, "I'll tell you someday."

128

So there I sat, on my hillside, overlooking the sea, exactly where I am now. I was in my midforties, and much of my life had closed down. Miss Fay had recovered, but she remained frail, and I saw her often. Sometimes she, Marian Killeen, and I went to a concert, or to dinner, or merely for a slow walk along the shore.

My parents flourished, though in a quieter way, and seemed to draw ever closer. I became obsessive about my house and, once the essential repairs were completed, embarked on a full, authentic restoration. I hired an architect who understood what I sought, and I lived the work, moment by moment, doing most of it myself.

Except the plastering. The architect found a genius. Plasterers have a reputation for lunacy. This man, Liam Jenkins, told me that he didn't want me near the house while he was there.

"But I live here."

"You'll have to go sómewhere else."

"Any reason why?"

Liam Jenkins said, "I work naked. That's why."

He got his way, and I got my walls—to a perfect standard.

"Where did you learn your trade?" I asked him one evening over a drink.

"I'm an accountant by training. And one day I asked myself, 'Is there any skill I admire more than any other in the world, and how would it benefit my country if I had it?' So I set out to become the best plasterer that anybody ever knew."

In the months it took to finish the house, his remark haunted me. I finished the plumbing, the electrical wiring, the flooring, the tiling, the painting, the wallpapering. Every room allowed me to take it up to a pristine state. I had been sleeping in a camp bed, in the smallest room—as close as I could get to replicating a prison cell. Now I retrieved from the warehouse in Cashel my own possessions, and those that Mother had passed on to me. They and the house seemed made for each other. I had to buy so little.

As my last job, I built a locked cabinet of aged fruitwood for James's notebooks. I astonished myself—I made marquetry inlays, cut in fine detail and feather-thin stripes. This took the longest of all, and as I worked I interrupted myself to read from the notebooks I was protecting—James's wisdom, snatches of verse, stories, cures, recipes, and quotations.

Came the day that I had no more work left to do. And could drum up none: every path, every pillar and post, every pocket of grass had been renewed. I had little facing me except to sit and look at my beautifully plastered walls. And think. And reflect. And mourn the loss of my inner decency. And seek a recovery—of any kind.

Is there any skill I admire more than any other in the world, and how would it benefit my country if I had it?

129

Please understand, Ben and Louise, that nothing romantic hung from my next decision. I had always leaned this way; I didn't necessarily know that about myself—but at that moment I saw it. Hence my fascination with James; and with the hundreds of men and women, of all ages, by their firesides; and with the generations gone before them, back to the time of the bards. And hence my living obsession with John Jacob O'Neill.

He replied to my careful letter (it took me a week to draft) with two words on a postcard: "At last." When I visited him, I assessed what he needed; a second visit set us up.

Here is the plan we made: I would apprentice myself to him as a storyteller, he would teach me everything he knew, and I would memorize all the stories he had in his head—or was prepared to tell me. I agreed without hesitation to meet his three conditions.

One: Nothing would be written down. "Back to the old days," he said. "The druids, the bards—they kept everything in their memories."

Two: I would see it as a true apprenticeship, with all the discipline involved. During my training I would spend as much time with him as I could.

And three: With me in tow, he might, he said, take to the road for one last week, as though traveling in the old days. I did persuade him to the concession that he would allow me to drive him.

130

We worked together for two years. On Monday mornings I left my house at seven o'clock and drove the long journey down the four seasons of roads. He'd insisted upon what he called "office hours"—from half past nine to six o'clock, with an hour for lunch. I made sure to dress as elegantly as I could, though never in anything other than a black suit, a white shirt, and a black tie.

In the first month, I loaded my daily clothes into the closet in my room. He inspected everything, asked to see my boot polish and brushes, my shaving kit. To my socks he paid especial attention, and made me change the kind I wore. We didn't have a vast range available to us in Ireland, but he made me buy pairs with more cushioning, of a wool less coarse.

He next put me through, in effect, a job interview. His focus centered on what he called "My own private three R's: rising, recreation, and retiring." And he dismissed—in his usual kindly way—my habits.

"Rise at precisely the same time every morning. Rest for at least three hours every day—one to include lunch, two around an evening meal. Retire at precisely the same time every night. And I mean retire to sleep. Allow for half an hour or so to read or to make tomorrow's lists. But make sure that you close your eyes at the same hour of the clock seven nights a week."

I asked him, "Why is the precision so important?"

"It will reduce your anxiety," he said. "You of all people."

"Does it show?"

"Takes one to know one," he replied. "I was so anxious that I had to travel the world."

"Were you easily frightened?"

"My own shadow startled me. Or a sudden cry from a bird."

And so my training began. Before we reached into the area of his famous narrative expertise, he said he wanted to talk about scheduling. "How did you plot your journey around the country?"

I said, "I didn't have a plan. Either I went where the wind blew me or I followed up contacts the Folklore Commission wanted me to pursue."

He shook his head. "You should have had a system. We can do nothing without systems," he told me, and he went on to describe his methods:

"I'd start in a town, any town, by the ocean. From there I'd travel all around the coast. Then I'd work my way inland by about ten miles or so and begin a second circle. And so on, and so on, until the circles became tighter and tighter by ten miles at a time, and I'd end up on the banks of the Shannon at Athlone, in the middle of the country. I called them my 'ring roads.' "

"Did you ever keep count of the distances you walked?"

"I used to think that miles traveled amounted to some kind of feat. And I suppose you could say that was true. I changed, though, and measured myself by how few places I visited. Because that meant that they liked my stories and didn't find me too bad."

We may think that we scrutinize our parents while growing up. And I know that I did. I could tell when either of them hit a bad-tempered patch, or grew excited, or morose. Easy enough with my father, whose face was a movie screen. Mother, though, tended to hide her feelings—until she couldn't, and then they became a lightning storm, flashing and crashing.

Never, though, not even with Venetia, have I focused on another human being as in those two years with John Jacob O'Neill. I watched everything he did, every gesture he made, every step he took. Now I can see that I was relearning life. Having not only failed at everything I had done but traveled to the very underworld of baseness and vile deed, I needed a lifeline. At the time I wouldn't have couched it like that; looking back, I can see it clear as day.

Was I tempted at all to confide in him? Of course I was. There were moments in almost every day when I felt the words of confession lingering behind my teeth. Why didn't they pour out? He stopped them. Not by anything he did or said but by his own simple being.

He had a reserve about him, a distance he could put between himself and the world. Nothing splashed him. Sudden and difficult moments didn't come his way. The humdrum pressings we all experience never wrinkled the fabric of his life. Not once in those two years with him—and never thereafter—did I see him having to deal with a difficulty.

How did he do it? How did he manage his world so well? It didn't look like control. He didn't chide people or challenge them. Things didn't go wrong—or so it seemed. His electricity bill arrived the first week I was there, claiming an amount eight times his annual costs. He wrote the agency a calm letter, enclosing a check for the same amount as the last bill, and asked if someone would look into it. The fish truck arrived one day with no fish. He joked with the man, and never asked him—in justifiable irritation—why he'd bothered to call with an empty van.

You must remember that I had never seen such a steady human being. My father, Harry, brought turmoil into every corner of his life. Mother dashed close behind him, putting out his fires. James Clare, with whom I had traveled a little, fought a rearguard action against his own lungs. Miss Fay tidied everything around herself—all the time.

And I? What was I like? I didn't know. Had you asked me, when you first met me, to describe myself and how I conducted my life—I wouldn't have been able to tell you. From John Jacob O'Neill, though, I learned that I had no life system worth anything.

He found only one part of my work ethic that he could applaud. (Not that he decried me: not once did he criticize me.) He admired only the neatness of my car interior and my briefcase and notebooks.

"If you were a tradesman," he said to me, "I can tell that you'd have all your tools in neat rows on the wall."

I still bask in that.

In short, he rebuilt me. Within days I had adopted his regime—not that I had a choice. I rose precisely, came to breakfast at exactly half past eight, took my hour and my two-hour breaks to the minute, went to sleep at the same time every night. And slept—which surprised me.

As to my soul and its guilt and remorse—that remained. Almost undimmed. Not a day passed that I didn't see those three riddled corpses, and the black pools of blood on the floors of that seedy house. At some point every morning I caught the smell; in fact, it often preceded the wonderful smell of John Jacob's baking, as though the gods wished to remind me of the foul odors I had caused to be released into the world.

He sensed that something deep troubled me. Or did I frantically wish him to sense it? So that I could confess to him. To anyone? I controlled, as best I could, my bad moments; their worst attacks came in the first two weeks, when my mind hadn't yet engaged with the material I had come to learn.

I persevered. We concluded that first learning period with a plan: when he deemed me fit, we would indeed take to the road, and he would indeed once again become a traveling storyteller. "We'll print a poster," he boomed, with mischief in his eyes. " 'Coming Attraction.' "

I so wished him to ask me questions about Venetia and me. He never mentioned her name. And I so wished him to ask questions about the Folklore Commission. He never did—but he did reply to a letter from the officials, refusing to see them, and he left the letter and his reply lying around before he sent it. So that I could read it.

A tiredness swept over me after a few days, and so afflicted me that I fell into a deep sleep every night. Yet the morning saw me refreshed and alert, with no stiffness or aches. It took days for me to realize that this was new. In due course I put it down to routine.

When I mentioned it to John Jacob, he said, "The cows of the fields have their routine, haven't they? They get milked morning and evening, and if they're not they let everyone know about it."

131

At last the training in narrative began in earnest. I wanted to drive down on the Sunday night, such was my excitement, but I held back, not wishing to impose upon his own routine. In fact, I arrived at his lane an hour early that Monday and parked a little distance away, backing the car up the same old cart track I had sped into with Venetia when fleeing Little Boy.

You know those mornings when you can hear a bell from across the sea? I heard a distant laugh, voices, then an engine being started. John Jacob's was the only house within sight or earshot.

The cart track gave excellent cover from the road. Through the bushes I saw a car, newish, emerge from the lane, driven by a woman. To judge from the confident way she drove out onto the larger road, she knew this place.

I had a fragmented view of her; condensation masked the windows of her car. Was she blond? Not sure. She wore a head scarf, and she had a stylish and well-to-do air, not at all the type of woman commonly seen in that countryside of farms and cottages. Age? Couldn't tell. Not a girl in her twenties; more mature.

She changed gears directly in front of me, slowing down a fraction to do so. If I had to swear to it, I wouldn't have been able to identify her. Nor would I have been able to swear that it wasn't Venetia.

I dismissed the thought. Who could be less likely to have visited John Jacob? And who could be more likely than I to imagine that he was spending time with Venetia? I glimpsed her everywhere. An illusion, as you know.

However, one assumption stood out: when somebody is leaving somebody else's house at eight o'clock on a Monday morning, they've likely stayed overnight. Or for the weekend.

Inside, I found no trace of a visitor. Nor did I see breakfast crockery, neither for one nor for two—he had cleared everything before I arrived. But he did that every Monday morning.

My storytelling lessons began with form, not content. We spent many weeks on technique. He began each frame of teaching with a question, his first being "Do you ever go to the cinema?"

"I do. Often."

"What's the first thing that happens when the picture begins?"

I said, "There's the title, and the names of the actors, and the most important people working on it."

"Anything else?"

"Often there's a piece of writing or a place and a date."

"And what's the purpose of all that information?"

"To tell you who everyone is," I said.

"But they often tell us about a whole lot of people at the end. So why don't they keep the information from the beginning till the end?"

"Because they want it to be seen? Before people get up and leave?"

"I always stay and watch every name," he said. "I feel I should. In order to honor their work. But that's beside the point. Before I answer my own question let me ask you something else: what do I do before I begin to tell you a story?"

"You fiddle with your pipe. You lay everything out beside you. You make sure to be organized."

"And why do I do all that?"

I said, "So that you'll tell the story better."

John Jacob nodded. "Fair enough. But what I'm doing is exactly the same as the cinema. I'm giving you time to settle down, and I'm creating anticipation. That's the first step in storytelling: appetite."

"Shouldn't I be taking notes?"

He said, "You can write all this down tonight, if you like, but if we were back two thousand years ago, you'd be memorizing it all. Now, what's the next step?"

I shook my head. "I don't know."

He said, "Authority. You must make the audience comfortable. To do that, you need authority. You have to make them feel that the story is entirely yours to command. You can do this in a number of ways—by making a quiet beginning or having a humorous start. Humor suggests confidence. Or a mischievous one—mischief is good, too. We'll elaborate on all these points every day. Two ingredients, so far, right?"

"Appetite." I counted on my fingers. "Authority."

"What's the third ingredient? Address," he said. "Did you ever play golf?"

"No. My father did."

"In golf, the golfer 'addresses' the ball. The storyteller addresses things in an even more vital way—he addresses the audience and the story. By this I mean he speaks to the audience as though they were his creatures, and nobody else's. And he behaves toward the words coming out of his own mouth as if there could be no other words feasible ever again. That's what I mean by Address. Intense focus."

132

The Three A's. That's how I began my master classes in storytelling with John Jacob O'Neill: appetite, authority, address. Session one lasted from half past nine to eleven; the second from a quarter past eleven to one o'clock, when we broke for lunch. Our third began at two o'clock and ended at a quarter to four, and our fourth session began at four o'clock and ended at six; it usually consisted of me repeating all that he had told me that day, and asking related questions.

During that first week I asked him why he had made the last session so long, especially at a time of day when people fell asleep.

"That's precisely why," he said. "So that you'll defeat the sleep demon."

Before we got to language and delivery, we visited every corner of physical technique. He spoke about hand gestures, movement on the chair, leaning in different directions, eye contact, inflections, how to use a prop such as a glass with liquor in it or a pipe—in my case, he suggested a pen.

What clothes should a storyteller wear, in general? He had two ideas: either conform to an image people might have of what a storyteller should look like (as with my black coat, black suit, black tie, white shirt, and black boots) or go the exotic route and wear a coat of many colors, like a Gypsy.

Each had its advantages and drawbacks. My habitual garb made me look, he said, "not unlike an undertaker—but it won't distract people." Were I to wear, say, a coat like a wizard's, all bright color and wild pattern, it would announce me, he said, as "exotic, and it might fascinate the people listening to you, but would they hear every word, or would they be too busy looking at your coat?"

He favored what he called "clothes with a strong identity."

"Explain?"

"I dress like an Irishman. Or, to put it more directly, nobody is surprised at the clothes I wear, and yet they're distinctive enough for me to be noticed. And taken seriously."

These practical teachings took months. They included how to knock on a door, how to enter a house, how to greet the people: "As though you're delighted to see them and as though you're bringing them something special—which you are."

He taught me how to charm a housewife who groaned at the thought of an extra mouth at the table and grimaced at the notion of her children being up till all hours. "Tell her," he said, "that you heard of her kitchen's great hospitality. She can't go against that."

If the storyteller knows the house has children, "wear a watch and chain across your vest. Finger the chain, and the child will surely ask you the time. Take out the watch, open it, and show it to the child, and tell the child a story about the watch."

I asked him, "What story do you tell?"

"I might make one up. I might say to the child, 'Until very recently, this watch was around the neck of a baboon.' Always use a notable word to a child—like 'baboon' or 'chimpanzee.' So: 'The creature took it off an explorer who was attacked by a lion in the jungle, but the lion couldn't digest the watch and threw it up. Now, it so happened that the explorer's brother went looking for him, and he saw the watch flashing and winking high in the trees above the jungle, and he lured down the baboon with bananas, and got back the watch, and that's how he knew that his brother had died.' "

He asked me, "In the middle of a story, how do you retain the attention of your listeners? It might be late at night. The fire makes people sleepy—so what do you do?"

I shook my head, aware that I wasn't expected to know.

"That's when your technique comes most to help you," he said. "You do things."

For the next few minutes he showed me all kinds of small movements. He searched for matches; he mopped his brow with his pocket handkerchief; he crossed one foot over the other; he paused on an upward inflection, as though interrupting himself with his own sense of wonder at the tale he was telling. At one moment he looked away, to gaze down into the fire and shake his head, as though he felt staggered by what he was about to tell. Next he clapped his hands hard together and exclaimed, "And do you know what?"

I hadn't observed him using many of these stratagems when he was telling me stories, and I said so.

"But you never fell asleep," he said. And chuckled.

Every night, by the fire after dinner, four nights a week (after Friday's final session, I drove back to my house outside Dublin), he told me a full story. Nothing was required of me but to listen.

He took me all over the world in those tales. I learned about a boy in Cuba who slew a blood-sucking creature that had been terrorizing a village. He told me a story about a dance marathon in Russia, where the prettiest girl in the village made her many young suitors dance all day and all night, and she would marry the last man standing. Who was blind.

From Italy he had a tale of a man who made a bargain with a witch and tried to renege on it. The island of Ireland has thirty-two counties, and for eight weeks he told me a story from each county—in alphabetical order.

He told me the shortest story in the world: "That evening, the last creature left on earth saw the sun going down in the east." The longest, he said, "would take seven years, seven months, seven weeks, seven days, seven hours, seven minutes, and seven seconds. And note," he continued, "that we use seven devices for measuring time—years, months, weeks, days, hours, minutes, and seconds."

Before he considered me ready for the exalted level of telling him a tale, he and I analyzed a number of legends. He showed me how to lead with a strong character. "Or, better still," he said, "with a weak character who grows strong, because the best legends are those where we learn how to overcome what besets us."

Conflict, he said, lay at the core of every story, because we face pressure all day, every day.

"Walking against the wind—that's the least of it. Getting up, going to bed, preparing food, eating food—we futile creatures must struggle all the time. Nothing that we need comes to us; we must reach for everything."

He boiled down "the things we call stories" into three simple components: "Somebody does something for some reason. Or," he said, "Who does what and why? After that, language is the toolbox. In there, you should find shiny, beautifully polished and honed tools, with sharp edges or hammerheads or needle points, and with those tools you will fashion your tale.

"But, as with all tools, you have to learn how to respect them, and how to use them with accuracy and elegance. I mean to say, you never see a master carpenter take his toolbox, open the lid, and toss the whole thing up in the air. How would he ever get his table made? And he certainly wouldn't get the lovely marquetry inlay done, and the dovetailing and detailing.

"And at the end of the day, after using his tools on the job to the best of his ability, the carpenter will be tired—and so he should be, because he has made an effort to work hard and with grace, to create something that is poised and admirable, intended to bring pleasure to people."

A great leap forward came when he sent me out of the house to the top of the lane and told me to walk back as though approaching the house for the first time, with the intention of telling stories by the fire. We opened the door to heavy rain. He didn't say, "Wait till the weather clears"; he said, "Well, you'll be out in all weathers, and you're used to it anyway."

My heart racing, I waited, then walked back down the lane as, so to speak, an actor. I knocked on the door as directed: three firm, spaced knocks. He took his time answering, and I said, "God save all in this good house."

"And yourself," he answered.

"Do you have room in your mind for a tale of life itself, a tale of wonder, wisdom, and delight?"

When he'd taught me that line I'd said to myself, *I wouldn't have been able to resist that if I'd heard it at my door.*

After what he called "some furnishing and burnishing," we moved on to embrace content. This training, naturally, took the longest time of all. During our tuition segments, he trained me in four stories. First he told me the entire tale, and then I had to repeat it to him. Then he went back over it piecemeal, and I repeated segments.

He criticized my pace—"too fast, too anxious." And my smile—"too frequent, too false." Of my language he said, "Not rich enough, not strong enough." And on we went, until I told those four stories in their entirety to him at night, in the time between dinner and bedtime, the time he usually told me tales I hadn't heard.

Monday night, the story about the chariot maker and the boy who could speak to horses: no comment on my telling. Tuesday night, the woman who tamed a whale and rode on its back down the coast to see her mother: no comment. On Wednesday night I told the old Irish legend of the children of Lir, condemned to live as swans in the cold places of the earth: he listened as keenly as a child and made no comment.

On Thursday night, I finished telling, as he had taught me, the story of the man who made a wooden horse and then breathed life into it, and went on to create from the same timbers a woman, whom he then married. As I spoke the words, "That is my story, and now that it has left my mind and gone to live in yours, another story will soon take its place," John Jacob rose from his seat and stood looking into the fire. After a pause, he spoke:

"It occurs to me to say, 'You'll do well.' But you work best when praised. Therefore I'll not stint on what I think and feel. You've taken on this training with vigor and conscience, and you'll be hailed as having donned the mantle of the great tradition. Wherever you go in the world you will be respected and welcomed, as long as you continue to honor the story in the way I heard you do all this week."

Children, I didn't let him see the tears in my eyes. That night, I think, counts as the only night in which I didn't sleep. His praise worked some balm into me—not enough, I know, to erase that awful stain, but it helped, and I lay in my bed, not hating myself as much.

133

A month later, John Jacob Farrell O'Neill made what he called his "final, final" appearances as a traveling *seanchai*. And I embarked upon a life that had once been his. We'd agreed that watching him work would count as my last tuition. After that, we would have what he called "an important conversation." I was to tell him my own philosophy of storytelling—which he expected me to have worked out by then. That had to happen, he said, before I'd be ready to go out on my own.

In our planning we'd agreed not to be foolish. Yes, we'd approach every door on foot as though we had been walking all day, but we would travel everywhere by car. And we would park just out of sight of each house to preserve the illusion.

As a second concession, to his age and the times we lived in, we would make it clear that we didn't expect to stay in the houses we visited.

"I'm too old to share a bed with another man," he said, "and you're too young," and we laughed. "However," he added, "if the lady of the house is free to make amorous overtures, I'll compete with you for her affections."

To which I said, and I knew it to be true, "I'm afraid I wouldn't stand a chance in that contest."

I think we were only half-joking.

It crossed my mind at that moment to ask him about the prosperous-looking blond lady I'd seen driving away from his lane that bell-clear morning. I'd never seen her since then—but I had taken care not to arrive early on a Monday again. True, I did sneak around the place once or twice on Mondays afterward, but I saw nothing evidential. Unless you count a new box of Black Magic chocolates sitting on the table in the scullery, near the sink.

He could, though, have bought them himself—he claimed a "weakness" for them. "Must be the name," he said. "I'd eat anything with the word 'magic' in it."

On the night before our road trip, I arrived at dusk. A car drove away mere seconds before I reached the top of the lane; I saw its red taillight as it headed for the mountain road. It occurred to me to follow it—and then, firm as a foot, I shut down that idea. It had nothing to do with me, no matter who it was.

At the house it took John Jacob half a second to open the door—and then he stepped back, startled.

"Oh, Ben. I thought—" He stopped and led the way in as normal. *He thought that the person who had just left had forgotten something and had come back for it. That's what he thought.*

He recovered fast. "I have all the maps ready," he said.

"And I have a question for you."

"Fire ahead."

I said, "You have to answer it."

He looked at me as if to penetrate my frontal lobes with his eyes. "This is serious. I'm listening."

I said, "You can probably guess what I'm about to ask—but I'll ask it anyway. Is it possible that I will tell a story somewhere, in some house, by some fireside, some night—and then find that it, or a version of it, comes true?"

He didn't hesitate. "Yes."

"What is that? A phenomenon of some kind?"

"Every storyteller worth his salt will tell you that. And I suppose, yes, it is a kind of phenomenon. I have a different explanation for it. Mythology is the emotional history of a country, the spiritual record. And when you're in that kind of mystical territory, anything can happen. And usually does."

I said, "What does that do to the storyteller?"

He smiled. "Just the kind of astute question I'd expect from you." He made me wait—and then said, very quietly, "It heals."

From there we turned to the maps. We had spent a great deal of time working out where we would go, and for how long in each place, and how we should schedule the trip day by day. Pursuing his system at its best, we intended to start in the north of Donegal, on the Inishowen Peninsula, right over at the border, and work our way down the coast to Sligo. If we got fine weather, we'd have a glorious time.

I knew by his face, though, that some new and important matter had seized him.

"Here's the map," he said. "We're going somewhere else."

"Where?"

We bent over the table together. He pointed to a village I knew well—Templederg, fifty miles to the west, out on the coast. "There. And only there."

"Why?"

That morning, he wore a tweed jacket I'd never seen before, dark blue herringbone, and the top pocket had a navy kerchief with white polka dots. He also wore a navy turtleneck sweater—he looked sixty, not eighty.

"In some countries," he said, "a storyteller can act as a healer. If there's been violence. A murder, say. And there was a man killed in Templederg recently. Nobody knows who did it, they believe it's a local person, and they'll all be in a troubled state."

"What do we do?"

He said, "We'll go to Templederg, and we'll go to three houses, and in each house I'll tell them a story. It will unite them, and that's a healing process."

Stooped as I was, over the map spread out on the table, a chill spread like a slow flood of ice water across my back. Why was he doing this?

134

He made me drive through Templederg at first—a prosperous place with a strong creamery, a village hall in good condition next to the church, and many of the houses well looked after. We found a place to park, sheltered and under trees, and we could see the lights of the houses ahead of us.

The first man to open his door blurted greetings and pleasure. No warmer welcome existed. Three children, aged about ten to fourteen, sat at a table with their schoolbooks. Down at the far end of the kitchen, a woman stood at an ironing board. That scene played every evening in hundreds, if not thousands, of homes across Ireland.

I discovered that John Jacob had visited this house long ago; these children formed the third generation he had met. They knew all about him here, and so did the wife, who came forward to greet us. Glasses of whiskey soon gleamed in our hands.

John Jacob said, "Do you know why I'm here?"

"It'll be a welcome thing you're doing," said our host, whose name was JohnJoe. "You'll see a crowd."

We ate with the family. Perhaps for the purposes of my education, John Jacob reminisced with JohnJoe and his wife about his visit to this house and, in another county, her family home.

He got them to tell their memories—of his arrival, how the evening built, the stories they remembered. JohnJoe's wife served heaps of the same diet that I knew from all over the country: bacon, eggs, soda bread, tea. Since I'd known him, John Jacob had always eaten more than I did, and it never showed on his big frame.

We pushed back from the table and found places by the fire. As though somebody had rung a bell, people began to arrive—neighbors, with and without children. Soon thirty people had gathered in that kitchen.

I had heard of this many times, in houses all over the country: some kind of unexplained bush telegraph. Nobody had quit the house since we'd arrived, and they didn't have a telephone—so somebody must have seen us walk through the dusk down the village street, as though it were a hundred years ago, and knock at this door.

Some houses did have the reputation as haunts of the *seanchai*— "rambling houses," or, to give it a Gaelic name, *cuartaiocht,* which translates as "visiting." In such houses, music and dancing would break out when the storyteller had finished telling his tale.

Not, however, on that somber night. The conversation hung at low decibels; few smiled; nobody laughed. One by one, the villagers settled, many of them anxious, and John Jacob began:

"When a visitor comes to your house, he brings the outside world with him. And he brings the feelings of the universe, for you to inspect them. And you may select from those feelings whatever you need at that moment. And that's why the magic of the world directed my feet to Templederg tonight."

He began to light his pipe. For the thousandth time I watched his technique. And I observed how people watched his hands and the tobacco and the tamping down and the flare of the match. They looked rapt.

"You've had an unfortunate occurrence in your midst. A man from your village was taken away and murdered. Many of you heard it happen, and that's almost worse than seeing it. And you saw his blood on the ground after he was hit on the head, and some of you saw him dragged away. Most of you heard him scream. But you haven't found his body, and you haven't found his murderers, and therefore you have no means of mourning."

He had a fire to him that night. His eyes sparkled, not with humor, no trace of that, but with something else. I reach for the word "zeal"—but that's an unsafe word; it smacks of evangelism. "Fire" might work; he certainly exuded some kind of flame.

"Worse than that, some of you fear that you might have brought this murder among you. That fear will divide you. And my job is to tell you tales that you can all listen to of an evening."

I looked around the room. JohnJoe's wife had her hand to her mouth. Other faces, male and female, defined the word "thoughtful." And never did the children know such a time to keep silence.

You must understand, Ben and Louise, where we were and who we were. A peasant society, certainly, but with high levels of natural intelligence. Now, in a time of acute pain and fear, these people needed something other than their norms. At one stride we had returned to a kind of spiritual paganism, an intense humanism almost, a reaching for primitive beliefs in the power of the human spirit to learn how to heal itself.

Nobody in the room would, of course, have put it like that. Except John Jacob Farrell O'Neill. I learned it from him. And from James Clare, and from the warriors and princesses and heroes and maidens and druids and wizards and chieftains and bards who stood in the shadows of that room that night, returned from the shadows of time and the universe to help their descendants to a better life.

This is what took place—and it went on until five o'clock in the morning. John Jacob now had the full and rapt attention of every body and soul in that room.

"I'm going," he said, "to tell three stories tonight in the village of Templederg, and I will tell them in three different houses. Some people among you here have seen this done before, by me and others of my wandering tribe. When I have finished the first story, I will leave this decent place and go to a neighbor's place, and any of you who feel like it, and who feel that the next house can accommodate us as our little band of people grows, will be welcome house by house."

Heads nodded without thought. *Will he need a field to fit in everybody? Or will this be some kind of magic whereby hundreds of people will stand easy in a room made for ten?*

He rounded off his opening thought: "Before the cock crows to tell us that the sun is on his way up from below the rim of the sky, we'll have heard the third and final tale."

PART SEVEN

❄ ❄ ❄

The Last Storyteller

135

And so we come to the final chapters of my *apologia pro vita mea*. You will see why I rank that night as the most extraordinary of my life—because so much flowed from it. Perhaps I should tighten that definition of "extraordinary" to "extraordinary and good." We already know what the "extraordinary and bad" was.

John Jacob told each of his three tales to exactly the length of two hours. He told me afterward that he did it "by instinct."

"But you didn't look at a watch. And I don't remember seeing any clocks. Not in your eye line, anyway."

"The world gives you a kind of rhythm," he said.

He did something else during the evening: he became a kind of timeless figure. As I watched him, he changed. A new spirit entered and took up residence in the well-dressed and well-tended old gentleman by the fire, in his natty tweed jacket and polka-dot pocket handkerchief.

Now I saw a man of no age, yet gnarled by centuries. Now I saw a man carefully holding himself together, yet assailed daily by the wind and the rain. Now I saw a man who did not live in a "strong farmer's house with all the modern conveniences" but a man whose roof was the sky, or a barn with swallows darting to and fro under the eaves, or the dense canopy of a tree in full summer leaf.

The commanding figure by the fire had not come there that evening; he had been here eons ago, when the houses were wooden, with one hopeful slot in the ceiling for the smoke to escape. He had walked into this place centuries ago, when the floor and the walls were made of mud

and sod, and the people shared with him their oaten stirabout and goat's
milk, which was all they had. He had walked into this village decades
ago, when the first gleams of freedom were banishing the dark angels of
poverty.

I looked at him and saw not the charming and muscular John Jacob
O'Neill with the twinkling eyes—I saw the figure who, without my
knowing it, had all my life been the most important portrait in my own
private gallery, the leading member of my inner cast. What was James's
word? The "culmination."

I was seeing an archetype. Not a local character, such as a ballad singer
or a blacksmith; this was a visitor from the world stage, a vital cog in
Man's spiritual machinery. In all the faiths, in all the hopes, in all the
belief systems of the world, one figure and one only held the truth for
me, and therefore the healing: the storyteller, the one who tells us who
we are, and who has done so since God was an infant.

John Jacob was that archetype that night, and as though to prove it to
my eyes, he shape-shifted, as if he'd been in an old legend. He changed
from the man who had been with me in the car, with the navy turtleneck
sweater, the ruddy cheeks, the impeccable hands, the power thrumming
away beneath the surface.

Now I saw a man in a long black coat, a black hat, and powerful,
shiny boots; a man with a face of stark, white parchment whose deep-set
eyes glowed like coals and whose hands punched each dramatic point; a
man who turned his head slowly, like a searchlight, seeking out every face
listening to him and compelling it not merely to hear but to *understand*.

I saw a younger man, still in black but with a hint of the clerical in his
shirt and collar, a priest or a schoolteacher, and I realized that I was seeing a fugitive, a man to be shot on sight because he possessed learning.
Shakespeare knew it: "He thinks too much: such men are dangerous."
This man was bringing to these people out under the trees and the hedges
the thrill of Ovid, the power and yearning of Dante, the beauty of Virgil
and Horace, and would, if caught by the red-coated soldiers, pay for it
with his life.

And I saw, too, a tall man in a robe with a staff, entering the castle hall
and being made welcome, and sitting on great cushions, and eating and
drinking, and then, invited to stand beside the king and queen, telling a
tale, in ravishing language and flowing verse and eternal feeling, a tale by

which a kingdom could be governed, on which a nation could be founded.

From the first house to the second we went, and from the second to the third, and no matter how humble one fireplace, or how comfortable another's parlor, the power escalated. Three tales he told that night, and he moved people to all the emotions they possessed; the tales touched on the five senses, too, and as they listened, people saw, heard, tasted, smelled, and touched.

Example: "The king reached forward, took her wrist, laid a gentle finger on it, and said to her, 'Feel. This is your life coursing through your body. I want to flow in that stream.' " I swear that most of the adults in that room and all of the children reached for their wrists.

136

We walked back to my car. John Jacob took my arm. Before we stepped into the shade of the trees, he stopped.

"Look," he said, pointing. The faintest sliver of light, milk white touched with yellow, had begun to open the sky. "I'm giving you that," he said.

Sad to think that there had been a time in my life when I wouldn't have understood what he meant. Good to think that I then grasped it in depth.

Back at the house, I took over. He slumped in a chair, exhausted, while I lit the fire and prepared the breakfast he liked, oatmeal with cream and honey, and, this morning, whiskey. I laid the table as elaborately as if for dinner, made tea strong enough to stand a spoon in, and led him to the table.

We ate in silence. The food revived him. I risked a compliment:

"You were magnificent. I don't own words enough to praise you."

He raised his great leonine head and looked at me.

"Thank you, Ben. I'll treasure that remark."

"It's true," I said.

I reflected, but didn't tell him, that he had moved several notches up the scale from the performances he had given for me, even including the drama of Ballyneety.

We ate on, and finished the pot of tea.

"You must be exhausted."

"Food always revives me," he said. "And we had a lot of food last night." He laughed. "That's how I kept going."

True: at every house in which we'd appeared, the people had insisted on feeding us.

"How much did you prepare? Mentally, I mean."

He said, "It's difficult to tell. I'm preparing all the time, in a way. My mind is always looking for new structures, new styles, new methods of stating things." He paused, reached for his pipe. "Do you have notes for me?"

Startled, I looked at him. "You mean—a critique?"

"Yes. What could I have done better?"

"Oh, dear God," I said. "How could I?"

He chuckled. "Did Leonardo make the Mona Lisa's nose too long? Is that what you're saying?"

"Yes. Absolutely."

"I'd have a lot to say about Mrs. Gioconda's nose. And tonight I went into the first story too fast, not enough preamble. And I flagged badly on the last story."

"If you say so."

He bristled a little. "I do say so."

"Well—do you know why?"

"Yes. I was nervous on the first story, and tired on the last."

"I can understand 'tired.' But 'nervous'? Surely not."

"Look at the reality. I've been training you for months and months, and now the teacher has to be watched by the student."

I conceded: "I know what you mean. But I saw no flaws. Anywhere."

He went to work on the tobacco in the heel of his hand, the pipe stuck in the corner of his mouth.

"We'll see how you like it when I come to hear you, soon."

I laughed. "That's not fair. And if you do, I'll be tongue-tied."

"No," he said, shaking his head. "You won't. I've found my true successor."

That, children, was almost too much. He knew it, too.

"Damn! I left my lighter in your car."

I think he did it to release me, so that I could hide my emotion in a few minutes of absence. When I came back with the lighter, he had begun to clear the table.

I said, "No. Not tonight, or this morning, or whatever time it is. You have to sit down. I'm doing this."

Meeker than I had ever seen him, he headed for his chair. By now the fire had taken heart and flared with beauty—orange and red flames, with flickers of green.

When I came back to the kitchen with everything washed up and tidied away in the scullery, he had recovered his energy.

"We talked," he said, "before Templederg about a philosophy for you, and perhaps a plan of what you're going to do now."

I said, "I'm taking to the road."

"I know that. How will you handle it?"

"Don't know yet. I'm still thinking it through."

"Can I help?" The pipe glowed; the blue-white smoke rose.

I said, "I need to know why I'm doing it."

He took the pipe from his mouth and looked at me; I didn't dare break the eye contact.

"We both know why you're doing it, Ben. Let yourself hear yourself say it. Out loud. Alone, if you prefer. That has always worked for me."

"How do I do that?"

"Open your mouth and be spontaneous."

I did as he said, and these words emerged and hung in the air: "I need to change myself. In order to heal myself."

"Good boy."

Neither of us spoke for some time. We both looked into the fire, each lost in—perhaps—the same thoughts. John Jacob broke the silence:

"I did something very bad once. Foul. Outright, black evil. Sometime later, I heard from an old, old man the stories that I told last night in Templederg. I followed him, I learned them, and I told them."

137

The next day I sat down with him and made my own plans. Thoughts, ideas, proposals, and arrangements flowed from me in a torrent. He approved everything I intended. For a time we were like children, high with glee at the speed and intelligence of our thoughts.

We agreed that the first year or so should continue to be a learning process for me, and then he planned what he called my "release," the moment when I would go out into the world alone on this brave, venturesome project. After that, on a date to be agreed, he would come and hear me. At my bidding. It would take place sometime after the year ended. In the meantime, we would not see each other.

As we sat back and rested from our great efforts, John Jacob laughed. I looked at him with a quiz in my eyes.

"I'm just wondering," he said, "whether you're poacher turned gamekeeper or gamekeeper turned poacher."

"I'll give you a John Jacob O'Neill kind of answer," I said. "Both."

As to my repertoire, we determined that I would not yet attempt stories in three different houses in one night, not until I had gained a lot of experience—some of it theatrical. "Theatrical"—John Jacob's idea—meant that I was to book village halls here and there and hope that the people would arrive.

My main thrust, though, would be the reconstruction of a *seanchai*'s life, the only difference being my car (and that didn't last long). I would tell stories he had taught me, and then move on to material I had collected.

Wasn't this all quite an undertaking? Indeed. Think, however, of the depth and degree to which it occupied my repeatedly troubled mind.

It also took my mind off my country. And how I needed that. I still wonder that we didn't fall apart. Ireland grew worse by the day. People emigrated by the thousands, to desperate jobs and worse circumstances in England, to promises of sunshine in the United States, but only if they had relatives there. Political myopia spread like a rancid fog across the land, as the church interfered more and more in the running of the state.

Ironically, the Border Campaign limped along, with pathetic attacks and sadder deaths. I say "ironically" because a case could be made that the rebels had waged the wrong fight—they should have tried to take over the south. We needed something to shake us out of our torpor. (We did in due course receive the impetus we needed, but not until the early 1960s, and only then when a golden visitor showed us what the power of glamour looked like.)

And so, on a Monday morning, with maps and schedules, I set off on my new road around Ireland, to become a storyteller in the great tradition. Was I nervous? Yes. And frightened. Anxious. Unknowing, and therefore uncertain. Full of doubt. The times had changed—how would I be received?

138

I made for the coast of Clare, for the small place not far from Doolin where James Clare had been born, within earshot of the Atlantic breakers. It seemed the perfect choice—and it had been my idea. I followed John Jacob's instructions to the letter: park a mile away; walk to the hamlet as though I had been walking all day; choose the house; knock on the door; and greet the inhabitants as he had taught me.

According to his directive, I had to select a house I didn't know, one I had never visited. Coward that I was, I yet drove through beforehand, in daylight, looking around for the cleanest, the most well-ordered place. I found a cottage with white walls and a new slate roof. Neat window boxes held geraniums, and in the tiny front garden hydrangea blossoms bobbed their heads like babies.

During the long Atlantic dusk I came back and knocked on the door. A woman answered, in her sixties, perhaps seventy.

"Yes?"

"God save all in this good house."

"There's only myself, but thanks anyway," she said, a spry and cautious woman.

"Do you have room in your mind for a tale of life itself, a tale of wonder, wisdom, and delight?"

She looked me up and down with her pale eyes. "What is it you're trying to sell?"

I took the question and transformed it: "A story. A long story. Of love found and lost. Of dignity and failure. Of grandeur and defeat."

She eased, in front of my eyes: so gratifying.

"Come in, so," she said and stepped aside.

I had chosen well; she kept her home shiny as a new pin, so clean I almost felt afraid to sit down. As I stood in her kitchen, feeling too big for the room, and awkward at being twice her size, she looked up at me and said, "I've had a chair here for years big enough for a man to sit in, and not a man has come yet to sit in it, so you might as well be the first."

She directed me to a great leather armchair.

"Thank you, ma'am."

"That was my grandfather's chair. And my father's. They were big men, like you. My name is Maura O'Grady."

She generated hospitality by way of the inevitable tea—I refused liquor, another part of my deal with John Jacob. When we had finished with the small talk—she had never heard of James Clare—I told her the story of the great Malachi MacCool and the girl Emer.

Such an attentive audience: still as a stone; pale eyes on mine; not a fidget or a move. I took about two hours, told a shorter version than John Jacob's, and not at all as accomplished, not by a long chalk. Not yet.

At the end she thanked me.

"I haven't heard a story like that since I was a child," she said, in quite a flat way.

This was a woman in whom joy would be difficult to perceive. I wanted her to tell me whether she had been moved, but she said nothing more. Except when I stood at the door and said, "Good night now, and thank you for listening to my story."

"The girl was right," she said. "To marry the young fella. Oul' Malachi didn't have the guts to fight for her. He should have challenged the young fella to a boxing match or a duel or something. If I had a fella, that's what I'd want from him."

I couldn't resist asking a question, even though it took me out of character: "Did you ever have a man in your life like that?"

She said, with no feeling discernible, "I never had a man in my life at all. I'm an only child, and my mother didn't like men, so she warned me off them."

So ended my first story. I made my way to Doolin and stayed in a bed-and-breakfast place. My last thought as I fell asleep? *This is cheating. I should be sleeping in a barn somewhere or the open air.* Soon I would be.

139

As I made my way through every place on my schedule, I remained steady and calm—for hours at a time. Yet, no day passed without a memory of that house in Cavan and its three dead bodies—which I now chose to see as vile in death. That's how I processed what I didn't wish to acknowledge: I demonized. The bodies were to blame for their own foulness, nothing to do with me.

And Venetia? Those were thoughts that I could and did control. How could I do otherwise? She had vanished of, I believed, her own accord. Had made her choice. Rejection. Of me, and all that I stood for, and any relationship that we might have. So—I demonized her, too. Arrested every thought process the moment it began. Didn't even allow myself to wonder whether she had mourned Jack Stirling. Note, however, that I thought of her as still alive.

For weeks I made my calls, on my schedule that had taken so long to plan. I told the stories John Jacob had told me, and soon I began to tell some of my own. Here, again, I obeyed directives; as soon as I had become accustomed to telling his tales I could include stories I had known from elsewhere, from my own collecting.

Now, at this far distance, it astounds me that I did it. But back then? Not a moment's faltering did I have, as though I knew I had no choice. And I didn't—that is, if I'm permitted to use the word "spiritually." My alternative? If you'd asked me, I'd have said, "Death."

An interesting cowardice rose to the surface. I kept choosing stories I might never see reflected in life. For example, after six weeks or so, I was almost telling the Malachi MacCool story in my sleep. From this locked pattern I had to break away—and I confess that I was curious to see whether anything I might tell a family had any bearing in real life. Or would prove to have.

This inquiry nagged me, especially as I had been so intrigued and, I believe, influenced by it from John Jacob's storytelling.

For my "breakout," I chose a Friday night, and again I set up everything in advance. This time I knew the house, had been there a number of times as a collector, and felt sure of my welcome. Also (and this will tell you how I tried to control things) I had calculated that I might afterward make things happen that would echo the legend I had chosen.

140

The children of the house had an appetite for narrative (and so, in truth, had their parents). So by way of preamble I merely said that it was a story of the ancient world, and I settled down to it.

Long ago and not too far away, on an island off the coast of Munster, where the sun shone through the leaves on the trees and made colors like stars on the ground, where the birds flew upside down when it rained because that's the easiest way of all to get a drink of water, where the horses held contests to see which of them could run faster than the wind, there lived a king who believed himself the finest king in the world.

His royal majesty liked to show what a fine fellow he was. He even insisted that his only child, a son, call him "Your Royal Majesty." As part of his royalness he held his head as though it sat on a pointed stick, and turned it this way or that only when he felt that he saw something worthy of his royal eyes. And he walked like a stork, tall and slow and stately, as though he had no need to keep up with the pace of the world.

This was the part of him that most troubled his advisers—the slow, deliberate, lordly pace, the way he looked at the universe down the long slope of his

royal nose. They, being wise men, knew that the planet spins at its own pace
and that we had better keep up with that.

He also had a third and, to some people, even worse characteristic: he
spoke in a very slow and orderly way. No hurried words, everything
considered—that was how he believed a king should speak.

So look at him for a moment: holding his head stiff and upright and
avoiding any sight of which he might not approve, because he was such a fine
fellow. Walking slowly, because he believed that he, being such a great king,
did not need to keep pace with the world; rather, he believed that it was the
world's place to keep up with him. And speaking in a measured and slow
way, believing that to be the royal manner in which a king should speak.

There were, however, those who believed that the king behaved like this
because he was a sad man. He had no wife anymore; she had disappeared
during a lightning storm one night and was never seen again. The king's son
had left, too. He had no wish to succeed to the throne, and he'd gone abroad
to become a scientist, interested only in the lives and habits of spiders.

Sad or not, for years and years and years the king went his royal way,
while ivy thickened into bushes on the castle walls, while his dog grew a gray
beard and went blind, while his marshes slowly became bogland that his
children's children would dig for peat to put on the fire.

And then one summer, on his sun-filled island, it rained. As never before,
it rained in the daytime. He had so ordered—or so he believed—that it rain
only at night. That happened to be the way the climate in that part of the
world ran itself, yet the king believed it to be his doing. When a great storm
up on the roof of the world changed some matters here and there, on the king's
island it began to rain during the day.

And it rained all day, every day. The ducks on that island, who had never
been very good swimmers, suddenly became champions at paddling. I don't
know if they have paddling at the Olympic Games, but if they had, those
ducks would have won all the medals.

The frogs became wonderful swimmers, too. The poor creatures didn't
know at first what to do with all this water, because in the past they had
depended on the charity of boys and girls who made special pools for them.
Now they jumped and they splashed and they turned somersaults in the
abundant water they found everywhere.

It didn't stop raining all summer, and in the rain the farmers couldn't
plant anything, and it rained all August and September and October and

November and December, and the farmers couldn't harvest anything, because there was nothing to harvest, and even if there had been the weather was too bad.

The island, therefore, had no food. The people used up all their stores, and by Christmas they had nothing left to eat. The people knew that they were living now in a famine.

They sent envoys from the island out into the world to ask for help. But each country said to them, "Oh, isn't your king that proud fellow who won't look at anyone, who will speak only when he wishes and at his own pace and who walks like a tortoise on stilts?"

When their ship sailed home empty-handed, into the harbor in the rain—because it hadn't stopped raining—everybody fell silent. Their clamor stopped. They said not a word, not a whisper. And then a child, its feet in the water, its cheeks drawn and pale with hunger, spoke the unspeakable.

"So I am going to die," she cried, "because the king is so proud."

She was dark-eyed and had straggly hair and a wild look. Everybody turned to see her.

"Tell us what to do," said an envoy, who wasn't at all haughty about the wisdom that comes from the mouths of babes.

"If all the children march to the palace, the soldiers won't kill us—because many of them are our fathers. We will talk to the king, and we will teach him our ways, and we will delight him with our play."

When the king heard the commotion at his gates, he sent his favorite footman, Faluta, to find out what it was about. The footman returned and said, "Your Royal Majesty of royalness, the children of your subjects have come to see you. They say that they want you to come out and play."

The king, quite a plump man—he, of course, had his own private store of food—sat up. He looked surprised, but, as Faluta the Footman later reported, he also looked a little pleased.

"Bring them in," he said. "Let them play here."

The children flooded in. They examined the buckles on his royal slippers, they fingered the beautiful royal hose that clung tight to his legs, they rubbed the velvet of his robe, they tried on his crown.

To the king's own surprise, he enjoyed the company of the children. He almost smiled. He showed them the jewels in the crown. And his great ring. And he let them handle the ornamental sword that hung above his throne. He patted their heads.

Standing a little apart from the group, the raggedy girl watched the king carefully. She observed how his head did not turn easily. She perceived that he walked like a stork in pain. She heard his speech, stilted as sour milk. And she knew what to do.

She walked over to the king.

"Are you enjoying yourself?"

"Oh yes, oh yes," he said. "This is wonderful."

"Do you feel happy?"

"Oh yes, oh yes."

You will note that she didn't call him "Sire" or "Your Royal Majesty" or anything like that. Then she turned to the children and said, "Tell the king why we came here."

As with one voice, they cried out, "We are hungry, we have no food."

The king looked startled—in fact, he didn't know where to look. Finally, after some spluttering, he managed to speak—and he spoke half at his own old, slow pace and half at the pace of the children.

"But. Is. This. My fault entirely, I mean—"

"You're a king," said the girl. "You have royal powers. The powers of gods. You must act."

"But. What. Shall I do, I don't know—"

The girl said, "Open your storehouses and release the food. But you must serve it to the people yourself, and you must walk among us at our pace, and you must hold conversations with us, and you must see us for what we are."

The king looked at her carefully and he didn't speak. But when the next day came, the king went to meet his people. He left the palace, his footman attending him a pace behind. They blinked. Never had they seen such a crowd. Down below them, at the foot of Palace Hill, all the people of the island had gathered. Tables had been set out by the king's men.

Slowly the king began his descent. In the heat of the moment, he had forgotten that he must not walk as he had always done. So he picked up speed and developed a nice brisk walk. He also turned his head from side to side like a normal person, and not at all like a king.

When the people of the island saw this, some clapped their hands in delight, but their applause didn't catch on. Until he spoke to one or two. To their astonishment he said, like a normal person, "How do you do?" and "Miserable day, I'm afraid," and "How are you keeping?" When he had passed by, those people to whom he had just spoken began to applaud.

Soon the entire multitude, despite their weakness, was making a thunder-ous sound—hands clapping, feet stamping, tables being rapped. The king, touched almost to tears, bowed—and began to ladle out stew.

He found that he enjoyed this task—so much that he couldn't stop saying so. When he moved on from that sentiment, he began to ask over and over, "Is there something else I can do?"

Nobody dared suggest anything—I mean, who would tell a king what to do? Until he came to a woman he thought he recognized. He didn't know her—but her face was familiar because it was her daughter who had led the children to the palace.

He asked her, too, "Is there anything else I can do?" and she said, in the forthright way that her daughter had learned, "Yes, there is, sire." The king looked at her and waited. "Come and live with me and my family for a few days, and you will understand your kingdom better, and your people will love you more."

The king took a pace back. He looked all around Palace Hill. Word of what the woman had asked went whispering through the crowd. They fell silent—so silent that you could hear the swallows chittering in the eaves over-head, so silent that you could hear the wind in the grass, so silent that you could hear the stream that gurgled down Palace Hill to the river in the valley.

As they waited, the king frowned. They knew what was going through his mind: would this be royal behavior? And still the rain poured down. It plas-tered his hair to his forehead. It drenched his royal robes. It ran down the faces of the people who looked at him, the woman and her daughter, and the children around them; everywhere the king looked he saw wet, expectant faces.

He spoke. "That is a most gracious invitation," he said. "And I am happy to accept."

For the next seven days the king lived in that woman's house with her husband and her children. They had one room, divided for sleeping arrange-ments by a rope hanging an old sheet. He ate their pitiably little food, he washed his face in the water they—or he—brought from a stream. He walked at their pace, he spoke in their tempo, and he looked at every wonder to which the children pointed. They all found him to be a most agreeable com-panion.

On the eighth morning, he stepped from their house, into the pouring rain. As he turned to say, "Goodbye and thank you," the rain stopped. As suddenly and definitely as if somebody up in the heavens had turned it off. The king had atoned. And never was there such prosperity on that island as in the following years.

141

I finished my tale, took in the wide-eyed silence of the children and the pleased smiles of the adults. They asked me where I had first heard it, and I told them that an old lady told it and many more on an island in a lake near Enniskillen. Afterward, they offered me a bed for the night, but I declined. I had other plans; I would begin to make the tale I had told come true.

I only had to make a short journey. Outside the village, travelers had camped. They had a horse-drawn caravan painted in the usual bright colors, and a couple of ponies grazing while tethered to the van. A fire glowed, neither high nor bright. Earlier, driving past, I had seen an elderly man and woman. Their ages I could not tell.

Though it was near midnight, they hadn't yet gone to bed, wherever that was. She sat on the step of the wagon, he by the fire, smoking a cigarette and crooning to himself.

You'll have seen, children, groups like these, usually larger, with children and extended families, and maybe a dog or two and a donkey or a mule. They suffered from us—we were what they called "the settled people," who lived in houses. The believed us to be bullies, we believed them to be thieves, and I know that much of our demonizing of them had to do with the fact that we treated them so badly.

Although they were supposed to have descended from our dispossessed chieftains, people all over the country moved them on with sticks and kicks. Once or twice, they burned them out, setting fire to their tents, their animals—and their children.

In terms of bloodline, I didn't know where to place them. Some claimed Romany blood, ancient tribes. None liked the names we gave them; instead of "tinkers," they wanted to be called "tinsmiths," and, indeed, they had a rightful claim with their hammers and their repairs. They didn't like "Gypsies" either.

"We didn't come from Egypt," they said, "and we never did," and they'd been known to fight anyone who said otherwise.

They drank too much and fought too much. Many of them trashed the roadsides where they camped and the pubs in which they drank. Reach for the word "pariah" and you get some idea of their status.

I parked the car a little beyond their caravan and walked back. The man by the fire had a bottle in his hand—beer, not whiskey—and he slugged it as I approached.

His wife said something I didn't catch; they spoke rapidly, some of it in a dialect.

"God save you all," I said.

The man with the bottle grunted; this wasn't the first time I'd been mistaken for a priest.

"Shtand up when the man talks to yeh," ordered the woman, and said not another word.

What had I expected? That they'd jump at my offer? They didn't. With no input from the woman, the man stalled. I pressed hard, finally showing him a roll of cash I had prepared. He wanted to finger the notes; I refused, said he couldn't touch them unless and until we had a deal. He walked around the fire, threw the empty bottle into the field, and walked around the fire some more.

And he muttered all the time, the same words in a kind of speech tune. By standing close to him I picked it up; he was saying, over and over, "I dunno, I dunno, I dunno now, I dunno."

But I pressed him, and he agreed. We struck the deal that I had been thinking about for some time. In return for cash and my car, and most of its contents except my essential personal effects, he would give me a leather satchel that hung from the door. Made by his wife, as I had guessed from having seen it earlier, it had a pilgrim sturdiness. Over and above that, though, came the concession to which he had been reluctant: I would live and travel with him and his wife for a month.

Ask me why. You know the answer. Atonement. Penance. Restitution. The stories I was telling had led me into a deeper self, a place of greater recognition. Down there, in the deep fastnesses of my soul, I had learned that true repentance comes harder. For a man who liked his comforts, a fastidious man, what colder shriving could I have than to go where I belonged—into the greatest daily hardship and unsanitary unpleasantness that existed in my own country?

It proved worse than I had imagined. I have to be careful here, lest I give the impression of criticizing or decrying people who had scant control over their lives. All they had—and they told me this frequently—was the freedom not to be "settled," meaning housed with permanent neighbors, in a crowded urban setting. That was the shape of government programs for travelers. For them it meant the death of the life they cherished—one on the open road.

Yet although I don't entertain in me a jot of criticism or judgment of them, I must report things as I find them. In a month I saw neither person wash. They seemed oblivious of such need. Due to the odor and the cramped space, I didn't ask to sleep in their caravan; I slept where they put me, in old blankets down between the wheels. Night after night, hail, rain, or snow—fortunately, we had almost none of those—I crawled in and lay down, deep under their wagon, in what most people would call rags.

During the day I walked out and washed my own face in streams and tried to keep clean, especially as I was visiting houses within twenty miles, telling tales if they'd have me. Some didn't. During the night I would wake up and hear muttering over my head, and never know which of them spoke, and whether it was sleep-talking.

Over matters of sanitation and the like, I draw a veil; all I need say is that I had never before been shouted at by passing children because I looked like a tramp.

As to food, you may dismiss any notion of romantic stew, of rabbit and game, caught and killed on rich estates by lovable rogues. We had tea, endless tea, without milk or sugar, unendurably strong, and we ate stale bread mostly, bought or pilfered or received through charity in the woman's daily round selling her lucky heather.

After about three weeks, in which we never moved from the same place, the police came by, and their glances didn't take me for anything other than a traveler. They asked the man—who was not old, but it took time to see that—when he was moving on.

"Any day now," he said.

"That's what you told us last month."

"Time flies," said the traveling man, whom the woman called "Joe." I never discovered her name, and she never spoke to me. I'd guess her age at early forties. Nor, in essence, did Joe have much to say, apart from a grunt here and there.

Yet they had some kind of tribal signals, because in the second week a rattling old van drew up, with six men. They all knew Joe and his wife, and they brought bottles of drink. One of them produced the necessary form for the surrendering of a car. In the box marked "Sale Price," I wrote, "Nil. Gift."

142

Had I been shriven? Did my burden of guilt and remorse feel lighter? Not then, not immediately. This house, where I'm writing now, sits, as you both know, on the side of a hill. Sometimes I get a little flooding at the end of the garden, as the water comes down after heavy rain. In my renovations, I had to take care that I laid wide, deep drains all around the walls, and they are effective; no water comes into the house.

The hill, however, brings a good consequence, too. When this house was built, the owners formed a loose cooperative with other houses on the hillside, and they built a reservoir near the top. It's fed by rain and, since the late 1940s, by local mains, too.

As a result of the constant and abundant supply and the steepness of the gradient, we all have excellent water pressure. I was therefore able to install something almost unknown in Ireland back then: a shower. I think, Louise, you were the one who said to me once that the force of the water could take the skin off your shoulders!

I said goodbye to my travelers, to Joe and his nameless wife. As my last act, I bought parcels of clothing for them in Ennis and brought them down to the campsite. (It took a moment or two, and some evident banknotes, before the shopkeeper would do business with me.) When I returned to Dublin, I removed all my clothes, dumped them in the bathtub, and stepped into the shower. I ran it until the water turned cold. Then, washed to my bones, I ate some real food.

Although reluctant to allow it into my life, I felt some ease beginning. I saw it almost as a distant light at night, and as I thought about it, I drew nearer to that light. Soon (and I know that I'm pushing the metaphor, but forgive me) I could look into the window of my own soul, as it were, and inspect the damage.

Call it considerable. Widespread. Deep. Savage. Once, in science class at school, we had to polish an old tin frying pan until we could see our faces in it. Then the teacher, with us watching from a safe distance, poured acid into it. We watched as the acid bit into the metal, and naturally we marveled, as we were expected to do—the teaching was in the emotion as much as the science.

In the next lesson, however, came the drama. The tin had blistered, and the blisters had burst, and now we had a surface of blackened, pitted metal. It looked like a dark moon seen through an unclean telescope. Here and there the acid had missed tiny spots, and they still shone brightly. The small places in my soul formed the areas that I had to expand.

That's when I began to cope with my guilt—when I saw the extent of the damage. Oddly, my giving away of my treasured and useful car hadn't helped as much as I'd imagined; in fact, I felt profound irritation at myself. So I went and bought another car. Had to. Couldn't, I felt, go on otherwise.

The descent into a reduced and blatantly unclean way of life—that had helped. I found shriving there, but I also accused myself of being patronizing. Which I had been. And had intensified it by giving the couple clothes and some cash when I was leaving. The message to myself? Be careful how you view what you see as your charitable acts.

I did, however, find that I had experienced genuine healing, or the beginning thereof. It fell into two neat halves: that from a source I could identify and that I felt had yet to come but from a source I knew.

You won't be surprised to learn what I first identified: the storytelling. Giving of myself in that way, sharing the delight I had always felt, choosing tales with some meaning—that's where the strengthening began. When I thought of each tale, it was as though the black pittedness retreated infinitesimally and another tiny area of bright tin began to gleam. Oh, sure, I had to polish it—but at least it was there to be polished.

So, in search of story, and in search of the food it provided, I went to work—in a way that paid dividends. Not only did I scan and devour James Clare's notebooks, with all their stories, and leads to stories, and proverbs, and gnomic, gnostic sayings, I went to an even deeper well. In that month I stayed in Dublin—to re-right my life and stabilize—I began to build a library.

When you first came to this house, on that wondrous and memorable day, both of you did exactly the same thing: you walked around my "bookroom" (I've never had the nerve to call it "library"—too grand) and you touched the shelves of books. You took one down here, opened another there, and I saw your excitement. Well, if it proved joyous to you, imagine what it did for me—night after night after night.

Shakespeare led—no surprise there, although I had never expected his poetry to contain so many rewards. Chaucer became my friend, a man both rambunctious and boring—in other words, normal. I saw Dante and Virgil as the two most important figures in my life after Shakespeare, until Horace came along. And then Homer, now that I had a chance to read him at leisure, all but blitzed the lot of them. Until Coleridge came along, and Keats, and Wordsworth, and Samuel Johnson, and Daniel Defoe, and Charles Dickens and Oscar Wilde and W. B. Yeats and John Millington Synge, whom my father had once seen walking in Dublin.

It's an easy picture to inspect, and although the world knows a great deal about self-healing today, we hadn't a clue back then; I was flying blind.

Gradually, the days became more tolerable. That unceasing and violent drone of accusation in my head quieted—a little, to begin with, and then some more, and then some more. And so on. The familiar and dreaded waking-up pit in my stomach didn't lurch so deep every morning.

I can't and won't put a time on any of this; I don't know how long it took for tolerable ease to arrive and settle; to be truthful, I still get disturbed visions of those stiff black pools of blood, but not more than once in a while.

Still, I hear you say, and it's accurate, "That reading of books and poetry—that was all impersonal. What about people? Isn't it the case that it's people who heal people?"

I smile at that. Some whom I've met could be seen as living proof of the opposite. But it's true, and that's where I had the most work to do.

143

Where to begin? Obviously, with my parents. At last, after almost thirty years, I hauled out what I had been concealing and faced it. When my father ran off with Venetia, both parents made me somehow responsible. Or so it felt. My father broke the news to me that he was quitting home, and left me to deal with it. Mother sent me off to fetch him back; I was eighteen. I behaved like an obedient son, but a resentment grew in me.

When I then married Venetia, my father hated me for stealing his love object, and Mother didn't wish to hear Venetia's name. Worst of all, they destroyed—and I don't know which of them did so—all of Venetia's letters and telegrams to me, imploring me to come and bring her back from Florida. And bring the two of you, also. I had fuel for my fire, didn't I?

Although I behaved courteously with them, and dutifully if required, the old warmth we'd had when I was growing up had gone. The jokes faded; the shared news, the funny, spiky gossip disappeared. For years after Venetia's first disappearance, I didn't go home. When I did, we moved around each other as gingerly as skaters on thin ice. We kept conversation to generalities, such as health, weather, politics, neighbors, farming.

I thought that I'd been the one who had wanted it that way. In my new easing out of my own spirit, though, it began to occur to me that they had felt betrayed by me when I married Venetia. A double betrayal, one for each parent. Perhaps triple—as I didn't tell them. In fact, I'd never told them face-to-face; they'd learned it by other means, such as Miss Fay.

Time to put all that behind us, and I knew what to do. With one simple, unprecedented icebreaker. Since I'd left home, in all my travels

I'd never brought them a gift. Not for Christmas, not for birthdays. That gauges the depth of my resentment. Now I resolved to visit them, and I wrote a careful letter, inviting myself; it turned up in their papers after Mother died.

For Mother I found a shawl of gossamer tweed, woven by a woman out in Connemara. It had all the colors of the rainbow, but muted and elegant. She hid it minutes after I gave it to her, a sure sign that she thought it precious. It's the shawl she wore in bed during her last illness, never parting from it.

For Harry I found something different. He liked to sing (I use the word in its loosest form) an old ballad about the racing greyhound Master McGrath, and by great good fortune, that expert in sanitary ware Mr. MacManus, the great bear of Limerick, found me a chamber pot with Master MacGrath's picture and some verses of the ballad on it.

By the way, Mr. MacManus never mentioned "Alicia Kelly" to me, not once.

When I gave them their gifts, we knew—without a shared glance or word—that the gulf had closed. We had healed the rift. All three of us began to speak at the same time about different things, just as we had in the past. That Sunday with them became one of the happiest days I had known for many years. No difficult topic raised its head, no awkward missteps, no fumbled remarks, no silences.

When I was leaving, they both stood at the car with me, and we talked on for another fifteen minutes. I promised to visit them every few weeks, as I did for the rest for their lives. Sometimes I went oftener than that—despite my own new circumstances.

Miss Fay, Marian Killeen, Billy and Lily Moloney—when I look back it seems as though I must have sat down and taken inventory of the people who had an important emotional connection to me. I shepherded Miss Fay from the planet. She fought every fight she could find: arthritis, rheumatism, cancer.

"No knockout punch yet," she'd say to me, and I'd ease her into the car in all her finery. She talked to me about James—that's what she wanted to talk about. When they both woke in the middle of the night, they had long conversations. That's what she missed most, that and watching him eat. "My mother didn't like James; she said he ate like a hyena. He did, and I loved that about him."

I went to Dan Barry's funeral—along with half of the government. Suddenly the old IRA had become respectable. The grieving widow wore a veil—Jimmy Bermingham's advice, I believe. Elma, Jimmy, and I walked from the cemetery together.

"Did he tell you?" she asked me.

"Go easy now," Jimmy said. "It'll take a while."

"He's going to run in the next election," Elma said. "This border thing is fizzling out."

Well, that circle has closed. Half gambler, half lounge lizard, looks like a bookie on a wet day. He'll hold ministerial office in no time. My God, he looks important already. Has some of her bloom dimmed?

Jimmy turned on her. "Whatcha tell him that for? You'll be putting it in the papers next."

He saw my irked glance at his harsh tone and scuffled off a few feet ahead.

"Does he speak to you like that all the time?"

Elma said, "I never thought I'd miss Dan as much."

Marian Killeen and I remained close. We met whenever I was in Dublin at any length. She came and stayed here; but you know that already. We had the most open friendship—even talked about what it would have been like had we married. She never wanted marriage, she said; she'd seen enough of it.

Her cleverness added to my fortunes. She had a nose for investments, so I took her advice and trebled my capital. And trebled, too, the proceeds of my parents' estate.

It became possible for my parents to hire back Billy and Lily Moloney.

"We did it for the entertainment," Mother said, and as Billy got older, he grew more tongue-tied in her presence, because he couldn't curse in front of her. This afforded her great amusement, especially if he was fixing or repairing something for her and it wasn't going his way.

"He'll walk away," she said, "and he'll stand in front of a tree or wall, and he'll address it as he would a human being. Sometimes I can hear him, and I wait for the wall or the tree to turn blue."

Who was it said, "A man must keep his friendships in constant repair"? My father said it was Abraham Lincoln; I said it was Samuel Johnson. He argued that no Englishman would have been that clever; one day

I will check. But it's what I now tried to do, and I believe it went well—I hope that my friends viewed me with the same kindness as I felt for them.

As you probably recall, I've described my father's death elsewhere. The pain of it lingers; I had no idea how much I loved him until he had died. I'd have forgiven him anything—well, I did, I suppose.

When Mother went, I felt orphaned. How could I possibly replace such a person? Ever. For weeks I dredged up every good memory of her, and I soon saw how resourceful this shy, awkward woman had been. Somewhere in my papers you'll find a recollection of mine about a stray horse that had broken its harness and looked prehistoric and dangerous. Mother soothed the creature with a word and a stroke. I wish she could have done the same for me, but I hold only the best feelings for her.

This new, careful, and deliberate behavior toward everyone had one sore outcome: I missed Venetia more than I'd ever done. No matter how I tried not to listen to the loss inside me, it reverberated. I coped with it; I had to. But time and again, leaving some village in the morning or arriving somewhere at dusk, I'd see her face in the sky—and I'd wish. Wishes, however, are frail things, smaller than hopes, weaker than dreams, and I put them aside with care and regret.

And so I went on, keeping my friendships in constant repair and telling my tales. A sense of good organization returned, and my welcome at firesides increased. Some counties became my favorites: County Leitrim, poor as its own marshland; Cork, in its power and glorious variety; Tipperary, with its political drive; Wexford, with its old customs and dark places, though none as dark as my darkest days.

144

At the two-year mark, halfway through my second full round of the country, I wrote to John Jacob. "Perhaps the time has come for my teacher to assess how I'm doing," I said. With him in mind, I hired a hall next to a church twenty miles from his home; it could accommodate a hundred and fifty to two hundred or so.

It filled to about three-quarters of capacity; knowing the countryside, I figured the rest would drift in around a quarter past eight. When I walked onstage at twenty past, people were standing here and there at the back, chatting.

No applause; it didn't happen that way in those days. I sat down on my kitchen chair (borrowed from the priest's house next door) and cleared my throat and clapped my hands. More nervous than usual—which is saying a lot—I checked the faces and saw John Jacob about ten rows back. *Is this man ever going to age or change?* I wondered. He looked as I had first seen him, ruddy and healthy and sound.

I opened by talking about the life of the *seanchai*.

"They were knowledgeable men, those old storytellers, with gifts of language and timing, with prodigious memories and a strong desire to tell the stories of the land. Through them we preserved our ancient identity, and even if every tale they told didn't relate directly to that audience on that particular night, they kept people alive to the Family of Man."

I tried not to look at John Jacob, but his nodding head kept drawing my eye back to him. No wonder he approved: my opening remarks came straight from his tuition.

And then I took the leap. I had been planning it for months—and I knew that I might never do it again. It contained a huge risk for me, and yet it seemed essential. After all, it observed, responded to, and put into practice the central piece of advice by which James Clare had guided me.

"One day you have to tell the story of your own life," he said, "and perceive it as myth. When you can do that—that's when you've finally grown up."

I launched into it. It took two and a half hours, and here you have, again, an edited version—you two children know it in its "real-life" form, anyway.

145

If we were sitting by your firesides tonight, and were we a hundred, five hundred years back in time, the tale that I'm about to tell you would last until cockcrow. But I'm mindful of the electricity bill, and the hardness of the chairs you're sitting in, and the fact that we all have to get up in the morning.

Long ago, if long ago means that many, many rivers have flowed into the sea, and if long ago means that many, many stones have rolled down mountains, there lived a chieftain's son. He had no sisters and no brothers, just his father, the chieftain, and his mother, the chieftain's wife.

A rich family, they had horses and cattle and pigs. They had sheep on the mountain too, and when it came to the first of May each year, the boy rose at earliest light and gazed anxiously into the distance, because he knew that if the peaks shone white with snow, they would have to pay no rent for the grazing of their sheep up there that summer. It gave him great pleasure to wake up his parents and tell them, "There's snow on the mountains."

They lived in peace, this chieftain's family, and the wheel of the year rolled over them in a benign way. The sowed and they reaped, they planted and they harvested, and when all their labors were closed down by the winter winds and rains, they sat by their fire of logs and admired the pictures they saw in the flames.

A hospitable house always welcomes visitors, no matter how inconvenient, and one day, the boy, his red hair flying in the wind, ran down the hill to the door of his house and called everybody.

"Look! Come out and look!"

Advancing up the road they saw a party of singing, dancing, swaying people wearing the wild motley of jesters and troubadours—pointed hats and pantaloons in variegated colors. One man turned cartwheels; another juggled silver balls that caught the light; a young girl cracked a whip that echoed up and down the valley.

At the center of their group, like their queen bee, strode a tall young woman who clapped her hands in a steady rhythm. As the breeze turned this way and that, the chieftain and his family and his household could catch the strains on the wind of a pleasant marching song.

The party drew closer and closer, and the boy grew more and more enchanted. As they crossed the grass sward in front of the house, the tumblers tumbled higher and faster, the jugglers switched from silver balls to gold, the girl cracked the bullwhip so hard and so fast that it sounded like branches breaking in the woods in a storm.

For five full minutes the troupe kept up this performance, accompanied all the while by their beautiful young leader clapping her hands and singing the song that gave the other performers their rhythm. When they had done, they bowed deep and low, and the chieftain and his household applauded.

Naturally enough, the chieftain and his wife called up food and drink, on tables set out on the grass. The boy spoke to each performer and asked how they'd learned their wonderful routines. Each promised to teach him, and never had the boy enjoyed such company.

But a cloud came into view—not a cloud in the sky, for it was a beautiful day of bees humming in the honeysuckle and birds warbling in the trees, but a cloud in his mother's face. She left the table and went into the house. The boy, so dutiful all his life, so caring of his parents, tore himself away from the troupe and followed.

In the hallway he found his mother standing with her forehead pressed to the wall. The boy walked over to her and said, "What's the matter, Mother?"

She waved him away and went upstairs; he heard her lock the door.

The boy went back to the table, where the troupe had begun to perform again. This time, directed and urged on by their beautiful leader, they startled the household with their speed and agility and talent. Foremost among them, their leader danced as they sang and played reed pipes for her and she beat a drum.

She danced as no woman had ever before danced, a swaying to the rhythm that grew wilder and faster. In the beginning she made lazy and friendly movements, and by the end she was spinning so fast that the tassels in her hair made a bright circle in the air. And, as the music came to a sudden stop, she threw the drum aside, sank to the ground, bowing low in front of the chieftain.

At that moment the boy, for no reason that he could tell, glanced back at the house. *Looking out from an upstairs window, his mother stood with her hand to her mouth in fear. As the dance ended, she turned away and vanished.*

The next morning he rose early, and felt something wrong. Down in the yard, he saw his father climb onto a saddled horse that had been loaded with bags and goods. He had always known when his father was undertaking a journey—for weeks the household prepared. They shod the horse, they polished the leather of the chieftain's bags, they prepared his best riding boots. But this journey must have been a surprise, an emergency.

The boy ran downstairs; he could just hear the clip-clop of the hooves as his father rode from the yard. With all his speed, he raced after the horse and caught up to his father at the gate.

"Father! Father! Take me with you," cried the boy—and he surprised himself with these words from his own mouth, because he hadn't meant to say that at all. The father turned in his saddle and said, "I can't. This life to which I go is too uncertain. Stay at home and take care of your mother and the household."

He spurred his horse and cantered off. The boy raced after him again, calling, "Father! Father! When will you be back?"

Of course he couldn't catch the horse, who had now been spurred into a gallop, and the father never answered. Or didn't seem to, although the boy thought he heard on the wind the single word "Never."

Back at the house his mother waited by the door. Do you know how your face looks when you feel both angry and sad? You frown, yet your mouth turns down. That was how his mother looked. The boy didn't know what to say—but his mother said it for him:

"I know what has happened, and I know where he has gone. From now on, you will devote your life to finding your father and bringing him back. To me."

For a year and a day the boy went into training for his great search. He learned how to ride a horse across a torrent of water. He learned how to look for plants that gave natural food. He learned how to take a stone out of a horse's hoof. He learned how to use a sword and a knife against bandits. He learned how to ask a question and get a straight answer—almost an impossible feat in Ireland.

And when a year and a day had passed, his mother stood by in the yard as the menservants saddled the horse and loaded up the bags and the weapons and the food and helped the boy—who had grown so much in that year—to mount the horse.

"Bring home your father," said his mother, and the boy rode away.

"Good speed," said the cook as he rode away.

"Good speed," said the kitchen maids as he rode away.

"Good speed," said the menservants and the yard boys and liveryman as he rode away.

He began his search by asking questions on the road he followed. "Have you seen a band of strolling players? They wear all the colors of the rainbow."

For a year and a day he received no answer to that question, and he reached the end of the road.

Next, he began to ride in circles that narrowed and narrowed. This time he asked, "Have you seen a man who can tumble as the clouds tumble across the sky? He wears all the colors of the rainbow." For a year and a day he received no answer to that question, and he reached the innermost circle. If he rode any farther he would be looking at his own face and the horse would not be able to turn around.

Finally he said to himself, "I have to do the thing I feared: I have to ride up the steepest mountains and down into the deepest valleys," and, his heart laden with fear and doom, he set out. This time he asked, "Have you ever seen a juggler who has all the colors of the rainbow flashing in his face from the gold and silver balls he juggles?"

For a year and a day he received no answer to that question—but mountains are high and valleys are deep, so he soon knew that he would need another year and a day to scale every peak, plumb every depth.

On the third day of the third month of the third year, as he rode his horse down a rocky path by a cascading stream, he met an old man cutting wood at the edge of a forest. He asked his question, and the old man, shading his eyes from the sun, said, "If I tell that I have seen such a sight, that I have seen a juggler who has all the colors of the rainbow flashing in his face from the gold and silver balls he juggles—what will you give me?"

The boy said, "I will give you the sun in the morning."

But the old man said, "I already have the sun in the morning, and most mornings I don't like it very much."

The boy said, "I will give you the moon at night."

But the old man said, "I already have the moon at night, and she's a cold mistress."

The boy sat back on his saddle and thought as deeply as a sage in his cave. Finally he said, "If you guide me to the juggler who has all the colors of the rainbow flashing in his face from the gold and silver balls he juggles, I will come back here and tell you legends and tales that will delight your mind for as long as you live."

With a cry of pleasure, the old man pointed to the high hills. "Up there, every morning at dawn, every day at noon, and every evening at sunset, I see all the colors of the rainbow flashing and dancing."

The boy spurred his horse and rode up the mountain. And oh, it was a hard ride. He had to ford a torrent of icy water. He had to take a stone from his horse's hoof. He had to find food from plants that grew under rocks. He had to fight off a lone bandit who wanted to kill him and steal his horse. But now and then, as he looked up, he saw the colors of the rainbow flashing and dancing just over the edge of an escarpment.

As the sun reached the highest point in the sky, he rode around the edge of this cliff and up onto the plateau. There he saw, laid out as with a great circus, tents of all colors and sizes. Weaving in and out among them went tumblers and jugglers and clowns and singers and dancers. The boy knew that his search had ended.

He walked forward from tent to tent, opening the flaps and peering in. In the first tent, he saw a man teaching two bears to waltz, and the man was so kind to the bears. In the second tent, he saw a man teaching a monkey to play an accordion, and the man was so kind to the monkey. In the third tent, he saw a man teaching an elephant the tightrope, and he was so kind to the elephant.

From the fourth tent he heard music. He lifted the flap and peered in. There, three musicians, playing a pipe, a fiddle, and a drum, kept time to the dance of the queen of the troupe while the boy's father, once a great chieftain of the lowlands, lay on cushions, watching, smiling, and applauding.

As the boy stood there, the dancer saw him. She snapped her fingers. The music stopped. She walked over to the boy and took his hand and kissed it.

"I have been waiting for you," she said. "Welcome. I need you here."

Though he still hadn't reached his majority age in life, the boy knew enough of the world to feel alarmed. His father stood up and, with great reluctance, greeted his son.

The boy felt the fear in his heart. Those are bravest who know fear and act anyway. He said to his father, "You have to come home."

"Who are you to tell me what I must do?" said his father.

"Your home needs and requires you," said the boy, standing his ground.

His father said, "I haven't taught you well enough or hard enough, but I will now," and he punched his son in the face. The musicians and the dancing queen recoiled at this violence.

Now, a father striking a son carries no taboos, though you may contend that it should. A son striking a father, though, breaks many laws, unless there is a larger and more human law at work. The boy hit back—for his mother, for their life, for the household.

A mighty battle broke out. They wrestled, they kicked, they gouged, they punched, and when the two bodies finally separated themselves, the boy was the one standing upright and, therefore, the winner.

Now all had changed. His father slunk from the gilded tent, found the boy's horse, and rode home to his wife and farm. The dancer took the boy's hands and led him to a tent where she bathed his cuts and bruises. Then she sat him down and fed him—meat and fruit and glorious bread of yeast and flour and golden butter. And she never took her eyes off him.

From that moment, the boy and his dancer saw little in the world except each other. They walked through meadows of tall grass and flowers, taking care not to step on the nests of larks. They watched fish swim in dappled pools, and nibbled at the trailing cress. They found berries where they hang richest, under the leaves of the bramble, and they fed each other until their lips and faces were stained black and red and blue, and they laughed at their reflections mirrored in the waters of the lake.

And after many, many weeks of this joy and laughter, there came a wonderful day when the dancing queen flung her arms around the boy and told him that he was to become a father. They held each other tight and wept.

The ancients, as you know, had gods for all purposes. And not all those gods had benign intent. One day, when the clouds came down on the mountain, the dancing queen vanished. Nobody knew where she'd gone. A girl said that she thought she'd seen her float away on a cloud. A young boy said that he thought he'd seen her ride a torrent down to the valley. The oldest man in the troupe, the chief juggler, said that he wondered if he'd seen her being plucked by the wind from the highest peak.

If there was one thing this boy knew it was how to search. And now he searched, and he searched, and he searched. All the straight roads, and wide and narrow circles, and deep valleys, and high mountain ranges where he'd *searched for his father—he visited them again. The questions he asked, the answers he received—for eleven years and eleven months and eleven weeks and eleven days and eleven hours and eleven minutes and eleven seconds he wandered the world looking for his love.*

He never found her. He never ceased to love her, either. He loved her more than he loved the sun or the cold moon or the bright salt grains of the stars, he loved her more than the first grass of summer or the first snow of winter.

And when a day came when he knew that his search yielded no fruit, he ceased asking questions. He kept his promise to the old man, and he still wandered the earth, from house to house, from door to door, from hearth to hearth. But instead of plying people with questions about his missing dancer, he told them the story of his love and his life. And that, ladies and gentlemen, is how the first seanchai, *the first traveling storyteller, was created.*

146

It's fair to say that the audience showed its appreciation. John Jacob applauded loudest of all, and he had that broad smile on his face that I now recognized as something I needed and sought. While the people filtered from the hall, and a few came and spoke to me, he waited in his hard chair as content as a pasha on a rich divan. Finally, he was the last one left. Up he rose, and held out his hand.

"Was it all right?" I asked, torn apart by the emotion of the tale.

He couldn't stop smiling. "Good boy," he said. "Good boy, good boy."

We began to walk from the hall. He took my arm. A few paces from the door, he relinquished his grip and said, "I'm going to leave you here. You'll be in touch, I know."

Quick as a whippet he was gone, into the night.

That hurts. Where's he gone? Has he abandoned me? Why so abrupt? How is he getting home?

We had no communal money in Ireland. You could never call that village hall, or any of the dozens like it, prepossessing. Shabby. Damp. Last year's decorations. Flitters of old colored streamers. Low-wattage electric bulbs that might not be turned off until tomorrow morning unless I found the switch.

Better turn off the lights. Where are the switches? Usually by the side door. No sign of them. The lobby, then. If I can't find them, I'll go. Why did he leave so fast?

I picked up a chair that had fallen over and walked out. The lobby had no light—but in point of fact it had all the light in the world, and would have for me evermore.

A woman stood there, unrecognizable, until she took off the heavy glasses and head scarf. And shook out her hair and smiled. And came over and held out her arms.

There my story ends. Truer statement: there I will end it. We sat on two of the hard chairs and talked until three in the morning. We made all kinds of rules, including no questions about or recriminations of the past. We found that deep down, where nothing true ever changes, nothing had changed.

From that night on, Venetia and I never stayed more than a few yards apart. If I went for the newspapers, she came with me. If she went to the hairdresser, I drove her.

Our lives returned, "at one bound," as they say in the best stories, to the days and weeks when we first became a couple. And they never changed from that; they retained that precious and superb texture.

147

Louise and Ben, our beloved children—I will naturally draw a seemly veil over much of our existence, Venetia's and mine, together. Let me close with two observations.

The pair of you lit our lives like the moons light Jupiter. We took such pride in you, every minute of every day, and we spoke of you all the time.

I proved insatiable for stories of you growing up as infants, as toddlers, as small children, and asked on and on, tell me more, more, and Venetia always obliged.

Here's my second observation. Do you recall something I wrote sometime ago? You can find it; I wish I could remember the page number, and I hope my handwriting has made all of this legible enough for you. This is what I wrote:

For our winter fireplaces I will have a woodpile. And a workbench for fixing things. I will be impeccable in my hygiene and my manners. You will never see me looking as decrepit as I do now. I promise to shave every day. I will never leave the house with unpolished shoes. And never, never will I go out without telling you where I'm going. I will be so kind to you, tender beyond your most romantic dreams.

How I will spoil you. Buy you things. Make you laugh, and never make you cry, unless through the telling of a touching story. I will come home to you with news of the outside world, and the strange things I hear in my daily work, and I will watch your eyes widen in wonder and delight and awe as I tell you. I will love you for being my finest audience, and for the talk we shall have, and the thoughts we shall share.

This isn't boasting; I did it all.

PART EIGHT

❊ ❊ ❊

Epilogue

148

New York, Winter 2008

We are the children of Ben MacCarthy and Venetia Kelly. We were born forty-five minutes apart, and have never been much farther than that from each other since. We live separately, in adjoining apartment buildings, 414 and 424 East Fifty-second Street. Although we have always done everything together, this is the first time we have written in collaboration. We are here to explain. Please bear in mind that we are lawyers, not writers, and excuse our prose style.

Thirteen years ago, in the spring of 1995, our father, Ben, passed away at the age of eighty-one. We had grown very close to him; he was a wonderful man, capable of an unusual depth of kindness. He also entertained us with his stories, of which we never tired. We assisted him through his last illness, and we were able to tell him how much we loved him. And we forgave him his naïve side.

On the day before he died, in his own home, he had enough strength to lie in the conservatory he had built. At the garden end he had included a raised sunroom, away from the plants, from where he could look out over the sea. We drew our chaises beside his, and we all three lay there together, him between the two of us, which he always loved, and he held our hands, and talked about our late mother, Venetia, who had died some years before.

The next day, taking an afternoon nap, he died in his sleep, and we cried for days and weeks.

When the Will was read, and we gained access to his house and papers, we found many astonishing things—not least an orderliness that we can't yet match.

As lawyers, we also appreciated the papers. Ben had set out the record of his life with impeccable care. (We never got around to calling him "Dad," and sometimes we called him "Big Ben," as distinct from "Little Ben," who is also the same height and build.) Not only did he list every one of his considerable assets, and the few, tiny financial liabilities not worth mentioning, he gave the names, addresses, and telephone numbers of every functionary in his life, down to the contact person at the electricity board.

He also left behind, in large notebooks the size of old cash ledgers, a handwritten record of the life he had lived, most of which had been dominated by his feelings for our mom, whom we adored too, but perhaps not as much as he did. His Will requested that we not open these papers until five years after his death and stated that we could, if we wished, publish his account of his life. When we opened and read them, we decided to shape his great record into manageably readable accounts, and to publish them in three volumes.

The story of his life can be found in those works. Over and above our family connection, we found them remarkable for the emotional history they contain. We can think of no man, especially in modern times, as courageous in his naked portrayal of himself, certainly no Irishman—and definitely no American male! Our purpose in writing this epilogue is simple: he left some gaps at the end, and in part of the tale as well, and we think that the story deserves closure.

149

To begin with, he never lied about the facts of his background. All his accounts and descriptions are true: we checked the details of his parents, Harry and Louise MacCarthy; the family farm, Goldenfields; our grandmother, Sarah Kelly; and our great-grandfather, King Kelly, and we interviewed many of the people mentioned, including Billy and Lily Moloney, the husband and wife who worked at Goldenfields and, later, at our grandparents' home in Goold's Cross. In Kansas we spent time with Mr. and Mrs. Charles Miller; she was the former Miss Begley, whom my father knew when she was a matchmaker in Kenmare, Ireland.

It wasn't that we doubted our father, no matter how often he described himself as an unreliable witness. Our pressure to check his facts came from disbelief that he had been capable of killing—twice.

In the first case, we succeeded in tracking down the war records for the Malmedy district of Belgium and uncovered the accurate account, including the name of the soldier: Sebastian Volunder, infamous even in his own German ranks. For the second, a murder that he had commissioned, and that he also witnessed by overhearing, we were granted access to a police file in Dublin, in which he featured at length. Charges had not been pursued, because of lack of proof.

We should say that we researched those two incidents first, because they so appalled us. But they did not change our opinion of Ben. The man we came to know better than we've ever known another human being had grown into a resolved and peaceful person who gave of himself in an almost miraculously generous way. Nobody we've ever known has had a deeper or more loving soul.

And we believe that we know why. He said that he had held on to an early dream, and although in practical terms he had had that vision snatched from him for the greater part of his life, and not once but twice, he almost never ceased to believe.

The word "almost" has an importance here. For a period of years in the late 1950s, he shuttered his life from his love. He turned away from all thoughts of Venetia.

When she returned, however, his feelings for her came flooding back, as you have now read. He understates, though, how he conducted his final relationship with her, and we want to fill in some of those blanks, if only to see that he receives full honor for his nobility, and his immeasurable care.

As we've said heretofore, he did indeed display a lovable nature, but the depth of our affection for him comes as much from watching the way in which he lived for her. Of Venetia we find ourselves more critical—but not crucially or, we hope, unpleasantly so. In part because of our insistence, she came to appreciate him, and in time did let him know.

We have other spaces we'd like to fill, other gaps to plug, and in some cases we don't know whether he knew what we discovered. In fact, we feel certain that he never inquired into one significant part of the puzzle. Mom told us the details, just once, and asked us never to tell him. Even then, she drew a veil over some of it, and although we both have our suspicions, we have no proof.

It concerns the period after she ran away from Ben by the seashore north of Dublin. He had parked overnight at Rush, a wide, sandy beach resort for summer Dubliners. In the morning, when he couldn't find her, Ben assumed that Jack Stirling, our late stepfather, had followed them and spirited Venetia away somewhere.

Then Ben stalked Jack, tried to attack him, and was beaten away by Jack's "associates," as he liked to call them. Those two men, as we learned (though Ben never mentions it), had been in jail with Jack, crooks together. Ben then had Jack killed by two Irish republican mercenary hit men, and was himself brought low by remorse.

He never knew that Jack had not "kidnapped" Venetia. Sometime during that night in the car, she woke up. With Ben still asleep, she took most of the substantial amount of cash he carried in his work case and hitched a ride from Rush into Dublin on an early morning delivery truck. Ben never mentions the disappeared money either, presumably because he didn't want to suspect her or cast her in a poor light.

From Dublin, Venetia, who had known the Irish countryside intimately since her road show touring days, caught a train to the town nearest Mr. O'Neill, the elderly storyteller whom Ben revered. Mr. O'Neill took her in, took care of her, and found her brief lodgings nearby. From there she got in touch with us. We came to fetch her, and all three of us returned to Florida together.

Venetia kept in touch with Mr. O'Neill and visited him frequently. She stayed there many times, and once or twice almost ran into Ben there—which she didn't seek to do. We never asked her whether she had a love affair with Mr. O'Neill. Ben, so far as we know, had no awareness of that relationship. We do know from Mom that when Mr. O'Neill was invited to see Ben perform, he sent for her, and then insisted that she accompany him.

Mom always remained vague about her feelings for Ben during that second period of separation. We asked her more than once whether she ever supposed that they would be reunited one day, and she said that when she heard news of Jack's death, she thought that a circle had been closed, and that all were intended to go their fated ways, and Jack's way had been death. She said that Jack had died as he'd lived—in violence.

In her daily attitudes we often felt that Mom should have been more demonstrative to Ben, considering the attention he gave her. Eventually we said so, and her response startled us. She told us that we were completely right, that she had been unfair to Ben in many, many ways—but she said no more than that, and didn't seem to change too much.

However, we found in her effects, after she died, a diary of sorts. Typical Mom, she kept it higgledy-piggledy; her lack of orderliness must have driven Ben crazy, but he never said. In one diary, for 1964, by which time they had been back together for some years, we found this entry; she was sixty-four, he fifty.

"Today I had a moment—another!—when it would have been fine to die, because I felt perfect emotion. He hurts my heart when I look at him. This is a Man."

We would also like to say something about Jack and Mom. For the first twenty-four years of our lives, Jack was the male parent we knew. In this we suffered a duality—because we had another male parent, whom we had never met but of whom we heard all the time, and always in whispers. Mom spoke of Ben constantly, though never in Jack's presence (she later told us that she was forbidden to do so), and in her words and feelings, Ben seemed everything that Jack could never be. That turned out to be true.

She never explained to us why Jack hadn't shown the same brutality to us that he showed to her. We both asked many times, and never received a satisfactory reply. Once she hinted that she had made herself a lightning rod, that she taunted him to draw his fire away from us. On another occasion she suggested that Jack knew she would kill him, or have him killed, if he, as she put it, "laid a bad finger" on us. We asked if she would have been able to kill him, and she said that she probably could, but that she knew somebody who would, and we understood that she meant Ben.

When news reached us of Jack's death, Mom didn't grieve. She said

that all bereavements are composed of grief and relief in different proportions, and she felt ninety-five percent relief, if not more. She added
that with Ben it would be "one hundred thousand percent grief."

One of Ben's accounts describes their meeting in Jacksonville. That
day had lived in our minds as a puzzle. We came home from school in
the afternoon and found Mom alone and weeping. Jack had a gig in one
of the hotels down the coast that night, and had long gone. Mom flung
herself around the house in a state and condition such as we had never
before seen. She couldn't speak and then retreated completely into herself and didn't come out for weeks.

Neither of us had ever even glimpsed that side of her. The good and
normal Venetia came across as Ben describes her—sunny and humorous,
always pleased with an opportunity to perform. The Venetia he tells
about on the night they stayed with Mr. O'Neill—that was the Mom we
knew when nobody else was around.

We can, however, confirm everything he says about her moody behavior in the days—and it was only days—they spent together after he
snatched her from the stage of the Olympia Theatre. She did have a ten-
dency to retreat into herself; we knew her capable of that. We'd seen it
more and more as we grew older, and went to school and college. This
infuriated Jack, and we had gone to Ireland with them to protect Mom
from his rage.

She hated being part of the show, felt it beneath her, and he knew it.
He had always hit her, but never so often as in their last year. In his sa-
dism, he never damaged her face, and he told her that the blows hurt
more when people couldn't see where they'd landed.

We don't believe that Mom knew who killed Jack, or any of Ben's part
in it. Venetia never commented on the manner of Jack's dying, and we
never elaborated. We didn't let her see the Florida newspapers, either; we
just said that he got caught up in something bad, and she said, "Well,
that's Jack."

Our life with Mom and Jack could have been a great deal worse. He
traveled, and all through school she stayed home with us. If he returned
sober, everything remained fine; if not, he baited and abused her, and she
had no fight-back mechanism, no inner army. We stopped much of it
when we reached our late teens, but we had no idea how badly he behaved when we weren't there, and Mom didn't say.

Once we asked her why she had remained with him, and she said that children in the United States needed a man to protect them.

She had, we believe, the best years of her life—of anybody's life—in the years that she and Ben finally lived as a couple. With nobody harassing them, they made it work in a way that set an ideal. They put together their road show, with Mom on Shakespeare and Dad playing the storyteller, and they packed in the crowds.

Sensibly—his idea—they toured for only a number of months every year and spent the rest of the time at his house, Goldenhill, which he had restored, and which we now own and visit several times a year. When we asked him once how life was, just a light throwaway question, he said, "Idyllic. But I always knew it would be."

They gave the impression that from that single moment when she removed the glasses and head scarf, in the lobby of the hall, everything was as it had first been—a true love match.

If all this sounds romantic, we apologize, but that is how it was, how they were. A psychologist told us one night at dinner that our father's single-mindedness and his refusal to let go of that obsession stemmed from his upbringing as an only child. He'd had a rich fantasy life, as imaginative sole children do, and he had also, of his own admission, wished to take care of his parents from an early age.

To detach from them he had to find another love object. It could have been a career, or a horse; it happened to be Mom, and he didn't know it until she ignited it. By wanting him, and saying so, she made it all right for him to be with her.

He seems always to have had the gifts by which we still identify him. Miss Killeen, who came to see him frequently after Venetia died, proved the most knowledgeable. Although we went to see Mom in Miss Killeen's house, and met Ben there for the first time, we didn't know of the night they had spent together until we read what Ben wrote. When asking about him, we didn't divulge the secret he'd recorded, and indeed we had to delay this publication until after her death, a year ago. (Mom didn't like Miss Killeen, and didn't meet her often.)

She longed to talk about him, and we encouraged her. Of all the people she had ever known, she said, Ben had the greatest gift of loving. He gave the impression of being self-important, moody and aloof, and sometimes boring, but he was nothing of the sort.

In one of the multiple conversations about him—because that's all she wanted to talk about—we asked her if she'd been in love with him. Without a minimal hesitation she said that she was, and had been since she'd first laid eyes on him, and was happy that she had met the one man who had made her think that human nature could be worthwhile. She hadn't needed to do or say anything about it—that's how content she felt with the knowledge of herself and her feelings.

Miss Killeen became one of the richest women in Ireland, and in her Will she left us, as Ben's children, a sum of money that can only be called "enormous." She also created a bursary to endow folklore studies, and every year the Ben MacCarthy Trust funds ten all-expenses-paid scholarships to students all over the world who wish to practice storytelling in the old fashion. "Ben MacCarthy" is the name by which the art is remembered.

In June 1978, Mom fell ill. She came home from a shore walk with Ben late one afternoon and felt out of breath when they reached the house; customarily the climb bothered neither of them. Ben, so alert to every moment in her life, called their doctor at once. That night, they moved her to a local hospital for observation, and the next day to one of the big Dublin hospitals, St. Vincent's.

A lung had collapsed; she had caught some kind of respiratory infection. That afternoon her condition worsened, but by nightfall she had stabilized. They kept her in the hospital for three weeks, though when she came home she seemed greatly reduced. We flew over to see her, and her pallor alarmed us. She had all but lost her voice.

While we were there, he hovered day and night, praising her, encouraging her, lifting her spirits. But he couldn't keep her alive, and when she began to decline fast he climbed into bed and held her until she died.

150

We had a rich time whenever we stayed with them. Both of us went—somewhat late—to law school at Yale, and we found our studies exhausting, so we traveled to Ireland at every opportunity and drank in the atmosphere in that adorable, always exciting house.

More important, we watched our parents share in a philosophy they put into practice. They believed that Ireland, the country they knew so intimately, needed to have its story told to itself, so that it would have a bedrock on which to build a much-needed new spirit. A kind of reconstruction began while they were on the road. The late President Kennedy's visit in 1963, alluded to briefly by Ben, who calls him "golden," energized many young people and licensed the notion of charisma.

Ben and Venetia believed profoundly that, for the country to know where it should go, it needed to understand where it—and the world—had been. The content of their wonderful theatrical evenings, with Mom's international cast of dramatic characters and Ben's tales from all over the world, reflected that passion. Ben saw his life as his country's life, and Venetia didn't disagree.

We know from his writings that we met the full range of characters in Ben's life. Miss Dora Fay's patent dislike of Mom amused but never dismayed us. Miss Killeen came to stay with us in New York. We can both do passable imitations of Billy Moloney's cursing. All of the people Ben mentions became familiar to us, either in fact or in conversation.

Except one. He never told us about John Jacob O'Neill. Mom did, but she said very little. We asked her once where Mr. O'Neill had lived, and she gave a vague answer. Mr. Bermingham didn't know either, nor did his wife, nor did Randall Duff, the painter, whose works we collect.

One day we made discreet inquiries at the Irish Folklore Commission. A clerk assumed us to be Americans in search of legends and gave us an address. We walked down a lane that answered the given address and Ben's description; we even smelled wood smoke; but no house could we find.

Louise MacCarthy
Ben MacCarthy

PHOTO: © JERRY BAUER

FRANK DELANEY is the author of the *New York Times* best-selling novel *Ireland,* as well as *The Matchmaker of Kenmare, Venetia Kelly's Traveling Show, Tipperary, Shannon,* and *Simple Courage: A True Story of Peril on the Sea.* A former judge for the Man Booker Prize, Delaney enjoyed a prominent career in BBC broadcasting before becoming a full-time writer. Born in Tipperary, Ireland, he now lives in New York City and Connecticut.